Lie Still

Renew by phone or ~r

ALSO BY JULIA HEABERLIN
FROM CLIPPER LARGE PRINT

Playing Dead

Lie Still

A Novel

Julia Heaberlin

This large print edition published in 2014 by
W F Howes Ltd
Unit 4, Rearsby Business Park, Gaddesby Lane,
Rearsby, Leicester LE7 4YH

1 3 5 7 9 10 8 6 4 2

First published in the United Kingdom in 2013
by Faber and Faber Limited

A CIP catalogue record for this book is available
from the British Library

ISBN 978 1 47125 986 9

Typeset by Palimpsest Book Production Limited,
Falkirk, Stirlingshire
Printed and bound by
www.printondemand-worldwide.com of Peterborough, England

This book is made entirely of chain-of-custody materials

With love to Mom and Dad,
advanced fans

PROLOGUE

The ring glittered, resting on the dirt of the forest floor, the sun catching it in the fractured afternoon light falling through the leaves.

The ring hadn't been there the day before. A week of brutal, ceaseless rain finally cleaned it up and washed it from its hiding spot twenty years too late, long after something terrible happened.

A hiker paused when he saw it, nearly turned away, and then recognized it for what it was. Plastic. Made in China. A prize from a gumball machine. He picked it up and briefly examined it. A pink heart-shaped jewel on a small, dulled band. He thought about taking the ring home to his three-year-old daughter, probably strutting around at this very moment in her Barbie princess crown, but he decided his wife would yell at him. Tell him the ring was a choking hazard. His daughter would ask why it was scratched. He dropped it as casually as he had flipped his empty Ozarka bottle into the brush a few minutes earlier and trudged on up the trail.

He didn't feel the eyes on his back, watching him disappear.

The crow swooped in.

It was the same crow that had been stealing the change out of a broken car-wash vending machine a mile down the road. Exactly $57.50 to date, all of it deposited daily into the sawed-out window of Joey Tucker's pine tree house that he built all by himself that summer. Joey told no one about the money. He thought it was a secret gift from God.

Few people – certainly not Joey or the man in the forest – know how smart crows are.

But the crow was done with Joey. Joey was rich enough. The bird flew through the trees, higher and higher, sweeping through clouds still heavy with water, a tiny black dot, taking his prize with him.

The crow recognized the ring for what it was.

For what it *once* was.

A bit of joy.

CHAPTER 1

For me, the rape is a permanent fixture on the clock, like midnight.

A point of reference.

I was nineteen years and four days old.

I remember because he treated me beforehand to a belated birthday dinner of scallops, chive mashed potatoes, haricot verts, and a bottle of mediocre wine. I was surprised when my plate arrived and haricot verts turned out to be ordinary green beans.

His name was Pierce Martin, one of those names that could work backward or forward. The sheets were Tommy Hilfiger.

I remember because he pressed my face into the pillow's red and blue patriotic design to prevent me from screaming.

After my birthday dinner, our third date, he begged me to come back to his fraternity house and spend the night in his bed. *No sex,* he promised. *Just kissing. Just holding.* The wine made my world spin pleasantly, and he smelled sexy, a hint of musk and a little sweat left from a pickup basketball game. Before I took my first sip of wine, he told me he had scored twenty-five points.

I said yes to his room.

I trusted him.

I'd told him I was still a virgin, one of the girls who signed the celibacy pledge at church camp in eighth grade and meant it. He'd told me with a solemn face that he wanted his wife to be a virgin. He didn't say anything about himself.

The first time he asked me out, also the first time he said hello, he slid an arm around my shoulders and walked me across campus as if he already owned the right. Sometimes I picture the moment, my face turned up to his, eager, a puppy, a lamb, a foolish girl. I want to slap her.

I was decently popular in high school but not material for the Pierce Martins of the world. So when Pierce – funny, smart, rich frat-boy Pierce – picked me out of at least fifty other girls in my college economics class, intoxication seeped its way into every insecure crack. He wasn't looking for the test answers for next Tuesday from the girl who scored 103 on the last quiz. He wanted the *other* me.

As soon as I stepped inside his room that night, it began to feel weird. The lights were off. Pierce's roommate lay sleeping across the top bunk, a long, dark lump, his face to the wall. Pierce had introduced him to me once, briefly, in the cafeteria. He was a legacy forced on the fraternity, a skinny freshman with random red splotches on his face from squeezing pimples, which he clearly despaired about when alone with the bathroom mirror. Pierce chose him for a little brother so he could abuse him the rest of the semester as a personal slave. He washed Pierce's dirty underwear, fetched Pierce's takeout, lied to Pierce's mother on the phone.

It seemed funny, before the rape. How easily I lost my center.

'It's OK,' Pierce assured me. 'He won't care. He's a deep sleeper. Like in a tomb. Nothing wakes him.' I crawled hastily into the bottom bunk, suddenly wishing I hadn't chosen a skirt over the pants I slid off at the last minute. I'd stay half an hour, tops, I decided, then say good night.

Lying flat in that dark cave, staring up at the bedsprings, I didn't realize Pierce had stripped to a T-shirt and boxers until he pushed his body against mine and swirled his warm tongue in my ear. Still, I thought: *This will be OK. Kissing. Maybe even a little more.*

I sank into him. I was butter melting along the path of nomadic, expert hands. His tongue roved lower, a friendly snake. I didn't want it to stop.

Minutes later, he slipped cool fingers up my skirt and yanked my underwear down. His nails raked the side of my leg, leaving a red scratch I'd find the next day.

'Please don't.'

I said it as urgently as I could, leg stinging, my brain flipped back on like he'd thrown a switch. My voice was soft, not wanting to wake his room-mate. Not wanting to humiliate any of us. I was still hopeful.

Those were my last words to Pierce Martin.

'You're a tease.' He clapped his hand over my mouth and flipped me over. *He's done this before,* I thought, struggling a little, still sure I'd get away, still trying not to wake his roommate, still wanting to limit my embarrassment. The roommate had an unfortunate name straight out of a historical romance. Pierce made fun of it. Wheaton. No, Haywood. That was it. Haywood Worthington.

Pierce gripped my hair and yanked my head backward, pain ripping through my skull. His lips brushed my ear like a lover's. The whisper floated into my ear, down the dark tunnel to my brain, settling inside me.

'Lie still,' he said.

The night with Pierce wasn't a fork in the road of my life because I didn't get to pick which way to go. More like a screeching U-turn.

I'm thirty-two years old. Up to this point, I've told only five people about that night: the campus police officer on duty at 3 a.m., a bored woman who put down her pen and said I'd never be able to prove it; Rosemary Jansen, my roommate that semester, whom I don't even exchange Christmas cards with; and my parents, who are no longer alive.

I still consider the rape a secret, but we all know there are really no secrets.

All of us walk around with ridiculous amounts of intimate information about strangers and acquaintances. We'd never get out of bed if we realized how much peripheral people in our lives know about us. What even the people we love most say behind our backs. The number of confidences broken.

A co-worker, a person named Anne whom I barely know, is the sister of a woman married to one of New York's senators. Anne told me once over a happy hour that her sister keeps a private apartment in San Francisco for her lover. The senator, her husband, doesn't know.

Just a stray fact, a shard of conversation that disappeared from her mind into the next tequila shot.

The senator is a regular on primetime news shows, and now every time I see him interviewed, I think, *You're famous. I've never met you. I've never met your wife. Our lives haven't touched. But I know this thing that could blow up your world.*

I wonder about the people on the periphery of my secret. My parents probably told Father Joe about the rape as they sought counsel from our family priest to help me. I'm sure Pierce bragged about that night to his fraternity brothers, who told their girlfriends, who in turn will use my story someday as a cautionary tale for their daughters.

I imagine my old roommate Rosemary bringing me up as a personal example of being touched by rape. *That happened to my college roommate,* she might say at a party of fellow suburbanites. *I tried to get her to turn him in, call the frat board, anything, but she wouldn't. She thought it was her fault.*

It *was* my fault. I don't care what a court of law says about the word *no* or my polite 'please don't.' I laid myself down in that bed. I was naïve, stupid, shallow, flashing my virginity around like it somehow made me better. A prize somebody could win.

Haywood might still be keeping my secret because it was his, too. That night, Pierce branded us both with humiliation and guilt, the kind that embeds in your skin like a tick and spreads disease.

When my mind travels back there, the shame flares up from the embers, licking at my soul until I find myself flushed and kneeling over the toilet. So I've worked at not thinking about it.

Until Clairmont, Texas. This small dot on the map, thousands of miles away from where my story began, is the place that my past and present exploded.

My mother believed that Fate is a compass inside us. If she hadn't met my father in college, she said, she would have found him somewhere else along the way. *We choose our steps,* she insisted, *but they always take us to the place we're meant to go.*

I don't know how she could reconcile such loosey-goosey mysticism with her belief in Catholicism, especially if she'd known how she and Dad were going to die.

If you follow her theory, we are responsible for running dead-on into the evil as well as the good.

8

Misty and Caroline turned out to be both. Good and evil.

My kindred spirits and my tormentors.

They were the catalysts to free my soul.

But their secrets almost killed me.

CHAPTER 2

If someone asked a few months ago, I'd say my compass pointed north. But a strange wind blew me here, and I held my breath.

I didn't want much. Just for every moment to be like this one. Blessedly normal. For the shadows to go *poof*, little vampires extinguished by the sun.

There was plenty of sun. Mike lay in a yellow patch of it, stretched out on the bed, nursing a bottle of Sam Adams, surrounded by piles of my discarded clothes. He flipped the pages of a *Sports Illustrated* while absently observing my state of fashion crisis.

I'd ripped open every U-Haul moving box that littered the floor of the room.

'Eyes up here,' I ordered. 'What do you think of this?'

'I think it looks good. Just like the last five things you've tried on.' He patted the bed. 'Why are you worrying about this so much? It's not like you're walking into a room full of celebrities. And, I'd like to point out, you've actually done that with a lot less drama beforehand.'

I propped the full-length mirror leaning against

the wall in a better position to see the side effects of a protruding belly.

'I'd think you'd want me to wow them, chief,' I said, tugging the orange top down so it wouldn't show the safety pin keeping my pants together. 'This makes me look like a construction cone.' I yanked the top over my head and slung it at his head.

I'd started to really show in the last couple of months, but the move and goodbye lunches with colleagues and friends left no time for maternity shopping. In the life I'd resigned, as director of a small SoHo art gallery, I would throw on something black, a gold cuff, and be done with it. But even in the two short weeks we'd been in Texas, I could see that would make me look like a fat crow among a flock of colorful, glittery birds.

'I don't want to stand out as too . . . New York. My father always said, "Make a bad first impression and you're digging yourself out of a grave for years, make a good first impression and people—"'

'"—will give you the benefit of the doubt forever." I'm familiar with the wisdom. And why do you think New York is an instant bad impression?'

'We're snotty, rude, walk too fast, use big words when little ones will do just fine. Steal their best baseball players.'

Mike moved from the bed to the floor, kneeling with his ear pressed against my bare tummy. 'Just

11

be your quirky, sweet self,' he murmured. 'Texas thanks God and the Yankees every day for stealing their overpriced baseball players. I hear they've incorporated it into the Lord's Prayer.'

My hand rested gently on his head, shaved bare to avoid the inevitable, the unexpected bonus being that it made him look even fiercer during his seven-year run as an ATF agent. Mike had led a brotherhood of men who carried recessive genes from cavemen ancestors to kill and protect the way others carry genes for cancer and beauty. I'd watched these men drink beer and tease one another in my kitchen like regular guys, but they never, ever truly relaxed. I sleep beside one of them, so I know. They are different from the rest of us.

Our mirror reflected a happy, loving union. No fear, no tension, no anger. No hint of three years of painful infertility treatments, miscarriages, weeks of utilitarian sex, and hot words that nearly ripped us in two.

My eyes remained glued to the couple reflected there, hoping it was real. In Mike's case, the bald look worked, like it did on men without ridged Cro-Magnon skulls, making him even more attractive than he was before.

'Come on, give me a more detailed rundown on my hostess tonight.' It was my practice to be fully equipped before negotiating a room of strangers.

'Three words,' I demanded. An old game we played. Mike shrugged. 'Rich. Widow. Tragic.'

'OK, need more than that. And your left hand needs to stop right there.'

'I think she lost a son,' he said. 'I don't know if she cast a vote, but she attended my final interview, so she wields power here in little Clairmont. Mostly with her wallet. I was told she provided seed money for some upgrades at the new headquarters.'

So far, my only impression of Caroline Warwick was a soft Southern drawl on the other end of the phone. Three days ago, she invited me to a gathering of the town's female elite and seemed slightly annoyed when I told her I'd have to get back to her. Despite his casualness now, Mike had urged me to accept. *Get to know people, Emily. Help establish our new life.*

Texas was not even a glimmer in our wineglasses on those late nights after the stick turned blue and we talked dreams with new urgency.

So Mike was lightly dismissive when an old FBI friend of his mentioned a position leading a well-funded police shop in a high-heeled Southern town, the kind of town rising on *Fortune* magazine lists. Clairmont, Texas, per capita the wealthiest, most highly taxed city of its size in the country, home to CEOs and Dallas Cowboy football players and Texas land barons and nouveau riche wannabes who carried mountains of mortgage and credit card debt.

But then there was a phone call from a persuasive headhunter. And another. Mike flew down first-class for two interviews. The salary shone

13

like a gleaming platinum carrot: $175,000 a year, plus a bonus plan tied to lowering the town's crime statistics, which were mostly connected to rowdy teens. In Texas, that amount of money meant something. Mike feared it also meant he'd been bought. I could tell it bugged him, this worry that he, the caped crusader, was selling out. That maybe he wasn't hearing the whole story.

When the mayor told him the job came with a brand-new, fully loaded, armored Hummer, Mike thought he was joking. He asked if most Clairmonters carried grenades and ran from crime scenes on foot, in which case the Hummer would be fine. When nobody in the room laughed, he said he preferred a basic high-speed cruiser.

I didn't press him too hard on his doubts.

'It's not forever,' he said, shrugging, and my relief flowed, a swift river.

Because, at that point, I wanted to go.

I wanted to run.

Two months ago, my past had snaked its way into our New York apartment on a rainy afternoon while Mike was hunkered down on a case somewhere. He could have been a hundred miles or two minutes away, dodging bullets or playing cards in a safe room, I never knew.

There was so much he never told me about the details of what he did for a living and so much I didn't tell him about what lay at the core of me. On the bad days of our marriage, our secrets

14

circled us like ghosts, blowing an icy draft between us. Would we love each other the same if we knew what the other was capable of?

I remember holding the violent message in shaking fingers, as the soft rain turned to hail, a thousand fingernails tapping on the living room windows, wishing Mike were there so I could finally tell him everything. He showed up at the apartment ten hours later, exhausted and bruised, after I'd tucked the piece of paper away in a shoebox with all of the others.

That is the short story of how we ended up here in the Southern hemisphere, seeking warmth. Mike turned in his resignation and I quit the gallery, promising to take it easy until the baby was born, with the idea that I'd take up my painting again. Life was suddenly an open, blank canvas that we could sketch with careful hands.

'Go away,' I said now, as Mike's fingers began to roam again. 'Go make out with yourself. It's acceptable in the second trimester.'

He stood, his large frame blocking my view of the couple in the mirror. Not budging.

Now it was just us. The *real* us.

Flesh and blood and flaws.

I fought a sudden urge to cry, which seemed to be happening about every fifteen minutes these days. Losing this man would kill me. I pulled his head down and traced my tongue along his mouth. I felt the rush of familiar heat that had sustained us through everything. He drew away for a second, grinning.

'Is this hello or goodbye?'

I pushed him back onto the bed.

Maybe I could help him out a little.

Fourteen minutes later, adjusting the seat in my newly purchased, pre-owned Volvo station wagon, I tipped down white wraparound sunglasses picked up off the streets of New York for ten bucks, and took one last pass at myself in the rearview mirror. Not too bad. My green eyes were made less weary by dark blue eyeliner, the splash of gold in the center of the iris more noticeable than usual.

I'd opted for a bold New York/Texas compromise: a body-hugging black cotton-Lycra dress that left no doubt about my state of maternity and over-the-top, gem-studded gold flats bought at a Barneys sale two years ago.

My body buzzed pleasantly. It seemed wrong to love the thing that had ripped my life apart. But sex set me free in a way nothing else did.

I plugged Caroline Warwick's address into the navigation system that Mike insisted I'd need as a person born without directional ability. He'd bought the GPS from a friend setting up an online business of British paraphernalia, so my guide ordered me around like a bored Hugh Grant.

As the sun slid down in an orange halo, I found myself on the outskirts of Clairmont, driving for 2.3 miles on a farm road, a field of rising corn on

16

one side and a rolling stone wall on the other. When Hugh crisply ordered me to turn, I did so with relief, away from the corn and toward the façade of a medieval-style gatehouse. Fields of corn always remind me of a gang of children wielding farm tools and a childhood slumber party where I didn't sleep a wink. Thank you, Stephen King.

I could see instantly that I had entered a land of surreal-dom. A little city of copper turrets and tile rooftops lay beyond the stone wall, a glittering mirage on the prairie. The gold letters set into the limestone wall announced THE MANSES OF CASTLEGATE. I rolled slowly forward and halted at a miniature stop sign that looked like it belonged at a Renaissance Faire. For a second, I wondered if Hugh had the magical powers to transplant this place from across the Pond.

A sun-beaten troll of a man in a beige uniform sat in cramped air-conditioned quarters, nursing a Diet Coke and watching *Wheel of Fortune* on a tiny TV. I wondered if his prior life involved tending the field across the way.

'Yep?' he drawled, sliding open the window.

'I'm here for a party at Caroline Warwick's. My name is Emily Page.'

Manses were supposed to be the homes of ministers, not vulgar rich people, a detail I remembered from a Scottish architecture course, and something I'm sure my troll friend didn't want to hear from an uppity New Yorker. He ran his finger down a small computer screen, found my name, punched

17

a button. The iron gates swung open easily into a pseudo-snotty fake England.

Why did people who could afford multimillion-dollar castles like this install their 15,000-square-foot homes on postage-stamp front yards, forty feet apart from neighbors on either side? While the general impression was grand, after a block or two, the cupolas, curved stony walls, and widow's walks blurred together like a theme park.

A few twisty detours on cobbled streets designed to invoke the feel of the Ripper's old London, and I turned off the ignition at 4203 Elizabeth Drive, a faux palace half the size of our New York apartment building.

The ivy-covered brick archway to Caroline Warwick's manor rose to the sky. Mike had told me that in Texas, the height of the front-porch arch directly correlated to the price of the house. It was like a house bragging about its penis size. And this was a top-dollar, porn-star penis.

As for my own house hunt, I had quickly abandoned the newer subdivisions after five days of drifting through bland, light-filled spaces with half the rooms already wired for flat screens. Our real estate agent expressed dismay when Mike and I stumbled across a wood-frame fixer-upper a few streets outside of Clairmont's historic downtown and fell in love. A giant live oak in the front yard, honeysuckle run amuck, a stone fireplace, a wraparound porch, sixty-year-old wiring, and a kitchen that felt cramped with three people in it, including the one in the womb. Still, it was twice the kitchen space of our Manhattan apartment. Now staring at the formidable home in front of me, I considered a U-turn back to my bed.

'Honey, open up. Don't be shy.'

My head whipped around to see a woman's pudgy hot-pink manicured fist banging vigorously on the window, the other balancing a plate of something triple-covered with Saran Wrap. I switched off the ignition and opened the door two inches, straight into the rolls of her stomach pressed against my window.

'Watch it. You're going to spill Aunt Eloise's Lemon Squares. They're not quite set. Here, carry them.'

She deigned to move a few inches back and I squeezed by, grabbing the plate dripping from her fingers. She didn't seem to notice that Aunt Eloise's Lemon Squares nearly fertilized the grass.

'You must be Emily,' she told me. 'I'd die to have had a little pregnant basketball like that but my family's all big-boned. That dress is a little tight on you, don't you think? You're a pale one. I guess it's New Yorky. If you want, I can get you into a tanning bed real cheap. My cousin Marsha Lynn Gayle runs the best facility, about seven miles from here, in Keller. Her motto is, "Tanned fat looks better than white fat." I told her she should paint it on the door.'

I watched a raindrop of sweat drip down her face, tracing a white line through her makeup. 'Not

19

to get you worried or anything,' she continued, 'but labor is like one of them Iraqis torturing you. All three of my kids were like poopin' frozen turkeys. Not to mention the hem'rhoids. I read on the Internet that I could dab apple cider vinegar on them, but all that did was make me stink like Easter eggs for a week so I don't recommend it.' That was a hell of a lot of similes in one breath.

She must have weighed 250-plus pounds, but she moved fast, her mouth a blur of candy-pink lipstick and her ass a giant, bobbing red and yellow flowered pillow. As she propelled me toward the house, I was trying to figure out if she meant she smelled like the vinegar you put in with the dye pellets or . . . I didn't want to know. She'd guided me halfway up the walk before I could think about asking her who the hell she was.

'I'm Leticia Abigail Lee Dunn. Everybody calls me Letty. I'm sure you've heard of me.' Her twang fell heavy into the hot air.

When I looked blank, she said impatiently, 'Oh, come on, honey. Wife of Mayor Harry Dunn the *fourth,* your husband's new boss. Daughter of William Cartright Lee *of the Robert E. Lees.* You know the General, don'tcha, honey? We've also got a long line of pageant girls in our family, too, but I don't want to brag.' She gave my arm a squeeze.

'I was fourth runner-up in Miss Texas. Miss Congeniality was outright *stolen* from me by Miss Haltom City,' she whispered, as if it were a secret.

I nodded mutely, struggling to imagine a crown perched on the top of that teased mountain of bleached-blond hair, happy that I didn't have to participate for this conversation to go on.

I wondered how she knew so instantly who I was. She swept her hand grandly at the nearby houses. The ripples of fat on her lower arm swung like dimpled bread dough.

'This tract used to be one of our ranches. I think my ancestors would like that it is now home to modern royalty. You aren't a Democrat, are you? That's one thing I told the girls, "We might have to brainwash the Hillary out of her." ' She narrowed her eyes at me. 'You don't talk much, do you?'

She didn't wait for an answer. 'We can just walk on in, honey. Caroline is real gracious that way. She's a bit of a control freak in other matters but you'll get used to it. Have you filled out an application?'

Application? I risked a breath instead of speaking, hoping that once again she didn't really want an answer. I needed to prepare myself. A roomful of unknowns churned up my insecurities every time. I liked a script, a purpose, when entering a room.

My best friend in New York, Lucy, is a chameleon like me. Assessing the audience, adapting as necessary. She's the only other person I've ever known intimately who is as deliberate and sneaky about it as I am. I remember our instant connection at a museum gala nine years ago, bonding over a Lucian Freud portrait, a mediocre glass of merlot, and our predilection for dark thinking. I wished Lucy and her biting humor were with me now as I navigated this land of twangy trolls and lemon squares.

Leticia grabbed the knob of the massive arched double door. She hesitated. One of her long pink fingernails tucked back a piece of my hair that I'd purposely styled to fall out of the bun on my head.

'I've got a little spray in my purse that will take care of that if you want to scoot off to the bathroom first. Be forewarned, this is a curious bunch. And we're tight. You'll need to suck up a little to get in.'

In where? The door? Was she talking about my stomach? Her stomach? Why, why had I said yes to this?

'Hey, y'all!' Leticia bellowed into the house. 'I got Emily here. The new chief's wife.' She swept me across a marble floor, past a jade inlaid mirror in the entryway and a barely glimpsed Miro sketch, down a hall of ancestral pictures in striking, contemporary frames. Twenty feet in, I stopped impulsively to admire the view.

A stunning garden room ran along the entire back side of the house, an atrium of tropical wonders – ferns, banana trees, and hibiscus I'd seen only on the Internet. Thirty or so women crowded around talking and drinking wine, a much more diverse, anorexic, and formal group than I'd expected after encountering Letty. A pale young harpist wrapped in a gauzy dress played

Mozart near a banana tree as if she were all alone, or at least wished it. A few of the women paused at our entrance, smiled, then turned back to their conversations.

'Gimme those squares so I can present them to Caroline.' Letty grabbed the plate and abandoned me, parting the crowd like a whale churning through water.

I felt a hand on my shoulder and turned to face two nearly identical women, with taut, Botoxed faces, breasts like tennis balls, $150 haircuts, spray tans, French manicures, white capris, and tight sleeveless tanks that showed off their Pilates regimen. Women who looked older than they were because they worked way too hard at achieving the opposite.

'I'm Red Mercedes,' said the one who appeared the tipsiest. 'And this is Beach House.'

'Stop it, that's not funny if she doesn't know us. Mary Ann's had a little bit too much to drink already. It's an inside joke. I'm Jenny, by the way. We have the same plastic surgeon in Dallas. And he owns a Mercedes convertible and a beach house, which we're pretty sure we paid for. I can't believe I'm explaining this. God, you look amazing. Do you even wear foundation? Oh, to have ten years back.'

'Thank you. It's very nice to meet you.' I felt like curtsying.

Huge diamonds in multiple forms and sizes glinted on their fingers as if they bred at night.

These were women who likely graduated out of college sororities straight into marriage, part of the pack of hausfraus I'd dodged this week in the local upscale grocery, Central Market. The women who pretended not to see you as they cut in line at the cheese counter and their Justice- and Abercrombie-clad children demanded Havarti over Gouda.

'Welcome to our butt-hole of a town,' Jenny told me. 'The gossip is that your husband is a modern-day gladiator.'

'Did Letty mention she was a pageant girl?' Mary Ann tipped the last sip from her wineglass. And, then, under her breath, 'She's such a *bitch*.'

I felt like I'd fallen into a Texas rabbit hole. Or maybe a tarantula hole. I'd gotten my first scary look at one of those suckers in the front yard yesterday. The six-year-old boy next door had offered to stick his garden hose in it and blast out the owner, an offer I politely declined.

I was unsure how to respond to this schizo-phrenic chitchat. Where was my hostess? My eyes flitted around a little desperately.

Mary Ann was rubbing a finger across a tiny red spot on Jenny's cheek. 'Pimple. Not skin cancer,' she slurred.

'I bet you're looking for a drink,' Jenny announced into the space left by my hesitation. In seconds, the two women had tugged me into the yard that spilled out of the atrium. The architect's optical illusion with glass and nature made it nearly impossible to tell where the inside stopped and the outside began. That is, until I reached the invisible line, where the air-conditioned breeze evaporated and a stifling wall of summer air took my breath away.

I spied not one, but two outdoor rooms with plush furniture to sink into on either side of a lagoon-like pool. The fire pits glowed, even though it was 95 degrees outside. I smelled an industrial amount of mosquito spray. Chemical misters at work. Not good for Baby.

'So, what can you drink?' Jenny demanded. We moved toward a mini-bar covered with a fake thatched roof, where a tuxedoed young man with a green and yellow tropical bow tie stood, bored and hot. No one else had even ventured out here.

'White wine is great,' I said. 'On the rocks. Makes it last longer. My New York doctor's a woman who recommends one glass of that and a warm bubble bath every night.'

'A Texan already. Ice in everything. If you need a rec for an OBGYN here, we all use Gretchen Liesel. She also cleans up our mistakes.' Jenny winked. 'Anyway, she's here somewhere unless she got an emergency call.'

Jenny leaned in toward the bartender, showing that her small perfect breasts didn't need a bra to prop them up. He didn't care. I caught a glimpse of a Steinbeck novel propped up on the Jack Daniel's. I was busily reworking my preconceived views of Texas. Abortions. Wink. Classic literature, but of course.

'José, one white and two reds, please,' Jenny commanded. I cringed at the Hispanic dig, until I saw that his name tag actually read 'José.' *Relax*.

'Let's sit over here and get acquainted.' She handed me my glass of wine and pulled us deeper into the mosquito jungle, toward a concrete bench set beside a koi pond. I breathed as shallowly as possible.

'First, we have a little bet going,' Mary Ann said. 'A pair of Mephistos ride on this. How long did it take for Letty to tell you she is descended from the Robert E. Lees? In seconds, not minutes, because we know she couldn't hold out that long.'

'I'd say thirty.' I swallowed a deep sip and wondered if a second glass of this elixir would hurt. I'd need it to get through the next two hours.

'Shit,' Jenny said. 'I guessed ten. Mary Ann said twenty-five.'

'It was right after she mentioned that her husband was "the fourth,"' I added rashly, sucked in.

'Ah, yes. Dirty Harry.' Jenny grinned.

She dumped the remains of her glass into a spiky plant that drank it like a greedy alcoholic.

'Lookie over there. It's little Misty Rich. The other new girl.' Jenny lowered her voice. 'In a white dress and red fuck-me shoes.' But by the time I turned my head, Misty Rich – whoever she was – had slipped out of sight.

'Misty's a freakin' weird one,' Mary Ann informed me. 'Pure trash. You can't dress it up. She's been here three months. Long enough for Caroline to become quite taken with her. Word is, she's already

26

invited Misty in.' She leaned closer. 'We think Misty is into recreational drugs. We saw some scars. Caroline does love to find things to fix.'

'Mary Ann, you're cut off,' Jenny decreed.

A low-pitched chime made all three of us turn back toward the house. Jenny pulled her friend up, gripping her arm a little harder than seemed necessary.

'Summoned by the royal gong,' Mary Ann said sarcastically. At the same moment, an elegant woman with coiffed silver-blond hair appeared at the opening of the atrium. It was impossible to tell if she had overheard anything. My two companions faded behind me like sullen little girls.

'So this is where you've been hiding my guest of honor.'

Caroline Warwick shaped thin lips into a smile, gliding toward me in ice-blue linen. I imagined the air chilling as she moved through it. Her grip was firm and dry on my hand, her voice Southern, but a violin, not a banjo. More Deep South.

I couldn't determine her age. Fifties? Sixty? Caroline had an ageless sex appeal that reminded me of Lauren Bacall, appearing both youthful and old, her skin near-flawless, her movements controlled, graceful, almost sensual.

'I hope this invitation wasn't an imposition, Emily. I'm sure you're not quite settled yet.' *Ema-lae.* My name falling from her tongue was like a caress. So why was I certain my hostess didn't give a flip if this was an imposition?

27

I smiled. 'Not at all.' I caught the flash of something white out of the corner of my eye. The newcomer stood several feet behind and to the left of Caroline, a nymph in a frothy shift and fire-engine-red stiletto heels. Short, casually spiked dark hair, a heart-shaped face. A small dollar sign encrusted with diamonds hung off the silver chain around her neck – a little irony with her last name that I'd bet was intended.

Misty Rich straddled the line between Peter Pan fairy and punker. She was instantly my favorite person within a radius of 11,000 square feet.

She raised her wineglass coyly at me, brushing her hand against a green frond, familiar, as if we were already playing a game.

CHAPTER 3

After two hours of a maverick card tournament that involved drinking, dice, musical partners, and trivia questions, my eyes blinked in slow motion. My mid-trimester bedtime clock had set itself at 9 p.m. and the alarm had buzzed about twenty minutes ago.

I was pretty sure I could fall asleep sitting up in this chair, in spite of the din of voices and laughter that rose with each bottle of Prosecco consumed. At Caroline's wish, we'd 'removed' ourselves to a game room set up with eight card tables of four chairs each. The buffet that ran along the wall was heaped with chocolate truffles, raspberries, and ice buckets chilling about a thousand dollars' worth of fizz.

I'd played Bunko before, but this oddball Southern version required more than tossing the dice and luck. Good for me, since luck had never been my thing. But I was good at facts. Ever since winning the sixth-grade geography bee by knowing that the smallest country is Vatican City (what good Catholic girl doesn't know that?), I'd realized the power of storing loose pieces of information.

To the delight of my multiple partners, including a frail old woman named Gert who called me Ruby all night, I was able to rack up bonus points by knowing that Audrey Hepburn won an Oscar for her debut role in *Roman Holiday*, that Van Gogh sold exactly one painting in his lifetime, and that the collective noun for a group of crows is a *murder*.

An hour and a half in, I gave up trying to remember too many names that ended in *i* or *y* or *ie*. I'd learned through rapid partner swapping that not everyone was a 'regular' and that permanent admission into this club required Caroline's approval, a 'donor's fee,' and maybe the selling of a teeny bit of one's soul. Caroline didn't play. Instead, she wandered from group to group, with her mouth drawn up like a coin purse. The purpose of a hostess is to make everyone relax, but her arrival had the opposite effect. Everyone swigged whatever she was drinking.

Caroline slipped past my table just as Marcy on my right began to yell into the most blinged-out, bejeweled phone I'd ever seen. 'Really? *Seriously?* You're bothering me with *that* right now? I have no idea where the frickin' weed whacker is. We have a *service*, for Christ's sake.'

She tossed the phone into a Louis Vuitton bag that could hold a horse's head and scooped up her cards. 'My husband just called to ask what I've done with the weed whacker because it isn't hanging on the hook in the garage. He doesn't want to use it. God forbid that he'd ever touch a tool. We pay someone $200 a week for that. He just wants to know where I put it. Jezus. Our son probably sold it on eBay. More power to him.'

Jenny's boobs bounced stiffly as she tossed a round of sixes. 'Last week, Rick called me at my best friend's fortieth birthday lunch at Le Cinq to tell me the dog crapped a loose one all over the upstairs rug. I'm in Paris eating things I can't pronounce and he wants to know what he should do. *He runs a multimillion-dollar business.*'

The owner of the Louis Vuitton purse smirked. 'What did you tell him?'

'To be sure that when I walked in the door, it was like it never happened. Jesus, call the professionals.' Jenny nudged me. 'What do you think, Emily? I thought New Yorkers had lots of opinions.'

The three of them waited expectantly, the dice still.

'Well,' I played it deadpan, 'I think these things are never really about the dog shit and the weed whacker.'

Right answer. Everybody laughed. Lots of wine, lots of man bashing, lots of exclamations involving Jesus, and lots of me keeping my mouth shut whenever possible.

Misty and I finally landed at the same table on the two-hour mark. She'd abandoned her ruby heels somewhere in favor of bare feet. A French pedicure. Long pretty toes, which she tucked easily up under her on the chair. Dark, purposely mussed and moussed hair framed an expertly made-up face. Not beautiful but highly cute. The kind of girl that boys like to throw in the pool. I guessed her to be in her late twenties or early thirties. Her only other jewelry besides the dollar-sign necklace was a wide platinum wedding band. Her fingernails were bare and chewed to the quick.

'Hi, newbie,' she said.

'Hi back,' I replied.

Gert was hobbling her way over to round out the foursome at our table, tipping most of her glass onto the carpet on the way. Her gray hair peeked out under the Bunko crown, a Dallas Cowboys cap covered with rhinestones and assorted political and memorabilia pins, including one that read I MISS W. I had been trying very hard all night not to roll a Bunko and receive the honor of wearing it. Gert stopped abruptly in the middle of the room, as if she'd suddenly lost her place in time. I left Misty to grab Gert's arm and guide her to the empty chair next to mine.

'Ruby!' she crowed enthusiastically, patting my hand. 'There you are!'

'Alzheimer's,' murmured Tiffany Green, who'd just rotated to the table. 'My husband is her pharmacist.'

Tiffany shot Misty and me a cold stare and stopped her first roll in mid-air. 'Have you two filled out your applications yet?' she demanded.

'What application?' I asked. Letty had mentioned

32

an application, too. 'I don't understand the application thing.'

'I never got in,' Gert confessed forlornly. 'I'll be with my dear Frank and Jesus before I get in. Will one of you nice girls scatter my ashes at Lake Texoma?'

'Your husband's name was Jasper, honey,' Tiffany said.

'I sure as hell know what my husband's name was.' I had the feeling she certainly did. Gert held the piece of paper in her hand closer to the thick lenses of her glasses. 'I also know that the phrase *rule of thumb* comes from an old English law that said a man couldn't beat his wife with anything bigger around than his thumb. Give me three points for getting that. Who makes up these questions?'

'Look, I'm just wanting to know who my competition is,' Tiffany persisted. 'There's one spot open for fall. I've been waiting since last year, so I'm hoping y'all can see that it's only right that it would go to me.'

'Will someone play a ghost hand for me?' I asked. 'I need to find a bathroom.'

'Down the hall, three doors on the left,' Tiffany instructed briskly. 'Or two doors. Or maybe it's to the right. Whatever. You'll find one. There's at least ten potty rooms in this place.'

She threw the dice harder than necessary, one of them bouncing into Misty's lap. 'Y'all be thinking about what I said,' she muttered.

I shut the heavy game room door behind me and sagged against the flocked wallpaper of the hallway, the chatter from the room instantly muted. Mike owed me big for this night. A series of closed doors trailed away on both sides of me. Low-lit sconces. Ivy creeping up the walls. The whole effect reminded me of an old luxury hotel.

Pick a door, any door. Your grandmother and hot tea behind Door One. An illicit lover behind Door Two. A maniacal Jack Nicholson with a bloody knife behind Door Three. All better options than returning to Tiffany's inquisition.

A dark maple staircase swirled up from the ground floor, breaking briefly for the second landing, and then disappearing above my head. *How many floors,* I wondered, *for one rich lady?*

The baby gave my bladder a swift kick. I counted three doors to the left and knocked.

Mary Ann's voice filtered out. 'It's going to be a while. I'm puking.'

I tried a few more doors, all locked, finally finding a knob that turned at the very end near a back servants' staircase. It opened up into a bedroom. I practically flew inside to the guest bath visible from the door. I barely made it to the toilet, shoving the door closed with my foot. Four glasses of water plus one roly-poly fetus was basic pregnant math, sort of like how a Ben & Jerry's Half Baked ice-cream bar plus a small bag of salt and vinegar chips equaled a nice afternoon snack.

porcelain sink with a large
l-painted inside the bowl.
. I dried my hands on my
back into the bedroom. I
rints stamped in the thick
fossilized dinosaur's. Sheer
ere tied back on all corners
poster. I imagined pulling at
ing there in a private purple

ner I should fluff out my foot-
ace behind.

Mew.

Startled, I swung around, knocking my knee painfully against the trunk at the foot of the bed. *What was that?* A kitty? Maybe trapped in the closet? There were two doors in the room besides the one to the bathroom, one with a key in the lock. I picked the door without the key and found myself staring at a red Miele vacuum cleaner, a tight row of empty wooden hangers, and built-in shelves holding extra linens and towels. No cat.

I stared at the door with the key. There were way too many doors in this place.

Mew.

Tiny, soft, polite. The universal cat distress call.

What the hell. I turned the key, pushed the door open, and found myself on the threshold of another bedroom.

Two thoughts, almost simultaneously.

That was one mean-looking cat on the bed.

Hadn't Mike told me that Caroline had lost a *son*?

This room belonged to a girl. A girl in transition. Pale pink walls and a cream-colored quilted bedspread with a battered teddy bear perched on top. Old-fashioned French Provincial furniture. A porcelain music box shaped like pink toe shoes rested on the dresser below a mirror. Postcards and random pictures were stuck inside the edges of the mirror's frame, arranged a little too perfectly.

A movie poster of *Rear Window* was tacked to one wall and a smiling Elizabeth Taylor in *National Velvet* to another. The room felt unused but regularly dusted, like a set piece in a museum. The whole effect was disturbing.

The cat, an enormous, whorled yellow and white tabby with wide gold eyes, bared his teeth from a predatory position on the bed. He looked like he benched his weight at the cat gym and needed no rescuing from me.

'Shhh, sweet-sweet-kitty-kitty.' It came out the way I worried I was going to talk to my baby.

The cat settled back on his haunches, glaring. His eyes followed me as I drifted toward the bookcase and several rows of neatly lined-up volumes. At least twenty diaries, the kind with the cheap lock that any kid brother could pop with a pin.

My Diary, in worn silver lettering, was printed

on each of the spines. No imagery of Hello Kitty, peace signs, or those *Twilight* guys. I shivered. I felt like I was standing in a pink funeral parlor. The little girl of this room didn't exist anymore, I felt sure. I doubted she'd ever stood in this spot. The bed, the bear, the pictures, the diaries – all of it transported from another time and place.

My eyes landed on a cat box in the corner, spread smooth with clean gray litter.

No kitty footprints.

The cat had dropped a small, curly brown turd on the floor right beside the box.

His little message.

He wanted out.

The party was breaking up by the time I slipped back, women milling around, chattering, saying goodbye. I threaded my way to Misty, who was bent over, strapping on her shoes. I guessed the heels at six inches. Knockoffs.

'What took you so long?' she asked.

'A cat that needs an antidepressant.'

She stared at me a moment, then grinned, displaying small, pretty, very straight teeth. 'I'm sorry we didn't get a chance to talk more. How about lunch this week? My place? My husband's out of town.'

'Sure.' I leapt at the friendly, casual invitation.

'Emily?'

I turned to acknowledge a fiftyish, plain, very

tall woman, one of the few in the room to let her gray hair sprout however it wanted to. 'I just wanted to introduce myself. I'm Gretchen Liesel. These girls are at full gossip tilt since your husband rode into town on his metaphorical horse.'

I'd gotten a good vibe off of Gretchen even though I had only observed her tonight from a distance. A nice, low laugh that carried. The night's high scorer on trivia, besting me by a point. A gray dove in a room of peacocks. I turned to include Misty, but she had drifted away.

'Everyone tells me you're the person to see about the baby,' I told Gretchen, smiling. 'My OB in New York recommended someone, but she's in Dallas. I've seen her once. At the Margot Perot Center. It's a little farther to drive than I thought.'

'Her name?'

'Herrera.'

'I know her. She's very good. High-risk pregnancies.' She paused as if thinking about that. 'It's not that far really. And the Perot center is state-of-the-art, embracing, even. Whatever you think of Ross Perot, you can't argue with his ingenuity. Or generosity.'

'I voted for him,' I said.

Gretchen laughed. 'Don't say that too loudly. Here's my card. I don't steal patients, but I'm available to you locally in a crisis.'

We exchanged a few more words, mostly her

admonitions about how pregnant women needed to be extremely careful not to get dehydrated in the brutal Texas summer. Eight tall glasses of water a day, at least. She urged me to stick a bunch of plastic water bottles in the freezer and grab one for the cup holder of my car every time I walked out of the house. Screw the environment for a few months. The water would melt just right, and I would be thirty percent less likely to faint.

Gretchen Liesel punctuated my evening with the most normal conversation of the night. I glanced around for Misty but couldn't find her. We hadn't set a day or a time. While waiting in line for Caroline to clasp my hand regally at the door, I wondered if I could make it home without dozing at the wheel.

Back in the Volvo, seatbelt buckled over Baby, I switched on the motor, only to be jolted by another *rap, rap, rap*. Letty.

Now what does she want?

Instead, when I rolled down the window, the face surprised me.

'Dr Liesel?'

She leaned in through the window, her voice lowered, her breath smelling pleasantly like peppermints and champagne, appropriately antiseptic.

'Gretchen, please,' she told me. 'This might sound strange since you don't know me at all. But be careful around these women, Emily. They like to pry and tell. A tip from one ex–East Coaster to another.'

Before I could respond, she'd straightened and tossed a little wave to Caroline, a spidery shape in the doorway, like something etched in a Tim Burton movie. Surely, this wasn't Caroline's message Gretchen was delivering?

My head pounded, the effects of the wine, my two-week withdrawal from caffeine, and one of the most bizarre social evenings of my life.

I watched Dr Liesel trot around the corner. No car. Gretchen lived in the kingdom, too.

I cranked the Volvo into gear and let Hugh take me home, away from that little girl's pink room, frozen in time.

I smelled honeysuckle and damp wood when I stepped outside the next morning onto the turn-of-the-century wraparound porch, *my* porch, the one I'd dreamed of while stuck in our hot box of an apartment on 57th Street.

I reached for the envelopes stuffed into the old metal box hanging by the front door and wondered if I would always feel fear when I retrieved the mail, even though there are lapses of time between her letters. A full three years before the one recently delivered to our old apartment. Maybe she had needed a vacation. Maybe she'd been sick.

Maybe she wouldn't track me down here, in our new home, thousands of miles from New York.

Sometimes she slams me with pages of obscenities and wishes for my early death in strong, angry cursive. Sometimes she details how she'd like it to happen.

Sometimes she just types a single word.

Murderer.

I'm not who she thinks I am. Until the most recent communication, I wasn't absolutely sure *she* was even a she. My letter stalker never signed a name.

Now I knew. The last envelope that arrived in New York, the last one dropped into the shoebox, signaled an ominous change. It held a picture printed off the Internet, a painting I recognized instantly even though she had ripped three-fourths of it away, leaving nothing but the grieving mother, howling, distorted, cradling her dead child, all sharp edges and pain. Picasso's cubist masterpiece *Guernica.* This latest message was directed at me, the artist with a bloody brush. Worse, there were no more pretenses about who she was.

I never told anyone about the letters. It was another of my secrets, one that would require too much explaining, lead to places I don't want to go again.

My eyes grazed across the picturesque street, taking in the tidy patches of lawn and renovated cottages, starter homes for the iPad generation.

Nothing out of place.

I watched two young men hop out of a white van across the street, both wearing clear hard plastic backpacks sloshing with gasoline. One held the long black leaf blower in front of him with two hands, gripped like a rifle, as if he was prepared to fire, to spatter bullets across this quiet street. It wasn't that hard to imagine that he was.

I wanted to stop thinking like this.

CHAPTER 4

'OK, what's the deal?' I asked, slathering my belly with Coppertone. 'Are they some kind of high society Texas cult?'

My sunglasses skied down the sweat on my nose as I leaned deep into the cushion of a lounge chair cushion. I was mesmerized by the drop-off edge of Misty's pool where water met flat blue Texas sky. It was as if there was nothing to prevent me from swimming right up into the clouds.

The sun felt good after the icy air-conditioning. A radicchio salad with fresh shrimp, takeout from Central Market, settled nicely in my tummy. Misty had called this morning to make the date for lunch and a little old-fashioned Texas 'laying out,' to hell with grammar.

'I should have helped you more last night,' she said. 'Those parties are like a Tilt-A-Whirl. I could hold your hand, but there's really no way to get off until the ride stops.'

I found Misty's own situation curious. She lived in a modernist's dream on an exclusive hilltop: a million-dollar-plus house with geometric windows that stared down on a few Mexican-tiled roofs peeking out from the lush greenery of live oaks. The nearest neighbors, I presumed.

Up close, the stones in Misty's dollar-sign necklace were fake, but the near-invisible, high-tech security system protecting us at the moment was worthy of a nutty dictator in Dubai. Most people wouldn't notice. I had a former ATF agent for a husband, whose hobby was spotting them.

The place was spacious but not huge. Maybe 3,500 square feet total. Black wood floors gleamed. Triangle skylights, stainless appliances, sharp corners. Scattered Oriental silk rugs lay in the open spaces and a vivid Kandinsky wannabe sat over the fireplace, warming things up.

My life had taken a dramatic leap, I decided, from antique-filled, four-story vertical townhouses of the old moneyed to cavernous spaces with high ceilings and air-conditioning bills that must hit at least a grand a month.

An hour earlier, Misty had grabbed a pitcher of iced raspberry tea and two salads in plastic containers from the near-empty refrigerator. I glimpsed milk, Dijon mustard, and a six-pack of Evian on the shelves before she shut the door. She ushered me to a sunlight-flooded room off the kitchen and we sat Japanese-style on the floor at a low dark-wood table. We leaned companionably against bright square cushions. Lunch had been filled with easy, shallow conversation. No jumping into emotional or intellectual depth.

I learned that her husband, currently on a trip

to Japan, handled international real estate and roamed the world. They moved here from California after her husband's company headquarters relocated to Dallas. She tried to give the impression that she happily played the role of corporate wife, but I didn't buy it. Misty seemed too intelligent and purposeful for that. I didn't feel comfortable enough with her to pursue the truth.

However, I did want to finagle a few more details about Caroline. I adjusted the tilt on my lounge chair and tried again.

'What's La Warwick's story?'

Something flashed in Misty's eyes. 'It's too late for me. But you . . . you should run the other way.' Seeing my bewildered look, she said, 'Caroline gets off on trying to fix other people's pain. She worms her way in, figures out where you're most vulnerable, how you can be useful. Your husband, for example. He could be useful.' It was a much blunter answer than I expected and it chilled me. My second warning. First Gretchen, now Misty.

'You've only known Caroline for a few months, right? Surely she's not that bad. For the most part, these women appear harmless. Rich and bitchy, but harmless.'

'One of those rich and bitchy women told me that Caroline got her drunk and then recorded her blabbing about an affair she was having with her kid's soccer coach. On video.'

'You're telling me Caroline blackmails people?'

Misty shrugged. 'Call it what you want. The next

45

day, when the woman sobered up, Caroline emailed her the iPhone video with a warning to stop having the affair, that it was immoral and potentially devastating to her children. So she did.'

Misty took another swig of water while I thought about that. I wasn't seriously bothered. A father's affair wrecked one of my childhood friends. Took a chunk out of her forever. My friend was now on her fourth marriage. Caroline's videotaping was sneaky, but apparently in a gray moral area for me.

'The women in that club aren't harmless,' Misty said abruptly. 'You weren't so far off with the cult idea. Caroline is their little Hitler. They need to *belong*. At whatever cost.'

I opened my mouth to respond, then thought better of it. For the third time since we'd settled outside, Misty tugged down the bottom of her white, conservative one-piece, cut low on her bottom and high around the neck, like a competitive swimmer's suit. It reminded me of something my mother used to wear. Misty wore a flimsy black coverup with sheer sleeves over it.

'I burn,' she said. From what I could see, Misty owned the body of a sixteen-year-old, without a dimple of fat or cellulite on her, so the modesty confused me. Especially since I was all out there, with my basketball belly, in a yellow-polka-dotted bikini. Especially since I knew Misty had funky taste in high heels. As Misty repositioned herself, I noticed faded scars on the insides of her thighs. So Mary Ann wasn't making that up.

'Car accident as a kid,' she said, seeing where my eyes landed. Her legs closed up tight. Embarrassed.

'I can barely see them,' I lied.

The conversation had veered sharply into dark and uncomfortable territory, derailing my single-minded purpose in coming here: to make a friend. I watched goose bumps prick up under a streak of rosy sunburn on my arm, where I missed a spot with the sunscreen. I lathered on more sunscreen and decided to ease us back the other way. 'How did you find this house? I love it.'

'An . . . acquaintance told me about it. The previous owner invents high-tech alarm systems for museums. Started messing around in his barn in Edna, Texas, at thirteen. One of his devices is now used in the Louvre.'

That explained the house's top-of-the-line security system. The artist in me liked the idea that the *Mona Lisa* was protected by a device born in a barn, like Jesus.

'Tell me about you,' Misty said. 'You ran an art gallery? And what's the story with your husband? The word is that he's a good-looking version of Michael Chiklis.'

I laughed. 'For his already giant ego's sake, I won't share that. Mike led an ATF team on special ops all over the United States, and he's still here. Alive, I mean. And all of his guys. Every one of them.' A little pride leaked into my voice.

'What made him take this job in Clairmont?

Everybody's wondering.' Misty rose to splash water on her legs and then stretched out again beside me. 'Seems like this place would drive him out of his mind after all that excitement.'

'Frankly, we'd both like a lot *less* excitement. Mike's thirty-five. I'm thirty-two. New York saps you. It's a very hard place to live. And we never knew when he'd be assigned to a case and have to take off.'

I laid a hand on my stomach.

'This baby is a reason to change. Even if it's just for a few years, this is a good break for us.' I was glad the sunglasses hid tears stinging behind my eyes. Damn hormones. I wasn't going to open up to this reticent new friend about the miscarriages.

'It seems like it would be hard to give up everything that you've both worked for.' Misty's voice sounded wistful.

'Don't get me wrong. I loved my job. Helping people pick out beautiful things to live with. Giving a break every now and then to a young artist. But I could easily slip into a seventy-hour work week before an opening, especially if Mike was working and I had nothing to go home to. I had no time or space in our apartment to paint. What about you?'

'I'm in an in-between phase,' Misty replied vaguely. 'Trying to figure out what's next.'

She said earlier over our salads that she attended USC but she didn't say when or claim a degree or say what she studied. She'd managed to sidestep all of my questions about her family or her childhood. She didn't spare any goopy emotion on her husband. I couldn't put my finger on her accent, blunted, an accent from nowhere.

Still, I liked her. I understood the layers of the private soul.

The house, oddly silent, felt empty of spirits other than Misty's. The stillness wasn't even disturbed by the friendly rumble of a refrigerator, but then hers was a sleek machine and not the ten-year-old Maytag that came with our home.

'When will Todd be back?' I asked.

'He's overseeing the building of a corporate headquarters in Osaka right now. I'd guess three months. Maybe four.' Alone in a grand house, lots of windows, no man. *Turn on that cowboy's alarm, girl.*

Misty tilted the Evian bottle toward her lips even though it was empty.

I had detected an edge in her voice, but before I could say anything she got up, murmuring about a kink in the pool sweeper.

I lay back and drifted, letting the sun soak my brain like crack cocaine.

She returned five minutes later and our talk grew superficial and drowsy, with longer and longer pauses in between. We fell quiet. When my eyes opened again, the sun had started its descent and the chair beside me was empty, Misty's towel tossed over the edge.

I must have drifted off. I dug through my beach bag for my cell phone. Almost four. Good grief. All the books said I'd be suffused with energy at this point in the pregnancy. Instead I was nodding off like a grandmother.

I took a quick dunk in the pool to rinse away the sweat and grease, and toweled myself off.

'Misty?' I entered the tiled mud room, although I guess in a modern masterpiece like this it was called something grander. A mini–washer and dryer were stacked one on top of the other, and a neat basket of clean rolled-up beach towels rested on the floor near the door, next to five pairs of size 6 flip-flops. They looked barely worn.

I ventured farther inside, past the kitchen, into the sunken great room at the front of the house, my own flip-flops echoing like little drum clicks in the cool silence. Goose bumps pricked my legs and shoulders, and I wrapped the towel more tightly around me.

'Misty?' I called louder this time, moving toward the spiral steel-and-wood staircase that hung in the air at the far end of the room, invisibly suspended, a work of art in itself.

I didn't feel good about leaving without a goodbye. Or staying there alone, for that matter.

A few more minutes and I'd call again. Probably she was in the bathroom.

I wandered aimlessly around sleek leather furniture, running my fingers over a large vessel sculpted and hammered out of copper. I recognized the artist, found her mark, wondered if Misty knew the heat and sweat and muscle and pounding that went into making it an object of beauty. Ayesha. I sold her jewelry in my gallery after she figured out she could make more money per hour of sweat by melting metal into beautiful *little* things.

I leaned in to inspect the piece hanging over the fireplace. Maybe not a wannabe. It looked like a genuine Kandinsky.

Der Blaue Reiter. The Blue Rider. A horseman riding with his girl, a blur across a green space, the background colors popping across the canvas. I'd seen it in person before, years ago. A small fortune in paper and paint. I couldn't believe it was in a private collection now. This had to be a glorious copy. Even my practiced scrutiny couldn't tell.

My eyes swept the black-and-white photographs that lined the walls, almost certainly snapped by the same artist, one who favored farm landscapes and small-town America from the less blessed side of the tracks. No signature, but the work was somehow familiar, like I'd seen it in one of thousands of catalogs I had thumbed through.

I was particularly struck by a shot of a frame house falling in on itself. An old Chevy was rusting on the lawn, and a man's T-shirt hung on a clothesline, bleached white and stark, more like a flag of surrender than a symbol of hope.

At the end of my tour, I found myself in the corner at a round glass table that held the few personal objects in the room.

I lifted a heavy silver frame with a recent snap-shot of Misty. Her arms were wrapped around a good-looking, dark-haired man I assumed to be Todd. He emoted nice and cute, like a really smart guy who came into his prime after high school and never looked back. But you never knew.

I replaced it carefully and picked up the other picture on the table, also framed expensively. It was faded and a little blurry and not particularly well composed, the kind of photo that usually ends up in the bottom of the box or tossed out as unworthy. But it was easy to love the cherubic little girl with gold curly hair who grinned out at me, perched on a boy's bike, shoving the toy bauble on her finger toward the camera, showing it off.

Misty? The eyes, something around the nose. Maybe. I'd had blond hair at that age, too, but nature took its course. I smiled back.

'Emily.'

I jumped, almost dropping the little girl, and knocking Todd and Misty over, onto the glass. She had slipped up behind me.

'Sorry, Emily, I didn't mean to scare you. Can I please have that photo?' She didn't wait for me to hand it to her, snatching it out of my hands. 'Probably not good to scare a pregnant woman. I was on the phone with Todd.'

Really? I wondered. Why was I so sure that she was lying? That – wherever she had been – she'd been watching me? Then again, hadn't I thought the same thing after I left that bizarre pink room last night? That someone besides Big Kitty had their eyes on me? When had I gotten this paranoid?

Misty's body language was tense. She was holding the photograph of the little girl flat against her chest. Not happy with me. Or the conversation with Todd hadn't gone well.

'Thank you so much for today,' I stammered. 'I'm sorry I fell asleep.'

'No problem. You needed it, I'm sure.'

She edged us toward the door. Why did she even display that snapshot if she didn't want anyone to see it? We walked up the few steps that led to the polished black granite landing by the front door.

Impulsively, I made a decision. It seemed more ridiculous not to ask.

'Misty, who is the girl in the picture? You?'

She looked at me carefully before answering, deciding, I think, whether I could be trusted.

Later, I would brood about her words, about her use of the present tense instead of the past, before I knew Misty's secrets and after. How stupidly I'd misinterpreted everything.

She said, without a trace of a smile, 'It is the happiest day of my life.'

CHAPTER 5

Two days after the rape, I purchased a hammer and a seatbelt cutter and taped them securely under the driver's seat of my car. They weren't tools to defend myself.

I was tormented by a new, unreasonable fear that I would drown, trapped inside a car as it tumbled to the bottom of a river or a lake or the sea. Again and again, I imagined myself choking on the rising water, my terrified face pressed against glass. So, instead of studying for a critical trigonometry test or getting rape crisis counseling, I learned everything I could about how to escape from a submerged car.

For example, it's actually possible for electric windows to work for several minutes even underwater. I learned that I should roll them down immediately to equalize pressure in the car, hopefully as soon as the car hit the water. If the windows wouldn't roll down, I knew to punch out a side window with my hammer because the windshield glass is made to resist.

After swimming through the broken window, I might feel disoriented, so I'd look for air bubbles, which always travel up. If there were no air bubbles or it was too dark to see, I must not panic. Relax. My body would then naturally float upward, showing me the right way. And, of course, always swim toward the light.

Eventually, like monsters in the closet, that fear vanished.

When somebody asks, I always say I am happy. I *am* a happy person. Like everyone else, I am suffused with colors, hopefully more light than dark. The rape didn't destroy me. It's not the worst thing that could have happened. Others suffer far greater traumas. Most of them still laugh, love, pursue careers, remarry, have children, go on with life. Buoy themselves up. Appear smooth on the surface even though there is an active, textured inside life no one has a clue about.

I can go months without thinking about the rape, but I'd be lying if I said it hadn't transformed me. How much did it alter my future? I'll never know. A teenage drunk driver killed my parents in a car crash a year and a half later, so it became a little hard to tell where one trauma left off and another began.

I switched colleges four times, eventually earning a double major in visual art and theater, with a master's in art history. A shrill, bitter acting professor was my earliest therapist, elated by my ability to mimic and disappear into someone else. At night, alone, I painted obsessively – the flowers on my kitchen table, the cracked mirror that the previous tenant left behind. Sometimes, the abstract slashes of Pierce's face. I usually threw my work into the dumpster behind my apartment before it dried.

I married a man professionally trained to rescue me. I love him more than anything on earth. I am afraid to tell him my whole story, although I feel that the time to do it is coming closer.

Every morning in the shower, I take my finger and draw good luck symbols in the fog on the glass: a heart with my initials, a four-leaf clover, a peace sign, a cross.

I don't think I'm an unlucky person. I just wouldn't call myself lucky.

I found myself back at the entrance to The Manses of Castlegate three days later. The twangy troll at the gatehouse was gone, replaced by a large-boned black woman named Shaunette, so identified by the Hobby Lobby name tag that she'd apparently forgotten to take off after her shift. Shaunette was working more than one job, and I mean *working*. Nothing was going to get past Shaunette.

While Shaunette grilled me about my business on 'the property,' I wondered whether her mother had been counting on a boy and had tacked on the 'ette' after an exhausting labor. I hoped Shaunette's zeal for security would save me from spending the next hour or so at an impromptu tea with Caroline that would probably involve a stilted conversation about Impressionism and God knows what else. I debated saying no on the phone yesterday, but Caroline cast her spell of charm and guilt and suckered me in. It is tricky turning down a Southerner. I was going to need to get better at it.

No lucky break from Shaunette. She handed me a forty-percent-off coupon for Hobby Lobby, and waved me through. 'We just got some good ceramic roosters in,' she imparted confidentially.

So now I stood under Caroline's arch, studying its careful geometry, thinking how I would sketch it. I tugged up the front of my sundress, which was sliding down provocatively. I had let a relentless saleswoman in one of the local maternity boutiques convince me that cantaloupe-sized black, white, and yellow polka dots provided a pleasant optical illusion for a woman in the second trimester. I paid $258.97 to look like a pregnant beetle emerging from the rain forest.

The door opened before I could knock, revealing a pretty Hispanic woman in traditional black and white maid garb. I remembered her moving silently through the background at the Bunko party.

'I'm Maria,' she said, all shyness and obedience. But as she led me a few feet down the hall, her swaying hips said something else entirely. She stopped abruptly in front of a lacquered black door marked by an intricate pen-and-ink drawing, which I had passed by without noticing the other night.

It was the first thing that set me slightly on edge.

A Chinese girl lounged on a couch like an exotic bird, provocatively offering a tiny foot to the man bowed and kneeling on the floor in front of her. A crown of pearls rested on her head. Her hands were bound behind her back by black string. The image was bluntly asking: *Who holds the power?*

Maria twisted the doorknob and nudged me into a mahogany-paneled, windowless room. It was dimly lit by the red and yellow prisms of a Tiffany floor lamp and the orange glow from a gas log in the fireplace. A weak stream from the air-conditioning vent in the ceiling blew the idea of winter on my bare shoulders.

I was not the only guest. Three other women, two of whom I recognized from Caroline's party, sat stiffly like posed mannequins in chairs placed in a careful semi-circle. Tiffany was closest to the fireplace, pressing a glass of iced tea to the sweaty sheen on her cheek. Three chairs stood empty. One for me. One for Caroline, who had risen and stepped toward me with a tight smile and an outstretched hand. One for someone else.

'Hello, dear.' Caroline's grip was perfunctory. A purple silk shift draped her slender body like a Grecian statue. Her lipstick matched the brilliant square-cut ruby nestled on a gold chain in the hollow of her delicate neck. The whole effect was bold, simple, and stunning. She gestured to the straight-back chair beside hers. 'Please have a seat. You remember Tiffany and Holly, right? And this is Lucinda Beswetherick. I don't believe you've met.'

Frozen smiles from the three women, like Best Actress nominees waiting for someone to rip open their fate. It reminded me of another room, a long time ago. A room I hadn't escaped. I had wanted to run then, too.

'Super-cute dress.' Tiffany was staring at my polka-dotted wonder. She was mimicking the exact words of the woman who sold it to me. I was pretty sure neither of them meant it.

'Thanks. Nice to see all of you.' My eyes were pulled to the behemoth image rising behind Caroline: a floor-to-ceiling oil portrait of our hostess as a teenager. She sat English-style on a white horse that appeared to have sprung loose from a fairy tale. Either the artist painted a sycophantic lie, or Caroline was devastatingly beautiful in her youth. There was more raw sexuality in this painting than in the implied bondage in the hall.

'We'll get started when our final guest shows up.' There was a tinge of irritation in Caroline's tone. She waited for me to sit before sitting herself. Her skirt slipped up several inches above her knees, showing off legs that reminded me of a dancer's, all sinewy muscle.

Holly, an interchangeable blonde with an inter-changeable Birkin bag, sprang to life and bowed her head to her phone, in the middle of a frantic text conversation.

'What's wrong?' Tiffany's hyper-whisper easily carried.

Holly didn't bother to whisper. 'Alan Jr just told me he needs to have a potato carved into a Russian dictator by tomorrow morning. I pay $15,000 a year to a private school and my reward is that I'll be up at midnight cutting out felt clothes for a freaking potato.' The phone grunted twice and her thumbs angrily tapped another response to the forgetful little person on the other end.

'Do Brezhnev,' Lucinda advised. She spoke with a slight lisp. 'Raymond did him last year. We got five extra points for the eyebrows and another ten for all the thumbtacks we stuck in him for medals.'

'Brezhnev had a fetish for them, right?' I asked. The women turned and stared at me blankly. 'Medals, I mean. Didn't he award himself the Lenin Peace Prize?' Silence. 'Black feathers would make great eyebrows,' I added weakly.

In New York, this was my skill. Carrying a room, using odd bits of information to insinuate myself and make everyone feel a little more comfortable. Here, I shifted in my seat, rebuffed.

More vigorous thumb action from Holly.

What in the hell are we waiting for?

It was boiling in this room, a hell entirely of my own making. I wasn't here just because of Mike. Part of me was still that nineteen-year-old girl wanting to be accepted. *Will she ever go away? Stop seeking assurance?*

'That's a lovely portrait, Caroline,' I tried. 'Very skilled. Who is the artist? Did you sit for it?'

'No one you would know, dear. It's actually a copy of a photograph taken when I was fifteen. My father sent the photo to an elderly portrait artist in Paris. He is long dead and forgotten, I'm sure. He painted it and shipped it over the ocean. I still remember the day they unbundled it from the truck and hung it in the parlor. My sister was so jealous.'

'And the horse?'

'One of many.' She spoke a little more curtly. The other women in the room tilted our way, like someone had pulled a string through their bodies.

'Are you able to see your sister often these days?'

'My sister is deceased,' she said coldly.

'I'm so sorry,' I stammered. 'I had heard about your husband and . . . son, but I didn't know . . .'

There was a sound at the door. Caroline's head whipped toward it.

Misty stood in the open frame, a living, breathing curse word. A rhinestone-studded T-shirt clung tautly to her chest. A white leather miniskirt hugged her butt, stopping one inch from obscenity. Bare white legs descended into short yellow cowboy boots. She could have passed for seventeen, Caroline's naughty child who spent the night out without calling. It occurred to me that she might have a personality disorder.

'My apologies for being late, Caroline.' She touched her hostess's cheek briefly with her lips, leaving a light lavender smear. 'Todd and I kept getting cut off. A bad overseas connection.' She plopped into the empty place next to me and made a face. 'We're having a few issues.'

Caroline's expression said she didn't believe Misty, not for a second, while I wondered about openly using a fight with her spouse as an excuse and showing up for tea dressed like a Skype hooker. After Misty's biting attack on these women at our lunch, I wondered about her showing up at all.

But, thank God.

Caroline didn't say a word. She reached for a small wooden box on the Louis XV end table beside her. The signal, apparently, that we were beginning. Every eye in the room was now glued to that box.

'As most of you know, there is one opening in my club this year because of Helen's unfortunate death. I thought this would be a good way for me to get to know the prospective candidates a little better.'

Who was Helen?

I stared at the box. *Human ashes?* Misty stared at her bitten nails. Tiffany eagerly propped herself forward. Holly appeared to want to power through this as quickly as possible and get after that potato. Lucinda of the multisyllabic last name tossed back two pills from a prescription bottle, a little too late.

'Your husband's resume is obviously going to be a huge asset to our little community, Emily.' Before I could respond, Caroline nodded at Misty. 'I'm sure not everyone will cotton to you two being

62

on the fast track. The other girls here have been applying for years.'

Tiffany shot me a death stare, while I made a vague mental note to Google the etymology of *cotton* as a verb, during the part of my pregnant day when I sprawled on the bed with orange Doritos and Googled random things. During the part of my day where I pretended there was only one of me, not two or three or four.

'In this box, there are five slips of paper,' Caroline continued serenely. 'Each one is a secret that belongs to someone in this room. We'll pass the box, and each of you will randomly pull one out and read it aloud to the group.'

Not the boxed remains of a dead person. But this – what *was* this? I waited for the burst of laughter. For rebellion. For people to jump up and say they'd left these kinds of silly games behind a long time ago, at around fifteen, with séances and slutty bathroom graffiti. But no one flinched.

Caroline passed the box to me. I took it. I had a decision to make. It was a lovely box. Dark mahogany. Old. An intricate ivory rose was inlaid in the lid. My hand shook a little as I fiddled with the brass catch.

When I raised the lid, I smelled the sea. Salt. Decomposition.

Guilt.

The box held a jumble of white slips of paper that appeared to have escaped from fortune cookies. I tried to buy time by running one of my fingers over the words etched into the inside of the lid. *The rose remembers the dust from which it came.*

Caroline leaned over and moved my fingers into the nest of paper.

'Pull one out and read it aloud.' Insistent.

What did she know about me? I fumbled to separate one piece of paper from the others and smoothed it out between my fingers. I heard a voice, surely not mine, because the smart me would already be in her car, turning the key.

'*I killed Alex.*'

CHAPTER 6

I wanted to take the words back as soon as they floated from my mouth. Words like insidious dandelion seeds, blown from a slight puff of breath. Poisonous words that would thrive in a room like this, where the soil was already disturbed. But that must be the point.

One of the women in the room drew in an audible breath, either of shock or guilt. I didn't care who.

This was not my secret.

I stared at the other slips of paper, wondering which one was.

'Pass the box,' Caroline ordered.

Reluctantly, I handed the box to Misty.

Misty glanced at her slip and then over at me, hesitating. Then she read in a clear, calm voice: *'This baby is not my husband's.'*

'Are you kidding me?' The words flew out of my mouth. 'How could you read that? Of course this baby is my husband's!'

Caroline's hand landed lightly on my knee. 'Emily, this is a bonding exercise. We hold our thoughts until the end. You do not know if other women in this room are carrying a child.' I sucked in a breath. Every other belly in this room was a washboard. Actually, Tiffany's and Holly's sank in, like small moon craters.

Tiffany eagerly grabbed the box out of Misty's hands. 'This is fun. It reminds me of the old days at Alpha Chi. We told each other everything.' She giggled nervously, smoothing out her piece of paper. 'This one is *bad*. It says: *I do not believe in God*. Well, I can tell you this is not my secret. Just ask the woman I witnessed to in the Kroger express lane yesterday.'

She thrust the box at Holly, whose hands were tightly clenched in her lap, a one-inch red nail digging into her wrist like an implement of suicide. It also looked sharp enough to mutilate a potato.

'Come on, Holly, you need to play.' Tiffany's voice was impatient. 'Hell, I'll just pull a slip for you. Do you want me to read it?'

'That's not allowed,' Caroline said.

'Give it here.' Holly snatched one out. I was mesmerized by the small crescent-shaped indent in her wrist. She read the words silently. Something I wish I'd done. But then her face relaxed. 'It says, *Look under my bed.*'

'It doesn't say that. That's not a secret. It's more like an order.' Tiffany ripped the slip out of her hand. 'Oh. It does.' She shrugged. 'Kind of ambiguous.'

What's under my bed? Nothing, I assured myself.

No old sketches. No diary. Just dust. Maybe a pair of Mike's dirty socks.

The box passed to Lucinda, and I could feel its weight, so much heavier now that it was a few slips of paper lighter. I prayed that she would be the one person in this gathering with the common sense to stop all of this.

'There is blood in my house.' Lucinda's lisp was a little hard to understand, but the word *blood* was unmistakable. She popped the slip of paper in her mouth and began to chew like a bubble gum addict on cocaine. I had guessed her to be the one who didn't believe in God, but maybe I was wrong. Maybe there was blood in her house. Maybe her husband beat her, or her children. Maybe all the bad things in her life, all her insecurities and decisions, sprung from her very first lisping word.

A trickle of sweat rolled down my back. I felt physically pinned to the chair by invisible forces. Waiting for the punch from a sneering bully. I was certain this exercise was going exactly as Caroline intended.

A butterfly brushed my arm. Caroline's silk dress. She was swaying slightly in her chair, falling into me. I leaned over to steady her while everyone else remained rooted, staring the other way, fascinated by Lucinda's vigorous chomping.

'Are you OK, Caroline?' I said it loudly to get their attention, struggling to fake concern. After all, this nasty creature was torturing us.

Us. Already, the bonding that Caroline sought, and a seed of fury sprouted in me.

Lucinda had ceased to be the most bizarre thing in the room. Something appeared to be very wrong with Caroline. Her face was slick and waxy. 'I'm getting one of my migraines,' she stuttered out. 'We'll have to finish this some other time. Misty, can you see me up?'

It was oddly intimate, the way Caroline said Misty's name. Maybe Caroline had already chosen. Maybe Misty was in on all of this. Maybe Caroline was acting. I couldn't tell. It was convenient timing. The box was empty, still sitting in Lucinda's lap.

Mike once joked that body language should be a high school requisite, like French or Spanish. He believed that everything you really needed to know about a person could be observed. And Misty was up and draping Caroline's arm over her narrow shoulders as if she'd done it a hundred times before.

Holly was the first of us to stand, finding her voice as soon as Misty and Caroline disappeared. 'Well, girls, I had a better time spreading my legs at my last Pap. Caroline can stick her club right up her ass. I won't be applying.' That was a lot of imagery my stomach couldn't handle right now.

Because I could taste the inside of that box.

Holly was halfway to the door when Lucinda spit. The wad of paper flew out of her mouth and landed right on the pristine red toenail poking out of one of Holly's Via Spiga sandals.

'Jesus, Lucinda, get some help, will you?' Lucinda flinched like a dog used to being kicked. Holly bent over to scrape the soggy ball off her toe with a practiced red fingernail. She stalked over to the fireplace and flicked it into the flames along with her own slip of paper. 'I recommend y'all do the same and that we all forget the last twenty minutes ever happened.' She paused at the door, flashing a sly smile. 'Not that it's any of y'all's business, but I keep a few naughty toys under the mattress.'

I wouldn't want to share a lifeboat with Holly, but in the last ten seconds, I had developed new respect for her. I bet she'd carve a damn good potato. Lucinda hobbled after her, mumbling an apology to her back. On any normal day, I'd be jumping up, not admiring Holly in the least, trying to soften Lucinda's humiliation, assuring her everything was OK.

Their exit left me alone with Tiffany and the flirtatious girl in the portrait. Tiffany slid over to Misty's chair and pulled it in so close to me I could feel her body heat, ramped up from the fireplace. She smelled like chocolate-covered pinecones, probably some designer perfume I couldn't afford. The two scars of her eyelid lift were barely perceptible. I thought that we weren't so different from the girl in the hall, whose tiny foot had been broken and bound for beauty. Whose hands were bound by black string.

'If that's all she's got on me, I'm in good shape.'

Tiffany snatched the piece of paper out of my hand. 'Alex needed to go.'

Am I dreaming? Still in New York, asleep on my couch?

'Stop looking at me like that. It was just a little antifreeze in his water. *Stop looking at me like that!*'

I wasn't sure what expression I was wearing. I couldn't feel my lips or my cheeks. I was perspiring from the top of my head, which I hadn't known was possible. The room was baking now, unbearable.

Tiffany began to pace like a feral cat in five-inch heels, desperate to be let out of her cage. Four steps forward. Four steps back. Again. Again. And again.

When did someone shut the door?

Tiffany halted abruptly in front of me, as if she'd made a decision. 'Unfortunately, Hannah Beth was the one to find him. He was trembling and frothing a little bit at the mouth. But I told her he just spit up a little milk. She's only four, so she probably won't remember anyway. I bought her that Louis Vuitton purse shaped like a Chihuahua the next day. Adorable, and it doesn't shit.'

It took a second.

She's talking about a dog.

I tried to shut off my mind. To not imagine the face of the presumably adorable Hannah Beth when she found the small furry pile.

'See ya around, Emily. Or not. I really don't think you have the stomach for it.' Tiffany's eyes

70

raked lazily over my belly. It felt like a threat. I wanted to strike out, but my hand lay dead in my lap, and then she was gone.

I gazed up at the girl on the wall, frozen in blues and browns and greens, and wondered what she knew. She had to hold clues to Caroline Warwick, to the reasons I was here contemplating all the things I had tried to forget.

The weeping willow in the portrait suggested that Caroline had been raised somewhere else in the South, maybe by a river. Georgia? Kentucky? That fit with the honeyed accent. Riding pants and high black boots hugged long, graceful legs. Her hands gripped the reins loosely, but there was no question about whether the horse or the girl was in control.

My eyes roved over the woodwork. The ceiling. I stood and stared into the shiny black pupil of young Caroline. I squeezed my eyes shut, trying to quiet my mind. Instead, I saw the teddy bear on the bed in the little pink room somewhere above my head. Abused by love. No eyes. One ear, missing. The seam, sewn flat.

'What is wrong?'

My heart slammed like a rock against my chest, and I jumped sideways, knocking the Tiffany lamp. *Too many Tiffanys*, I thought crazily.

'I did not mean to scare you. Did you lose something?' Maria steadied the lamp.

'No. I'm sorry. I should go.'

I didn't tell Maria that before I closed my eyes

71

I had been looking for tiny cameras, because it would sound absurd. Or that I felt like I had stumbled onto a stage three days ago, in the smack-dab-middle of a play, and everyone knew their part but me.

And I didn't tell her that the relief coursing through my body was like when Daddy pulled back my swing, high and taut, and let me fly into the wind.

That lovely wooden box that stunk like the morning breath of the devil?

None of its secrets was about me.

The praying mantis is a stick figure that has five eyes and can turn its head 180 degrees to stalk his prey. All the way home, this is how I thought of Caroline, as page 44 in my mother's insect book.

Odd what pictures the brain chooses to keep. Me, age ten. Cross-legged on the kitchen floor. Opening up to the right page, as directed. My mother flipping pancakes and describing the beauty of the praying mantis despite the fact that it is a brutal and clever killer. The mantis pretends to be praying before thrusting out its spiky fore-arms and sinking its teeth into the neck of its prey. Not to kill it, but to paralyze it. Because the mantis likes to eat its victims alive.

I unzipped my dress and let it fall to the middle of my kitchen floor. My belly was a white balloon.

I wrapped a throw from the living room around my body, naked underneath except for a bra and a scrap of panties, opened the kitchen door, and walked purposefully across the backyard to the alley.

Mike had purchased two large plastic trashcans, preparing for the avalanche of diapers. I studied them, glancing both ways down the alley. No sign of life. I passed by our plastic bins and ventured another hundred yards to one of three old metal garbage cans in the tall grass between the houses. The alley was narrow, its road rutted like small-town alleys are, barely big enough for the garbage truck to pass.

I lifted the lid of the can and smelled the perfume left by thirty years of dung and rot. The can was empty, black on the bottom like a hole into the earth. I stuffed the dress all the way to the bottom. At the last minute, I slipped off my new sandals and threw them in, too. I slammed down the lid. It echoed in the afternoon silence, a dissonant cymbal clash.

I carefully retraced my path back on the dirt road, barefoot, trying to avoid the bits of glass and metal that had been spit back out by garbage trucks.

Three houses ahead of me, a man slipped from a yard into the alley. He wore the yellow and black nylon palette of Livestrong. He didn't wave, but his eyes never left me. He moved into the middle of the alley, stretching his body as if warming up for a run.

I was keenly aware how vulnerable I was. How

easy it would be to rip away the afghan hugging my body, the one that used to lie neatly folded across the back of my grandmother's couch.

How no one would hear while the glass and metal and rock bit into my back.

He watched me until I disappeared behind our fence.

CHAPTER 7

Mike was propped up by a pillow on the bed, reading glasses slid down on his nose, as he studied a thick manila file folder. A stack of folders toppled over on the floor on his side of the bed.

All through dinner and a little late evening yard work, I hadn't said a word about my visit with Caroline or the club membership she dangled like a glittery prize. I'd rattled on about a quick trip to Whole Foods. About the baby clothes that arrived in the mail from his sister in New Jersey, the one who would glue an Apple product to her ass if they invented one to go there. She had wrapped up a tiny onesie stamped with IPOOD and another that read, GET OFF FACEBOOK AND FEED ME.

The onesies made me laugh. That laugh, a long nap, and three small plastic cups of Jell-O chocolate pudding temporarily flicked Caroline back into the weeds where she belonged. She was nothing more than a Vegas psychic in Southern drag, I told myself. The carved box, the obscenely hot room, that giant, ridiculous portrait – her props. She had picked at our scabs, hoping they'd

75

bleed, probably having no idea how we got them. Except for the specificity of the name 'Alex,' the words on those pieces of paper could apply to thousands of people, if not millions.

But now, in bed with Mike, Caroline the mantis was creeping back, one green blade of grass at a time.

'I think there is something weird about Caroline Warwick,' I said abruptly. 'She is really pushing the issue of me joining her little club. The one I told you about the other night after her Bunko party.'

Mike rested his glasses on his head and put the folder down. His face wore the 'You are six months pregnant so I'm going to stop what I'm doing and listen to you' look. Usually, I loved that look.

'Did I tell you about the pink room? Her collection of diaries?' I knew that I hadn't, but I needed to ease in. 'I came across a room on my way to the bathroom the night of Caroline's party. It was like a creepy museum to some little girl. Very . . . pink. Old movie posters, a teddy bear, a bunch of old diaries on a shelf. I'm beginning to wonder whether Caroline replicated the room from her own childhood. If those diaries are hers.'

'So? We've all got our quirks. I still dream about a Derek Jeter–themed bathroom.'

'Uh-huh. We've discussed. I'm not going to listen to a lifetime of No. 2 jokes.' I punched him lightly on the arm.

'The club might be a good way for you to get to know people.' He said it absently, his eyes roaming back to the folder on the bed between us.

Not that interested. Part of me was glad. The part that wanted to figure out a few things first. I reached over and placed the folder back in his hand, glancing at the name on the file tab.

'Who's Jimmy Cooper?' I asked.

Mike had committed every single night to reading at least twenty old file cases from Clairmont's criminal history. He wanted them wired in his head before they were wired into a new, high-tech computer system arriving at his office next week. The database was Mike's first request after taking the job. He had figured it would take two years or maybe never to get approval. Instead, a big fat check to pay for it landed on his desk the next day.

'Jimmy Cooper is a man with a lifetime of drunk and disorderlies.' He scribbled a few notes, presumably about Jimmy Cooper, on the yellow legal pad in his lap.

I watched my stomach contort like a circus show, the baby punching out his nightly workout.

I juggled myself over onto my side, rubbing Mike's thigh.

'Stop doing that unless you're serious,' he said.

'Does anything bad ever happen in this town?' I asked.

'The last homicide was about two years ago. Domestic. A trailer park case just inside the city

77

limits. The city council conveniently redrew that line two months later so it didn't show up in their statistics. In the last seven years, the city has recorded two murders and two suicides in its jurisdiction. The man in the trailer park who beat his wife to death with a coat hanger. And an unsolved in 2002 – a Jane Doe from God-knows-where dumped on the side of a county road west of town. FBI profilers came in on that one because of similarities to the murders of two young females in Boston and Philadelphia. The same ligature marks.'

He reached for the half-empty Abita on the nightstand. 'A couple of recent suicides. A local high school student hung himself in his bedroom after a girl broke up with him.'

'Who found him? His mother?' My gut twisted into the complicated knot that it performed earlier in the day, with Tiffany breathing into my face.

'I shouldn't tell you any of this,' Mike said. 'You should be thinking nice baby thoughts. Bunnies and flowers.'

'Who was the other one? The other suicide?'

'Really?'

'Really.'

'The wife of the First Presbyterian minister over-dosed on a cocktail of prescription drugs. Helen Mayse. Three months ago. That's all you're getting out of me tonight.'

'Helen?' I sat up. 'I think Caroline was talking about her today. I think she's the woman who died and left a spot open in that stupid club. Caroline didn't give any hint of a suicide.'

'You saw Caroline again today?' He gave me an odd look. 'You didn't mention it.'

'It was just a quick glass of iced tea with a few women at her house.'

Mike shrugged. 'Suicide still carries a stigma. People won't talk about it.' He banged me on the head with the folder. 'Come on, honey. This is just your run-of-the-mill small-town stuff. Relax. I'm glad you're getting to know people.'

Caroline's macabre performance this afternoon was stuck like a clot of bread in my throat. It was just as much a lie because I held it in, an excruciating lesson I had learned over time. This lie of omission was already casually walking over to the little nest inside I'd made for the others.

The baby was operating the dimmer switch for my brain. My eyes drooped.

'I hear you.' I fluffed up my pillow and laid down again. 'Bunnies and flowers.'

Eleven hours later.

My name, 'Emily Page,' stood out in bold type on the printed label.

The package was thin and brown, stamped crookedly several times in red ink with PRIVATE. No stamps. No return address.

The package, propped up against the doorframe, had grazed my feet as soon as I stepped onto the side porch to water a dying pot of impatiens. A familiar flutter of fear, but I pushed it away. She'd never hand-delivered anything before. She was old. Far away.

She could have hired someone. You don't really think she's going to kill you herself, do you?

I headed back inside to the kitchen and snatched a paring knife out of the wood block on the counter.

The package was thin enough to be empty, but I knew better. I slid the knife under the flap and reached my hand down deep, pulling out a sealed legal-sized envelope. Blank. White. No writing. I dropped the knife and slit the envelope open with my nail. I unfolded the single piece of paper inside. Surely it was a leftover form from our real estate agent we still needed to sign.

It wasn't anything nearly so simple.

The type blurred in my shaking hands, but a cop's wife instantly recognizes a police report. I caught a name, and a terrible verb.

I could see Pierce's face in my mind. Hear his voice. *Lie still.*

I smoothed it out on the kitchen table. I'd never seen this – didn't even know it existed – but Officer Marilyn Hinks got all the basic details right. Thirteen years ago, a sophomore female, Emily Waters, entered the Windsor University campus police office at 3:13 a.m. to report a rape.

I quickly read the brief summary of the complaint:

Emily Waters asserted that she'd been raped by another student, Pierce Martin, at the Theta

Chi fraternity house two hours previously, about 1 a.m. The complainant was calm and composed, wearing black sweats and a clean white T-shirt with a Windsor logo. She admitted she had gone back to Martin's room of her own free will with the idea of spending a little time. However, she insisted she did not agree to sex. There were no visible bruises on her body and she refused to allow an officer to see or take any pictures of her back, chest, or legs. The complainant said she had taken an hour-long shower in her dorm before showing up to report the rape. She would not agree to a Breathalyzer test to determine her alcohol level.

I felt faint. The paper was going gray around the edges. Warned me that I should put my head down between my legs. But I couldn't stop reading.

Based on her demeanor and a lack of evidence, I suggested Ms Waters drop the complaint and be more careful in the future. I cautioned her to stay away from fraternity boys. She appeared to be a standard case of a girl exacting revenge on a guy after a bad breakup. I suggested several times that she think about her role in the events of the night before filing a formal charge, and Ms Waters got up and left without doing so.

81

This level of fury had coursed inside me before, and the outcome wasn't pretty. But to see the policewoman's sloppy work in black and white, to feel her derision and judgment jumping off the page – everything I'd wondered if she'd thought that night – was waking an angry demon from his nap.

It's not like I don't blame myself, but intellectually, I knew this ill-trained campus officer shouldn't have dared to. Rape lite. It came unbidden to mind, the derogatory term I'd heard used for date rape.

It occurred to me suddenly, belatedly, that I needed to be more focused and distressed about *why* this piece of paper rose from its grave in a file cabinet far, far away and landed on my doorstep.

There were no clues, no note was attached. I dug my fingers into the bottom corners of the envelope again and came up empty. Caroline? It seemed too soon. I'd been sitting in her house less than twenty-four hours ago. And, yes, maybe she was faking, but she appeared to be genuinely ill.

I pictured Caroline trotting up to the door in her pearls and running away in a senior citizen version of Ding Dong Ditch. It wasn't a genteel lady move.

The scarier possibility, of course, was that my faithful, hateful mail stalker had gathered momentum. Something had taken her rage to a more intimate level.

The phone – a red, old-fashioned dial-up still

attached to the wall – shrilled two feet from my head, and I let out a short scream.

Calm down. You aren't a nineteen-year-old girl anymore.

I picked up the receiver, ready to give the caller everything she had coming to her. To let her know that I wasn't a person who could be blackmailed, although another part of me tried to speak up, saying I was exactly that kind of person.

'Emily?'

Not a female voice. Mike.

'Yes.' I battled a wave of nausea.

'You aren't answering your cell phone.'

'It's . . . on the bed. I think.'

'Hold on a second,' he said. The phone chilled my burning cheek. I could hear a small commotion on the other end. Several voices.

Could I tell Mike about the rape now? After all these years?

He'd be angry, hurt, that through all of our shouting matches, hours of marriage counseling, the ups and downs of our marathon sex life, I had never trusted him enough. Keeping the rape from him was one more dent in our marital armor. It would erase all the progress we'd made in the last six months. I'd thought about this thousands of times, relentless waves lapping at the shore.

I closed my eyes, hating myself. For the rape. For the things that followed.

But Mike's curt words quickly erased any thoughts of telling him anything. 'I'm over at

Caroline Warwick's house. She's missing. Em, you were one of the last people to see her.'

My fingers involuntarily crumpled the police report until it was a wad in my fist, the size of a small grenade.

CHAPTER 8

Was I imagining the soft sound of crying in the background? Maria?

'Oh, Mike.' I cleared my throat. 'When?'

'Caroline complained of a migraine all afternoon, then went to bed around seven-thirty last night. Maria claims she stayed on her shift longer than usual before going home, to make sure Caroline was OK. This morning, when she didn't show up for breakfast, Maria found her bedroom empty, the bed rumpled, but the covers still in place, like she hadn't ever pulled them down.'

'Maybe she made the bed and went on a late morning walk?' Why was this being treated as such a crisis when it had been less than twenty-four hours? And why was he calling me? Mike never included me in his investigations. Never.

I aimed the ball of paper at the kitchen wastebasket ten feet away, playing a game with myself. If it went in, I didn't have to tell Mike anything at all. If I missed, I would come clean.

'Maria says Caroline tells people that she hasn't made her own bed since she was six,' Mike said.

85

'She's fired three housekeepers who didn't change the sheets by eight on the dot every morning.'

'Maybe she took a late night drive? Got in an accident?'

People like Caroline always came back. I arched my wrist and fired. The paper ball bounced off the wastebasket's rim and under the kitchen table. Stupid game.

'We're checking the hospitals. But all of her cars are in the garage. Three Cadillacs.' Mike lowered his voice. 'I don't feel good about this.' At once, I understood. Mike's well-trained gut was talking.

'You think something has happened to her?'

'There's a little blood on the back of a pillow. An open window. A footprint in the flower bed. Ladder marks in the dirt. A gutter with a dent in it. It could be a week-old nosebleed, a desire for fresh night air, a diligent gardener picking weeds, and a little hail damage. It's not like I have a crack CSI unit.'

'There's something else, I can tell.' Mike's sarcasm had whipped up a new batch of paranoia in my head. Was Caroline's bedtime reading a copy of my rape report? Was someone sweeping my past into an evidence bag? Mike couldn't find out this way.

'There are three empty prescription bottles on her nightstand. Prozac, Percocet, and Vicodin. Exactly the drug cocktail that killed her friend Helen. Prescribed by Dr Gretchen Liesel. The painkillers are for migraines, so that's consistent at least. But the Mayse suicide is extremely fresh in my mind.'

'You think Caroline killed herself? She was definitely not suicidal when I saw her.' Anything but.

'It's not my top scenario. And there's another odd thing. Maria says Caroline always kept her Bible on her dresser. Wouldn't let her touch it, even to dust. Onionskin pages. A relic. There's an inscription. *To our blessed daughter, on her tenth birthday.* Someone ripped a page out of it and underlined a passage. One of my guys found it on the floor by the window. Hold on, let me get it. It's already been bagged.'

Mike came back on the line.

'Matthew 23:33.'

'It's not top of my mind at the moment,' I said.

'*You serpents, you brood of vipers, how are you to escape being sentenced to hell?*'

Tearing a page out of someone's Bible was like burning the flag in front of a soldier. Maybe worse.

'What do you want me to do?' I asked. *He wants me to tell him the truth,* I thought. *Tell him that the five women who sat in a room with Caroline Warwick yesterday, including his pregnant wife, would make a nice little lineup of suspects.*

'Stay home. I'm sending an officer over for your statement.'

'Mike, I . . .'

He'd already hung up.

Cody Hill was a young, redheaded policeman who topped out at about 6'5" and held a glass of ice water in sprawling hands that belonged to a former

Clairmont High School All-State quarterback. It was a fact he mentioned about himself immediately after dropping onto my couch.

I forced my fingers to stop twirling a strand of hair into a tight rope. The crumpled campus police report now resided in the pocket of my jeans, a ball of lead. When did paper become so heavy?

'I don't really know how I can help,' I told him. 'I don't know Caroline Warwick well. She invited me to a party at her house several days ago and then yesterday for a glass of iced tea with a few other women.'

'How did she seem?'

'Yesterday? Fine, I guess. Again, I don't know her well enough to say. Her headache came on suddenly.'

'She didn't say anything that indicated she was worried?'

'No, the conversation was . . . just small talk. Benign.' If you considered a puppy murder and sex toys under the mattress to be benign. Maybe Cody would. I wasn't sure why I was lying, setting more traps for myself. But yesterday Caroline wasn't the victim in that room. I wasn't about to start my sentence in this town by ratting out the people who were.

The officer, tapping out his notes on an iPad, paused over the word *benign,* and I stopped myself from spelling it for him.

'What time did you leave Ms Warwick's home yesterday, ma'am?' He stuttered a little over the *ma'am,* and I began to sympathize that he had drawn the short straw to interview the wife of the new boss.

'Let's see. I looked at the clock when I got home. It was three-fifteen. So I probably left her house around three.'

'Did you have any contact with the housekeeper? Maria Valdez?'

'Yes, Maria let us in. She let me out. I was the last one to go.'

He paused for a beat, as if that was significant. 'Did she show any animosity toward Mrs Warwick?'

'Absolutely not.'

'Do you know if she's an illegal?'

'*Illegal* isn't a noun.' My voice was clipped, not liking where this was going. 'If you're asking if she's in the country legally, I don't have any idea.'

'Yes, ma'am. We'll be checking on that.'

Patronizing. No more trace of a stutter. Maybe he'd faked it. You'd think at this point in my life I could read people faster. Like last month, when that New York plumber charged me twice what he should have, swaying any doubts about the price with a story about being a single father who struggled to braid his daughter's hair that morning.

People are adept at getting what they want these days, mingling the lies and the truth, fooling you, wriggling into your soft parts. Maybe people always had been like this.

I was beginning to think that underneath Cody Hill's fresh-scrubbed face, a redneck bully thrived.

'That's an interesting little club she's got set up,' he drawled. 'I've heard some weird rumors about it from my girlfriend. Like they all have special tattoos in a private place. A lot of pissed-off women in this town, both the ones who get in and the ones who get blackballed. My girlfriend, she's still hoping for an invite.'

'I'm not her ticket,' I said. Tattoos that said *liar* or *whore* or *killer*? Nothing seemed too far-fetched at the moment.

Cody frowned, not liking my answer. 'Did things seem normal between Ms Warwick and her guests?'

'I don't know them. I don't know what normal would be.'

'Did anything at all stick out at you yesterday?'

'You're just asking the same question different ways. Maria could surely tell you more about these women than I can. Did you ask her? She speaks English.' *You jerk.*

He flipped the iPad cover over his notes, and stood. 'Mostly, I was just after a timeline.' The words flowed in a syrupy drawl. 'I 'preciate it, ma'am.'

He towered over me as we walked to the front door. He stopped short, four inches from my stomach, invading my baby space, nauseating me with the smell of bitter sweat and an overdose of Old Spice deodorant.

'One more thing, ma'am. Your husband's already thinking about calling in the FBI. It ain't even the usual forty-eight yet. It's tough being the new guy, trying to please the mayor. We all get that. But we can handle this. So maybe you could assure him, since you're a friend of Miss Warwick's, that wouldn't be such a good idea. Give her a little time to come home on her own. Prevent her some embarrassment.'

He glanced down, and I became distinctly aware of the paper bulge in my front pocket, and then the one in his pants. I realized that his eyes weren't trained on my belly but on the sliver of bare skin showing above my jeans.

His gaze rolled up to my breasts, a C cup for the first time in their lives. My nipples tingled like he was physically touching them, and I felt the familiar flush of shame. The experts say the body is cued to respond, even under attack, even when we don't want it to.

'Watch where you look.' My voice pulsed with anger.

'You seem a little on edge, Mrs Page.'

He stepped over the threshold to the porch, and I slammed the door.

I waited for Mike in his favorite armchair, facing the door, my feet propped up on a moving box. I pulled my grandmother's afghan tight around my pajamas. When I was five, I liked to waggle my fingers like little puppet people through the crochet holes.

There is blood in my house.

Staring at the door, I thought about how I could

never survive Mike leaving me. About how ironic it was that I married a man immersed in violence when I can barely make it through a full episode of his favorite cop show on cable.

Mike takes my idiosyncrasies in this area in stride. He knows what's off the table. Horror movies with the word *Saw* or a Roman numeral in the title. Torture scenes that involve fingers, clippers, knives, cigar cutters, or water. Children in peril.

The truth is, I was like this before Pierce raped me. Ever since Beth died in *Little Women*, I'll check out the end of any book that foreshadows the death of a character I love. As long as I know what's coming, it's OK. But don't surprise me.

Yet I have no problem at all murdering Pierce Martin. I see him in my head right now, arms crossed, lazy grin. I'm pulling the trigger. One, two, three, four, five. Always five. This isn't the first time I've killed him. It helps that I *know* he's going to die.

His body lurches like a floppy fish with each blast until he crumples, finally harmless. I've never felt any guilt about making this bloody mess. I haven't successfully reconciled that with my belief in a loving, forgiving God who asks me to reflect His image.

In my night dreams, when I'm not on guard, Pierce is alive. He lurks while I'm soaring through a happy, nonsensical plot, vanishing the second I turn my head.

While I sleep, my rapist is still my stalker, even though I've killed him over and over in the daytime. Even though I know he can't hurt me anymore.

When Mike walked in the door, my Cartier watch said it was 3 a.m.

'I have to tell you about the box,' I said.

Except that when I woke up, I wasn't wearing a Cartier watch. I didn't own one. A pillow from our bed was tucked under my head. I hadn't put it there.

When I woke up it was morning, and Mike was already gone again.

CHAPTER 9

The sign near the receptionist's desk had promised WOMEN CARING FOR WOMEN, as if that was worth bragging about, and so far, so good.

Dr Gretchen Liesel's waiting room was like a giant womb, bathed in warm red tones and indirect light, without a harsh fluorescent bulb in sight. Somehow, I hadn't expected Texas to be like this.

After filling out a little paperwork, my body nestled itself into one of six overstuffed chairs as a classical music station played faintly, the way I imagined the baby could hear music in his insulated cocoon. I dug into the Sunday Arts section of *The New York Times,* a treat, because I'd started reading it on Mike's iPad since we moved, and it just wasn't the same. I had taken exactly one bite from a chocolate chip granola bar from the loaded snack basket when a sweet-faced nurse named Anna called my name.

I obediently followed her into an exam room, outfitted with the same soft lighting, a couch, and custom oak cabinets that hid the cold, glistening tools that made every muscle in my body clench.

Or maybe they used those awful disposable plastic ones here. Surely women caring for women knew that, for some reason, cheap, hard, disposable plastic hurt more than steel. Anna left the room, and I shed my clothes and pulled on the cuddly, high-thread-count, blue cotton gown folded on the exam table.

I lay back on it and thought about my sole reason for being here.

Paranoia.

Paranoia about an ache in my belly this morning that was either a sign that I was losing my baby or that I shouldn't eat red Doritos every day.

Paranoia about Caroline's ridiculous fortune-cookie secrets. About yesterday's vile package on my doorstep and whether the missing Caroline could possibly be responsible. I wanted to believe that Dr Liesel had the answers to all of these concerns, all of it covered by doctor-patient confidentiality.

When I called several hours ago, the receptionist heard my first sentence about pain in my lower abdomen and immediately plugged me in as a new patient at 4 p.m.

Two raps on the door. Dr Liesel stepped inside, dressed in pale green scrubs.

'Hello, Emily.' She gave my shoulder a gentle pat before heading to the sink to wash her hands. The pat. It changed the entire dynamic of the doctor/patient relationship. Perfecting the patient pat should be a medical school graduation requirement.

'So what's going on?' She dried her hands on a paper towel and rolled her stool over, unhooking the blood pressure cuff from the wall.

'It hurts all across here. Probably something I ate?' Hopeful.

'Don't talk.' She pumped up the cuff.

The blood pressure machine hissed like an angry snake, the only sound in the room. I thought about Mike, who had no idea that I was here, or that something might be wrong. My worry was all I could carry this time. He was more afraid of losing me than of losing another child he didn't know.

But *I* knew this child. He had wrapped his little fingers tightly around my soul. So had all the ones before him.

I breathed deeply and tried to focus on the cool and gentle fingers pressing on my wrist, feeling my pulse.

'150 over 90.' Dr Liesel ripped off the Velcro cuff. 'Not ideal. Your pulse is a little fast. When did you last see Dr Herrera?'

Why was this always a surprise to a doctor? That pulses race faster and blood pounds in the presence of someone who could rock your world with a few words of irrefutable science?

'Several days ago. Everything checked out fine.'

'Lie back and let's untie your gown.' She flipped a switch on a screen above my head, pulled out an ultrasound wand, and squirted warm jelly on my stomach.

Searching, searching, searching for that elusive

96

heartbeat. I squeezed my eyes shut, and wondered where women caring for women heated up the goo.

I tried not to imagine a tiny, curled-up form perfectly still on the screen above my head. Too still. I didn't realize I was holding my breath until I heard horses galloping through a stream and almost choked on air. My baby, beating away.

'From what I can see so far, your baby looks and sounds perfect.' She gently wiped the jelly off with a soft washcloth.

'Lie back for a second.' Careful hands massaged my stomach. From my angle, it appeared to be protruding about two more inches than yesterday. She pressed a stethoscope to my belly before pulling it out of her ears and adjusting the exam table into a sitting position. 'It's noisy in there. Maybe eat some plain yogurt. Do you know the sex?'

'Yes.' Overflowing with gratefulness, indebted, as everyone is to a doctor who delivers good news, as if they're somehow responsible for it. 'A boy.'

'Relax, OK? You've made it well past the first trimester this time. I see here in your paperwork faxed over from Dr Herrera that you've had a number of miscarriages. The percentages are with you at this point.' She paused, frowning at my paperwork. 'Is this right? A glass of wine a day?'

'More like every other day.'

'Cut back. One a week.'

'OK.' Timid. With doctors, always timid, whether

they were assholes or angels, ones who patted my shoulder or ones who coldly told me that my future adorable first-grader who cut out construction paper butterflies was now a dead fetus that needed to be harvested by a machine.

'Do you take someone . . . like me? High risk?' The words rushed out unexpectedly.

She studied my face. 'You want me to follow this pregnancy?'

'I think so.'

'My first delivery was twin calves in my uncle's barn in Massachusetts. Sticking my arms up that poor cow at age sixteen prepared me for just about anything. I'm not worried if you aren't. Still, Dr Herrera is an excellent doctor and her facilities are a little more impressive. So what will it be?' She glanced up for confirmation, and I nodded.

You. I don't know why I trust you, but I do.

She started pecking with two fingers into a small laptop on the counter. 'I could do a full exam, but I don't like to bother the baby unless it's absolutely necessary. My nurse will set up a schedule of appointments. Call me anytime you're worried. No big deal.'

Eat some yogurt. No exam. No big deal.

'Any other questions?'

I hesitated. Things were going so well.

'Do you have any idea where Caroline could be?'

'No. Unfortunately, I don't.' Clipped.

She stood up, patted my shoulder in exactly the

same spot, and headed for the door. 'You can get dressed.'

'Wait. Please.' I sucked in a breath. 'Caroline invited me over with some other women. We passed around . . . a box.'

Her hand stilled on the doorknob.

'And yesterday someone left a pol – a piece of paper on my doorstep. I need to know if Caroline's behind it. It's about something that happened to me a long time ago.' My voice began to plead. 'You warned me. I need to know why.'

She turned to press the intercom button on the wall. 'Anna, I'm going to take a few minutes with Emily in my office. Call Mrs Lindstrom on her cell and check on her, will you? She's in labor in her car in the emergency room parking lot. She's hoping she can make it till midnight. If the baby has other ideas, let me know.'

She turned back to me, smiling, as if there were no undercurrents, no torture instruments behind the cabinets, no fears about a baby who could die regardless of statistics that said he shouldn't. No ridiculous thoughts of blackmail and no missing Caroline.

'Mrs Lindstrom's insurance company pays for only two days, and the day starts whenever you show up. But she likes to get her full forty-eight hours. This is baby number six. She could probably deliver it herself.'

I wondered what it would be like to be so blasé about a pregnancy that I'd sit in a parking lot in full-blown labor, playing a game of chicken with the insurance company.

'Meet me in my office,' Gretchen said. 'The door on the right at the end of the hall. Just come on in after you get your clothes on.'

A few minutes later, I found her sitting in fresh blue scrubs in one of two overstuffed purple chenille armchairs. The chairs faced a massive cherry desk, the top barely visible under a slough of papers, medical journals, two iPads, and a large flat-screen computer monitor glowing with what looked like a tiny white rat in a man's hand. A baby? I peered closer. No, it definitely appeared to be a rat.

The doctor gestured for me to sit in the other chair. Equals. No power moves, with her behind the desk.

My eyes skimmed a diploma from the University of Texas Southwestern Medical School. Medical journals were crammed up against John Irving and Emily Dickinson on the bookshelves. A small bar in the corner was set up with crystal glasses and a few bottles of premium hard stuff. 'It took me a second to get that.' I pointed to a small wooden sign that hung over the bar alcove. 'Oh-be-gin. Clever.'

'A gift,' she said, 'from a very relieved wood-working daddy.'

'Cute, cute.' I sounded idiotic. Absurdly nervous. Filling the space. How the hell was I going to start this conversation? It turned out, I didn't have to.

'First, call me Gretchen, Emily. Second, you need to know that Caroline is an extremely complex person. What is that line Jessica Rabbit says? "I'm not bad, I'm just drawn that way." Anyway, it's always reminded me of Caroline.'

Gretchen's eyes were an unusual color. Almost lavender. Lavender, and bloodshot. No makeup. A short nose, blunt chin, a casual bob of hair shot with gray. Not a beautiful face, but a compassionate one. I felt guilty about taking up her time. One of the Bunko girls had told me that Gretchen delivered as many as five to ten babies a week. A third of the time she was paid in tamales. Besides her own practice, she volunteered at the county's free clinic, which served mostly illegal immigrants.

'Thirty years ago,' Gretchen told me, 'we were just a small group of women trying to find their way in sexist and repressive small-town Texas. Not all of us were born in the South and held pedigrees. It was a shock to our systems, like it probably is to yours.'

She pushed herself up from her chair and walked to the bar, pulling out two bottles of Dasani from a small refrigerator underneath. 'Don't kid yourself. The good old boys' network is still thriving here and will be long after the two of us are dead. It's like racism. A lot of people just spray on more whipped cream and keep serving it up. It's so ingrained, we don't even acknowledge that it's there. These are the same men who pat themselves on the back for not being racist like their daddies and then suggest electrifying a large wall on the border.' She handed me an ice-cold bottle of water, and sucked two-thirds of hers down while I waited for her to continue.

'It couldn't even be called a club at first. Most of us were either in the early stages of careers or were wives supporting men who were. We drank. We shared. We traded our secrets in little living rooms, long before careers took off and money rained down. Caroline burst into our lives maybe a decade after we began, when we'd already started meeting regularly, once a month. She said she lost both her son and husband in a house fire in Kentucky and all she had left was a pile of money and a sister she hardly ever saw. She needed a clean start. What she really needed, it turned out, were people to take care of.'

A sister, I remembered. *But Caroline told me her sister was dead.*

I couldn't believe Gretchen was actually sharing all of this. She finished off the water, and leaned forward to toss the bottle into a bin for recycling. The bleach on her scrubs hung in the air. It reminded me of hiding in the freshly laundered sheets my mother hung on the line. Everything lately, it seemed, was reminding me of people I had lost.

'We were those people,' Gretchen was saying. 'Caroline became our mother confessor. She made herself available at all hours, on the phone, in person.

She delivered instant intimacy. Unconditional friendship. It was like being seduced, without the sex. She paid hundreds of dollars for therapy for women in this town who didn't want their husbands to find out the real person they'd married. One was drinking and slapping her kids after school if they brought home anything less than an A. Another was molested by her father as a child and had been faking orgasm ever since. Intimate, scary stuff. Caroline took our friendly little club to a whole new level. And, yes, there were copious amounts of liquor and that little box involved.' Gretchen forced a tight smile. 'Caroline puts so much money in the clinic, it should have her name on it. But she won't let the board of directors do it. How do you hate a woman like that?'

I wasn't sure how to respond. I hadn't asked Gretchen if she hated Caroline. Was she trying to ease my mind by pouring forth all this information? If so, she wasn't. I'd only seen hints of the do-gooding woman Gretchen raved about. The whole thing sounded way too Southern gothic, an overwrought Pat Conroy novel. And wasn't Gretchen, a doctor, just a little too smart and cynical to be pulled into this?

'It wasn't until a year ago that I realized that Caroline was . . . losing it a little,' Gretchen said bluntly. Defensively. 'I should have seen it much earlier.'

My head snapped up. It was like she heard my thoughts. Just as easily as she had conjured my child's tiny, beating heart a few minutes ago.

Gretchen ran her palms distractedly down her thighs, ironing out wrinkles in the scrubs that weren't there. 'She wasn't as discreet with our private lives. She taped our meetings, even personal lunches. She was clearly in a mental tailspin. Suspicious all the time. Of everyone. One night about two months ago, she called at two a.m., sobbing, asking if I knew where Alice was. I had no idea who she was talking about. The next day, she acted like the conversation never happened.'

'So maybe she *did* harm herself.' Or maybe she had pushed someone in the club too far. Maybe someone who was Alice in another life.

Gretchen didn't appear to mind-read that one. She shook her head. 'Emily, she's my friend and my patient. I'm skirting a thin ethical line here. In fact, I'm well over it because I want you to understand why you should stay out of this. I'm not going into more details. The *club* has someone looking for her. We've hired a private professional. And to be perfectly clear, I know nothing about Caroline attempting to blackmail you.'

'But she's done it before,' I persisted. 'Hasn't she? I get that she handpicks the club, so there's loyalty. But maybe some of them didn't want to play her party games anymore. Not with so much at stake.'

She stared at me intently before replying. 'I don't think one of the girls made off with her, if that's what you're asking. She's been gone a little more than a day. If it weren't a small town, the police wouldn't even be paying attention yet. We'll find Caroline in a few days, and we can resolve this quietly. I'll have a word with her. I'm trying to help you, Emily. I obviously can't stop you, but I'd prefer that you didn't share all these details with your husband unless Caroline doesn't show up soon. Maybe put him off a little.' The overall tone was now less warm, less polite. The message was the same as the cop's. *Lay off.*

I suddenly wondered whether Gretchen was manipulating me, not the other way around.

Anna peeked her head in the door, which I'd left cracked.

'Sorry to interrupt, Gretch. The emergency room called to say that Ms Lindstrom just delivered in her car.'

Gretchen stood. 'All's well?'

'Yep. Although she is out-of-her-mind ticked off at that poor baby for not waiting it out. The resident, that Duke snot, wants to know if he can give her two mils of Valium. Wants her to stop cussing at him.'

'No, he can't,' Gretchen said. 'Tell him I'm leaving now.'

Anna stared at me pointedly. Office hours were over.

I walked to the Volvo slowly. Happy, and not. My baby was fine. But I was as confused as ever about Caroline and her little club. The parking lot was crammed, and a white, late-model Lexus SUV crept behind me, a little too close for comfort, apparently hoping to grab my spot. I turned, annoyed. The glass windshield was too black for me to make out the driver, an illegal tint job, which I'd seen plenty of here in Texas.

Except that a few minutes later at a red light, I could swear the very same Lexus was right behind me. When the light turned, I pulled off into a McDonald's and flipped my head to watch the SUV gun by. The sticker on its back window urged me to HAVE A BLESSED DAY. The right bumper declared the driver an ABORTION SURVIVOR. That was a brain twister.

My eyes lit on the neon pink graffiti on the McDonald's window heralding the 'return' of the McRib.

My stomach really wasn't hurting anymore. I promised myself I'd eat better, starting tomorrow.

I rolled up to the drive-through and ordered.

On the way home, I decided.

I was going to tell Mike about the rape.

CHAPTER 10

'He's a rookie.' Mike kicked a box out of the way as he sat down to the night's pitiful dinner offering: a Spa Lean Cuisine with an apple. Mike would compensate by downing a whole bag of chips later in front of the Yankees game. 'He's a kid. Cody doesn't know how to handle himself yet. He also happens to be the son of a city councilman who has the ability to make my life very easy or very difficult.'

He took an aggressive bite out of the apple. 'Did you have to shut the door in his face?'

'Is that what he told you?' I fired back. 'You should be supporting me. He's a walking sexual harassment case for the city. Not to mention his racial remarks and the little underlying threat about not stirring things up. He bears watching. He's a redneck tattletale.'

'Oh, come on, Em. Did you really just say *redneck tattletale*? He said he brought the whole thing up to me because he was worried that he upset you . . . in your condition.'

I rolled my eyes, feeling a sudden kinship with Gretchen Liesel. Good old boys.

'*You seem a little on edge, Mrs Page,*' I mimicked, pitching my voice lower, drawling it out. But my anger at the young cop had started to dissipate, one of the benefits of riding the roller coaster of second-trimester emotions. He wasn't worth the energy.

'I'll stop egging you on,' Mike said. 'I know there are some issues there. God, it still creeps me out that you can manipulate your voice to do whatever you want, even sound like a guy. Although I'd be happy if you want to bring a little Scarlett O'Hara into the bedroom tonight.'

'Hey,' I said lightly. 'Those voice-over gigs paid for my master's degree.'

All at once, I missed Lucy. She had been fond of me rummaging around my bag of accents. Pulling one out as a party trick. I once convinced one of her new boyfriends that I was a princess from Bulgaria seeking asylum.

'*Redneck tattletale* is going on the list.' Mike spit an apple seed into his empty microwave dinner plate, which once held the meal he'd eaten in five bites. He nodded toward the piece of paper on the refrigerator held up crookedly with a magnet the shape of New York State.

It was titled 'Pregnant Thoughts,' in Mike's barely decipherable scrawl. He'd introduced the list in the second month of my pregnancy, to record my hormonal pearls of wisdom. Currently at the top: *Just because I'm crying doesn't mean I don't have a point!*

The list of pregnant thoughts was one of the first things he dug out of a box when we moved. They were always funny the morning after, and it kept the other list company – the one scribbled with possible baby names. Over the years, that list got shorter. Mike didn't know, but I had named each baby we lost.

'So where do things stand with Caroline's case?'

'I'm wondering whether I overreacted. Wondering whether I'm reacting enough. Feeling my way through small-town politics. By the way, Harry and his wife would like to meet for dinner tomorrow night. At Ruggieri's. About seven.'

'Harry . . .?'

'Mayor Harry Dunn. As in the mayor. My boss. You met his wife at Caroline's.'

Letty. I didn't want to think about two hours of spaghetti twirling with a former pageant queen who was probably on board with the Confederate flag license plate. I swiftly changed the subject. 'I saw Dr Liesel today. You know, the woman at the party who was recommended as a good local OBGYN.'

'Why? I thought you just had a checkup in Dallas. Did she look at the baby?'

'Yes, we heard the heartbeat. I'm fine. The baby's fine. I was having a little intestinal distress. I'm trying to tell you something else.'

Mike eyed me carefully. He knew about more than a few paranoid trips to the doctor, some that made me feel embarrassed and neurotic and others

109

that painfully assured me I wasn't. He tossed his tray and apple core in the trash and walked over to where I was standing near the window in the fading light.

'I'm glad everything's OK,' he said softly. He didn't wait for me to speak. 'That light, that blue shirt . . . you look like the Madonna. I'd paint you right now if I knew how to paint with something other than a roller. Maybe you should look in a mirror and paint yourself. You have to be the most beautiful pregnant woman ever.'

He bent over to nuzzle my neck and to feel up the C cups.

'I have some things to tell you . . . about what Dr Liesel said . . . and . . . other things.' I leaned back into him, distracted by Mike's roving hands and mouth and liking it enough to not make him stop.

He paused. 'Didn't you tell me everything is fine with the baby?'

'It's not about that.'

'Can we still have sex?'

'Yes.'

'Then let's take this discussion to the bedroom.'

This was it.

This was the moment I should tell him. When he felt the most in love with me, after his last shudder, while we spooned, my padded body snug against his muscles, his arm curved around my belly protectively.

The safest place in the world for me to tell.

Our lovemaking had been especially simple and intimate tonight. Not a lot of foreplay. Our faces so close that I could feel his breath, his eyes locked to mine, blue to green, for each slow and deliberate thrust. A good, sweet hurt inside, like when a masseuse's hands find the right spot.

Mike came quickly. I didn't.

I didn't want to.

I turned over, squeezing my eyes shut, preparing myself, thinking that every moment after this one could be different.

'I was raped in college.' A rush of words. A whisper buried in my pillow, too low for him to hear. Nothing like I planned. No easing in. No waiting for his body to recover.

I said it again, too loud this time. The word *raped* cracked the air, a gunshot across the water. His arm around me loosened a little. Retreat? I was flooded with instant regret.

Two seconds had passed. Now three. Enough time for an Olympic runner to cross the finish line well ahead of everyone else. My body began to shake, like it might explode. Mike was pulling me to his chest.

'It's OK,' he said urgently. 'It's OK.'

Sobbing, I clutched his arms around my belly. When I squeezed my eyes closed, I spiraled in a black universe. Mike said things, soothing things that I didn't hear for all the noise in my head.

After a time, my breathing grew less ragged. The spinning carousel slowed.

'Emily?' Tentative.

Nothing came out of my mouth, even though I willed myself to speak, and my body to stop trembling. I tried to identify the one emotion that hadn't been wrenched out of my gut. I felt relief. But not healed. I wanted desperately to feel *healed*.

'I've always suspected something like this.'

I swallowed a hard rock in my throat. 'You aren't mad?'

'Why in God's name would I ever be mad at you for this? I'd like to kill the guy.'

I didn't say anything. Mike didn't make empty threats. The last thing I wanted was for him to go hunting.

'There were signs.' Mike shook his head. 'I saw them. Marguerite saw them. She said not to push you. That it would happen. That you were almost ready. Because you loved me . . . and wanted to change. You wanted *us* to change.'

Marguerite, our last therapist, our *best* therapist, a University of Chicago Ph.D., the only professional who told me with unwavering faith in her Supreme Being never to be afraid to try again. She was only in her late twenties, but she knew about losing things. She'd grown old on the streets of Detroit before she was sixteen. She had told us that much. She didn't say that she'd been raped in that city of decay. But I knew.

'I don't think I can live without you,' I whispered.

'Why in hell would you ever have to?' He arranged a few pillows on the headboard and patted the space nearby. Familiar territory. I scooted up and leaned my back against his stomach, staring at a pattern of nail holes in the wall, at the three oval shadows in the paint left behind by a set of framed vintage flower prints. Now the orchids were permanently gone, and so was the old lady who hung them.

Words stumbled out of my mouth. I told Mike excruciating, inane details, like the empty Domino's pizza box sitting on the floor of Pierce's dorm room. I avoided dragging him along razor-sharp wounds, like how there was another person in the room. Mike didn't seem to need any more than I was willing to say, murmuring encouragement, never interrupting.

Not until I mentioned the package.

'Someone sent the rape report here?' he barked, rolling away. 'You don't know where it came from? Where the hell is it?'

'In my purse. On the dresser.'

He jerked himself off the bed, and I immediately felt a chill, the moment disintegrating. Zero to sixty, tender to tense, in a split second. Our pattern.

'How the hell can you find anything in here?' Mike was back on the edge of the bed, pulling things out of my purse recklessly: loose coins, lipstick, my wallet, receipts. Dumping it all onto the tangled sheets. No woman can bear this kind of invasion of her purse, especially when it's a nuclear disaster inside, even when it holds no secrets.

'Mike, calm down. Stop. Please.'

I grabbed the purse from him and opened the zipper compartment. The crumpled sheet was now smoothed, folded in half twice.

'You wadded this up? Were you not going to show it to me?' His voice held disbelief. 'Never mind.'

He read quickly down the page, detached, professional, not the lover who had moments ago curved his hand around my breast.

'This cop, if you can call her that, should be shot like a dog. I don't like this, Emily. Did you ever think this could be from him?'

'No,' I said, truthfully, thinking I didn't like that expression. *Shot like a dog.* Any rabid dog was better than the man who raped me.

'Frat-boy rapists like him don't stop at one.'

No, I thought. *They marry shy little wives who homeschool their kids, they go to church every Sunday, rail against homosexuals, and continue their sexual perversions on the side.* I closed my eyes and pictured a Christmas card photo with Pierce and an imaginary family: a lovely wife and two sweet-faced children posed with him in front of a simulated forest, everyone wearing forced smiles and coordinating black shirts and worn jeans. Trying too hard.

The pitch of Mike's voice was rising, the cadence more and more frenetic. 'A friend of mine who works sex crimes calls date rape "the last frontier of crime." Women won't report. If they do, juries don't like them because they are traumatized and look guilty because they *feel* guilty and can only paint a picture of fragments. But the rapist, he isn't confused at all up there on the stand. He's not feeling guilty. He's got the whole picture. He *drew* the fucking picture.' Mike dropped back onto the bed, resting a hand on my leg. 'I shouldn't even call him a frat-boy rapist. He's a serial predator. A planner. These guys operate in their social network, careful not to leave marks, assessing targets less likely to tell. You know that he *planned* to rape you that night? Maybe for weeks.'

Mike was making a noble speech in our bedroom, rushing to fill the space with his experience, with facts, to attach some kind of sense and reason to something that couldn't be tacked down by either one. He was meaning to make it less, not more. But his ferocity and the cold, antiseptic words flying out of his mouth – *target* and *predator* and *social network* – only broke loose more pieces of that night.

The cloying odor of Pierce's shampoo. My first, absurd thought when he flipped me over. *He's not going to marry me.* The sting as my roommate dabbed alcohol along the path where his fingernail had raked my leg.

It was almost unbearable, the pain and guilt I felt for that naïve, humiliated girl. But Mike was trying so hard. I couldn't let him know he was making it worse.

'I don't think that Pierce Martin sent this.' I hadn't spoken his name out loud in thirteen years. He was like a roach crawling out of a sink drain.

'Where's the envelope?'

'In the kitchen trash.' He grabbed his boxers off the floor and pulled them on. I swiped at his arm but too late. 'Wait. Mike.'

Already, I could hear him tossing the kitchen trashcan, slamming a drawer shut that was in the way, silverware rattling. It didn't take long, but long enough for me to urge my heart rate slower.

'This it?' He stood in the doorway in old blue boxers, holding a piece of paper, red-faced and half-naked, and it struck me not for the first time how there was never a moment that he looked vulnerable.

I nodded and spoke quickly, hoping to diffuse things. 'I keep thinking . . . this might be Caroline's work. Mike, where are you going?'

Let me tell you about the box, dammit. About a club of pretty Texas vipers entwined by their ugly secrets.

'To take a shower.' His response was brusque. 'Then to work for a while. To butt in.'

When Mike reappeared, he was dressed in his new uniform of crisp khakis and a dark blue polo shirt with CLAIRMONT POLICE DEPT. embroidered over the pocket. He strapped on the gun lying on his bedside table before leaning in to simultaneously brush my forehead with his lips and run a swift hand over my belly, always part of the goodbye now, like rubbing a Buddha for luck. But it was the tiny Buddha inside me who needed all the luck he could get.

He turned at the door and spoke gruffly. 'You good?'

This was typical of Mike, to acknowledge as he was walking out the door that we'd just experienced something of a breakthrough.

'I'm fine. Really. Thank you.' This was typical of me, not asking him to please hang around.

I knew the uselessness of telling Mike in this mood that it was too late to go back to work – 8:13 p.m., by my clock radio – so I lay back on the bed listening for the front door to click shut, to hear his key locking it from the outside. I wondered what he planned to do with the police report, whether he would search for Pierce Martin and find out the rest. Untie the ribbons of my secrets all by himself.

The brittle ring of the phone interrupted.

I couldn't think of anyone on earth I felt like talking to. Reluctantly, I picked up the receiver on the bedside table. Something was screwy with our caller ID because of the old telephone lines in the house, but Mike insisted I answer the landline no matter what. He didn't like when he couldn't reach me, which he declared was half the time lately. The pregnant me forgot to charge my cell phone, left it in the car console or buried in the chair cushions, turned off the sound.

'Hello.'

Nothing.

'Hello? Who is this?'

I felt a presence on the other end, waiting me out. The thick silence spun me back to a phone call in college, months before I even knew Pierce Martin's name. The caller had paused his rapid breathing long enough to whisper that he was watching me through the bare window of my basement apartment. The cops who showed up ten minutes later assured me that the caller was some gutless wonder lying in his own bed, jerking off. But, I always wondered, how did he know I had no curtains?

Anger at Mike surged, for leaving me alone and not letting me finish. I sat there in my nightgown, slick with sweat and tears, gripping the phone and willing the intruder in my bedroom to hang up first.

I won.

I woke up, sitting ramrod straight, staring at the face of a frightened, wild-eyed woman.

It took a moment to realize that the woman terrifying me *was* me.

My eyes were locked on a murky reflection in the mirror leaning against the wall on top of the dresser. The white moon of Mike's head rose beside me in the glass before his arms pulled me down into a warm embrace. He had slipped back into bed around 1 a.m.

'The dream again?' he asked, half-awake. 'The little girl?' And then he promptly started snoring.

'Yes. The dream.' I snuggled tighter into his arms even though my body was steaming, soaked with perspiration.

'The little girl,' I said.

The little girl in my dream stands on top of a steep hill. Her expression is solemn. An ancient stone church looms behind her with dozens of pointy turrets rising like thick, sharpened pencils against the clouds. I can see every detail of her face and every microscopic blade of grass on that hill in high definition, a magic trick of dreamland. After the third miscarriage, Mike had made me bring her up in one of our marriage counseling sessions with a woman whose name wasn't Marguerite.

Yes, the little girl in the dream looks like me, I told the therapist, who gave off a polite, bored vibe in our sessions, as if I wasn't interesting enough to be a good anecdote in the unfinished self-help book glowing on her computer screen. If only she knew.

The therapist persisted.

Did I know that the little girl probably represented my vulnerability? My fears?

It wasn't a deep thought worth 150 bucks for a forty-five-minute hour.

Yes, I'd heard that.

But, of course, I knew something different.

CHAPTER 11

The uneasiness began with the moms, like I guess it usually does. A tiny flame of gossip, texted and tweeted and Facebooked, all of it leaked from Mike's office. The blood on the pillow. The damning Bible verse. No family stepping forward.

It was a churning, collective small-town kind of worrying unfamiliar to me, an ex–New Yorker who knew exactly seven people by name in my last apartment building. In New York City, there were 99,000 calls to 911 a *day*. People disappeared into the ether all the time. No one bonded about it.

Three PTA officers had hounded Mike's office yesterday until he agreed to place an extra cop at the elementary school during recess and for end-of-the-day pickup. Their concerns weren't specifically about Caroline Warwick but about the idea that this could happen *here*, to someone rich and ensconced behind a fortress wall.

'"Paranoia is knowing all the facts."' I said this nonsensically to Mike, on the third morning that Caroline was missing. 'Woody Allen.' I was making myself a breakfast of cut-up bananas with sugar and milk, one of my mom's old tricks.

'Not helping,' Mike said. 'Facts aren't even part of the equation yet. One of those PTA moms bordered on maniacal. She mentioned the Lindbergh baby. First Baptist wants to hold a vigil. I want to hold off hysteria.' He grimly dumped his coffee in the sink and kissed the top of my head. 'What you are eating is disgusting.'

As soon as he closed the door, my smile receded. In seconds, I was punching *Maria Valdez* into a White Pages search on my laptop, which returned 113 listings for either M. Valdez or Maria Valdez within a sixty-mile radius. I took a guess and focused on the M. Valdez who lived closest, in the nearby town of Boon Hill, which was mostly Hispanic. A random decision on my part, because odds were that Maria Valdez was living in a house under a first name that belonged to a father or husband or boyfriend with one of twenty-five initials other than *M*. But this was the plan I'd made last night.

Mike had brought up Boon Hill in a recent conversation because he was amazed that it was mostly minority and poor with almost nonexistent crime stats. About four hundred people, mostly low-income Hispanics, some illegal, some not. Primarily good people, working hard. Scrubbing toilets, pounding nails in roofs that reflected 200-degree heat, making sub-par wages. No one seemed to mind, Mike said. The Clairmont elite cast their gaze the other way, to the far, far left, when it came to immigration papers for people who snuggled with their children and made their lives immeasurably better. For people they *loved*. The Hispanics hunkered down, hoping that they wouldn't get booted back, that Washington and Texas politicians would remain hopelessly mired. It seemed a very good bet for Boon Hill residents.

Clear directions to Boon Hill did not exist in Google or on the Texas map in the glove compartment, which meant I couldn't plug in the most accurate coordinates for Hugh. I snapped him off after he directed me to drive straight into a barbwire fence and rolled into British freak mode when I ignored him. *Bloody hell! You've missed it! Mum, turn around!*

'Bugger off, Hugh,' I responded, in my best Cockney.

I bumped along on the two-lane country road, feeling lost even though I was traveling in a perfectly straight line. The leafy trees on either side formed a drooping canopy over the road. Eerily isolating. Maybe this drive wasn't such a good idea. There hadn't been a single living thing in the last ten minutes except for the crow with nice aim who dropped a splotchy white present onto my windshield.

For the next five miles, I felt increasingly unsettled. The sun was shining but something was off. Every few minutes or so, I checked my rearview mirror. I had answered two hang-up calls this morning after Mike left for work. I was trying to convince myself that they were a glitch between a telemarketing company's computer dialing and our house's frayed wiring.

I woke up this morning with Maria on my mind. I figured Maria would have a pretty good handle on whether it was Caroline Warwick's habit to send out obscure threats to prospective club members. Maybe Maria herself had delivered this special present to my door as part of her duties. I hoped, prayed, that Caroline was at the root of this, because the alternative – that it was all somehow connected to Pierce Martin – was far scarier. I could handle a depressed rich old lady with an overly obsessive interest in my life. Maybe Caroline had voluntarily booked herself into a comfy psych ward for a couple of weeks. Maybe Gretchen had put her there and just wasn't saying.

I almost missed the sign. Weeds were growing halfway up the pole: BOON HILL, POP. 212, obviously a few years behind the census. No hill in sight.

When a colorful row of wood houses suddenly appeared on either side of the road, I pulled over with relief. Civilization. I almost ran into a small sign planted in the sloping lawn of a boxy house with peeling sky-blue paint. QUILTS AND ROCKS! SE VENDE! BARATO!!! Maybe not *quite* civilization. My high school Spanish translated: FOR SALE! CHEAP!!!

My eyes traveled past the litter of rusty tools and a huge pile of limestone rocks to the west side of the home. Wildly colorful, Mexican-inspired quilts fluttered on the clothesline like free-spirit Picassos. This house seemed as good a place as any to knock first.

I slipped out of the car, sidestepped a broken tractor seat and an old-fashioned hand pump, and delicately maneuvered up crumbling concrete steps to a small porch. I peered through the patched screen door, but could only make out the dark shapes of a couch and a chair. Every shade was drawn to shut out the sun. Somewhere in a back room, an industrial floor fan roared like an airplane taking off.

Just as I was about to knock, the chair moved. Or rather, a shadow rose out of the shadows. I found myself eye to eye with a fiftyish Mexican man on the other side of the screen. He wore a guarded expression and a faded red-and-blue-checked work shirt. A silver crucifix hung around his neck. Catholic. One of my people.

'I was about to knock,' I said quickly. I offered him a practiced smile, which he ignored. His gaze traveled from my sweaty face to my belly to the old pink Skechers on my feet. I hadn't taken much care with my appearance this morning, throwing on maternity jeans with a kangaroo pouch that the website promised would expand with me up to forty more pounds. This seemed possible, even probable, at the rate I was eating iced animal crackers out of the bag. I'd also pulled one of Mike's faded old T-shirts over my head, emblazoned with the New York Fire Department logo.

Definitely pregnant, possibly lost, certainly harmless. That's what I read in his face when he stepped out on the porch and let the door slam behind him.

'Do you know Maria Valdez?' I asked. *'Por favor.* I'm looking for her. *Por Maria. Me llama Emily.'* I pointed to myself unnecessarily. The man was silent for so long I considered turning around and trudging back to my car.

'I speak English,' he said, finally. 'I'm Rafael.'

'Good. Great.' I felt myself blushing. Awkward. 'I need a babysitter.' I patted my belly. Lying again.

'There.' He pointed across the road to several small boxy houses.

'Really? The pink house? The yellow?' I couldn't believe this was going to be so easy.

'Yellow.'

'Gracias, sir.' And then, impulsively: *'Cuanto?* For a quilt?'

'You want to look?' He asked it almost shyly. A paying customer. There couldn't be many of us meandering by.

'Yes. Please.'

He stepped off the concrete porch, avoiding the stairs entirely. *'Cuidado,'* he told me, offering a hand down.

Six masterpieces hung by common wooden clothespins, one every few inches, like a row of sparrows on a telephone line. I stopped at the first quilt, stunned, and moved slowly down the row, my fingers running lightly over the intricate quilting.

126

Each block was powerfully original and yet clearly born from the same artist's hands. Bold colors and clever, whimsical designs alive with frogs, flowers, turtles, fish, and birds. At a distance, the patches flowed together like a glorious mural; up close, it was hard not to fixate on the complex geometry of the stitching. I could look at these quilts a hundred times, a thousand times, and see something different.

I wanted to buy them all. A quilt under glass at the Smithsonian Craft Show last spring wasn't even close to this level of artistry. Price tag on that one: $10,000. But it seemed greedy, almost offensive, to strip all this beauty off the line.

'Incredible.' I waved my arm to encompass all of them. 'Your wife?'

'No, no. My wife died last year. Breast cancer. Me. My work. Always, my work.'

He bent over and violently ripped a large milkweed out of the ground.

'I'm so sorry.' I turned back to the quilts immediately, because that's what I'd want someone to do for me.

'The sewing passes my time. I sell the quilts every Saturday at the flea market.' He shrugged. 'But those people do not want to pay. They want everything for one dollar, two dollar. I make more on my old bottles and rocks.'

I think about how my connections in the art world could change the life of this grizzled man. But maybe he didn't want change. Maybe he wanted to be permanently fixed to this land, near things his wife had touched in life, where her spirit had settled.

I chose one, the smallest, which was strewn with a flock of colorful birds that I'd never seen in nature. For the baby's room. Maybe it would inspire me to abandon superstition and set it up. I'd sold off one piece of superstition already: the brand-new crib we'd bought three years and several miscarriages ago.

'I'll take this one. How much?'

'One hundred.' I could tell by his expression that he was up for bargaining. He turned away to free the quilt from the clothespins. Brown, wrinkled hands folded the quilt. His nails were as clean and well manicured as a surgeon's.

I opened my purse and pulled out a $20, my only cash aside from the emergency $100 bill in the back flap of my wallet that I had always carried to appease would-be muggers in the city. I tugged it out and gave Rafael that, too. I knew that it wasn't nearly enough, but his warm smile said that it was plenty.

'It is lucky,' he said. 'You pick well.'

'What do you mean?'

'For your son to sleep under birds. *Mucho suerte.*'

A burst of euphoria coursed through my ragged nerves. How did he know I was having a boy? That the quilt was for *my son*? The cross around his neck glinted in the sun. The heat spread through my veins like warm tequila. The air smelled like dirt and honeysuckle. I had just been blessed by a misplaced priest with a chipped front tooth.

'Muchas gracias.' I held out my arms, thinking I'd sleep under this quilt every night until the baby was born. But Rafael wasn't ready to hand it over.

'There.' He pointed to a tiny black cross stitched to the bottom edge of the quilt. 'That is my signature. *Dios es infinidad.*' Infinity. *God is forever.*

Before I left, he said, 'Sure, it's OK, take a few pictures with your phone.' I shot the quilts from every angle. It wouldn't hurt to email them to a few people. Spirits have been known to travel.

After I tucked my purchase into the backseat, I stood on the tidy, well-swept porch of the yellow house across the street. The very pretty Mexican girl who answered the door clutched an SAT study guide under her arm. Maria wasn't home, she said. A toddler clung to her legs, hiding her head under the older girl's skirt.

I told this young woman the same lie I'd told Rafael, only slightly more elaborate. That I was looking for a babysitter. That Maria was recommended to me. That I would pay very well. I overdramatically wiped sweat off my brow. I asked for a drink. She opened the screen door somewhat reluctantly and let me into a tiny cave of a living room. The rumble of an aging window air conditioner blended with the sizzle of something frying in the kitchen. Whatever it was made my mouth water.

'I'm Rosie,' she said. 'Maria is my sister. This is

Violet. My daughter.' Rosie couldn't be more than seventeen. Violet, no more than two. Rosie took the child with her into the kitchen while I flopped down on a small couch covered by a cheap fleece blanket that instantly made my legs sweat, perspiration working through my jeans. There were two small end tables, one with a tiled image of the Virgin Mary. Three straight-back dining room chairs. A heavy wrought-iron cross that looked like it might bring down the wall where it was hanging. Maria needed her job.

There was suddenly a little person crawling into my lap. Violet had returned, alone. She snuggled around my belly and began playing with the silver charm bracelet I rarely took off. Her fingers were soft and sticky and she smelled wonderful, like a human cinnamon bun.

I heard an exchange of voices in the kitchen and the sound of an ice tray being cracked. I took in a deep breath of little girl.

'Violet.' Rosie stood over us with my glass of water, served in a plastic Winnie-the-Pooh glass. 'Get down. Stop playing with her jewelry.'

'Pooh,' Violet said.

'No, it's OK,' I interposed. 'Leave her. This was my mother's. I used to play with it when I was little. It reminds me.' I gulped the water gratefully.

'My mother says Maria will not be back soon.' Rosie planted herself on the edge of the couch. She wanted this to be a short conversation. 'Maria

130

works very hard. The woman she works for is not
. . . very nice. Maybe Maria will take your job.
Please write down your name and number.' She
handed me a pencil and a piece of notebook paper
stuck in her SAT book. I wrote my name and
number carefully, thanked her, and gently lifted
Violet from my lap to her arms.

As I walked back to the station wagon, I hovered
inside the shade of a giant live oak, where it was
at least ten degrees cooler. I was glad I'd come,
even if I found out nothing. I wanted to carry the
peace of this lovely road for a long time.

I wriggled my awkward body into the Volvo,
thinking about showing Mike our new quilt. As I
switched on the ignition, a rusted pickup rumbled
past. That's when I saw the cigar box on my passenger
seat.

A box that hadn't been there a few minutes ago.

My belly knocked sharply against the wheel,
my breath seizing, my gut telling me to *get the
hell out of the car,* but I sat paralyzed, unable to
move or take my eyes off of it. Even in panic
mode, my artist self appreciated the aesthetics of
the cedar box and the evocative label glued to the
top.

On it, a large-boned blond woman was set
against pitch-black, draped in a swirling blue dress
and a snaking purple scarf. She had a rakish patch
over one eye, a bundle of tobacco leaves dripping
from one hand and in the other a cigar raised
jauntily over her head. Empowering, right down

131

to the bare feet with red toenail polish. She was left-handed, I thought distractedly, like me.

Black Patch Cigar Co.

I'd never heard of it – but then, I'd never puffed on a cigar.

I didn't move. I held my breath and listened for ticking sounds, although Mike had taught me that bombs don't always tick. His voice in my head screamed for me to *get out* even as I reached over and lifted the lid with a fingertip, touching nothing else. A single cigar was tucked inside, wrapped tightly in cellophane, dressed up with a bow made out of cheap pink curling ribbon. No note. *A congratulations for the baby? Or a threat?*

I didn't think Rafael had done this. The pink was wrong, wrong, wrong. Color would be important to an artist like Rafael. He wouldn't break in to my car, even though I left it unlocked.

I thrust open the door and ran to the wayback. I locked the doors with my remote before peering through the rear window. I saw nothing but the six-pack of water that Mike insisted I carry for emergencies.

I shot a 360-glance around me. Not a soul. Everyone was hiding out from the heat. The air was perfectly still, waiting.

My fingers fumbled to hit speed-dial 1. Mike's voice said he wasn't available at the moment, but would return my call as soon as possible.

'Your concerns are important to me,' he said politely. 'If this is an emergency, please dial 911.'

I got back in the car, yanked it into gear, and spun out, kicking up gravel and a choking cloud of dust. I reminded myself to tell Mike that no one wanted to be instructed to dial 911. People weren't idiots.

Ten miles down the road, it belatedly occurred to me to glance into the backseat.

My lucky quilt was still there, folded in a neat square.

CHAPTER 12

The three of them waited for me at a white-clothed table in the corner, set with half-drunk glasses of Chablis and littered with crumbs from a basket of hard French rolls. It was a full house at Ruggieri's. The lights were low. Votive candles flickered on tables, illuminating tiny bud vases of sturdy white carnations.

Christmas greenery pretending not to be Christmas greenery wound around a metal arbor behind the hostess stand. Nice try, with the fake orchids and daisies stuck here and there. In harsh daylight, this place probably didn't look much better than a diner, but it supposedly dished out the best Eye-talian in town.

A man rose up out of the crowd to wave me over. I was confused for a second, but, yes, this stranger was waving at me. Harry Dunn, I presumed. The mayor's eyes traced like a snake up and down my body, settling in the middle, surprised, as if he hadn't known I was pregnant. But that was nothing compared to how radically off my own assumptions had been about him.

Whenever Mike mentioned his new boss, I had

pictured Harry Dunn as a potbellied, balding, boisterous politician, with hopeless zeal for the Texas governorship. Instead, Harry Dunn was a stunner. An 11. Or a 12. An instant vote-getter. Dark wavy hair, an aristocratic nose, a sexy, slender frame, broad shoulders, a gorgeous black suit, a loosened tie around a stiff white collar, a very, very nice watch, and no ring on his left hand.

Leticia stood up, too, her chubby fingers curling possessively on her husband's arm as I wove my way along narrow paths to the table. Next to Harry, even sitting down, Mike stood out like a bruiser, his rolled-up sleeves baring thick, dangerous forearms. I felt sorry for Letty. Despite her size and a bright yellow sundress, beside her husband she appeared shrunken and outclassed. Mike had mentioned that Harry had risen up from less than gracious beginnings. Maybe behind closed doors, where Letty wrote the checks, the score evened out.

Harry shook off Letty's grip to lean over and kiss me, saying everything about their relationship I ever needed to know. The spot where his lips touched my cheek felt damp and clammy, like a tiny frog had landed there. I pushed down the urge to wipe off any residue. My heart started a steady pound.

I smiled coolly. This was the archetype of the guy I didn't do well around. The grown-up Pierces. Harry Dunn would have sex with me, pregnant and married, tonight, in the back of a car, hell, in

135

the one-holer bathroom in the back of this restaurant. He'd said it with his eyes and with the hand he casually drifted up and down my back while his lips brushed my cheek. I hated myself for the primal physical response he elicited. Attraction and abhorrence at the same time.

Right now, Letty's plump face reminded me of a pot of water about to boil. I tried to picture Harry and Letty in bed. Letty on bottom. Letty on top. My mind couldn't wrap around it.

'I'm sorry I'm late,' I rambled nervously. 'I decided to put on makeup. Then I couldn't fit into those capris that I wore last week . . . I really need to unpack . . . I left my cell phone and had to go back . . .'

Mike didn't know yet about the cigar box, which was sitting on our kitchen table. When I called Mike's secretary, he'd been stuck in meetings. I'd been careful. I removed the box from the car using latex gloves Mike kept under the kitchen sink. I checked the car out thoroughly before getting back in to drive over here. Under the hood, in the trunk, beneath the seats. Nothing.

Harry, lazily stretched back in his chair, smiled as if my flustered appearance utterly charmed him. Not Letty. Not Mike. His lips were stretched tight, an angry white line around them. Because he was jealous of the visual undressing I just got from his boss? That was no doubt Letty's grievance with me tonight. As for Mike – well, I thought we doused those jealous flames in a therapist's office a long time ago.

I sat down in the empty place across from Letty, trying not to stare at the mountain of snowy cleavage on display that reminded me of a toddler's bottom that had never seen the sun. I offered her the warmest smile I could summon, thinking I could use that gin and tonic at Harry's elbow.

'It's so great to see you again, Letty. And so nice to meet you, Harry.'

My tone gave nothing away. But while Letty and Mike buried their heads in the menu, I met Harry's gaze directly across the table with my answer: *No way.*

Harry quirked an eyebrow as if he'd just engaged a worthy foe. He'd silently declared another open invitation to me, even though I was pregnant, even though Mike could take him down in five seconds. Why, why did men like him still think I was an easy target for their invitations?

'I need more lemon slices for my water,' Letty yelled out at a waitress.

'Here, take mine.' I picked the lemon wedge out of my water with a spoon and tried not to stare while she squeezed it into her glass and doused the whole thing with the pepper shaker.

'It's a pageant-girl trick.' She said it like she was confiding state secrets. 'Although it's supposed to be red pepper. Beyoncé used it to lose all that weight for *Dreamgirls*. Stunts the appetite right off.'

She took a swig of her nasty concoction without any obvious ill effects, although it had an ill effect on me. I held down a gag reflex behind the menu, a tall plastic-coated affair that hadn't been wiped off lately.

'I'm kind of in between diets. I was on the Hallelujah Diet last month, the one where you just eat foods specifically mentioned in Genesis Chapter 1, Verse 29. Mostly vegetables. Janice Marstead recommended it. She's the second-best soprano in the First Baptist choir, after me. My stomach was like a lawn mower at work 24/7. I had to drink five Sonic milkshakes a day to calm things down. I don't think it's really all that God-approved anyway. In Genesis, Chapter 9, Verse 3, God lifts all those diet restrictions.'

The waitress ventured over to the table with a small bowl of lemon slices.

'It's about time,' Letty said. 'Get out your pad. I'm going to have the fettuccine alfredo with chicken and extra pancetta and a bowl of Parmesan cheese on the side because you never put enough on. Also, a Caesar salad, and don't be chintzy with the croutons.'

Harry seemed immune, as if he pretended his wife didn't exist most of the time, and Mike wasn't interested in sharing any silent humor with me. He wouldn't even meet my eyes. *What the hell was up with him?*

After we ordered, Mike and Harry might as well have been sitting at a separate table. They started with Caroline's case, then lit into a semi-civilized argument about a *New York Times* piece on Fort Worth's resident hanging judge and moved on to the Preston Trail Golf Club, so exclusive that members had to die before a spot opened up. Mickey Mantle had been a late and beloved member. Harry was bragging about his status as No. 548 on the waiting list.

I listened with half an ear while Letty gushed about how Suzanne Somers was the last legitimate fitness expert and that it was a shame she had to give that up to cure cancer. While Letty rattled on and Mike re-engaged with the wine list, Harry tossed me a wink.

'Well, Emily, what do you think about Caroline disappearing?' Letty demanded. 'It's been almost four days. She missed an interesting prayer breakfast this morning. The choir director took up about a third of it praying for her safe return. He's gay as a daisy. The scrambled eggs could have used more cheese.'

It was hard enough to follow Letty's non sequiturs when I wasn't exhausted and worried about a stalker who left presents wrapped in pink ribbon. 'I don't know Caroline very well,' I stuttered. 'Mike thinks it's . . . of concern.'

'Caroline took a fancy to you right away. Just like she did with your friend Misty. Some of the girls don't much like the idea of either one of you getting in. Me, I'll go along with Caroline.' Leticia slathered butter on a roll. She leaned in closer and lowered her voice, a breathy advertisement for the garlicky croutons stacked so high on her salad I couldn't see any green.

'I told that booger-nosed cop, Cody Hill, what I just told your husband. Neither appears to be taking me too seriously. It's annoying because I'm breaking the club's oath of secrecy here.' Leticia vigorously stirred her water with her butter knife. The pepper swirled like a polluted snow globe.

'Caroline and Misty Rich had an argument the day before she disappeared,' she continued. 'I saw them in Misty's Lexus going at it in the park off of Parr Road. Caroline—'

'A white Lexus SUV? Tinted windows?' I interrupted.

'Every car window's tinted, honey, when you live in Texas. But her Lexus is green. A sedan. I think it's a lease. My Lexus is white.'

I leaned back to allow the waitress to remove my salad and replace it with an enormous serving of spaghetti and clam sauce.

'That looks like somebody blew their brains out,' Letty said, wrinkling her nose. My spaghetti instantly morphed into blood and bits of gray matter. Add to that the smell of odiferous clams and Letty's pepper and lemon pageant trick with a glass of water, and my appetite had officially shut down. I didn't think it was possible.

'Don't you think that's weird?' Letty persisted.

I covered my plate with two paper napkins, watching a red stain slowly spread. 'I don't know. I've been here three weeks. I don't think you should openly accuse Misty of anything without more information.' I wondered if Caroline had been blackmailing Misty, too. The blurred photograph of that little girl on the bicycle crept into my brain. All that weird awkwardness.

Letty was still assaulting me with her garlic breath. My right temple pounded. 'In fact,' I added, 'I'm not interested in hearing your gossip about her. Ever.'

'Listen to *you* defend *her*.' Letty was in full sarcastic throttle. 'I didn't know you'd become such fast friends.'

Mike and Harry stopped their conversation to stare at us, like they had been watching a G-rated movie and suddenly somebody took off her top.

'Did you see those shoes she wore to Caroline's the other night? Whore shoes. Misty's a slut. Word is, so are you.' Letty's words sliced the air at a decibel that carried to every corner of the restaurant. I tensed. Mike's hand gripped my arm in warning. At last, some attention from my spouse.

'You think I don't know about *you*?' The room was now completely still, as if a conductor had raised his baton. Waiters balanced trays, forks froze inches from open mouths. No one spoke a word, all eyes glued to the four of us. The maître d' nervously maneuvered his way in our direction. I was sure he was dreading breaking up a brawl at the mayor's table.

Harry scooted his chair back loudly, nearly knocking it into the horrified waitress behind him. His face was filled with the kind of disgust I reserved for . . . well, I didn't reserve that kind of disgust

141

for anything but the Texas roaches the size of silver dollars that I found clacking across the kitchen counter last night. But Harry did, and he was aiming it at his wife. Leticia withered. It was as if she'd lost weight in front of my eyes.

'My wife has been struggling with a new medication.' Harry tugged Letty roughly to her feet like she was an obnoxious child about to get a whipping in the restaurant bathroom. 'My apologies.' He turned to the maître d'. 'Please put this on my tab and add in a thirty percent tip. Mike, I'll see you tomorrow. Emily, I'm sure we'll meet again.' That thirty percent tip was Letty's money, but Harry Dunn clearly threw it around like confetti.

Harry took my hand before I could refuse, bending to kiss it. I felt the tip of his tongue. It was a dead tie as to which of these two people was more repulsive.

'Good night,' Mike said, for both of us. I'm not sure whether he knew I was wiping the back of my hand along my pants leg.

On the way home in the car, Mike said nothing. I wanted to tell him about the boxes, both the one at Caroline's that held secrets and the one that held the cigar. About Harry's tongue. But now my own anger was blazing. He couldn't blame me for the disastrous evening. He'd set up this little dinner party and informed me of the details in a text, making it very hard for me to say no. Sure, I could have been more tactful. But the woman called me a slut, and her husband licked me like a dog.

142

We reached the front porch, and I trailed behind him. Mike turned the key but the old, swollen door stuck like it usually did. He thrust a fierce kick in the middle of the frame and the door swung open, slamming against the wall, leaving a star-shaped hole in the living room plaster.

'You think I'm angry about tonight? About that shrew of a woman and her ambitious asshole husband? Here's what I'm angry about, Emily.'

He spit out every syllable of my name like a bad taste in his mouth. He pulled me by the arm to our bedroom, to the pile of papers on his nightstand that I assumed were part of the Kilimanjaro of police files he reviewed as bedtime stories.

'See this?' He removed a sheaf of five or six pages from a folder, shaking them inches from my nose before letting them fall like autumn leaves. 'What else is there, Emily?'

I shrugged off his hand and knelt clumsily to gather up the papers, to give myself time. My eyes blurred with tears, but I could see enough words and phrases to get the gist.

Homicide.

Gunshots.

My hands froze. On the page resting at my feet, a crime scene photo was replicated on a scratchy fax. I could make out a bloody black soup near Pierce Martin's head.

'Why didn't you tell me the man who *raped* you

was shot to death three weeks later?' Mike was now on the floor with me, pulling me to him. His fury was hot and close. Too close.

I couldn't breathe. *When did Mike put these papers on the nightstand?*

'Did you do it?' Four words, each one hitting my brain like an ice pick. 'Why?' His voice was despairing. '*Why can't you talk to me?*'

'Because I was a different person then.' My voice was cold and far away, not at all the way I wanted it to come out.

I tried again, and this time my voice broke with my pathetic confession. 'Because you might not have married me.'

He dropped his hands from my shoulders.

'I've got to get out of here,' he muttered.

'Wait. Mike, please.' I sucked in a shaky breath. 'I didn't kill him.'

But he was already gone.

One sheet at a time, I picked up the papers scattered across our bedroom floor. My tears were falling like fat drops of rain, smudging the ugly words.

Of course Mike had checked out Pierce Martin. What cop in his right mind wouldn't check out a vicious crime against his wife, even if it happened thirteen years ago?

No, Pierce Martin never fulfilled his imaginary destiny as a nasty husband with two children, a dangerous roving eye, and serial rapist status.

My rapist was dead. I didn't need to see the crime photo staring up at me from the floor. I knew with the certainty of someone who has stood over his casket to be completely sure.

Pierce's mother had caught me when I'd crumpled over her son's coffin. It had been harder to confront a dead Pierce than I'd thought. With the kind of irony only God can dish out, his mother grabbed my elbow as I wobbled, offering support, asking how I knew him, murmuring that he was a 'wonderful boy.' This was before I became a suspect. Before I knew about the other girls.

I wanted to scream at his mother so loudly that I woke that evil son of a bitch in his coffin, so that all those mourners could know: *You raised a monster!*

Instead, I had pretended to be too overcome to talk.

When she turned away to find better consolation, I opened my fist, which clutched a chain with a tiny gold cross, a $30 diamond chip dropped into the center.

It was the cross hanging around my neck when he raped me.

The necklace that lived under the glass in a JCPenney store before he purchased it at the last minute, all part of his plan.

The one he gave me during the chocolate mousse course at my nineteenth birthday dinner two hours before he jammed himself inside me, then rolled off nonchalantly to pee in a bathroom a few feet away. Like I was nothing.

Standing over his dead body, I had lifted his suit flap and tucked the cross inside his crisp shirt pocket so he could take it with him to hell.

CHAPTER 13

'Miz Emily. You came. *Gracias.*'

It had taken four or five rings of the bell before Maria answered. She was an extremely pretty girl who didn't look at all pretty right now. Hungover, maybe. She teetered a little in Caroline's doorway. She was dressed in that frilly maid's uniform, only it looked like she'd slept in it. Blotchy skin, runny mascara, brown hair slashed with unnatural maroonish streaks. An inch of black roots. The uniform transformed Maria's curvy figure into a sexual cliché. The wrong kind of man would push her to her knees.

I didn't look too hot myself: no shower or makeup, drained and exhausted from my fight with Mike, anxious about everything I needed to say to him. The cigar box was back in the front seat of the car, still a secret, now a secret in a Ziploc bag.

When Maria called that morning, crying, peppering me with an English-Spanish pilaf I couldn't translate, it was tempting to say no. Even though my mission yesterday had been to track her down, I was too distraught today to deal with the problems of Caroline. Four days missing. I had my own messy life to get in order. Two of Maria's words finally convinced me.

Cops. Help.

'Your husband. He left with his policeman two hours ago. After the search.'

'What search?'

'They had a paper. Official. They looked all over her bedroom, disturbing things. I am trying to fix. She will be unhappy. Blame me. She will fire me, I know it.'

Maria used her hand to shade her eyes from the sun, on its way to high noon, and peered down the empty street. Luxury cars and trucks were tidily ensconced in four-car garages, their owners chilling out in refrigerated homes. For me, fresh from Manhattan's twenty-four-hour cacophony, the absolute stillness in late morning was eerie, as if everyone had fled a nuclear threat.

'What exactly do you want me to do?' The heat beat on my shoulders, and my throat felt parched.

'Your husband. He is in charge, no? He seemed nice. But the other one.' She pointed to her head. '*Rojo*.' Red. Cody Hill. 'He said he would look into my family's legal status if I didn't cooperate. I need to know. Is he going to give my family trouble?'

'Are you here illegally, Maria?'

'The problem is not *me*.' She said this impatiently. 'Can you talk to your husband about the *rojo* cop? Please.' The way she said *rojo*, it might

148

as well have been *asshole.* Something we agreed on wholeheartedly. While I remained silent, considering this, she burst into tears and spun into a torrent of solid-gold Spanish.

'Maria,' I said gently. 'English, please. I'll try to help. Maybe I can talk to Mike.'

'Everything is a mess now,' she sobbed. 'They took her drawers and closet apart. I can't clean it up by myself. I'm afraid I will get in trouble if I bring in my sister to help.'

I was shoveling a grave for myself simply by standing on the doorstep of a possible crime scene. Mike had returned home at dawn to shower and re-dress for work while I pretended to be sleeping. We were pros at that double maneuver.

Violet's sweet face flashed in my mind. A little girl who depended on her aunt for survival.

'I have about two hours,' I told Maria.

Maria swung the door wide with a shaky smile and led me to the kitchen. State-of-the-art stainless-steel appliances, miles of white granite counter space, stacks of generic white china behind the glass cabinets. A caterer's dream.

Maria opened a door in the corner to reveal a servants' staircase. The modern dumbwaiter was big enough to hold Maria and me cross-legged playing a comfortable game of patty-cake. As a kid, I'd always wanted to ride in one. Maria was already climbing the stairs in the narrow opening, quickly, two at a time.

'How many flights?' I was surprised to be slightly

out of breath on the first landing. Maybe I should sign up for the No Baby Fat exercise class advertised in the window of the Clairmont Y.

'Four. Miz Warwick's bedroom is on three.' One floor above the pink museum.

I tried to swallow my huffing and puffing once we reached the third floor. How could I be out of shape so fast? I ran a half marathon last year. Maria didn't notice or didn't care, hurrying around the curved hallway. This floor was identical to the one below it: closed doors, deep-red flocked paper, wall sconces dripping with painstakingly Windexed chandelier beads.

'Here.' She paused at a door in the middle. 'We must be quick. Any minute she could return.'

She threw open the door to a room that took my breath away. No one settled back against these pillows on this bed to watch a rerun of *Downton Abbey* and eat potato chips. The creamy antique linens and embroidered pillows must have cost thousands. The walls curved in a semi-circle, inviting us into a painted garden. Clouds from a muted sky drifted on the ceiling. Everywhere, the muralist invoked the gardens of Versailles at twilight.

Maria compulsively smoothed out an invisible wrinkle on the duvet. No crime scene tape, no blood on the pillow. The window by the bed shut tight, filmy curtains draping either side.

'We must work first on the bureau,' she said, 'and then the closet.' She nodded toward two double doors.

'OK,' I said, uncertainly. She pointed toward my foot. I was standing in a trail of silk underwear, tossed from a nearby bureau. I bent down, not really wanting to touch an old lady's panties. *Whoa.* This was expensive, sexy honeymoon underwear. It also appeared to have never been worn. I didn't think Mike would rake through a stranger's underwear drawer and toss it in this perverted fashion. But Rojo probably would.

I began to fold. Maria disappeared into the closet. Too far away to carry on a conversation. It took about a half-hour to sort out the underwear and nightgowns scattered across the room.

'Maria?' I called her name toward the closet. She appeared instantly.

'Are you too tired to help me more?' she asked, a little petulantly.

I glanced at my watch. 'I can work with you in there for a little while.' In closer quarters, where I could quiz her about Caroline and her damn club.

I wanted to snatch those words back once she reopened the doors, automatic lights flooding a cavernous white space. I should have started in here, to hell with the panties.

Two or three hundred shoes rested on floor-to-ceiling glass shelves, individually spotlighted, toes pointing every which way. And plenty of empty shelves where the piles dumped on the floor were supposed to go. Only the hanging clothes were undisturbed, hanging in neat, tight lines, organized by color, and Caroline liked color. Especially red.

'Every shoe must have two inches between each, with toes pointing straight out,' Maria recited. 'Exactly. Like this.' She demonstrated on a pair of glossy black evening shoes. I half expected her to hand me a ruler. Maria slid a small ladder in place and proceeded to climb it. 'The *rojo* . . . thought she hid something in her shoes. I'll do top. You do bottom.'

'Did he find anything?'

'No.'

'Maria, where do you think Caroline is?' I kept my eyes on the pair of Josef Seibel leather clogs in my hands. They seemed very un-Caroline.

'I don't know. I told the police this.' Defensive.

'Was she depressed? Her friends say she had become a little paranoid.'

'I'm not sure what this word – *paranoid* – means. What friends? They are all bitches.'

I appreciated her rude assessment. The woman who washed Caroline's underwear, who picked her hair out of the shower drain, who spent more time with her than anyone on earth, would know.

'They are all calling here, all the time, leaving messages. Checking. Like they care. Last night, I found Miz Jenny and Miz Mary Ann creeping around the backyard in bug masks. I recognize Miz Jenny's *tetas falsas* or I might have called the police. They said they were making sure that Miz Caroline hadn't fallen behind a bush.'

I thought for a second. 'Night vision goggles?'

'*Si*. Miz Jenny said she borrowed them from her husband's hunting closet.'

Maria stepped carefully off the ladder. Her own shoes were white, clunky, and rubber-soled. Nurse's shoes, before nurses started hipping it up with Crocs and New Balance.

Color flared on her cheeks. 'Why did you show up at my home? I do not think you are the type for a babysitter.'

'Truthfully, because I need you. I'm out of my element here. Caroline invited me over to pass around that ridiculous box. Then someone dropped off a little blackmail package at my house. Was that Caroline's idea?'

About six expressions played across the maid's face. First, surprise. So she *didn't* drop off the package. None of her facial tics after that were terribly sympathetic. In fact, the one she was wearing now could almost be described as . . . happy.

'It's OK,' she assured me eagerly. 'She blackmails all the ladies. Me. She provided fake papers for my sister and niece. This is what I am worried about with that cop. Violet was only one year old when she rode across the border in the trunk of a car. So sometimes Mrs Caroline threatens to expose them. She helps but there is always a price.' Her voice trailed into bitterness. 'If you are not going to hire me right now, I can't say more. I will make you lunch. For *el nino*.' She pointed to my stomach and walked out. Conversation over.

153

It felt both safe and illicit to be alone. It reminded me of the naïve middle-schooler I once was, snooping in my parents' closet, discovering a box of condoms and my mother's vibrator. Excited and a little horrified. Guilty.

I shook it off. Maria had asked me here, to help. We were almost done. And I *was* hungry. My head felt a little light. I ran my hand along a row of historical romances stuffed neatly in a bookshelf at the end of the closet. Maybe where Caroline got her ideas. They weren't real books, I realized. Even in her closet, Caroline was creating a façade. I leaned back against the shelf and closed my eyes. Suddenly, top to bottom, my world was moving. I fell backward, almost stabbing myself with a five-inch heel.

The bookcase was a camouflaged door.

I'd just read about this trend while thumbing magazines in my OB's office in New York. High-def, high-concept secret rooms that whisked adults back to the fantasies of their childhoods while conveniently soundproofing them from their own kids. At the time, I thought it was ridiculous. But here I was, staring into a black crack, wondering what Caroline would hide. Hopefully just the comfortable Hanes granny panties she really wore.

'Don't let anything shock you,' a friend said when I told her about our impending move to Texas. 'Guns, babies, reputation. They'll do anything to protect them.'

154

I let go of the absurdity of the moment, of the foghorn warning in my head, and stood up.

I laid my palm flat on *Romancing Mister Bridgerton* and *How to Woo a Reluctant Lady*.

I gave the shelf a push, wondering whether I was entering Caroline's tomb.

A foot in, and I was still blind. I slid my right hand up and down the wall until it touched a switch that flooded light into a decent-sized room, about 12 × 15 feet.

It took a second for my eyes to adjust.

I didn't see a lonely, crazy woman decaying on the floor or rolling around in a mad tryst with Mr Bridgerton.

A gorgeous antique Oriental rug lay at my feet, free of blood.

I smelled roses. Air freshener, I thought, until I saw the vase of fresh flowers on the built-in desk that held a state-of-the-art iMac. My gaze swiveled to a well-stocked glass-fronted refrigerator, a TV/stereo console, and a Kindle resting on a cushy leather chair. I wouldn't starve or die of dehydration or boredom if Maria shut the door behind me. My eyes fixed themselves on a built-in row of file cabinets lined against the left wall.

How long had Maria been gone? Five minutes? Ten?

I walked over to the computer screen. The pink room's nasty cat stared back at me from the screensaver. Then he howled, I screamed, and he stalked casually off the screen. Not a screensaver. A video? I peered closer, into that hideous pink room. I checked my watch. The cat was licking his paws. On the wall above him, a Barbie clock was keeping real time.

Caroline was spying on her cat.

I took a shaky breath. My eyes wandered from the screen to the neat stack of flat manila folders of varying thicknesses resting beside it.

The one on top had my name on it.

My hand poised to open it just as my cell phone vibrated in my pocket. I jumped like the cat had leapt out of the screen. *Dammit.*

I glanced down. A text from Misty.

Lunch tomorrow?

I texted back, *K.* And thought, *Now go away, Misty.*

I sat down at Caroline's desk and balanced the folder on my lap, my heart running laps. I flipped it open. A two-year-old color snapshot of me at an art gallery opening was paper-clipped to the top left corner of the first page. Caught in profile, holding a glass of champagne. I wore a pale blue silk dress from a designer thrift shop in Chinatown and Lucy's high silver heels. I was slightly drunk, trying to sell an A-list painting to a B-list celebrity.

It was attached to the first page of a report from a private detective agency in Dallas named Diskreet. Not a discreet name. Not even klever.

I refocused on the page.

Birth name: Emily Alena Waters.

Birthplace: Peekskill, New York.

My Social Security number, elementary school, middle school, and high school, college transcripts, SAT scores, hospitalizations, miscarriages, the crash that killed my parents.

The prisoner number assigned to the teenage drunk driver who killed them.

My job history, wedding date, husband's name and occupation, closest living relatives – every bit blazingly accurate.

It mentioned nothing of the missing year between my sophomore and junior years in college. I thumbed impatiently to the second page.

I learned that my husband was faithful, that a New York adoption agency hesitated to give us a baby because of Mike's occupation, and that our net worth totaled around $370,000. I shivered, because I knew what had to be coming.

I tore through the file but couldn't find a duplicate of the rape report. I settled on a paper-clipped bundle of Xeroxed newspaper stories, a more complete set than my own. Each headline drove me a little deeper into panic.

College senior shot to death in car near popular club

Windsor flies flag at half-mast to honor murdered student

1,000 turn out for campus memorial

Police eliminate drugs as motive in frat-boy murder

Five co-eds interviewed in shooting death

My history in a few tidy words.

I was mesmerized by a row of five headshots, a youthful me and four other girls unlucky enough to crawl into Pierce Martin's web. It could be the same girl photographed five times and cropped into a one-inch square. Pierce's type. Smooth, shoulder-length brown hair, dark eyes, fresh, bright faces worthy of Neutrogena commercials. Virginal.

Thirteen years ago, we five became sisters of sorts. We'd waited together nervously in a make-shift holding cell outside the campus librarian's office, the small sitting area where the police came to get us one by one for an interview.

'Fact-gathering,' the police told us.

I was the last one to arrive. The pretty Chi Omega, dressed in a blue cashmere cardigan and about five hundred bucks of Brighton jewelry, raised a hand to go first. I heard something indignant about 'my daddy' before the door clicked closed.

The co-ed beside me on the couch compulsively rubbed the rosary trailing out of her purse. The prettiest of us stuck out her hand, introduced herself as 'Lisa, pre-med,' and then calmly studied for a biology test at a small table.

A long-legged yogi named Margaret sat in a lotus position in the middle of the carpet and meditated, much to the chagrin of the police officer in charge of making sure we didn't speak to one another. I guess he decided that even he shouldn't interrupt a conversation between Margaret and whatever higher power she was channeling.

That left me, chewing my thumb raw, wondering how I ended up here, sucked in by a sexual predator, thinking I should have called my parents for a lawyer even though the police said I didn't need one.

That turned out to be true. They never even made it to the interview stage with me or Rosary Girl. Maybe some of her vigorous bead rubbing worked, although I didn't believe so much in the power of prayer at that point. More likely, the police realized they had opened the gate on a rabid dog. Pierce's parents were major endowment contributors. Alumni royalty.

I had watched the three other girls exit their interviews. They'd obviously been crying, except for Lisa, pre-med, who rolled her eyes at Rosary Girl and me on the way out the door.

'Fucking not guilty,' she mouthed.

The detective in charge directed his attention to the two of us. 'I think we have enough for now.' His face had the look of someone who'd eaten a plateful of bad shrimp. What he didn't appear was the slightest bit concerned about a girl gnawing her thumb bloody and another running rosary beads through her teeth. 'We'd like to speak to the Martin parents about our findings before continuing our interviews. This is a delicate matter for you and the campus. We'll stay in touch. Keep your mouths shut. That's best for everyone.'

Three weeks later, I stepped off a plane in Rome with a new hair color and never heard a word from the police again.

Now my fingers lingered over a narrow column copied crookedly on a sea of white paper, dated a month after I'd run out of town.

A black pen had made a loop around the third item, which announced that police were declaring Pierce Martin's murder case inactive 'due to lack of witnesses and evidence.'

Who did I have to thank for this lifetime reprieve?

The Chi Omega's rich daddy? Rosary Girl's direct line to God?

The incompetent campus policewoman who dismissed my rape report? Pierce's mother, to protect his reputation, her reputation, after learning more than she wanted to know about her precious son from the police?

I hadn't been the only girl in that interview waiting room whose body and soul had been torn apart by Pierce Martin. The police *knew*. I'd lay my life down on that.

I'd buried everything as deep as I could thirteen years ago. I'd vanished for a year, cutting ties to everyone except my parents, who agreed to support a year abroad at a small university in Rome. They hoped the experience would help heal me. I never even registered at the university. My parents wired a monthly check to a Rome bank. An anonymous person forwarded each one to me after the first month without a single bit of hassle, even though I asked them to address the envelope to another girl's name, two hundred miles away. The Italians understand that questions don't always need to be asked.

I wrote my parents pure fantasy about my life: how I painted and studied during the week and backpacked to European landmarks on the weekends with a sisterly roommate who didn't exist. I sent them little pencil sketches, all drawn from postcards I bought in a secondhand bookstore.

I returned home to my parents as myself, with my old name and my real hair color, hoping to leave my guilt and bewilderment behind. Instead, it chased me across the ocean, receding, crashing, teasing, always threatening to drag me under for the last time.

I glanced at my watch, a cheap piece with a flat yellow smiley face and a fake white leather band that I bought in Times Square for $7. It always ran about five minutes slow, which I figured was more than fair for the price.

Eleven minutes plus five had passed since Maria left me alone in the closet. I'd thumbed through the rest of the folders on the desk but didn't recognize any names. I stuck my own file in my purse without any hesitation.

I walked over to the row of file cabinets and tugged on the first one. It opened an inch. Unlocked. A more aggressive pull and the drawer revealed a row of orderly files, each with a name printed on a color-coded tab – red, green, or blue. Some files appeared yellowed and aged, others brand-new. All were neatly stored like the diaries in the pink room. Alphabetical. Organized by the same compulsive fingers.

Last names. I needed to remember last names. *Beswetherick.* Nope, there was no Beswetherick. I thumbed through the first row of files and found *Cartwright, Jennifer.* Jenny, one of the blond Southern stereotypes who cavorted with me in Caroline's plush Garden of Evil? Beach House or Red Mercedes, I couldn't remember which. I pulled her file and set it on top of the cabinet.

Dunn, Harold and *Dunn, Leticia.* I yanked them out. This was almost too easy.

I thumbed my way along the *D*'s and *E*'s. There had to be hundreds of files here. Caroline's voracious information-gathering apparently extended far beyond the club. I glanced at the door. How much time did I have? *Camel.* I remembered that Mary Ann's last name was 'Camel,' something she mentioned during that drunken Bunko game. The other woman in the Garden of Evil, she of the Mephisto habit. I went back to the *C*'s. No Mary Anns. I tried the *K*'s. *Kimmel.* Bingo. I hadn't factored in the Texas accent.

162

Five files away was Gretchen Liesel's. Thick. My stack was getting tall.

I opened another cabinet. *Rich, Misty*. Thin. Maybe empty. Onto the pile anyway.

I racked my mind but couldn't think of the last names of either Tiffany the Puppy Killer or Holly Who Had to Carve a Potato. Twenty-three minutes now without Maria. I yanked open another file cabinet and my fingers searched for *Valdez, Maria*. Nothing at all in the *V*'s. Had Maria taken it?

My brain was shrilling, *Light a match and get out.* What I was doing was illegal, not to mention immoral, and the two weren't always the same thing and one was bad enough.

But I had to get some idea of what I was dealing with, of what Mike was dealing with, right? And this seemed as good a place as any to start. I tucked the stack of files I'd pilfered into my bag, alongside mine. Thank God Lucy had talked me into this monster of a fake-patent-leather purse.

When Maria showed up with a tray, the shelf was clicked in place and I was pretending to finish up a row of walking shoes. Everything felt unreal, including the beautiful plate of food she set on the dressing table where Caroline probably sat to fiddle with her earrings. An egg salad sandwich on black rye bread cut into perfect, crustless triangles, a pile of plump, chilled purple grapes, a homemade oatmeal cookie with chocolate chunks, and a glass of what appeared to be fresh-squeezed orange juice. Impossible to resist.

I stood up and stuffed a triangle of sandwich into my mouth.

'You find the room, right? I give you enough time?'

I stared at Maria blankly, still chewing, thinking I'd misheard her. She shrugged. 'I left the catch loose. I don't want to get in trouble for showing you. I put your file on top.' She hesitated. 'I don't read it.'

Right. A rush of heat flooded into my face. *Is Maria with me or against me?* I purposely kept my eyes off my purse, lying at my feet. Should I scream at her? Or say thank you?

I slipped my purse casually over my arm. I decided to play nice.

'Maria, you don't have to stay here. To work for her. Whatever is going on . . . you don't need to be part of it.'

'I have to find my file. She showed it to me once when she was angry. I know it is somewhere.' Her face wore a mask of tight desperation.

'How much time did she spend doing this? Snooping on everyone?'

'Every afternoon. Two to four. I brought her peach tea and dry wheatberry toast every day at four *exactly*.' She snatched my plate. 'I will wrap this up for you. You need to go. You should never be here. It was a mistake.'

Her eyes were glued to my purse. She seemed to be considering whether to rip it off my shoulder.

164

'I read your file,' she said calmly. 'Whatever you have put in your bag, you will need to bring it back. Talk to your husband about *Rojo*.'

It was no longer a request.

CHAPTER 14

After pulling in to my driveway, I rolled down the windows, opened the sunroof, adjusted my seat into a more comfortable position, and picked out Harry Dunn's file.

The top sheet detailed an efficient list of Harry's trysts for the last year, courtesy of the Diskreet Agency, for whom my respect was growing. Fourteen different lovers, times and dates, most of them anonymous women met in roadside motels, only one person I knew.

Mary Ann had dallied with Harry for three weeks last October, once in the back of his Escalade. A telephoto lens had been able to showcase the crack of his ass. I wondered if Caroline had shared the details with Letty. Maybe she had blackmailed him into behaving and Letty was none the wiser. Caroline, the diabolical Dear Abby.

I glanced into Mary Ann's and Jenny's files. The first women, other than Letty, whom I met at the Bunko party that night. Official members of Caroline's toxic little club. And right in my lap, their private applications for membership.

Caroline required that hopefuls answer invasive,

truth-or-dare questions. They ranged from the softball, *When did you tell your first lie?* to *What's the biggest mistake you've ever made?* to *Who is the person you like least in Clairmont?* A little beyond your average college sorority crap. These were very, very bored women.

The undertones rang clear to me. Hold back and you won't get in. A bold line at the bottom promised that all applications were 'strictly confidential.'

As for Jenny and Mary Ann, they wrote the answers to Caroline's questions as if they'd sucked down a couple of pitchers of margaritas together and let their baggage and poor spelling fly.

Between them, they'd lain down for five abortions, seven plastic surgeries, and two arrests for public intoxication (literally, the cop had ordered them flat on the ground). They always voted a straight Republican ticket – except for Obama, because they both had always wanted to 'do a black man.' The person they liked least in Clairmont was, not surprisingly, Letty Dunn, crossed out with the pen in a blink of sobriety (but not well enough to keep me from figuring it out) and replaced with 'the pharmacist at Walmart because he won't refill our Ambien without calling Dr Gretch.'

I wondered whether the pharmacist they complained about was the one Tiffany mentioned was her husband. And whether that would aid or hinder her efforts to get in. I was beginning to understand the entanglements of small-town society. Take a step and your high heel was stuck in somebody's net.

Jenny and Mary Ann shelled out their secrets for bonus points, leaving little need for Caroline to fill out the space she'd left for her own personal critique. What else was there to say? Caroline admitted both of them as members on the same day six years ago, maybe because Jenny's husband ran a local branch of Bank of the West and Mary Ann's owned half of Grandes Cielos, a popular upscale restaurant and shopping development at the east edge of Clairmont. I think that because those were the only facts highlighted, presumably by Caroline, in fluorescent yellow. I absently bit into the half an egg salad sandwich that Maria had wrapped up for me.

The only things that Caroline did personally note about the two women, scribbled and dated after a monthly meeting several years later, were that *Mary Ann's in heat all over town* and *Jenny's breasts looked as hard as rocks tonight.* I couldn't see either of these women, who thrived on self-imposed drama, as interested enough in anything but themselves to be involved in Caroline's disappearance. What was their motive? These two weren't hiding a thing.

I'd avoided Letty's file, intimidated by its thickness. A headache ebbed and flowed and the baby kicked, suggesting that I needed to get out of this cramped space. I tackled the cookie. Delicious.

Maybe one more file. Misty's appeared to be a fast read. Thin. Probably a single page.

A tiny moth of paper fluttered out, onto the floor of the passenger seat. I bent down to pick it up. I felt like a rope was being pulled tight against my stomach.

Caroline's pretty handwriting was upside down. I righted it.

A stranger is someone you know.

I turned the piece of paper over. A single word, scribbled in pencil.

A question really.

Alice???

An hour later, I swung open the door of Copy Boy.

I didn't want anyone in Clairmont to see what I was doing, so my iPhone led me here, to a low-end, family-owned Kinkos competitor in a town fifteen miles away. Seven former customers had posted online that the service sucked.

For ten minutes, the high school kid behind the counter lazily watched me struggle to figure out an off-brand Japanese copier the size of a small Toyota. The machine was loaded with enough buttons to fire a cruise missile. Actually, there were probably fewer buttons involved in firing a cruise missile.

'I just want to make a fucking copy! Where the fuck's the button that says *"make a fucking copy"*?' I didn't normally cuss at high school boys – I'm a good Catholic girl who normally doesn't cuss out loud at all – but the hormones were coursing and I was furiously tugging on a Yankees sweat-shirt even though it was 102 outside. Retail air-conditioning in Texas summer is like a brisk fall day in Manhattan.

Copy Boy sighed heavily. New Yorkers aimed the F word like a Smith & Wesson into city streets and cafés, at perfect strangers, over the mildest of infractions, and the rubber bullets bounced right off. Here in Clairmont, it occurred to me that I hadn't heard the word in polite company, only on HBO.

He strolled over, hit the 'reset' button several times, thrust his hand out for the first stack of papers without looking at me or them, slapped them into the correct slot, punched four more buttons, and we watched them happily collate.

In the kind of voice reserved for small children, Copy Boy explained how to repeat those steps for the next batch of papers. He stood a foot from me at all times, like he feared I might bite. Actually, I might. After a paper jam and brief battle with the credit card scanner, I was good to go.

The edges of the other files stuck out of my purse. Tempting. Was it *more* illegal to copy other people's files? I glanced over at Copy Boy, all plugged up with his iPod, head down, and thumbs moving like the legs of a speeding roach across his phone. He would be a terrible witness in court.

I reached over to my purse, opened another file, slid the papers in place, and pressed 'collate.'

'I didn't do it.'

I laid the police reports that Mike tossed in my face the night before neatly onto the shining glass surface of his desk.

I had driven directly to his office from the copying store. I gave him no warning. Angie, the temp secretary that Mike said was living a second life as a dancer in a cage at Cowboys Stadium, cheerfully waved me into his office 'as a surprise.' She scored the best flat-abs-to-big-boobs ratio I'd ever seen. Mike had conveniently left that part out.

Mike glared at me, then took a tense stroll over to shut the door. I glanced around the room, the first office he'd ever occupied that didn't roll on wheels and come fully loaded with a trunk of armor.

The interior designer had opted for saccharine. Creamy walls. Wedding-cake crown molding tacked into every nook and cranny possible. Forgettable modern paintings with bright slashes of color. Two floor-to-ceiling windows overlooked a bare, plant-free courtyard open to the blazing sun. I wandered over to look out. A dead vine drizzled over a gazebo. Four iron benches at the corners, probably heated to 150 degrees, waited to grill somebody's rear end. Designed, I guessed, by a non-Texan.

'I can't hear the screams of the prisoners,' I said. The architect of this three-year-old building had stuck the booking area and soundproof holding cells in the basement. Mike found this an oddly primitive concept. He'd joked about people disappearing off the Clairmont streets, never to be seen again.

He pressed an intercom button on his phone and spoke roughly. 'Hold my calls, please.'

'Just like in the movies.' I was trying for a way in.

I dropped into a hard upright, green-striped upholstered chair in the corner and couldn't help but think how good he looked in blue.

'Can I be Katharine Hepburn?'

'You think this is funny?'

Just like that, he turned me on, and not in a good way.

'No, Mike.' My words were taut with anger. 'I do not think this is funny. I think it is shocking that you think that I could kill a man and then hide it from you for our whole marriage.'

Mike's eyes bored into me, disbelieving.

'How can you possibly put this on me?'

The words were in there, ready to go. About how I tried to confess everything to Mike the night before our wedding and give him the chance to opt out. How he had deserved to know what he was getting into. How I stopped myself from telling him on a blanket in Central Park and after I met his mother and on the night we wrote our wedding vows.

'I don't think you killed a man, Emily. Christ, you can't even watch *CSI* reruns without changing the channel. What I think is that you will never, *ever* tell me the complete truth about yourself. I think we're done with the surprises and then Whoops, look out, here comes another kick to the nuts.'

'I did it for you,' I insisted stubbornly. 'I didn't think it would look good for your career if you married someone who was once a suspect, however briefly, in a murder. I knew you'd feel obligated to share it with your superiors. This way, no one had to know.' Not the whole truth, but part of it.

Mike cracked his knuckles in annoyance, something I'd never seen him do. 'First of all, my guess is my superiors know. They just didn't find it significant enough to talk about. You weren't an official suspect, right? Did the police even interview you? If so, there's no record of it. It's only significant to me because you chose to hide it. Am I getting through to you at all?'

He whipped around and faced the vertical painting behind his desk, a swath of gloppy red, with a saffron dot of color drifting off the canvas in the left corner. I could have painted it in sixty seconds with my eyes closed. I wasn't sure what the artist intended as the message. But I felt like the yellow dot.

'If it weren't for the baby . . .'

He said it under his breath, with his back to me. But I heard.

'What?' My voice rose, surely carrying through the thin, cheap walls that were a given in showy, taxpayer-funded buildings like this one, unless you were locked up in the basement.

'What's the if? You wouldn't stay with me? Say it, Mike. Say you want to leave me.'

'You're ridiculous, you know that? I've had almost twenty-four hours to think about this. And you want to know my grand conclusion? If it weren't for the baby, I'd be stupid enough to sleep on the couch in the reception room for another night. Maybe two nights. But it appears there is nothing you can do . . . *nothing,* do you hear me? . . . that will ever make me walk out on you. I figured that out three therapists ago. And right now, with all this weirdness . . .' He gestured to the air. 'I'm not leaving you alone at night.'

The tears fell in a dismal trail down my face. Still, he refused to look at me. I couldn't blame him.

'I'm so sorry, Mike.' My voice wobbled. 'I'm so sorry.' I didn't stop repeating it, couldn't, until he walked over and pulled me tightly to him. We stood that way for a long time.

'You look more like Ingrid Bergman than Hepburn,' he said, finally, nuzzling my neck. 'Let's go home.'

'I love you, Mike.' I whispered it, half wishing he'd push harder right now, for real, interrogating me like one of his suspects – but then, Mike never did turn that side of himself on me.

174

He smiled gently, still expecting the best of me, and rubbed my stomach.

'Let me guess your next surprise. It's twins?'

'No,' I said, slowly. 'It's a boy. Just one boy.'

'What's that?' He gestured to the Ziploc bag that I'd rested on the desk.

'I'll tell you at home.' I scooped it up.

In the car, I pressed my head back against the seat and screwed my eyes shut, physically whipped. Surely I wasn't doing the baby any good. I needed all of this to stop.

Mike stared straight ahead at the road as he flicked the wipers on to take care of a fine mist settling on the windshield. And then he asked, as casually as he'd ask if I wanted to order a pizza for supper. I knew the question was coming eventually, and it might as well be now, in the twilight of this strange day.

'Do you know who shot Pierce Martin?'

'No,' I said, automatically. 'But if it counts, I wished him dead every day.'

There was one thing left. The thing that had been sleeping and waking inside me every day since I was nineteen.

The mist crept over the car, shutting out the world.

'I have a daughter from the rape,' I said, and Mike nearly ran off the road.

I was nineteen years old and three months pregnant when I first met Lia.

She was sitting with her small pile of possessions, cross-legged on the cobblestones of an Italian court-yard, counting out fifty-nine stones. When I bent down to hand her a euro, she grabbed my hand and begged me to pray the rosary with her.

Lia was blind. Most days, she hung out a few footsteps away from Mary's Refuge in Ravello, which rests on a promontory above the Mediterranean Sea. Lia taught me that pretty beads are unnecessary. The counting is the important part.

I found the flyer for Mary's Refuge on a bulletin board in the vestibule of my college's Catholic chapel, a tiny stone building on the edge of campus with one small stained-glass window. It was the day after I learned that I was pregnant from the rape.

A student Catholic organization was trying to drum up money for Sister Abby Francis and her small endeavor by the sea for unwed mothers. I tore the piece of paper off the wall. I would go there. For a while, I would become someone else.

When my baby was born on a chilly September day in a 900-year-old villa in a city hanging off a cliff, an ocean away from its conception, I didn't want to even see the face, to think of it as human.

She is perfect, one of the sisters assured me gently. She counted and blessed all of my daughter's fingers and toes like a living rosary. I glimpsed a tiny pink face.

We will find her a good home.

The little girl who haunts my dreams stands at the top of a hill, waiting. She gets a little older each year. In a month, she turns thirteen.

CHAPTER 15

'This is it? This is everything?'

Mike ran a tired hand across his scalp, the wrinkles around his eyes, in his forehead, etched more deeply than I could ever remember. It was after 1 a.m. We sat at the kitchen table, an empty pizza box between us, while I tried to help him understand the events of the last thirteen years. The last week. The last twenty-four hours.

The rape. Pierce's murder. The baby girl I left behind in Italy.

I had brought out the shoebox stuffed with the obscene letters I'd received for years after I returned from Europe. No signature, no return address. While the rain drummed a steady rhythm on the roof, I had told him about all of the hang-ups and the delivery of the cigar.

I didn't answer. I let him assume that was everything. I couldn't tell him about Caroline's files. Not yet. What I'd done was illegal. He would never keep it from his boss, from that insufferable Harry Dunn, because Mike's that kind of guy. He would get fired. I'd be responsible for a black blot on his pristine record.

'I saved a few things from college,' I said. 'I think they're in one of the boxes we stored in the sunroom.'

Mike closed the pizza box, tossing our paper plates on top.

'I want everything, Emily. Every scrap of information you kept. There is no detail too small. Whenever you remember something, in the middle of the night, while I'm at work, I want to know. Wake me up. Call me. You're sure there's nothing you know about Black Patch cigars? No significance? Pierce didn't smoke them?'

I shook my head.

'This is a high-end cigar. I'll send the box to a Dallas lab for testing tomorrow.' He fingered the top of the Ziploc bag. 'The box is raw Spanish cedar. Most cigar companies don't go to the trouble of packaging that way anymore even though it's one of the best ways to preserve cigars.'

He walked over to the other end of the table and put the lid on the shoebox of letters. He'd pulled on latex gloves and read every one before the pizza arrived.

'I don't have much hope for good prints off these. Explain again why you think your letter stalker is Pierce's mother. What's her name again?'

'Elizabeth Martin. She was a lunatic after Pierce was shot. She got my dorm room number from the campus police and just showed up, screaming horrible things at me in the middle of the night. She woke my whole floor. She called me a lying whore.' And other, worse things. I drank the last sip of soda water from my wineglass. 'I was always ninety percent sure it was her. The writing is feminine. The rage is personal. The picture of the grieving mother from *Guernica* . . . it seemed pretty spot-on.'

'Most of us unartsy types wouldn't make that connection. So maybe that's a reach.'

'And there's the point. She knew *I* would know.'

'What about the other girls who were suspects? They must have gotten letters, too.'

'I have no idea about that. I haven't seen them since the day of the interviews. The police told us not to speak to one another. I didn't know any of them personally. Different majors and dorms. Only one sorority girl. We were scattered across campus.' *On purpose,* I thought. *So we wouldn't be able to warn each other.* 'Pierce's mother saw me at his funeral. We met over the coffin before I became a suspect. Maybe she fixated on me.'

'Maybe. But here's the thing. The letters were delivered by mail for years. A variety of postmarks, all hundreds of miles from you.' His finger traced a circle on my arm, a habit of his. 'Hand delivery, that's a big step up.'

He reached across the table, and I slid my fingers on top of his.

'You believe me, right? You know that I'm OK about your daugh – the little girl? You could have told me from the beginning.' There wasn't reproach in his voice, just reassurance.

'Yes.' I wondered at how something that had built inside of me like a terrible storm could end like this, without casualties.

Mike's reaction to my news about my daughter said everything I would ever need to know about his love for me. He had pulled the car over immediately, switching off the ignition.

'I don't know where she is,' I had said stonily. 'I gave her away.'

It was several interminable seconds before he turned and grabbed my shoulders. His eyes had shone like slick blue glass. 'I can't believe you held this in. I wish you had told me. Although I can understand why you didn't. That kind of violence . . . it's intimate. Worse than a bullet.'

My heart physically hurt inside my chest at that moment. I had realized almost too late that Mike was one of the few guys who *could* understand, who wouldn't take it personally, who knew up close and personal that victims of violence don't follow a playbook. Some people let it go; the rest of us don't.

'It wasn't the rape or the murder that made me keep secrets from you,' I told him. 'It's just that it all led to the baby. I hated myself for giving her away. The guilt overwhelmed me. I had worked up the courage to go back and get her. Then my parents died and the grief took over everything. I could barely get out of bed. I called the nuns once, hysterical. She'd already been adopted. To talk about it made it more real. By the time I met you five years later, it was buried so deep, it seemed more normal *not* to talk about it.'

That was hours ago. I'd finally breathed all my secrets into the air and it felt like they'd flown away, at least for the night. Mike flipped off the kitchen lights and I followed him to bed. Too tired to make love, we wrapped ourselves around each other. For a little while longer, while the rain fell, no one was missing. Mike shut out everything else but me.

'Three words,' he murmured in my ear.

'Just one,' I replied. 'Lucky.'

Day five missing.

Someone had looped a scraggly yellow ribbon around Caroline's mailbox.

I stood once more at the door of her house, knocking for the sixth time. Maybe Maria had car trouble. Or changed her mind. It was still awfully early. A little after eight. On the phone, I had told her I wanted to return the files. I now had a full set of copies. I wanted to put everything back and then figure out how to drop a hint to Mike so he could execute another search warrant with everything in place and no one the wiser.

Almost a week now, but part of me still didn't believe Caroline was anything but alive and crazy, probably in Mexico at this very moment, a Four Seasons spa employee wrapping her in seaweed like a human sushi.

As I considered sitting down on the stoop and

giving Maria another fifteen minutes, the door opened a crack.

Her face was red and puffy, and she'd abandoned the uniform for jeans, sneakers, and a tight black gold-lettered Santana T-shirt that showed off her plump breasts.

She pulled me inside, gripping my arm tightly, setting off a trickle of fear.

'What's wrong? Did something happen? Is Caroline back?'

She shook her head.

'The FBI is getting involved,' I assured her. As was First Baptist. Flyers of an unsmiling Caroline littered the trees, store windows, and bulletin boards. I felt Caroline's disapproval, sure she would consider it demeaning to be displayed in something other than a gilt frame.

Maria's thick brown hair stuck up like a hip-hop artist's; her eyes were dilated, black and wild, rimmed by dark crescents of smeared mascara. *Is she high?*

She channeled us on a straight path up the formal staircase without saying a word. The house was still asleep. Lights off. My presence felt more wrong than ever. Still, I followed her back into the closet.

The bookshelf had already been pushed away, a rectangle of bright light behind it.

I stopped short at the doorway, the threshold of disaster.

Papers littered the floor, the desk, the reading

chair. The file cabinets gaped open, a few lonely folders still hanging, spared. One small square of Oriental carpet stood out in the debris, as if that is where Maria stood while twirling and flinging files and papers like a human tornado.

'I know,' Maria said. 'It is bad.'

I found my voice, and it moaned.

'Maria, what have you done?'

'I had to find it. My file. I spent all night going through them. I thought maybe mine was mixed up in someone else's.' She fidgeted with a strand of hair and spoke so fast I could hardly understand. Her eyes were like two black moons. 'Maybe it is not *so* bad. I put all the old files over there.' She gestured toward the desk. As far as I could tell, every file had been trashed and tossed aside, completely compromised. 'And the newer ones here.' She made a circular motion that encompassed the floor space.

'No, Maria. It's bad.' I knelt on the floor, distractedly picking up an empty file folder. Whoever the hell Meredith Lindstrom was, her life story was now scattered somewhere on this floor. My head pounded. Caroline's files, organized in alphabetical order, tidily stored in a cabinet, had been overwhelming enough to consider. I couldn't imagine how, in a day or even ten days, anybody could make sense of the maelstrom beneath my feet. And what Maria and I were doing in this room at all . . . well, now, amid the destruction, it struck me in the gut as not just wrong, but dead, dead wrong.

'Maybe she doesn't even have a file on you, Maria. Maybe she only said she did.' My mind was charging ahead, recalculating my plan.

Throw the files from your purse on the floor with the rest. Get out. That's what my little voice said.

'I told you, I *saw* it. She showed it to me. My file is *bad*.'

With a burst of clarity, I realized Maria wasn't talking about illegal relatives being shipped back to Mexico.

'What is it, Maria? What does she have on you?'

'I don't want to say.'

'Say.'

'OK. OK.' She took a breath. 'When I first came here, I could not find good work. I danced in a club. It was the only way I could make enough money. To send home. My mother and sister . . . don't know how I supported them.'

'You were a . . .?'

'Puta.' She spat out the word.

I was going to finish that sentence with *stripper,* but OK.

'A whore. For one year. I said to myself, three hundred sixty-five days. No more. A police friend of Mr Dunn, he came to the club a lot. He saw me there. One day, soon after I got this job, Mr Dunn, he came to the house. He tried to make me, you know, down there on him.' She pointed to her crotch. 'Miz Warwick came home and found us in the kitchen. She made him stop. She scared him. She didn't fire me. She paid off many lawyers

185

for me to get my papers. You see?' She blew her nose messily into one of the papers from the desk. 'I love her. I hate her. She will never let me go. What if she comes back and sees this?'

'Take a deep breath. We'll just start in one corner and go at it a page at a time.'

I slid my purse off my shoulder, and shoved papers aside with my foot, creating a path. I snatched up four empty Diet Coke cans, a spilled bottle of NoDoz, and a lime-green bottle of a scary-looking energy drink called Ammo. Maria was fully loaded.

In less than an hour, we had cleared a quarter of the carpet space. The desperate, super-caffeinated Maria was surprisingly focused and fast. We placed the empty files in alphabetical order in a circle around the room, and then sorted tediously through the giant pile of papers, matching them to their files. It didn't take long for me to realize that much of what lay at my feet wasn't blackmail material at all: innocuous newspaper clippings that went back as far as twenty-five years, Caroline's notes about somebody's illness, a birthday party, a society club dinner, a community play.

If somebody died, she dutifully included the local death notice and wrote *closed* on the outside of the file. Compulsive work. Sad work. A lonely old lady keeping track of a town's minutiae when much of it could be found in online archives with a few keystrokes. How dangerous could this be? Would someone have been angry and crazy enough to yank her out of her bedroom window?

A green tab marked all of the files allocated to club members. A typed label recorded both the 'anniversary date' of when the women joined the club, and their state of membership: active, moved, or deceased.

Someone romantically named Claire Elise Dubois stood out in a category of her own as 'ejected.' Maybe a woman with special anger toward Caroline? I paused to read her story. Claire Elise, who liked to be addressed by both names, thank you, had been summarily thrown out three years ago 'for consistent failure to properly RSVP.'

I wondered if, in Southern culture, this was worse than child abuse. I almost laughed out loud.

A high, musical voice stopped me.

It was frighteningly close, right outside the closet door, and it sounded very much like Letty Dunn.

CHAPTER 16

'Yoo-hoo, Maria? Caroline?'

Maria worked faster than I did. She was over to the door in a split second, clicking it shut and throwing an inside lock.

'Who is that?' I hissed.

'*Letty*.' If *rojo* was *asshole* in Maria's vocabulary, then *Letty* was clearly *bitch*. Maria's fingers were quickly bringing the Mac to life. She clicked on an icon of an ugly cartoon baby labeled NANNY CAM.

'My cousin put this in for her. A camera on the front porch, in the hall. In her bedroom, living room, kitchen. To spy on me and that *estupido* cat to make sure we aren't peeing on her rugs.' Her hands flew expertly across the keyboard. 'He teach me. My cousin is very good with computers.'

I could see that.

Letty Dunn was in resplendent HD quality on the screen, bouncing up and down on Caroline's bed like she was the star of a bad porn movie. I hoped Caroline's bed could take it.

Her body was squeezed into a tight pink velour tracksuit. A matching pink baseball cap with NIKE etched in rhinestones perched uncomfortably on her massive yellow puff of hair. The diamonds on her hands blinked in the light, like a Morse code to outer space. She wore a gold bracelet weighted with oversized charms, the largest one emblazoned with the initials *UDC*. The jingling sound that accompanied every bounce was the industrial-sized key ring in her right hand. It looked like it belonged on a janitor's belt.

Letty had a key.

'She will go away,' Maria said hopefully, under her breath.

Or maybe not.

Letty launched herself back on the massive bed, moving her arms and legs vigorously like she was making a snow angel. Perhaps it was some new cellulite-busting workout she'd seen on TV.

It was a mesmerizing show: her jiggling fat, the miracle of personal technology, and the general weirdness of Letty Dunn.

'*Ma-REEEEEE-aaaaahhh,*' Letty sang out. Her voice was an icy finger in my eardrum.

'Turn the volume off,' I whispered. Maria shook her head.

'Not to worry.' She pointed upward. 'Soundproof. Miz Caroline likes to hear no noise while she listens to her classical music.'

'Caroline? You home yet? It's *LETT-eeeeeee.*' Still, with the singing sound.

Then she abruptly changed tone.

'Maria, are you here? Lazy girl!'

My cell phone vibrated, a rattlesnake underneath a stack of papers across the room. I dropped to the ground, crawling toward it on my hands and knees. I read the text, trying to tamp down panic.

Misty. Lunch. *Not now.*

'Does she know how to get in?' I whispered.

'She can't hear you,' Maria said. 'And she is already in.'

'I can see *that*. Does she know how to get *in here*?'

'Oh. I don't think so. I locked the door.'

Like that nasty cat, Letty disappeared from the screen to roam around. Maria fiddled with the buttons and split the screen into four sections. Since the nanny cam was a fairly low-tech affair that didn't cover every room in the house, Letty wandered into view, then out of view. I felt like I was playing a kid's video game, on a hunt for the evil pink sorceress. My fingers itched for a zap button.

Letty was taking her sweet time with her house tour. She ripped open drawers and cabinets at random, appearing to search for nothing in particular. She swept her finger over a living room lamp shade. She checked the moistness of the soil in a potted palm.

'That is *supposed* to be dry,' Maria mumbled angrily.

If I had any inkling of doubt about Letty's character, which I didn't, it vanished when she deliberately knocked an Oriental antique vase off

190

its pedestal in the dining room. The crash tinkled through the speakers like a fake sound effect on an old radio show. A little smile played at the corner of Letty's mouth.

'Yoo-hoo! Caroline? Maria? Are y'all here? Is everything all right?'

'She probably is the one who took Miz Caroline,' Maria said bitterly. 'Or that Holly. One time she asked Miz Caroline to loan me to her so I could wash lice out of her dogs. That club will probably kill me, too. Think I know something.' Her eyes flashed with a little triumph. 'Which I do. I know plenty.'

Before I could process any of this, Maria pointed to a fish-eye view of the front porch. 'Look. A police.'

A man in uniform was stepping up to the door. I didn't recognize him. He laid his pointer finger on the buzzer and didn't take it off. With his other hand, he rapped a sharp, rapid drumbeat. Three more uniformed cops joined him on the porch. All carried evidence boxes and bags.

'We have to get out of here.' I searched the faces on the porch. No Mike. But he had to be the one who'd finagled a more expansive search warrant. He probably wasn't far behind.

'Where's your car?' Maria's voice was eerily calm.

'A couple of blocks away. Diana Street.'

'Good. You can drop me at Brake-O. My cousin works there.'

On-screen, I watched Letty throw open the door to the cops like she owned the place.

Maria turned up the volume.

'. . . I wanted to peek in on her maid. Daddy always said, you can't trust anyone who makes less than $15,000 a year or more than $200,000. You're probably all in the clear on that front.'

The cops didn't seem to know what to do with her. Letty was attempting to squeeze by them, using her double basketball of a bottom as a weapon. In the meantime, my mind had landed on an excellent idea. Don't budge. Hunker down in Caroline's secret lair with the loaded little fridge until the cops finished their search. They didn't know this room existed.

But, no. Maria had flipped off the computer and was now shoving the door open. 'Let's go,' Maria said, suddenly urgent. 'While she is here bothering.'

Only a second of indecision on my part. I wanted to get the hell out of there.

As Maria led me down the hall, I worried that her escape plan might involve the dumbwaiter, especially when we stopped in front of it, at the back staircase.

'These stairs go to the basement. We can go out that way. *I* could stay if I wanted to. I have a right to be here.' She said this defiantly.

Maria picked up a flashlight from a shelf in the stairwell that held five different odors of Oust. 'The light is broken,' she told me. 'You might trip. I will go first.'

Three and a half flights down. As we hit the

bottom landing, my eyes registered forms in the darkness: large paintings leaning against the wall; chairs stacked on top of one another; cardboard boxes; a still, human shape ten feet to my left.

I stifled a scream, realizing I was staring at a life-sized Western version of Saint Nick. Cowboy hat. Boots. A sign that said, Y'ALL BE GOOD. He likely ventured out once a year to stand on the front porch. By now, I could make out sliding glass patio doors on the far wall. The vertical blinds were shut, letting in only a trickle of light.

I almost lost it when the glass door stuck and Maria muttered under her breath and I heard the trample of feet above my head. But Maria gave the door a good, competent whack and we stepped out of the crazy Spanish novella of the past hour into dazzling Texas sun, onto a small patio, in a cranny of Caroline's expansive backyard.

'I am afraid for my family. That they will be stolen away.' Those were Maria's last solemn words to me as she hopped out of my car at Brake-O. I wasn't sure whether she meant by a boogeyman who crept in windows or one who came with an immigration badge.

I saw no reason to mention that I'd left the bookshelf door cracked open for the cops.

Our fingerprints, everywhere.

Let it all blow up.

Tiffany. Letty. Mary Ann.
Jenny. Lucinda. Holly.

All those *y*'s. All those boob jobs. All those strangling little secrets.

Southern sisters, linking arms, spinning and dancing a jig in my head until I couldn't tell them apart anymore. One face, one body, one voice, one killer. A glittering, faceted diamond. *The club.*

Right now, in Caroline's private little cave, everything that those women and a hundred others might kill to protect was being stuffed into evidence bags. Because of me. My mouth, meanwhile, was half-stuffed with a bite of Chef Joe Bob's burger of the day. I had decided to order it the second I saw it lettered in hot pink chalk across the blackboard: FOUR-CHEESE-BARBECUE-JALAPEÑO-BUTT-KICKER. In New York City, Joe Bob could sell these for $20 apiece, if he laid them out on designer pottery with an organic sprig of something green and exchanged smoked Gouda for the pepper jack. Here at Joe Bob's Diner on Clairmont's Main Street, the cook in the black cowboy hat threw it on a chipped, white-on-its-way-to-gray diner plate, along with a sloppy helping of half-ripe tomatoes, dill pickle chips, and a glop of a questionable mayonnaise-based item that I assumed was slaw.

Misty picked at a Caesar salad with dark wilt and mundane croutons, clearly not a menu item where Chef Joe Bob put his creative powers to use. I wondered why she picked the town's burger joint for our lunch date if she was the health freak she appeared to be. I'd never seen her eat anything but a lettuce-based entrée. She couldn't weigh more than 105 pounds.

'Did you see the WFAA news truck setting up across the street?' I asked her. 'A woman on the sidewalk told me they're doing a piece on Caroline.' I gathered a handful of paprika fries, stuck them on a napkin, and slid them over to her. 'Here, have some.' My not-so-subtle way of trying to get Misty to say something, anything about Caroline.

Misty shrugged, as if neither the fries nor the truck interested her. She displayed a stunning lack of curiosity about Caroline's disappearance.

And what about the secrets in that box? *This baby is not my husband's. Look under my bed. There is blood in my house.*

Melodramatic. Laughable, if it weren't that Caroline was so twisted. Was one of those secrets Misty's? Or was the whole thing a giant hoax and the entire club in on it?

'Do you know what *UDC* stands for?' I asked randomly.

'*UDC?*' She rattled off a list. 'University of the District of Columbia. United Doberman Club. United Daughters of the Confederacy. Unicorn Dunces Club. Take your pick.'

'I pick number three. United Daughters of the Confederacy. Although two and three could be the same thing. And four is an interesting concept.'

'Why do you want to know what *UDC* stands for?'

'I saw it on Letty Dunn's charm bracelet. She

certainly believes in her elevated place in the world.'

'Really, you think that? I think the opposite. I think she has no idea who she is. But then, I think most of us don't.' Misty stared at my chin, motioning for me to catch the dripping burger juice. 'You have a voracious appetite for red meat.'

'I know. It comes with the hormones. Mike says the next step for me is to dine with wolves at a fresh kill.'

Today, Misty had adopted the look of a rich suburban housewife. An all-white Nike jogging suit flashed against a new, deeper tan. The symbolic 'diamond' dollar sign nestled in the hollow of her neck. I looked surreptitiously for scars. There was the faint outline of several on both inside forearms. If you weren't looking for them, you wouldn't notice. I wondered if she had used makeup on her body or had instead made a date at the spray tan shop operated by Letty's cousin.

'I heard that Letty used to be a completely different person,' Misty said. 'Before Harry. Did you know she was a model? A Miss Texas contender?'

'She mentioned it.' I tried to rub a spot off my iced tea glass. It didn't budge. The thick glass was so scarred from dishwasher use it was impossible to tell if it was clean. 'That doesn't mean she was ever a decent human being.'

Misty moved first, leaning over to brush her hand gently over the top of my head. Intimate. 'You've got something in your hair.' A tiny, frilly pink flower drifted into my iced tea glass.

'I think it's from a crepe myrtle,' I said stiffly. 'I took a walk.'

I took a walk, all right. Less than an hour ago, I'd walked right out of Caroline Warwick's basement door, camouflaged by a bounty of crepe myrtles, while cops flooded the house behind me. I'd walked briskly with Maria through the backyard, to the gate, made it without incident to my car, dropped her off at Brake-O, drove home to change clothes and then on to Joe Bob's Diner for lunch. All of this, without going into early labor.

'Harry Dunn slept with at least three women the week before they were married. Including Letty's sixteen-year-old sister and one of the bridesmaids. And it didn't stop. Caroline knew.'

'So what? Half the town must know that Harry is a dog. He hit on *me*. I'd bet he's hit on you.' For God's sake, he tried to get a free blow job from Maria by the pots and pans.

'It was different with Caroline,' Misty insisted. 'Harry hated her. She hated him.'

'Are you trying to say that Harry has something to do with Caroline's disappearance?'

'I'm just saying it's an area to explore. You might mention it to your husband.'

'Was your secret in that box?' I was barely able to tamp down my next question. *Was it about that little girl?*

197

Misty pushed her crystal-studded Anne Klein sunglasses more firmly in place on top of her head. 'Caroline hires professionals to spy on people. She keeps a file cabinet of dossiers.' Misty knew? Had she been in Caroline's closet? I tried to keep my face expressionless. I dug into the white glop. Marshmallow, not mayonnaise. Interesting. Not terrible. I took another bite to relieve some of the jalapeño.

Misty pushed aside her half-finished salad. The fries were limp and cold. 'Letty tipped off the cops to an argument I had with Caroline the day before she disappeared.'

'I heard. That's why you should be the last person to defend her. Letty's a borderline sociopath.' An image of her knocking that vase to the floor sprung to mind.

'She wasn't lying. Don't you want to know what we were arguing about?'

'I guess.' My head was starting to hurt.

'You.'

I wasn't hungry anymore. The burger was settling in a lump near the baby, who was probably setting up to kick it like a soccer ball. I was tensing, waiting for it, for whatever Misty was about to say. 'That makes no sense,' I said.

'I told Caroline she should leave you alone.'

'You know about the rape?' The words shot out of my mouth before I could stop them.

'What are you talking about?' Misty's confusion appeared sincere. 'What rape?'

This was one of the most schizophrenic conversations of my life, and I'd played it all wrong. But now I had nothing to lose.

'Did your name used to be Alice?'

Misty's fists clenched. Her face blanched white under her tan.

'I need to go,' she said.

She laid a $20 bill over the $14.59 check and stalked out, a cue we were done, maybe with everything.

CHAPTER 17

The key turned a little too easily in the front lock, which should have been my first clue. But I was tired and distracted, my belly rebelling against the Butt-Kicker's jalapeños and my unsettling lunch with Misty.

Two feet inside the door, I almost stepped on it. A mirror. Mike's grandmother's mirror. The same mirror that scared me to death the other night by reflecting the ghostly specter of my face.

I wondered when Mike had moved it from the bedroom to the front alcove of the house. Why he'd laid it flat on the entryway floor where I might trip on it. I stared down at my image in the antique glass. Slightly cloudy, as if one of me was imprisoned in another dimension.

Not a bad idea to hang it on this wall. It would open up the tiny space. Had Mike come home for lunch with a fit of decorating inspiration? Maybe he figured I was using the back door these days.

I gazed down at my reflection, wondering whether to try to move the massive mirror by myself. At least lean it against the wall. I lamented what a crappy housekeeper I'd become. The mirror was dirty. Smeared.

Kneeling, I realized the dirt spelled something. Three words. A love note from Mike? A wry comment on my seriously declining domestic skills?

The first word was *see*. At least that was definitely an *s*. The last word, *her*. I knelt to get a grip on the heavy frame and tilted the mirror up into the light so I could see better. The *s* vanished. The message was disintegrating.

Heavy gray dust. I was a worse housekeeper than I thought. The mirror smelled dank, like my great-grandfather's sweater when I used to hug him.

Like cigarettes.

Or cigars.

My breath, coming faster, blew the first word away. It tickled my nose.

This wasn't dust.

This wasn't a message from Mike.

But it was a message from someone. Someone deranged.

I knew I should run, but my eyes were glued to the damn mirror.

Concentrate, Emily. Hold your breath. The second word, before it disappears. Or was it two words glued together?

The first letter? *A? F? T?* Seven letters? Eight letters?

The second word was *though*. I was pretty sure. No, *through*.

First word, *see*. Second word, *through*. Third word, *her*.

See through her.

I jumped back and the mirror fell from my hands, violently hitting the floor. The glass that had shone with the faces of Mike's ancestors for almost two centuries now lay at my feet in pieces, like hundreds of tiny knives.

I backed out of the door, my hands fumbling inside my purse for my phone. I needed to call Mike. A dark curtain in my brain began to draw closed.

I clutched the outside of the doorframe, one foot on the porch.

See through her.

Was the message a warning?

About Misty? About Caroline? Any one of the women in the club?

Who hates me this much?

My enemy, as always, was baffling. Inscrutable.

I slid down, the curtains on the stage swirling shut, the show over.

I woke up on my front porch with my head in the lap of a stranger.

'Are you all right, ma'am?'

A man with his hands near my throat. I wanted to scream, but I'd lost my voice. Maybe stolen by the spirits I felt whoosh out of that mirror when it shattered. 'Your husband and an ambulance are on the way, ma'am. I took the liberty of checking the emergency numbers in your cell phone. That's a helpful little thing Verizon's got in the contacts list, letting you put it right at the top. I got my kids' phones all set up. And mine. I've got the diabetes.'

I heard the faint wail of a siren in the distance. I pressed a hand to my chest, as if that would slow the irregular flutter of my heart. Could this man be telling the truth? I'd seen a UPS van parked on the street when I pulled in to the driveway. The man gingerly holding my head was wearing a brown uniform shirt. But it was always the man in the van.

'I didn't do CPR because your husband told me not to after I checked your breathing. The baby and all. By the way, I watched you go down from my truck across the street, and you landed pretty good. On your butt. Then you kind of keeled over real gentle. Just like an angel laid you down. So you're married to our police chief?'

It didn't seem like a question he expected a response to. Even in the bizarreness of the moment, with this stranger's sunburned, porous face peering down at me, I was reminded how Texans are the most natural people with the simile that I'd ever met.

Like an angel laid me down.

'I'm going to close my eyes,' I announced.

'No, ma'am, I'm sorry, I can't let you do that. Your husband made it real clear that if you woke up to keep you wide awake.'

Vehicles screeched up to the curb, sirens on mute. Blue and red lights flashed in the living room window like a patriotic Christmas display.

Footsteps, crunching up the walk. Mike's voice saying, 'I'll take her.' Familiar tree-trunk arms lifted me up.

'You OK, baby?' His breath was warm in my ear.

'Which one of us are you referring to?' I put my arms around his neck. I breathed in his minty aftershave.

'Both.' He carried me down the walk to the ambulance while a cop I'd last seen this morning on a computer screen kept pace beside us. Two black-and-whites were parked at the curb.

'Ron,' Mike said. 'Get the name of the delivery guy and his driver's license, will you? He gets a free ride on tickets for a while. Find out what his favorite beer is while you're at it.'

'Yes, sir.'

'Really, I think I'm OK.' Mike plopped me in the open end of the ambulance and a frowning EMT attached a blood pressure cuff. 'It was just a shock.'

'What was a shock?' he asked distractedly.

Of course. He had no idea about the mirror. 'Inside.' I pointed to the house. 'Someone broke in. They left a message on your grandmother's mirror. I think it was written in ashes.'

'My grandmother's mirror is in the bedroom.' He said it soothingly, but he looked concerned.

Probably about whether I'd banged my head too hard on the concrete porch.

'And now it's in the front hall,' I insisted. 'Somebody moved it. I nearly stepped on it when I walked in the door. Someone tapped out a message, maybe with the stub of a cigar. *See through her.*' It sounded crazy. I needed to make him understand. 'But it's gone. The message. I blew it away. The mirror broke. I'm so sorry.'

As if the message had never been there at all.

It was like watching a Transformer convert for battle. Mike barked something and two cops appeared at his side within seconds. That's the way it was with Mike. He led and cops followed him. Anywhere.

It was, he said in one of his more revealing moments, an awesome burden, and he meant awesome as in huge. Heavy. He'd never lost a man, and I dreaded the day he did. Mike was not one for telling big stories about himself, and every day on the job in New York was a story.

I knew, only because his mother told me on our wedding day, that Mike had saved two lives before he was twelve. A cat that a teenage boy was about to hang from a tree and, a year later, a little girl who almost stepped into a child molester's van to pet a golden retriever puppy. Mike caught her arm and yanked her back. He memorized the license plate for the cops. The guy had been listed on the Sex Offenders Registry and was hauled straight back to prison.

The boy with the cat had just looped a noose around the animal's neck when Mike showed up. Pretty quickly, the cat was watching the action from a safe perch in the same tree that was almost his gallows. Mike was bloodied and rolling on the ground when the cat's owner, an old neighbor lady, showed up with a can of Lysol and shot the bully in the eyes. Mike escaped with a cracked rib, a commendation from the SPCA, and free home-made cookies after school until the old lady died his junior year. His mother loved to tell the details, and I loved to hear them, over and over.

I often wondered why his mother told me about his early heroic nature on the day we got married. Whether she knew I needed saving. What has always been perfectly clear between us is that she steadfastly believes that her only son is an instrument of God. It is one thing we agree on.

A half-hour later, I sat on the sidewalk in a lawn chair Mike brought out from the garage. Two cops were loading the mirror frame, now swathed in plastic, into the trunk of their patrol car.

A tech was just finishing up dusting the front doorknob and random surfaces inside that the intruder might have touched. The lock had shown signs of being greased and picked but not enough that all of Mike's new colleagues had swallowed my story whole.

'Probably pointless,' Mike said. We watched the lid of the trunk slam shut on the mirror. 'We aren't likely to get prints. Whoever this was probably

206

wore gloves.' He turned to me. 'Come on, let's go in. I'm home for the night.'

At the door, the fingerprint tech slid by us shyly, offering up a sweet smile, probably thrilled about a job that involved more than a stolen car radio. She barely looked old enough to babysit, but she was professionally attired in bootie-covered tennis shoes, latex gloves, and the Texas requisite Wrangler jeans.

Mike gripped my hand as we stepped over the threshold. It was like a bitter wind had blown through our home. The space felt tighter, compressed. The air smelled metallic.

'I've hired someone to clean up the powder.' Trying to reassure me, as if I was actually concerned about a little more dust. 'I've already called a place in Dallas to install a new security system for us. They do some crime scene cleanup on the side. They won't leave until there are alarms on every window and every door. They'll be here at ten in the morning. I can justify keeping a unit at the curb for twenty-four hours. We'll figure this out as we go along.'

I was suddenly feeling lonely and scared, very pregnant, a lot sorry for myself and ticked off. I didn't have alarms on every window in New York City, but I needed them here. I missed my parents desperately, with a physical ache, like I hadn't in years.

Mike and I ventured into the kitchen, a room relatively unscathed by the day. At least I could pretend the fingerprint dust in here was flour or, in the case of the graphite on the white Formica countertop, spilled pepper.

'I changed my mind,' he said. 'Let's go out. Get a burger or something.'

The thought cheered me up a little. A two-hamburger day.

'Oh, geez, I forgot. Wait a minute.' Mike was already out the back before I could stop him. I heard his car door slam. He returned in seconds with a large cardboard box, the flaps loosely closed. He set it on the floor and opened up the top.

'I was at Caroline's today,' Mike said. 'Didn't think this little guy should be there alone.'

I heard a low and perturbed growl. Mike reached inside and lifted out my furry orange nemesis.

CHAPTER 18

After Mike left for work the next morning, I threw on my old pink chenille bathrobe with the torn peekaboo hole in the rear, folded my new lucky bird quilt into a precise rectangle at the end of the bed, reassured myself by confirming that the cop car was at the curb outside. Then I headed to the kitchen to fix myself a cup of decaf and a bowl of Frosted Mini-Wheats with fresh blueberries. Before the pregnancy, I didn't know what a frosted mini-wheat was.

I washed the bowl and spoon and left them to drain on a faded blue dish towel, hand-stitched with a puppy face and the words IRON ON TUESDAY. The towel was a remnant of the previous owner, Mrs Elsa Drury, who had lived in the house for forty-six years before dying peacefully in a chair by the window.

I stood in the approximate spot where Mrs Drury met her Lord and lifted the curtain in the living room again. My bodyguard, still there.

After retrieving my purse from under the cabinet near the computer, I pulled out the copies of two of the files I had yet to read: Letty Dunn's and

Gretchen Liesel's. According to the reminder note Mike propped by the coffeepot, it would be two hours before the alarm company showed up.

Two sips of coffee and three sentences into the life of Leticia Abigail Lee Dunn, I sensed a presence moving behind me. I jerked around, the chair leg banging against an angry yellow ball. He yelped. I yelped.

'Don't sneak up on me, or a few of your lives will be cut short during your time here,' I warned. The cat sailed into my lap like a bag of Gold Medal Flour with legs. 'Is this an apology?' I scratched tentatively behind his ear. He dug a claw painfully into my thigh.

He leapt off and wandered over to the bowl of dry food that Mike had picked up at Walmart on a midnight run. He ate grumpily. The message was clear: *The food's not great in this joint.*

He jumped onto the windowsill, licking one of his lionesque paws. Caroline probably called him something cuddly, like Butterball. He was no Butterball.

I turned my attention back to Letty. I wondered if someone at the police station was reading this file simultaneously, if that person would be discreet, if the slip of a fortune in Misty Rich's folder had fallen out and was lost somewhere in the deep green grass of Caroline's yard. If that even mattered.

I skipped down to Caroline's comment section. It shouldn't have surprised me, but Caroline had known Letty for a long time, in the Before Harry years. When Caroline showed up in Clairmont, Letty was a freshman in high school. I guessed that the town was still just a spot in the road then, mostly working ranchland.

Caroline's remarks about Letty were relatively kind. She took only a few stabs. *Letty's senior homecoming queen mum was so large it would have been more appropriate on a coffin.* And several years later: *Letty's wedding dress was a $10,000 piece of Chinese crap that my girl could have sewn.*

Letty and Harry had settled in Houston after their marriage, but four years ago moved home to Clairmont after what Caroline intriguingly referred to as 'Harry's setback.' A newspaper article neatly paper-clipped to the page cited numerous possible SEC violations by the Driscoll Investment Co., which mostly specialized in handling the multimillions of Texas and Oklahoma oil- and gas men.

The last paragraph of the story, faintly underlined in pencil, read: *The SEC investigation follows last month's firing of a high-level executive involved in questionable overseas investments, including Asian pornography and German sexual gadgetry.* From what I could gather, three months after this little 'setback,' Harry accepted a job from Letty's daddy, overseeing Lee family real estate.

My eyes roamed to the part of the application filled out in Letty's loopy hand. She married Harry two weeks after graduating from Southern Methodist University with a 3.82 GPA in biology and a declaration of pre-med. Wow. She was smart.

She just didn't put it out there. Maybe this was a Texas thing. After all, George W. Bush matriculated at Harvard.

Shortly after she graduated, Letty's father rented Bass Performance Hall in downtown Fort Worth for her wedding. The painted clouds and sky in the dome hovered over seven hundred guests, including a former president (first name, George). In the reception that followed at the Fort Worth Botanic Garden, the flower girls set two thousand monarch butterflies free. Twelve bridesmaids (but only two groomsmen) traveled down the aisle in Oscar de la Renta black. The pearl-studded train on Letty's gown measured fifty feet. *Style* magazine featured the near-architecturally impossible, ten-tiered white macadamia nut rum cake in its June bridal issue. The two honeymooned in a luxuriously appointed hut staked over aqua waters in Tahiti.

Letty had so much to say about the wedding that she jumped to a separate page of personally engraved stationery, inserted when she ran out of space.

Her dissertation was in answer to a single question: *What was the most memorable moment in your life?*

A wife and mother, and the best moment of her life was like a day at Disney World – not real, ephemeral, and in her case a harbinger of bad things to come. Harry Dunn, a black crow in a tuxedo.

Maybe I was just jealous. Mike and I tied the knot at the justice of the peace with only his parents; my best friend, Lucy; and Mike's best buddy, Leroy, as witnesses. I wore a creamy, ankle-length antique lace number from the twenties, scored from an estate sale rack at Poppet on 9th Street. Every second, I wished for my parents to show up, courtesy of the same random, illogical forces that stole them from me.

Letty was a piece of work, but I felt less hateful toward her.

I thumbed through to the last page of the file. A document from the Robert E. Lee Society declared that the Lees of Clairmont were not part of their official ancestral rolls and that 'our research points to them being related to the Lees of Coal Hill, Arkansas.' Now, *that* was blackmail material.

I moved on to Dr Liesel, fully aware that I needed a shower and that Caroline's files were like a drug I couldn't stop mainlining.

I expected this file to resemble everybody else's, but it was very different, almost like a diary. Notebook pages filled edge-to-edge with Caroline's A-plus-worthy cursive writing, the kind nobody takes pride in except people who came out of elementary school before 1960. Mike's eighteen-year-old niece had told me last summer that the hardest part of the SAT for her was the instruction to copy out three sentences in cursive.

Caroline's writing flowed like the great Mississippi.

12 NOVEMBER: *Gretchen is a lovely girl. And a doctor! She welcomed me here with an invitation to lunch at the local café. (I sipped at a terrible attempt at onion soup, probably from a packet, can you imagine? and a very weak iced tea.) She asked me to come over in several days to play cards with some of her friends. I believe I will go.*

16 NOVEMBER: *I had an enjoyable evening at Gretchen's home with 'the girls,' even winning the door prize (a sad little autumn wreath that I will toss directly or give to my girl). And a warm Brie appetizer with some kind of store jam spread on top! A very nice try. I told them about the accident with my husband and son and they were very sympathetic. I'm beginning to think moving here was a very fine idea. I believe I can help these women.*

Caroline's assessment of Gretchen grew more critical in tone as time wore on. Gretchen's lack of care with her appearance (*people might think she's lesbian*), her husband (*stubby-chinned and Jewish-looking*), her son (*not worth the price of tuition at his fancy-pantsy university*) – all were noted in the file. But affection wasn't absent.

14 MAY: *Gretchen saved a breech baby today and delivered Clairmont's first triplets! I am so proud. There is a spot for her in heaven. I had my girl make her a lovely chicken pot-pie.*

214

Again with *my girl*. Why was it that some Southerners still thought it perfectly OK to attach a possessive pronoun to someone who worked for you? And to rank domestic help? There was 'hired girl' (to remind us that she was actually paid, not a slave), 'my girl' (to imply some kind of benevolent relationship), 'cleaning lady' (totally impersonal, somebody filling in), and 'maid' (requires a uniform).

I flipped a few more pages. I'd never finish Gretchen Liesel's file in the half an hour I had left. My eyes stopped short on a word.

Nazi. What a load of power in that shorthand.

Nazi, the abbreviation for *Nationalsozialist.* My father, a World War II history buff, made me learn to spell it. Taught me that the swastika was an ancient symbol for good before the Third Reich got hold of it.

I backtracked to the page before, the beginning of the entry.

2 JULY: *I found out quite by accident that one of Gretchen's ancestors was an officer in Hitler's army. Her husband is an extremely Jewish professor, who specializes in Israeli studies or some such. He even wears the little hat occasionally. I'd just stopped over for a visit and Gretchen's worthless maid stuck me in the library. Gretchen hadn't yet arrived from the hospital and I found a stack of old picture albums simply by lifting the window seat to see how much storage it could hold. Her family did*

*not carry the gene for good looks. I picked up
the knit afghan on top to admire the stitching.
And quite a shock! Underneath those, a Nazi
uniform folded neatly in a plastic zip-up bag
with a picture of the young man who wore it.
There was some kind of World War II family
tree drawn out by hand. I could not make head
nor tails of it. Of course, when I see her, I will
not say a word. The whole thing reminded me
of that framed Hitler stamp collection that
Dickie inherited from his father when he died.
It was one time in our marriage that I put my
foot down. I let Dickie hang the Confederate
flag from that pole outside, but I wasn't going
to let him hang Hitler in my house.*

So, Caroline's husband had been a Hater. His
name was Dickie. As for Gretchen, plenty of
people saved artifacts of war, especially those tied
to family. A SoHo artist I knew framed the photograph of a child that her father stole out of the
wallet of a Korean soldier after he shot him to
death. To me, swiping that picture was almost the
equivalent of taking his life again. But to his daughter,
the artist, it was somehow a reminder that we were
all the same. She silk-screened the child onto one
of her canvases and someone paid the $25,000
price tag without blinking.

Ironic. Hadn't Misty called Caroline a little
Hitler?

The phone shrilled on the counter. I jumped

guiltily, and Caroline's cat skittered around the corner. I let five rings go by before walking over to check the caller ID. Mrs Drury's red dial-up was no more. Mike had installed a top-of-the-line Sony with three lines, an answering machine, and a lot of other buttons I planned not to touch.

The small window read PRIVATE CALLER, which annoyed me even more than call waiting. 'Private' callers were people angrily clinging to the crazy idea that there was still such a thing as privacy. In this case, the call was either from my elderly aunt in an assisted-living center in Minnesota who never talked less than forty-five minutes or from the anonymous person set on driving me out of my mind.

Neither was good, but I picked up the phone.

'Hello?' A slight sound. In old movies, that meant the line was tapped. Now it probably meant my caller was clicking a pen. Audible breathing.

I slammed the phone down.

Leave. Me. Alone.

My house had barely recovered from yesterday's assault. Evil had found a way back in again, traveling through the phone line like lazy electricity. The yellow morning light was suddenly dimmer, my coffee colder, the daisies on the wallpaper no longer cheerful. He was invisible but there, a presence in the kitchen, *my* kitchen, trickling his fingers down the back of my neck, so real that I reached out behind me to grab them in the air. I wondered if he was preparing another surprise for me. I wondered why I was so sure, for the first time, that my tormentor was a he.

The phone rang again. I was pissing him off. My eyes raced to the kitchen door, the deadbolt still secure from last night, although what I feared was already inside. I walked as calmly as I could to the front door. Twice more, the phone rang.

The front door was locked, of course.

The clock on the mantel read 9:32. Only thirty minutes until men began turning my house into a prison. I checked on the cop car and drew the shades in the living room.

I walked back to the kitchen.

I picked up the phone on the sixth ring.

'Don't hang up.'

I swallowed a gasp. Not the voice of a man, but of a woman.

'Lucinda?' My voice was shaking, but the snake squeezing my gut had loosened its grip. Lucinda. The woman at Caroline's little gathering with the tortured voice and the tortured last name. Not my tormentor.

'I'm sorry to bother you.'

'It's no problem at all,' I lied.

'I just wanted to talk to you about . . . the other day. The secret that Misty read. I just wanted to know whether that was really your secret. About the baby. Whether it's your husband's.'

The snake wriggled under my ribs, to the center of my chest. I tried to picture Lucinda's face, but it was a pale blur. All I could remember was her lisp. We had never been closer than five feet apart. We'd never spoken to each other directly before this phone call. I'm not sure our eyes even met, because she mostly kept hers cast on Caroline's floor except when offering advice on dressing potatoes like dictators. Maybe this is how life sucked for her. Her voice defined her.

'Don't hang up again,' she pleaded. 'Please.' I could hear soft sobs.

I didn't like situations like this, where the person on the other end is apparently hurting, yet is simultaneously throwing a knife at my heart. Which one of us would I sacrifice?

I took a breath. 'What's wrong, Lucinda?'

'That was my secret.' *Thecret.* Her lisp took the edge off the word. For a second.

'What?' It registered. Shock. And, yes, judgment. *Her* secret, not mine. She could have rescued me in that room.

'It was two months ago,' Lucinda said. 'The last night at my sister's. She lives in Maine. I go see her sometimes to get away from . . . things. He walked in the guest room. It was so hot and I couldn't sleep, and I'd thrown off all the covers.'

He walked in.

'I thought it was my imagination. But he crawled in with me. I could feel the heat pouring off of him. And his skin. I could feel that. He wasn't wearing anything.'

Please don't tell me this.

'For a second, he just hugged me, kind of. Pulled

219

me real close. Then he lifted my nightgown. It was such a shock. I didn't want my sister to hear.'

'I'm so sorry.' *She didn't scream,* I thought.

'He made fun of my lisp in high school.'

'Who, Lucinda?' But now I had a pretty good idea.

'Wilkie. My brother-in-law. Stupid name, isn't it?'

My head began to pound.

'He never said a single word. He made a baby inside me *without a word.* It couldn't have been more than three minutes. It wasn't rough at all. Then he kissed me on my cheek and left.'

It wasn't rough at all.

'I'm scared that Caroline will tell,' she said. 'My husband has a very bad temper.'

I found my voice. 'He raped you, Lucinda.'

'Oh, no,' she said. For the first time her words were clear, like she'd drunk from a cool stream. 'I wanted it.'

Buck up, Emily.

Take a shower.

These women are crazy, but that doesn't mean you are.

The new person who had taken up residence in my head was calm and insistent and bugging the hell out of me. I pushed her away and twisted the cranky knob in the bathtub to the right until the water shooting from the showerhead was almost too hot to stand. I stepped into it.

Maybe Lucinda wasn't raped, but you were.

I dug my nails into my scalp painfully while I washed my hair. Why was everybody in this godforsaken town reminding me of what I should have been able to let go of years ago? My past and present were like two silvery necklaces in a drawer whose chains were now inexplicably, impossibly knotted together.

I wondered whether Lucinda would keep her baby. Why I always assumed that people with a handicap of some kind were somehow more pure. About the hundreds of moments between Lucinda and Wilkie that led to that night, about whether she'd been lying in that guest bed for years, waiting for him to show up. About the sometimes shaky line between rape and seduction that no one ever wants to talk about. About whether a psychiatrist would say Lucinda could even understand what rape was.

And Caroline. It was like a gong resonating. Caroline had gathered up the most confused, spiteful, vulnerable, damaged human beings she could find for her little club. To fix them? Or prey on them? Had Caroline really known about Lucinda's baby? Or did she just sling her random arrows, knowing she needed only one dead-on hit to wield power over every person in the room? Had Caroline stirred the cauldron in this town to the boiling point and been forced to run because of it? Had she already secretly put that monstrosity of a house on the market? I should tell Mike to check.

Ten minutes later, hair dripping, mind still whirring, I dug through various unpacked boxes in the bedroom. I reluctantly tugged an olive-green maternity shirt over my head that reminded me of a miniature Lands' End tent. Just as quickly, I ripped it off. The clock said that I had three minutes before Mike's security goons arrived. I wrestled deeper into the box for my favorite sweatshirt, one of Mike's, big and cozy enough to take care of the low-60s nip that some bow-tied TV weatherman said was 'an unexpected cold front down from the Yankees.'

No luck. Maybe it was in a box of winter clothes in the sunroom at the back of the house. The sunroom, designated as my future painting studio, was crammed with boxes I hadn't gotten to yet. I grabbed my robe off the bed and padded down the narrow hallway, stopping abruptly at the sunroom. The door was wide open.

I felt a familiar trickle of dread.

My easel wasn't where I stacked it three weeks ago, folded and leaning in the corner near the blue plastic tub that held all of my art supplies.

It was now erected in the center of the room, facing toward the door, boxes pushed aside to make way. A sheaf of art paper was clipped in place, the top one blank. A tube of paint was set out along the easel's edge, the cap off.

I hadn't painted in two years and I never left the cap off a tube of paint. After yesterday, I wasn't stupid enough to think that Mike had set this up as a gesture of encouragement.

And why would the crime scene tech or cops

mess with stuff that was packed? *Well*, said the third person in my head, *they probably wouldn't.*

My eyes searched.

A cigar, half-smoked, lay on the floor by the leg of the easel.

Dust danced in the light that streamed through the wall of dirty windows. Or was it smoke? I don't know how I traveled those few feet, but my hand reached up and ripped off the first page, and the second and the third and the fourth and the fifth, faster and faster and faster, a blur of frenetic motion.

Because I knew there was another message.

I was inside the mind of my tormentor, like he was inside mine.

It was neatly taped to the last sheet of paper. A snapshot of Mike and me.

Exiting the restaurant after dinner with Harry and Letty.

Mike's expression, angry.

My expression, undetermined.

That's because a perfect red thumbprint, every ridge discernible, obliterated my face.

CHAPTER 19

The crime scene tech blamed the cops, the cops blamed the crime scene tech, and a furious Mike blamed himself, but everyone agreed that I shouldn't worry, the easel had been set up at the same time by the same intruder who drew the message in the mirror. The stalker hadn't re-entered the house. The police had simply missed the sign of an upright easel as being significant yesterday. They were positive the thumbprint was red paint from the open tube, not blood, which didn't comfort me in the least.

One of the female cops, Justine something, her face scrubbed shiny, her blue uniform so tight and starched that I wondered whether it was rubbing her skin raw, told me the thumbprint was a good sign. He could be identified. Her voice mentally patted me on the head.

'Really?' I asked sarcastically. 'I think it's a sign that he doesn't give a flip anymore. That he has an endgame. That he's not in the system. So do you really think that's a good thing, *Justine*?'

Even the guys operating on my living room with drills and hammers stopped their noise long enough to watch Mike drag his hormonal wife into the kitchen.

Three men from the alarm company had arrived minutes after Mike screeched up to our curb with his siren wailing. They climbed out of their van and took note of the cop cars, apparently unruffled by an emergency in progress. From a distance, the trio appeared identical: soldier-cropped hair, pale skin, army boots, and dark green jumpsuits that showed off Y physiques. They had strolled into my house like a bunch of Timothy McVeighs, a marketing image likely dreamed up by a right-wing Texas entrepreneur. The company played on both patriotism and fear, claiming it used only experienced war veterans as employees.

Right now, for me, that was working fine.

God bless Texas, and come right in.

I sat at the kitchen table across from Mike, who was as uptight as I'd ever seen him. I was hungry but I felt like throwing up. My head already hurt like hell but I had a desire to bang it against those yellow daisies as hard as I could.

One of the blond clones had just finished attaching several high-tech warts, some kind of motion sensors, to the 98-year-old ceiling. The head clone briefly had explained all the perks of this new security system to me while I sat on the couch and nodded numbly, but the only thing I really remembered was, 'A house fly won't be able to get by it when we're done,' which made me imagine laser beams shooting from the ceiling like a giant bug zapper.

Mike's finger explored the nicked lip of his coffee cup. The cup was a memento from a night at *Wicked* on Broadway. The chip was courtesy of our movers. He stood up, moved to the sink, dumped the dregs, and tossed the cup in the trash under the sink. I'd decided two days ago when I unpacked the mug that it was worth keeping because we'd had amazing, (almost) fully clothed sex against a tree in the park on the way home that night.

'I'm done in this room.' The clone nodded curtly to me as he carried the ladder out the back door.

Mike pulled a skillet from under the sink, tossed in a good chunk of butter from the refrigerator, and set the burner on low.

'What are you making?' It didn't take more than the sight of melting butter to distract me. 'Don't you need to get back to work? To Caroline?'

'Grilled cheese.'

'I want two,' I said. 'No, three. On whole wheat. No, white.'

'Plastic cheese or real?'

'The good stuff.'

'I repeat, plastic or real?'

'Well, maybe a little of each.'

I pushed myself away from the table to retrieve a few accoutrements: sweet pickle chips, a bag of Ruffles, and carrot sticks, today's small concession to health.

'What's happening to us, Mike?' I shut the refrigerator door with my foot. 'There is an *alarm company* booby-trapping our bedroom right now. Who is doing this to me? *Why now?*' My voice was shaking, teetering in hysterical range.

'I think it's tied up with Caroline's case,' Mike answered bluntly. 'I just don't know how yet. Still, I'm pretty sure it's not a person from your past, but someone in the present who's using it against you. Or more likely, against me.' He avoided my eyes as he flipped a sandwich onto my plate. 'Emily, have you ever thought that you *want* it to be someone connected to . . . your rapist? That the baby is a catalyst for all this emotion? That you are trying to finally confront it?'

'That's ridiculous.' Inside, I wasn't sure at all.

'Let's go over this again. How many people knew about the rape?'

'Who really knows? My parents. Pierce. His roommate was there.' Mike lifted his eyebrows at this new piece of information but didn't say anything. 'None of those are possibilities. Three are dead. The roommate was a wimpy guy who had his own problems with Pierce. I don't think he'd want to hurt me.'

'Who else?'

'Well, *my* roommate. But she was so good to me . . . afterward. She has no reason to scare me. I haven't talked to her in years. She's a marketing executive in Minnesota, I think. Then there's the cop who took the report that night, obviously. The police never actually interrogated me and I was known only as "one of the ex-girlfriends" in a couple of front-page stories in the Newark and New York newspapers. Rape was never mentioned as a possible motive for his murder. Only jealousy.'

Mike placed the rest of the grilled cheese sandwiches on a plate between us and dropped into a chair. I had deliberately pulled a newspaper clipping out of the file tucked in my purse and left it near the saltshaker. Before I left Caroline's, I'd put every original file I'd stolen in its alphabetical place in the circle. Every file but my own.

'What's this?' With his little finger, Mike slid the newspaper article over in front of his plate.

'It's the campus newspaper article.' I didn't say where I'd found it, and he didn't ask. 'We were told our names were removed at the last minute to protect our privacy because we weren't official suspects. But our photographs ran on the front page. One of the girls' fathers, some hotshot alumnus, protested to the chancellor after it hit the stands, and our photos never made the papers again. I heard that the student newspaper editor who made the decision to run them was fired and lost an internship at *The Wall Street Journal*. He thought he'd gotten the scoop of his life. Some sleazy cop slipped a reporter our names. The cop was fired, too.'

'Which one is you?' he asked, pointing to the row of headshots. 'You look alike.'

'Pierce had a definite type. I'm the fourth one over.'

'Really?' My husband stared at my face like he'd never seen it before, and then back at the picture. 'I'd never know it.'

'No one recognized me from that picture. Even girls on the wing of my dorm. It's one of the outtakes of a campus ID pic that was too blurry to use. I'm not sure how the editor got it. Or any of the pictures.'

Mike's eyes bored into mine, searching. 'Emily, do you really think he raped all these girls? The few old police reports we've been able to retrieve from Ithaca are unclear on that point.'

The quiet in the kitchen was like a silent church prayer going on too long.

'Yes.' My voice was steely. I was back in time again, defending myself. Defending *them*.

'I know you think this could be the work of your rapist's mother. Can you think a little harder about whether any other relatives, or a friend, stood out as especially angry? Someone who might decide to avenge his death? Maybe you aren't the only one of these girls being threatened.'

'Why not Pierce's mother? Why *not* her?' Even though I was reaching the same conclusion.

'She's old, Emily. We tracked her down. She's been on a tour of Africa with a church group for the last five months. Lots of God-fearing people confirm that.'

'Why didn't you tell me?'

'I just found out this morning.'

'I don't want to talk about this anymore.' I pushed away my second sandwich, half-eaten. He'd waited an hour to tell me about Pierce's mother. That should have been the first thing out of his mouth when we hit the kitchen.

'There is another reason I think this is connected to Caroline,' he said abruptly. 'We found an office off Caroline's closet in our last search of the house. You weren't wrong about her. She's a nut. Kept files on half the town. It has expanded my suspect list exponentially.'

'Really? Wow.' I hoped to sound believable. I hated the lie. But I didn't want to fall backward again. And what difference could it make now?

'Your instincts were right about Caroline. Do you have a feeling about any of the women you've met so far? Whether they'd want to harm her? Or taunt you?'

I'd spent more than a few minutes thinking about this before I shut my eyes the last two nights. Letty was too eagerly loyal, a Saint Bernard trying to keep up with the greyhounds and poodles. Red Mercedes and Beach House, aka Mary Ann and Jenny, seemed the type to leave clues when they were dragging a body out of a window. A Xanax pill that fell out of a Chanel bag, a little spit-up from the fourth martini they ingested the night before, a fake fingernail resplendent with DNA.

Gretchen Liesel was The Saint, above the fray. Tiffany, Puppy Killer, was deep into Caroline's game and loving it. She probably thought hazing was as necessary as water-boarding. Lucinda? Holly? Maria? Giant, swirly question marks.

'Emily?'

'What about Harry?' I asked finally. 'Maria told me he tried to get a blow job out of her, and Caroline intervened. You said he was mixed up in illegal stuff. And he'd be strong enough to drag her out of the house. She had a file—' I caught myself. 'I'm assuming there's a file on him. It must be loaded with reasons.'

'One file among hundreds. It's going to take forever to get through them,' he said. 'Caroline is now officially a missing persons case. The FBI is all over it.'

'I know. I know.'

He reached across to cover my hand with his.

'Whoever is behind all of this . . . they're going to be very sorry they decided to pick on my wife.'

It was a tone I'd never heard before.

I was seven years old the first time I realized that I was capable of a deliberate, immoral act.

It was a little thing, I suppose, but then it's the little things that turn the dial of our character slowly, a notch at a time, one way, then the other, until we reach the point in young adulthood where the dial is firmly stuck in place and it takes a lot of torque to coax it along again.

231

My mother didn't believe much in the value of Barbies as role models for little girls, so the only one I owned was an old Skipper doll that I'd bought for fifty cents at a garage sale. I'd painted her bald spot with a brown marker.

The lady behind the card table threw in a pitiful wardrobe of a pink-flowered bikini. One inch of fabric, *maybe*. And a strapless wedding dress with a ripped hem and most of the beads missing. All a girl needs if she's planning to live out her days with her lover on a desert isle.

But my friend Robin across the street owned an elite collection, so many Barbies and Barbie cousins that twenty of them served as mere decorations on a high, unreachable shelf that her father had nailed around the room. The plastic women were trapped inside their boxes, fake-smiling behind the cellophane. More well-loved Barbies were tossed in a large plastic bin in her closet or forgotten under the bed, arms and legs in unnatural positions, in embarrassing stages of undress.

Robin was fanatic about the accessories, using a tall plastic fishing tackle box with tiny drawers to store sun hats and veils, necklaces and hosiery, and the tiny, tiny shoes. My favorites were a pair of white heels with a minuscule white feathery puff on top, held down by a rhinestone that I imagined was a piece of a star.

Those shoes were stored in the third row, fifth drawer across. My fingers itched to see how they'd look with Skipper's pitiful wedding dress. I wanted them. And one day, when Robin slipped away to the bathroom, I opened the drawer. She wouldn't even miss them, I reasoned. It wasn't fair.

I did hesitate. For a few seconds, I stared at them in my small, sweaty palm, wondering if I could do this, thinking how disappointed my mother would be if she found out.

'Those are pretty, aren't they?' The voice wasn't angry but it was adult and knowing. Robin's mother.

'Yes.' Heat rushed into my face.

'Are you ready to put them back?'

'Yes.' My heart knocked against my chest as she opened the drawer and I carefully dropped them in.

She never accused me of anything, never told my mother, or even Robin as far as I knew. She saved me from myself, giving me the benefit of the doubt even though she was certain of my guilt. I loved her for it.

At my parents' wake, three days after the crash, I told Robin's mother that I'd never forgotten that moment, an early lesson about kindness and trust as a powerful teacher.

While mourners circled like restless birds, she spoke the words that comforted me the most that wretched week. I was certain by then that my lies had killed my parents. That if it hadn't been for me, they would have been taking care of the granddaughter I gave away, instead of driving back from the mountains that day.

'You're a good girl, Emily,' she told me. 'But you've always been too hard on yourself.'

CHAPTER 20

A call from Mike's office mercifully put a stop to our lunch conversation. I could hear the unmistakable chirp of the police records researcher on the other end of the line, a stout, fifty-three-year-old farmer's wife named Billie Rhine. She often called Mike around midnight. He had told me that her mood for the day depended entirely on whether she had time to drive through for chicken biscuits before she got to work. Mike didn't care. Even grumpy, she was dogged.

From the chattering I could hear, Billie sounded full of chicken and biscuits. I flipped on the TV in the corner of the kitchen for the first time since we'd moved in, keeping the sound mute. I flipped around the channels, stopping at the sight of a pretty brunette reporter perched in front of the Castlegate subdivision, gesturing animatedly to the seemingly impenetrable wall of stone. The news ticker underneath asked: POSSIBLE SERIAL KILLER?

Not the crew from WFAA. The local Fox News channel was now going at the story, too. Mike hung up the phone, and I slid over a little to hide the screen.

'Something popped,' he said. 'You good?'

He was under crushing pressure, I knew. He wanted to insulate me, the pregnant me who'd lost all of our other babies. He scribbled out a check with way too many zeros for the clones, who'd just finished up; grabbed my uneaten half sandwich; and jogged out to his car.

I turned back to the TV. Caroline swallowed up the whole screen now, staring out at me from a flattering photograph of her I'd never seen. She looked like someone's extra-pretty grandma. Like she wanted to please be found so she could go back to playing Scrabble and making chocolate scones. I clicked her off.

Mike's exit left me with the cop outside, a fat primer on my new alarm system that I'd never read, a greasy skillet to wash, and blinking little red dots all over the house. I chose to tackle the skillet first and fix a hot cup of decaf before moving myself to the living room recliner. Every speck of fingerprint powder was gone, like it had never been there.

For a half-hour, I flipped the pages of a pulpy paperback thriller that a woman I met while roaming the book section at Walmart recommended, but it turned out to be less interesting and well written than Caroline's files. My eyelids drooped a two-minute warning. I did love to sleep, so in that respect, pregnancy was a lovely drug. There had been countless nights in my life when I stared at the ceiling, my worries chasing their long cat tails.

I thought about Caroline's files, just the few that I'd read. I should have lit the match.

I pulled the chair lever, propping up my feet, and stared at the yellow and pink polka dots on the fuzzy socks Mike gave me in the hospital after miscarriage No. 3. Unable to shake the sudden, certain feeling that we were both looking the wrong way.

My cell phone, resting on the arm of the chair, tinkled the cheerful notification of an email. Lucy, I hoped.

I stared at my inbox, scrolling slowly.

Lucinda Wells Beswetherick wants to be friends with you on Facebook.

Leticia Abigail Lee Dunn wants to be friends with you on Facebook.

Jennifer Foster Cartwright wants to friends with you on Facebook.

Mary Ann Pratt Kimmel wants to be friends with you on Facebook.

Twenty-three friend requests from Caroline's subjects, one after the other, like they were sitting in the same room, deciding.

Like they had voted.

One by one, I killed them all.

The flap on the front porch mailbox clanked, startling me awake. The mail usually arrived closer to 10 a.m., not 5. I hesitantly padded over to the door and cracked it, relieved to see a man in a postal uniform retreating down our walk.

I opened the door another foot. He appeared to be wearing a skunk on his head. Our postman was a semi-reliable night school student named Harold who was fighting off his name with a rhinestone stud in his left nostril and two white stripes that ran through jet-black hair. Harold had introduced himself by dropping his mailbag to help me dump a large bag of compost in the front flower bed.

He was now crossing the yard to make better time, about to hurdle the low iron fence that squared off our small front yard. Another police car crawling down the block paused a few houses down.

'Hey, dude,' Harold called out.

Apparently, the sight of a punk mailman wasn't cause for alarm, and the two carried on a genial conversation in low volume before Harold plugged his iPod into his ears and strolled off. The cop car curved around the cul-de-sac and slowed to a stop, pulling up even with the cruiser already glued to my curb. The two policemen rolled down their windows and spoke, before the second car moseyed back down the street.

A little lazy cop chatter. I wondered what my neighbors thought of all this action.

My stationary cop waved to me. I waved back.

I turned my attention to the lumpy manila envelope protruding out of the old-fashioned metal mailbox. Apparently, the cop had not thought, as I did, that this package appeared mail-bomb size. With one finger, I nudged the envelope over a little to see the return address . . . and read: *143 East 57th St, New York, New York.*

I breathed a sigh of relief.

The concert violinist who occupied the apartment next to us in New York had offered to mail anything that sneaked through despite our change-of-address form. Shutting the door and plopping back in the chair, I slit the envelope open with a screwdriver the clones had left behind. I shook the contents into my lap.

I wasn't going to catch a break. Right on top, in priority position, was an envelope that wavered in my hands when I picked it up, not because I didn't know the sender but because I did.

The return address was loud, clear, and official.

The New York State Board of Parole.

I didn't have to open it to know what it was.

More than a decade ago, Luke Cummings was a twenty-year-old Syracuse University sophomore, almost exactly my age, asleep at the wheel, when he slammed into the back of my parents' Chevy sedan on the outskirts of the Finger Lakes. He flung their car into the kind of action-movie spiral where only Matt Damon gets to walk out alive.

My flesh-and-blood parents flipped over at least four times, the coroner ruled. For years afterward, I saw my parents' surprised faces in my dreams. In real life, the impact had startled Luke Cummings awake. He screeched on his brakes only seconds before a minivan plowed into him from behind. A little red-haired girl named Zooey was in that van. She died three days later in the hospital, pulled off life support.

I saw a picture of her once. Well, a picture of her shoe. A white tennis shoe with pink sparkly laces tied in a perky bow. It sat upright in the middle of the highway, all alone. Three hundred feet from Zooey's body.

My parents were returning to Rochester from a day of nature hiking with friends while Luke sped home from Syracuse University after his first-semester finals. Luke was coming off three beers, a tequila shot, and two all-nighters in the library.

During Luke's sentencing, I stared at the back of his grandmother's shaking blue-green cardigan while Zooey's twelve-year-old sister hiccuped her sobs in the row behind me.

The judge hammered Luke with the maximum for intoxication manslaughter in the first degree. Fifteen years. Luke's first letter, a ten-page apology, arrived five months after his trial. I didn't write back. I was angry that he ripped open every wound.

A year later, near the anniversary of the accident, he wrote again, telling me how he'd been promoted to food service for good behavior and that he was finishing his degree in business from behind bars. He didn't mention the accident.

I sent one sentence back. I told him he could write me once a year.

At Sunday Mass, I prayed for the life of the

man who killed my parents while I prayed that the man who raped me was burning in hell.

Luke worked on his degree, slopped tasteless mac and cheese onto prisoners' trays, and earned day passes to speak at colleges and high schools about drinking and driving.

I painted. I fell in love with Mike. I sold art. I lost babies.

When Luke first came up for parole, the parents of little Zooey offered gut-wrenching personal testimony to the parole board. I had marked the day on my calendar like my dead aunt's birthday, something to note and do nothing about.

I glanced at the postmark on the envelope and ripped it open. It was a little late in getting to me. Luke Cummings was up for parole for the second time in the intoxication manslaughter deaths of my parents and three-year-old Zooey Marshall. He was scheduled to appear very soon at the rehabilitative unit outside of New York City, where he was serving the rest of his sentence.

I wrote furiously at the kitchen table until my hand cramped up.

Four pages, five pages, six pages.

My plea to the parole board.

I read it, and instantly tore it up.

I drew out a fresh sheet of stationery, wrote one sentence, and signed my name.

Please set him free.

It's funny, how one sentence is often all you need.

★   ★   ★

241

Mike arrived home late, about ten, in a bad mood and tight-lipped about anything that 'popped.'

I made an attempt at conversation while he stripped to his boxers, then gave up, turned off the lamp on my side of the bed, and fell asleep. When I woke about 9 a.m., he was gone. Ten minutes later, the phone rang. I stared at the caller ID.

WARWICK, CAROLINE. A week since she had vanished.

I picked up.

'Why did you tell your husband where my house was?' I had to pull the phone away from my ear. The decibel of Maria's voice was at least two octaves above middle C.

'Maria, I didn't.'

'Really?' For a second, she seemed to want to believe me.

'He came alone, without that *rojo* cop. But he threatened. He said to stay out of Caroline's house and to keep my mouth shut about anything I knew about Caroline's business. That I probably had nothing to worry about from the courts if I didn't talk.' Maria's English was pretty darn slick and shiny today.

Mike was never one to massage his message. Maria didn't know it, but I was certain that his real purpose was like mine: to quiz the person who knew Caroline best and make sure the cameras didn't follow.

'That doesn't sound like a threat. More like good advice. I suggest you take it.' I said this while thinking that Mike and I were living separate lives again, omitting key parts of our day. He would say it was to protect me. I would say the same thing.

'You people, you *white* people, have no idea how the world works for brown people like me.'

'Mike is a good guy, Maria. He lives by his word. He will keep your family out of this if he can. This is a *good* sign.'

'I like you, Miz Emily, but you are a fool. Men never live by their words, especially ones who carry guns.'

I refrained from telling her that Mike's best friends in the ATF were every shade of brown on the color wheel, figuring that would sound patronizing. Like Sarah Palin hauling out her invisible gay friend.

Instead, I asked pointedly, 'Why are you at Caroline's house when the chief of police specifically told you to stay away?'

'Why are you being so nasty when I could tell your husband about the files you stole? About that man you killed?'

I heard a clatter, like she'd dropped the phone. Muffled voices. A man and a woman speaking urgently. Intimately.

More clatter. Maria was back on the line.

'See,' she said. 'You can't trust men. I told him not to say a word. Goodbye, Miz Emily. I don't think we need to talk anymore.'

And then, with a touch of sarcasm, 'Say hi to Belmont.'

It took me a second.

The cat.
Caroline had named her cat after a horse race.
And Maria thought I killed a man.
How many other people did?

CHAPTER 21

My nerves were buzzing like angry little bees when I opened my door to Misty Rich an hour later. She was garbed in white jeans, gold sequined thong sandals, a black T-shirt with white letters that read REMEMBER THE MISSING, and a small white flower pinned to one side of her head, a look that could work on maybe one out of a million people.

She was the one.

'I heard about the break-in,' she said. 'Are you OK?'

Several things occurred to me in the space of a few seconds.

First, how did she hear about the break-in? Second, she seemed genuinely concerned about me, despite our last, awkward parting at Joe Bob's. Third, she had opted for fake nails to hide her habit of chewing them. Fourth, and certainly not least, who the hell was missing? Surely, the T-shirt didn't refer to Caroline. It had a well-worn look about it.

'I'm OK. I think.' I waved reassuringly at the cop car and opened the door wider to let Misty through. She stepped over the doorframe with purpose, surveying the small living room lined with unpacked boxes. The clones had stacked them neatly aside, making them even less tempting to open. Her eyes lingered on the spanking-new security keypad by the door. I waited until she turned away before resetting the alarm.

One good thing about the pregnant me was that I didn't hang on to grievances for long. Misty showed up. That was enough of an overture for me. I couldn't discount the instant connection I'd felt when I first met her. It had been like that only a couple of times in my life. Lucy, my best friend. Mike, my husband. For right now, I was going to trust it. I *needed* to trust it. Because I wondered whether I was about to lose my mind.

I moved aside the magazines on the couch to offer a place to sit. Misty remained standing, hands on her hips like a tiny Superwoman, all bridled energy, surveying the room as if she'd already emptied the boxes and was contemplating paint colors. It was a normal, practical side of her I hadn't seen.

'How much have you unpacked?' she asked.

'Mostly just the kitchen.'

'Are you depressed?'

'I'm pregnant.' Automatic indignation.

'My aunt was pregnant for six years in a row and ran a sewing business nine hours a day out of her utility room. This looks like the house of someone who's depressed. At least, it is a house that is *depressing*. Why are these blinds shut?'

She strolled over to the large picture window and zipped up the blinds along with some dust. Then she muscled open the ancient crank-out windows. She was probably setting off an orchestra of alarms, freaking out the dudes who monitored these things in their anonymous cubicles. The keypad by the front door appeared unperturbed, its red light blinking cheerfully.

'You know, three months ago I was a working professional,' I said indignantly. 'I ran an art gallery and was on a first-name basis with every museum curator in the city. I was tidy. I wiped my window-sills every other week. I scraped the crumbs off the butter in the morning.'

The word *butter* ran smack into a gulping sob. Misty tossed off sparkly flip-flops and pulled her bare feet up under her knees on the couch. She patted the place beside her for me to sit. A slumber party move. Instant intimacy. All at once, I was spilling everything about the stalker. The rape. *Everything*.

Misty inserted the right questions to speed along my catharsis. 'Are you OK now?' she asked finally. 'You scared me. I haven't cried since I was twelve.' She rolled her lips tight. Maybe it was a remark she regretted.

'I do this every week or so, stalker or not.' I said it lightly, but what the hell was I doing telling her all this stuff? Yes, it had felt good. Now it felt bad. This woman wasn't Lucy. I wasn't even sure she was my friend.

'I'm going to wash my face.' I pulled myself up.

My ravaged eyes stared back at me in the bathroom mirror. I wondered how it could be that Misty Rich hadn't cried since puberty. I wondered about where she put the tears over the inevitable, casual betrayals by high school friends and awkward first love, over death and wistful goodbyes and even over sappy Lexus commercials at Christmas and reruns of *Grey's Anatomy*. Her question about whether I was depressed hovered like a shadow I couldn't catch. Because I knew she meant *clinically* depressed. Did she think I was imagining things? Making them up? Did Mike think that, too, but was too afraid to say?

When I walked back into the room, Misty was sliding a box out from beside the wall.

'Let me help you a little,' she said. 'I have a couple of hours.'

I hesitated only briefly, too wrung out to protest.

I thought about the little girl in the picture while Misty sliced through tape on a box with a sharpened Swiss Army knife that hung on a keychain she pulled out of her back jeans pocket. The girl in the picture couldn't have been more than eight years old. Misty said that it was the happiest day of her life, as if things had crumbled from there. So what made her weep for the last time at age twelve?

'It's impressive that you can still do that.' Misty pointed to my round belly hanging over a full-lotus position. A productive hour had passed without much talking, and we were now cross-legged on the floor, sorting books and DVDs out of five open boxes.

'Mark Twain, John Irving, Patricia Cornwell, David Halberstam . . . eclectic tastes,' she mused. As she flipped over a Pat Conroy novel, my eye caught the long scar on her left arm, a vertical six-inch white line between her wrist and her elbow. She had made no effort to cover it today, and I stared at the permanent reminder of something awful on her soft white skin.

'My parents died in a car crash,' I blurted out. 'When were you in a crash? When you were twelve?'

'That would make sense, wouldn't it?' She traced a finger absently along the scar.

It made no sense, of course, unless it was true, because I was simply grasping, reminding her of what she'd told me that day at her house.

'Caroline said that your parents died when you were still in college. I hope you're not upset that I know. It must have been . . . terrible.'

I'd never kept this aspect of my life a secret. What bothered me more with each passing minute was that Misty remained as impenetrable a mystery as ever. Every one of my questions was like a bullet ricocheting back at me.

I gestured to her T-shirt. 'What does "Remember the Missing" mean?'

'I started doing a little volunteer work for the Texas branch of a missing persons organization. Mostly, I insert information on sightings and new cases into their website. It's about two hours a week.'

'Nothing more?'

'Why would there be more?'

'Do you know where Caroline is?'

'You seem upset all of a sudden.'

'It's just that . . . I don't really understand why you'd warn me off Caroline even though you clearly have some kind of relationship with her. *Do* you know where she is? You don't talk about her. You don't seem that concerned about her disappearance.' I barely squeezed *The Catcher in the Rye* into the bottom shelf. 'That didn't come out right. There's not even anything in your fi—' I almost said *file*.

Misty didn't seem to notice. 'Next, you're going to ask me if I killed her.' Her voice was surprisingly even.

'Of course not,' I said quickly. 'I'm sorry if my questions are . . . intrusive. Really. I know that you haven't known her that long, either.'

Oddly, that was the arrow that hit the mark. My anemic apology. She slammed a book into the shelf. Her pretty face was twisted.

'Time doesn't really matter when it comes to relationships, does it, Emily? You can spend a long time never really knowing a person or a short time knowing them too well. If you were trapped in a room with a serial killer, you'd know him better than his mother does in five minutes. I'd say I know Caroline better than most.'

Was she hinting that it was a serial killer who carved those ugly marks on her body? That it wasn't a car crash that scarred parts of her I could see and God knows what parts I couldn't, hidden behind soft T-shirts and tight jeans?

I was suddenly sure of one thing. Misty was a victim. Of what, I didn't know.

'Misty, you should make sure that alarm system is on all the time. Even in the daytime. The cops . . . Mike . . . they are recommending that to everyone who has one.' The baby began to hop on my bladder like it was a mini-trampoline. I sucked in a few deep breaths, the cleansing kind taught by my old yoga guru.

'I can take care of myself,' Misty said quietly. 'Believe me.'

She went quietly on with the business of organizing my library, and when she spoke next, it was about a new bakery in Clairmont's old downtown, run by a young couple from France. They paid their mostly Hispanic help $2 an hour more than minimum wage, provoking concern from other local shop owners, who didn't want this to upset the equilibrium.

I let the dark thread of our conversation drift away.

Four hours later, my house was revived, as if it had seen a good therapist. Mike's Raymond Chandler books sat companionably next to my Charles Dickens collection on the built-in shelf in the corner of the living room. The steady light of the Blu-ray player glowed. Misty had hooked it up with the efficiency of the Geek Squad and placed it on the shelf below Mike's precious plasma, the remotes lying neatly beside it.

The fuzzy beige rug that Mike and I bought at a flea market in the city one summer day was rolled out, accenting the warm tones of the wood floor. Familiar old lamps were in place, plugged into sockets. The buttery leather couch, the dark purple go-to recliner that Mike affectionately named 'Barney,' and the two red and cream dragon-print armchairs were arranged for intimate conversations. A Tahitian woman counting shells by an aqua sea, a thank-you from a young artist I championed, was settling in over the fireplace. Empty boxes were broken down by the back door, ready for recycling.

The evil polished and tucked away.

'Misty?' I walked into the living room carrying a tray of hot chai tea, swirled with cream, and dark chocolate scones from Harry & David. They were two New York parting gifts discovered sandwiched in a box between my signed copy of *A Prayer for Owen Meany* and a DVD of *Revolutionary Road*.

I'd left Misty unloading guest towels and random toiletries in the bathroom, which she'd insisted on finishing. Apparently, that's where she still was. I should go help her. She shouldn't be sorting out half-empty bottles of shampoo, sanitary pads, toothbrushes, and old, clotting nail polish that I should have tossed before leaving New York. Instead, I set the tray on the coffee table and fell back onto the couch, propping my well-worn UGG slippers next to the tray, placing my hand lightly on my stomach.

'Hi, Baby.' I closed my eyes.

My body slung forward, like I'd been rear-ended in a car. All I captured of the sound was its last, whispering echo from the back of the house. I glanced at my watch. Dammit. I'd been asleep twenty minutes. I needed a shock alarm collar or something. Where was Misty? What woke me? Had she fallen?

The red lights were blinking. No alarm sounded. I didn't even know whether the alarm was silent.

I kicked off the slippers to walk silently across the living room, toward the hall that led to the bathroom where I'd last seen Misty working.

I passed our bedroom, the future guest room, and the cozy study we planned to use as the nursery. The last door on the right at the end of the hall opened into the bathroom. It was equipped with a pedestal sink; a pink claw-foot bathtub; the circa 1980 pre-fab glass shower I used every morning; cranky plumbing, circa God-knows-when; and the small linen closet that Misty had been stuffing with my life's toiletries. It was not, however, equipped with Misty.

The narrow hall dead-ended in front of a small oval stained-glass window of a purple tulip. A sharp left led to the sunroom. I stood at the threshold of the bathroom door. The light was off and everything in place except for the dripping piece of yellowing rose-and-vine wallpaper over the commode that I'd peeled back this morning to reveal a print of little girls in blue bonnets.

I inched reluctantly toward the passage that led to the sunroom. Where was the light switch for this part of the hall? A spiderweb tickled my forehead, and I swung frantically at it, imagining its architect crawling on my head. Wasn't the security system supposed to take care of him? But it wasn't a spiderweb. It was a pull chain, which I'd forgotten about, attached to a naked bulb in the ceiling. I tugged on it and was unrewarded with about 40 watts of light.

I moved toward the sunroom, its French door shut tight, old newspaper superglued over each pane of glass. The previous owner, the elderly Elsa, had done a painstaking job. Her mind was eventually eaten with too much paranoia to live alone. But maybe she knew something everybody else didn't.

I'd left the door open, I was sure, because we'd experienced unseasonably cool Texas weather the last couple of days. I liked to think the warm sun crept its way down the halls, keeping our gas bill low and Mrs Drury's ghosts from lingering.

Maybe Misty had gone home? But without saying goodbye? I heard a slight sound behind the sunroom door, like a cat's paws hitting the floor. But I'd found Belmont in a box of clothes before my nap, and he'd indicated that I should not remove him, ever.

My mind called up an image of Misty, sprawled on the floor behind that door, a man holding her Swiss Army knife at her throat. I marched the last few steps, twisting the glass knob with a sweaty palm. Pale yellow light poured into the hall.

Misty knelt over a box, her back to me.

She quickly snapped around, only losing composure for a second, but it was one of those critical seconds that causes you to rethink everything.

A fusion of hormones and fear and loneliness must have thrown off my instincts about people.

I didn't speak. The late afternoon sun struggled through grimy windows that overlooked the backyard, a bramble of bushes and trees cooked to a crisp for the past four months.

I had a mindless thought that the windows needed scraping and new hardware before the baby was born. Most of them were painted shut. Mike's and my child would breathe fresh air.

'I thought I'd get a start in here while you napped,' Misty said, brushing off her knees. 'I see you've already begun on those baby boxes over there.' She gestured across to the other side of the room and an assortment of half-unpacked shower gifts.

Was the awkwardness real or imagined? I was focused on the box at her knees. The one she'd been bent over. It wasn't open.

'I didn't want to wake you.' She gestured to the room. 'I was just getting a sense of how much is left to do.'

The excuse she'd thought up, maybe, just in case, before digging the tip of her knife into a box.

She took a few steps toward me. 'It's getting late. You look tired.'

We moved wordlessly out of the sunroom, down the hall, into the living room, past the lukewarm tea on the tray.

'Maybe we can talk tomorrow,' she suggested.

'Maybe,' I replied stiffly.

As I slid open the deadbolt, I wasn't thinking about her snooping in the sunroom or her jumpiness and I certainly wasn't thinking about how she deserved a grateful thank-you at the door for bringing order to my house and, surely, to some extent, my marriage.

I was thinking about her eyes.

Maybe it was nothing.

A whim.

A fashion conceit.

But the first time I met her, Misty's eyes were a deep brown like a golden retriever collie mutt I once loved.

In the light of the sunroom, they were blue.

CHAPTER 22

Misty Rich's master bathroom was probably a chrome and granite affair with perfectly folded, impersonal white towels, nothing like the motley collection she unpacked for me, worn thin and soft, accrued over many years, combined in marriage and now ready to clash with Pepto Bismol–colored tile.

Were her bathroom drawers stuffed with every hue of contact lens, five different shades of brown and blue and green, including that Caribbean aqua so mesmerizing and so utterly wrong on the face of a human being?

Who was she?

Did she feel like I did? That she hosted infinite people inside her body, who slipped in and out seamlessly, with no one ever noticing, transforming her into what she thought people wanted?

Twilight was casting its gray pall in the sunroom, but I could still make out the words scrawled on the box that Misty had been kneeling over.

OLD DISHES/STORAGE.

Misty could have been telling the truth.

I began to dig through the boxes, tossing them

aside, dumping them on the floor, a small well of panic rising. *Where was it?* There. The box underneath a round container that held my wisp of a wedding veil.

EMILY/PERSONAL.

The mover's tape securely in place.

I scraped my nail under the edge of the tape and ripped it open.

Since I was a kid, I'd stuck any piece of paper that meant anything to me in one place.

An old lover's poem, my parents' obituaries, a handcrafted birthday card from a friend, a *New York Times* review of the best books in the last decade, a napkin with the scribbled names of my foodie friend Delia's favorite San Francisco restaurants. All of it, stacked neatly into folders and envelopes for future reference, most of it unlikely to ever be touched again.

I pawed my way to the bottom until I uncovered the corner of something red. An ordinary, college-ruled notebook – notes from a Shakespeare class that confounded my nineteen-year-old mind with imagery and metaphors and obscure, clever references to the politics of another time. Why doesn't anyone admit that Shakespeare is so damn hard to understand?

It wasn't until much later, as an adult, that I had my epiphany. Shakespeare's words were not meant to be read and highlighted at a tiny desk in the hushed stacks of a university library. Shakespeare was meant to be roared out loud, and breathed in like a brisk wind.

I barely pulled out a B in the course, but I tried, at least until after the rape.

After that, before each class, I had swallowed two Vicodin prescribed for a toothache six months earlier, enjoyed a nice buzz, and doodled in the margin of this notebook.

I looked up from the box, frustrated by the waning light. Beyond the smeared glass of the sunroom, twisting, bare tree branches drew a sharp black outline against orange sky. A wicked Elizabethan set design for someone out there, watching.

I regretted not bringing the flashlight from the hall closet. This room had never been wired for a fixture. Mrs Drury apparently didn't enter it after dark. I wondered whether the cop was still out front.

Shivering, I flipped toward the back of the notebook, to my carefully rendered cartoon of a man with horns.

He lay on his back, a knife in his gut.

Rude ram, to batter such an ivory wall!

Angry words scratched across the page.

Words about Lucrece.

About me.

I was the crazy girl who did this.

Five names floated in the empty spaces, circled in heart balloons.

Brook E.

Margaret S.

Renata T.

Lisa C.

Emily W.

That's how the policeman called our names, like a teacher reciting first-grade attendance.

I wrote those words, drew that awful thing, on the same day that I met Rosary Girl and Lisa, pre-med. I'd been only a few minutes late to my Shakespeare class after the police dismissed us. I raced there from the library, eager to turn in my final semester paper, a mad, rambling piece of crap.

The professor had assigned us to write a fifteen-page analysis of any Shakespeare poem. It would count as forty percent of our final grade. Most of the class settled on *Venus and Adonis* or 'The Phoenix and the Turtle,' because those papers were for sale on campus for about seventy-five bucks. Twice that if you wanted an A.

I'd picked *The Rape of Lucrece*, the first words of Shakespeare that truly engaged me, a balm to my anger.

> *Here with a cockatrice' dead-killing eye*
> *He rouseth up himself and makes a pause;*
> *While she, the picture of pure piety,*
> *Like a white hind under the gripe's sharp claws,*
> *Pleads, in a wilderness where are no laws,*
> *To the rough beast that knows no gentle right,*
> *Nor aught obeys but his foul appetite.*

I had no trouble getting the gist.

Where are no laws.

A cockatrice, I learned in a Google search ten years later, is a serpent hatched from a cock's egg, with the power to kill with a glance.

I didn't keep the red notebook for the drawing, an embarrassing, vengeful thing.

I kept the paper for the names.

The headlights flashed through the kitchen windows like a lighthouse strobe as Mike turned his cruiser into the driveway. I heard the crunch of his shoes on the pebble driveway, the clank of the mailbox opening and shutting on the front porch.

Familiar, safe sounds.

'Emily? What happened? Were we visited by a fairy?' The front door slammed behind him, and I counted the electronic pings as he punched the numeric code, my mother's birthday plus a random 5 and a 3, into the keypad.

I had turned up the cozy factor in the living room. A few logs stacked by the garage now glowed in the stone fireplace, even though Mrs Drury's outdoor thermometer with the sunflower face pointed at 68 degrees. A couple of cheap candles flickered on the coffee table.

'Emily, where are you? Am I in the right house?'

'In the kitchen,' I called back. 'Very funny.'

I whacked the bottom of a tomato soup can with a wooden spoon, releasing the congealed glob into the pan, then dumped in a mixture of water and milk from a Pyrex measuring cup. With the other hand, I stuck a pan of open-faced tuna and tomato melts into the oven, upgraded with five-grain bread and Havarti.

Mike's black industrial backpack – he still wouldn't concede to a briefcase – dropped from his shoulder to the linoleum floor. It held things with a dark history that I didn't want to know about. I always imagined that if I stuck my hand in there, something inside would yank me into an abyss.

Mike walked up behind me and slid his arms around my waist.

'The place looks great.' He pressed warm lips against my neck and reached for my glass of red wine on the counter. His touch after a long day without it still left me a little breathless. In New York, pre-baby, we'd be on the floor by now.

'Hey, stop that.' I slapped his hand. 'Get your own. I'm rationing. I measured six perfect ounces. As for the house, it wasn't all me. Misty helped.'

'What?'

'Misty Rich dropped by. She spent most of the day here.' The easy mood cracked like the delicate glass it was, and he abruptly released me.

'Why do you look that way? Not that long ago, you were encouraging me to get out and make friends.'

'A lot has changed since then. Let's talk about her after supper. The fire's lit, the soup is simmering, the mood is light.'

'Now my mood sucks a little. You shut me out last night and you're doing it again.'

'Thanks for the brew.' Mike popped the top of

a Xingu he'd grabbed out of the refrigerator, a pricey black beer that he loved, my affectionate offering to lubricate the night.

'I was frustrated,' he said. 'A computer crash prevented me from seeing what Billie rounded up from the national databases. A brand-new $3 million system, and it blows up. I spent two hours trying to get someone to fix it. The tech company that installed it didn't send someone out until this morning. Their guy got the thing up and running in fifteen minutes. He's now number three on my speed-dial. I promised I wouldn't hesitate to rouse him out of dead sleep.'

'Why didn't you just tell me that?'

'Baby, I'm stressed. Wondering if I should just quit this job, pay the contract penalty, and get us the hell out of here.' He took a swig of beer. 'And it's hitting me. That you might want to find her. What that entails.'

Her. No lead-up, but I didn't need one. She hovered over us like a confused bird blown off-course. We'd avoided the subject since that night, never once broaching the obvious question of whether I could leave the daughter I'd abandoned to a life of fantasy.

'I don't have any plans . . . to disrupt her.' I spoke haltingly, not sharing how often my fingers had poised for a Google search. Or that I'd sketched her face in my imagination, on napkins, on scrap pieces of paper, a million times.

'Sorry, move, I'm burning the tuna melts.' I

pulled out the pan and dropped it on the stove, shutting the oven door with my knee. 'Get the paper plates and napkins, will you? The bowls are on the stove. Help yourself.'

After a few efficient seconds, we clinked his beer and my wineglass in lieu of saying grace and settled in to another of my 1950s suppers. Belmont, secretly renamed Golden Turd in my head, joined the party and rubbed against Mike's legs. My husband, everyone's hero. Last night in bed, Belmont actually spooned him, flipping over when Mike did.

'So if the computer's up and running now, what did you find?' I asked.

'We ran about thirty names from the files found at Caroline's. It turned up what you'd expect. DUIs. A little tax evasion. Shoplifting. Harry Dunn's corporate shenanigans in Houston, which I already knew about. Completely denies it, by the way.' He slugged the last of his beer. 'It's Caroline Warwick who turns out to be very interesting. She's not the widow she claims to be. Her husband and son are alive. So is a sister.'

My mouth dropped open in the middle of a bite and I rescued the piece of tuna dripping down my chin. I don't know what I was expecting, but not this. 'She specifically told me her family was dead.'

'She apparently told everyone that for years.'

'I don't understand. Why would she go to such elaborate lengths to reinvent herself? Where are her husband and son now?'

'She grew up in Kentucky, which is where her

264

husband still lives, in their house.' That meshed, I thought, with the portrait of the horse and her musical Southern accent.

'Her husband's name is Richard Deacon. They separated twenty years ago and divorced a few years later. Richard stayed in Hazard. Caroline reverted back to her maiden name.'

Richard. Dickie. The Hater. I knew of Hazard. It was in one of the most poverty-stricken areas in the country. I couldn't for a second picture Caroline there.

'Her son still lives in Hazard, too? What's his name?'

'Wyatt. We haven't found him yet. Wyatt was briefly shipped off to a juvenile detention center. It coincides with the time Caroline arrived in Clairmont. The Hazard police are not being too forthcoming with us about why, so I may take a little trip there. The son eventually landed in an expensive boarding school for rich kids. The folks at the school are equally zipped up on the subject. They would only tell us that he graduated as expected, at eighteen. There's not much of a trail after that.'

'Is he at the top of your suspect list?' I was adding quickly in my head. Caroline's son would be in his thirties now.

'He's up there, simply because he is suddenly alive and linked to a previous criminal history. The obvious question is, why would he do anything now, after all the years in between?'

'Maybe he didn't know where she was.'

'I don't think so. Caroline didn't make herself that hard to track backward or forward. Any PI could have done it. We're having a little trouble with Misty Rich, though. There are 42,000 people in the United States with "Rich" as a last name. The computer spit out ten Misty Riches, all of them over forty and easy to locate. None of them is your Misty. My guess is that "Misty" is a nickname. Billie, who seems to know these things, thinks chances are that her legal name could be "Michelle" or "Melissa." Billie is also tracking a list of Todd Riches. There are plenty of those, although none who are legally married to anyone named "Misty." Or "Michelle" or "Melissa."' He had emphasized the *your Misty* part a little too much.

'She and her husband came from California,' I ventured.

He nodded. 'I remembered you saying that. No pops there yet, either. Frankly, I wasn't that interested in Misty until a few hours ago. One of my more ambitious young cops followed Caroline's financial trail straight to that glass house Misty is living in. It's owned by a trust in the name of Caroline Warwick. Caroline's real estate lawyer flips houses for her. Caroline currently owns five homes in a fifty-mile radius. Two of those houses are on the market, two are being updated, and Misty Rich lives in the other one.'

All of this information was making my head throb. Other parts of me already throbbed. The

266

soles of my feet, my neck, the back of my legs all the way up to my butt. And now the suspect was flesh and blood. He had a name. *Wyatt.*

'Why don't you just roll up to Misty's house and ask her to show you a driver's license? I could ask her, for that matter.'

'No.' Mike's voice was tight with irritation. 'I'm not ready yet.'

'OK, OK. I don't know if you could trace this, but she was in a car crash when she was twelve. Or that's what she says. She has scars.' As soon as I said the word, it felt like a betrayal. Mike had moved to the sink and stopped in the middle of rinsing out his beer bottle.

'What kind of scars?'

I spoke reluctantly, wondering why I felt like I'd made some sort of silent pact with her. 'A six-inch narrow line on her left forearm. Vertical. Not suicidal. I saw a couple of marks inside her thighs when we sat out by the pool that day. I didn't get a good look. She seemed embarrassed by them. Some of the gossip . . . is that she is or was a drug addict. I think that's jealous crap,' I said firmly.

'How do you know it wasn't suicidal? People serious about suicide slice vertically along the vein between the wrist and the elbow. It takes about a second on Google to find explicit instructions. The slash-across-the-wrists method is movie folklore.'

I guess it was a positive thing that I didn't know this.

'What else?' Mike pressed. 'Even if it's little, it could be helpful.'

'She said something about taking classes at USC. But I didn't get the impression she got a degree from there. Today, for the first time, she mentioned her family. An aunt. No name.'

Mike, familiar with the signs of my nightly meltdown – the higher tone of my voice, fingers stripping through my hair like an angry comb – spoke gently. 'Don't worry about it for now.'

'Are you going back to work?'

'Not tonight. My deputies shoved me out the door. Told me to sleep for six hours or I wasn't going to be of any use to anybody. What's this?'

He'd been thumbing through the mail lying on the counter, his usual wind-down for the night. My red notebook was suspended between his thumb and pointer finger.

Something stopped me from telling him. Old habits. The shame I still wore, like a tattoo from a drunken spring break in hell.

'Just notes from a college Shakespeare class. I found it today when we unpacked. I'm thinking of reading a little more Shakespeare now that I'm more equipped to understand it. And since I have time on my hands.'

'Maybe you could write me a sonnet sometime,' he said with a smile. He set the notebook back down. I let out my breath. 'Good night. And good morning, too. I'll be out of here before you're up.'

He kissed me on the forehead, not the neck, or

the lips, or my cheek. This meant two things. He wasn't mad anymore and no sex tonight. Both good.

As usual, Mike didn't doubt my words. The guilt in my gut was familiar, but growing less bearable every day.

The newspaper article slipped out of the notebook so silently I only saw it on the linoleum because I bent down to reposition my slipper and found my nineteen-year-old face looking up at me. I had just finished straightening the kitchen and was about to turn off the lights and follow Mike to bed.

That stupid front-page story from the college newspaper. Before starting supper, I had swept it up from the kitchen table and tucked it inside the notebook.

Five little brunettes. The only time my picture made the paper except for our wedding announcement in *The Times*.

The byline leapt out at me.

Bradley Hellenberger.

The name that ran flush left over the top of the best campus newspaper stories. A titillating and anonymously sourced piece on a student's affair with a lit professor in line for dean. A first-person exposé after four weeks inside an insidious campus cult.

The murder of a rich college frat boy.

Everybody knew this reporter was going places.

So where did he go?

Did the ripple effects of Pierce's violence take Bradley Hellenberger down, too?

I never seriously thought about him as anything but a peripheral character, run over by this story along with his editor. But as soon as my eyes hooked on his name, the incident flowed back in slow, chronological pieces.

I shook the notebook over the table, and his business card fell out, the edges soft like a worn blanket. I was surprised it was still there.

I knew for a fact that Bradley Hellenberger was angry. I knew he was ruthless. I knew he felt cheated. I knew he suspected that one of the five of us killed Pierce because he waited for me after my Middle East history final, the class where I learned that sometimes there is way, way too much to forgive.

Bradley fell in line with me as I walked down the steps of the liberal arts building, his business card proffered as his first and last gesture of civility. I was slightly awed for just a second, because he was a campus celebrity of sorts. He wasn't at all how I imagined he'd look, the big man behind the byline. Short for a guy, not even 5'8', skinny, nondescript eyes, pinkish skin, a bad haircut, and wire-rimmed glasses. His written words blew like a force of nature but, in person, he appeared to be more of a light breeze.

'I know you're one of Pierce Martin's ex-girlfriends. I need to know what happened with the police. They interviewed you and the other girls, right?' He'd stopped me on the last step by holding my arm in a weak pinch, but it hurt. I decided Bradley was less like a breeze and more like a bug.

'Let go of me.' I shrugged him off. I'd been ducking calls from Bradley Hellenberger for days. 'I'm not going to tell you anything. You ran our pictures, you unbelievable asshole.' I couldn't stop staring at his nose. He had the tiniest nostrils I'd ever seen, like a baby's. I wondered how he could breathe through them when he got a cold.

I maneuvered around him to the sidewalk, students rushing by on either side of us. I had nowhere to be for hours, until 5 p.m., when I'd promised Rosemary I would meet her in the dining hall for the last supper of the semester. I fell in with the pace of the crowd, hoping he'd get lost. Ever since the rape, Rosemary watched over me like a mother, never leaving me alone too long, but on that day, she had finals stacked up.

'Did all of you conspire to kill him?' He yanked me to a stop and said it with such fierceness that a guy walking by with his arm slung over his girl-friend's shoulders stopped short, forcing the crowd to detour around them. It seemed like Bradley *wanted* other people to hear.

'You OK?' The towering, buffed-up stranger was talking to me but shooting Bradley the 'I can beat you into cherry pudding' look he'd probably been shot his whole life.

I answered for him. 'Yes. I think so. Yes. He's

leaving. Aren't you leaving?' I didn't want to make a scene. I didn't want anyone to recognize me, or him.

Bradley let go of my arm, seething. A dark flush crawled up his face like an angry surf.

'Yeah, I'm leaving.'

'Good thinking, bud.' My anonymous protector reattached himself to his girl and walked on, but slowly, his face turned toward us, making sure.

'Is this the kind of finesse you use to get all your stories?' I asked heatedly.

'They're firing me, bitch. I can't let that happen right before I graduate. I need to know what you girls said to the police. If they're arresting anyone.'

'So this is personal.'

'Yes,' he said. 'This is personal. Don't forget it.'

He seemed so small in person that I had forgotten him. A spider I flicked away.

Three weeks later, I was on a plane to Italy.

CHAPTER 23

Mike was already snoring on top of the covers, chest bare, boxers on, black plastic reading glasses slid halfway down his nose, a file placed open and upside down on his chest. Tanner Kohl's. Someone else I didn't know.

The small TV on the bedroom dresser exploded with a low-volume cheer as an Illinois coach lost it, charging a ref, screaming, permissible unless he took that behavior out into the street.

I snapped it off, along with Mike's reading light. I slipped off his glasses and set them on his bedside table, picked up the file and rested it on top of the short stack on his dresser.

His files, my files, Caroline's files. Way too many files.

I shook out my new quilt lying at the end of the bed, watching the lucky birds fly and gently float back down.

As soon as the fabric brushed his skin, Mike shifted on his side, still sleeping, to settle into a more comfortable nest. I prayed that I was doing this mundane routine for him when he was eighty, when every bit of passion was dried up, settled into memory fuzz like a good book.

Sleep did not come so easily for me. My mind circled like a Ferris wheel in a never-ending loop.

Questions with no answers.

Round and round, round and round.

One person in particular was still stuck on the ride. I couldn't see her face as she whizzed past. She was just a name on a slip of paper.

Alice.

The next morning I approached my laptop, tucked into a tiny alcove in the breakfast area. The built-in desk was designed for old-fashioned writing with a pen or pencil. There was just enough room for my laptop, not an inch to spare.

A few wooden slots attached to the wall above it were perfect for mail and bills, and we'd dutifully started filling them up. Mrs Drury's relatives had bequeathed us the small scratched wooden stool that slid out of sight underneath. I noticed my rear end didn't fit on it as easily as it did five days ago when I'd paid the electric bill.

I ran my fingers across the laptop keys like it was a piano that needed tuning. Four months ago, this Mac laptop loomed large in my world, an addiction. Technological crack. I'd never been a big texter, but I checked my Facebook and email so obsessively in New York that Mike whined that it interfered with our sex life.

As soon as I passed the riskiest stage of the

pregnancy, the need to reaffirm my existence every day disappeared. I no longer wanted to update my status on Facebook to share a picture of an especially nice pastrami sandwich from Zabar's with 522 friends. I was connected to another human being in the most intimate way possible and it filled me up.

Since we'd arrived in Clairmont, I checked email once a day and had fallen completely off the Facebook wagon. Now I was thinking Facebook could be a very useful tool.

But first, Bradley Hellenberger. I typed his full name and *journalist* into a Google search, immediately rewarded with dozens of hits. He hadn't fallen into a ditch. He was a managing editor for a prominent online newsmagazine in New York. This was going to be easier than I thought.

I clicked the third link, which promised a bio. When the picture flashed up, I thought I'd made a mistake. The guy who appeared beside the short profile was dark-complected with brown hair. Intelligence and ego radiated out of his eyes. This man was definitely *not* a light breeze. And definitely not poor, skinny Bradley with the small nose holes.

My eyes traveled over the bio. By the second paragraph, I began to get the sense that something was very wrong. This Bradley was that Bradley. Or at least, their history was the same.

Bradley graduated magna cum laude from Windsor with a double major in journalism and history the same year that I was raped. He began his career as an investigative reporter on the Windsor newspaper, with stories that received national attention in papers around the country.

He worked as a writer and editor at *The Wall Street Journal* and *The Philadelphia Inquirer* before going to work for magazines. So *The Wall Street Journal* hadn't blown him off after the controversy. He was a two-time finalist for the Pulitzer Prize. He made his home in New York City with his wife and three children.

It didn't mention a cosmetic surgery overhaul.

The Bradley I met thirteen years ago on the steps of the liberal arts building wasn't the real Bradley. I'd met an imposter.

Why?

My hands were suddenly ice-cold.

It entered my mind that maybe Lucy could help. Maybe she even knew Bradley Hellenberger. My best friend happened to be a reporter in New York journalism circles, with a generous freelance contract writing for *Vanity Fair.*

Lucy had the voice of a poet and the eye of a cynic. She told me she'd never write fiction, because life was way more bizarre and fascinating than anything she could dream up. I specifically remember the day the Joseph Fritzl case broke. The Austrian monster who had locked his daughter in the basement and proceeded to rape her for twenty-four years and father her seven children, never letting her see the sun.

I remember saying, 'And nobody knew. *Nobody knew.*'

Lucy and I were sitting companionably on the patio of a small SoHo café, finishing a bottle of wine. She tapped out her cigarette and threw me an intense look I won't ever forget.

'Emily, honey,' she said quietly, 'of course somebody *knew.*'

That's one reason I picked Lucy as my best friend. She was at home with me in the scarier places.

I punched speed-dial No. 3.

'Hello. Lucy Blaize.'

'Lucy, it's Emily.'

'Emily!' No one had sounded that happy to hear my voice in a while. 'I miss you. Nobody else understands that when I whine about my problems, I'm not looking for advice on how to solve them.'

I got right to the point. 'I need a favor. Do you know a Bradley Hellenberger? He's an editor in New York.'

'Brad? Sure. I see him here and there. We got hot and heavy at a Condé Nasty party last month arguing about whether newspapers should disappear from the planet. Brad's turned into a complete Internet whore. Ezra and I can't live without *The New York Times* lying in little piles all over our bed every Sunday morning, can we, Ezra?' I pictured Lucy scratching Ezra's chin. Ezra was her ten-year-old cat, snow-white except for one black paw, and her most consistent male partner in life.

'So you know him well? What's he like?'

'Smart. A pretty decent guy. Has a reputation for taking risks, sometimes running with things without enough sourcing. His reporters adore him. He's married and never hits on me at these silly parties, which always makes me respect a boy. Why do you want to know?'

That did say something about Brad, because Lucy was beautiful, even from behind. I'd seen dozens of strange men stare at her, waiting for her to turn around, because they already knew. She moved at parties like royalty or a ballet dancer. What they didn't know is that her Polish grandmother forced her to walk around with an encyclopedia on her head every day after elementary school and for an hour on Saturday. Lucy found it ironic that one of the things people found most beautiful about her rose out of childhood torture sessions with a sadistic granny.

That's not to say she can't disguise herself. When I first met her in line at the bagel shop underneath our building, she looked about fourteen, with a smattering of freckles, no makeup, and glasses. Cute. The kind of cheeks you wanted to pinch. The second time, I didn't recognize her until an hour into a museum gala. She had snaked on a little black dress, her shiny auburn hair swinging like silk when she moved. Lithe body. No jewelry. Tall black pumps. The only adornments were clear green eyes and a slash of red lipstick against pale skin. A painter's dream.

The good thing and the bad thing about Lucy is that she only sees herself as the freckle-faced girl.

I'd never told Lucy about the rape. How great it would be to spill everything now, to pile it all on her. But I couldn't. Not on the phone.

So, another lie.

'A gallery friend of mine is desperate to get a little feature in his magazine about one of his collectors. Could I give him a call and drop your name? Help her out?'

'I guess.' Lucy sounded dubious. 'He might be interested if the collector is someone powerful who's shunned an interview in the past. He'll need a hook.'

'Do you have his number? I'm afraid of getting put off by a secretary.'

'Not his cell, but I'm pretty sure I've got a card with his direct line at work. Never know when *Vanity Fair* will tire of me. Hold on.'

About thirty seconds elapsed before Lucy came back on the phone.

'Ready?'

'Yep.' I typed Bradley's number onto my computer screen.

'How's the baby?'

'Great, great. Fingers crossed.' Lucy had wiped enough tears away after my miscarriages to fill the Trevi Fountain.

'Hey, I might be down to see you in a couple of months. I've been assigned a "think piece" about signs of the apocalypse. Jerry Jones and that space-ship of a Cowboys stadium made the list. Do you know it costs a family of four a thousand dollars to go to a game?'

'Who's Jerry Jones?'

'You artists are hopeless. Let me know how it goes with Mr Hellenberger. And, Em – call me anytime. *Anytime.*'

I hung up, knowing how much she meant it. And thinking how odd life was. Lucy knew Bradley.

I punched in Bradley's number while I still had the guts. Right as it started to ring in New York, someone began banging a fist on the side kitchen door like the world was ending.

CHAPTER 24

O ver the pounding, I could hear the sounds of a shrill argument outside on the stoop. I clicked off the phone call on the second ring, crept over to the kitchen door, and lifted the corner of Mrs Drury's blue-checked curtain. The Puppy Killer's red, sweaty face was pressed up to the glass, trying to see through the fabric. We both jumped back, startled, and I dropped the curtain.

What exactly was the point of having police protection?

I opened the door.

'I'm not going to argue about it anymore, Tiff. That was your shot to take, not mine. I can't believe we lost a match to two Jenny Craigers.'

Holly, dripping, her face the shade of water-melon, was addressing her friend furiously from the bottom of the stoop. Tiffany was inches from me, holding a plate of deteriorating lemon squares that appeared to have been abandoned in the backseat of a very hot car at some point. She shoved them at my belly and eased past me, with Holly not far behind.

Both were dressed in black sports bras and tiny white tennis skirts. Their hair was pulled up in painfully tight ponytails that popped jauntily out the back hole of their Nike baseball caps. The hairstyle had the added effect of stretching their wrinkles flat and slanting their eyes, exacerbating the sharpness of their features. They wore the exact same kind of Asics, glowing like little neon-green alien feet.

I stared at the plate of lemon mush in my hand. The plastic wrap appeared to have melted into them. One square, I noticed, was missing.

'Welcome to town and all that,' Holly said. 'Tiff gave a piece to the cop out front. And then she offered to lick the powdered sugar off his lips.'

'It was a *joke*. Wow, this place is a dollhouse.' Tiffany yanked a chair out and plopped into it, her skirt flying up to reveal a hot pink underlining. Belmont yowled from under the table and careened to the windowsill. Apparently he recognized the neon-green feet of a possible cat killer.

'Thank you,' I said. What the hell was I supposed to say?

Holly pulled out another chair and kicked over a third one for me, as if this were her house.

'Sit. We can make this quick. Is your husband going to make Caroline's files public in any way? If so, we need to take some pre-emptive action.'

'I'm not sure what you're talking about.'

'Hmmm, not buying that. We know you got an up close and personal look at them.'

My mouth dropped slightly open.

'The maids, they talk,' Holly said. 'Like, I know that Tiff here is probably in foreclosure. She bought a ten-thousand-dollar oak dining room table for her New Year's Eve party and then returned it January 3, claiming it was scratched. Half of her six bedrooms have only mattresses on the floor. She's like a homeless person with a Lexus.'

'Jesus, Holly, you're so pissed off about that shot. I'm soooorrry. Shut up, already. This is about *her*.' Tiffany flipped her face to me. 'We're figuring you've got something to hide just like the rest of us. That we can join forces.'

Like hell.

I remained standing, thinking they might take a hint. 'I didn't know Caroline well at all, and she certainly didn't know me. But I'm sorry she's missing.'

'Uh-uh. No one's all that sorry about that. And Caroline wouldn't invite you over unless there was material to work with, honey.' Holly examined a small bruise on a very taut, very tan thigh. 'There'd be no point.'

'I was about to take a nap.' I looked pointedly at the door.

'Kind of rude, girl.' Tiffany hadn't budged. She was focused on the black wart on the ceiling. I wondered if she ate more than 300 calories a day. I could see the white bone of her knee through her tan. She pulled her left leg up into a half-lotus position and tugged restlessly at Belmont's tail. He growled. Finally, someone he liked less than me.

'What do you think happened to Caroline?' It burst out. What I meant to say was, *Get out.*

'Hol and I have our little list of suspects. Whoever or whatever happened to Caroline, it's not good, honey. She was a pain in the ass but you could always count on her to live by Caroline Warwick's Golden Rules.'

'She stood us up,' Holly explained. 'As prospective members, we got our invites a month ago to her annual candlelight séance. It was supposed to be last night. It's like her best party of the year. Scares the pee-Jezus-crap out of people. Half of us showed up on her lawn to see if she'd conjure herself out of thin air.'

Tiffany pushed herself from the chair. 'Think about those files, Emily. Women need to stick together. It's why the club is so successful.'

Before I could answer, Tiffany was out the door, yelling something sugary at the cop car. Holly followed more slowly, before languidly turning back. The muscles in her bare arms and legs were sleek and buttery smooth. Every molded piece of her was high and tight. Chop off her forty-year-old Botoxed head, and she was sixteen. I felt fat and clumsy and about seventy, with or without my head.

I met her eyes, bracing myself for a final threat. But her eyes were a surprise. Little blue pools of fear. Hurting. Then they blinked, a magician whipping away his cape, and the real Holly was gone. Whatever had been reflected there was about way more than the sex toys under her mattress.

Holly was like me. Acting. All of these women were actors. Stars of a TV drama that had gone on a few too many years. Speaking in the same sarcastic cadence, weighted by their mistakes, a parody of themselves. How I felt more days than I wanted to admit.

What Holly said next was perfectly scripted.

'You scratch our backs, Emily, we scratch yours. Ask our husbands. Our nails are long, and they hurt.'

Eight very unsettling minutes with those two women and the possibility of plastic wrap cancer did not stop me from prying loose a drippy lemon square and taking a bite as soon as the door shut. It was like the sun bursting in my mouth, if the sun was tart and yummy and a few degrees cooler. I licked my fingers and decided the best thing was to stick to my plan. My past. Something I could try to follow in a logical line. However illogical Mike thought that was.

He picked up on the third ring.

'Brad Hellenberger.' A pause. 'Anybody there?' Busy. Already irritated.

'Um, yes. This is Emily. Emily Page. You knew me as Emily Waters. At Windsor. But you probably don't remember. We never actually met. Although I thought we did. Lucy Blaize gave me your number.'

What a ramble.

He fed silence back to me. This call was a mistake of monumental proportions. The unpregnant me always thought ahead in practical steps, but that me was long gone, taking a break somewhere on a sunny shore, decked out in a bikini and downing a rum drink.

'I remember,' he said.

Two words, so heavily weighted on the line that I knew without a doubt that I held significance for this Bradley Hellenberger.

'What do you remember?' I asked quickly.

'I remember a story that shouldn't have seen the light of day.'

'But you wrote it.' Bitterness clipped my voice.

'I wrote it, without names. As per the rules of the Windsor journalism program and any credible newspaper, I was required to give the list of those names to my editor. I did.'

'And the pictures? What about the pictures?'

'The student editor-in-chief hacked them. The department investigation after the story ran uncovered that's how he got a lot of his tips. In your case, he took the list of names I gave him and downloaded ID outtakes from a trashed campus directory file. Today, those photographs wouldn't even exist, erased in a digital second as soon as they were deemed imperfect. I didn't know he had those pictures or was planning to run them until I saw the paper the next morning.'

I wasn't sure whether to believe him. He was certainly at the ready with a defense after all these years. I heard the rustle of papers and another line ringing.

'I'm not sure exactly why you're calling, Ms Page, but this seems like it's going to be a longer conversation than I can do right now. In five minutes, three enormous egos will be descending on me to pick next month's cover piece. Are you in the city?'

'No. I live . . . near Dallas. We moved from New York a month ago.'

'Well, here's a coincidence. I've got a meeting in Atlanta tomorrow and I have a layover at DFW . . . wait a minute. Let me call up the ticket. I should have about forty-five minutes around noon tomorrow. Can you swing by the terminal?'

I wasn't sure what to say to that. It seemed beyond coincidental. And why would a professional editor book any domestic flight with a layover?

'Yes,' I said. 'I can swing that. I'd like you to consider giving me the names of the other four girls. I only have first names. I want to contact them.'

'I'm not sure I'm comfortable with that.'

'You might be after you talk to me. Could you check your old notes in advance of our meeting? I ask that fully realizing that you're regretting that you even picked up the phone when you saw a strange number on your caller ID.'

'I pick up all strange numbers. My best stories arrive that way. And I don't need to check my notes.'

What did that mean exactly? Was I still a story to him? Was he really refusing to look at his notes out of ethical concerns? Or were our names branded in his memory?

'This is nice of you,' I said cautiously. 'To meet me.'

'I figure I owe you something, I trust anybody Lucy Blaize would send my way, and I'm curious why you're finally calling me back after thirteen years. It's a little late to give me a quote.' I heard voices in the background. 'Gotta go. The egos are descending. I'll text you my flight info in a few hours and we can arrange a place to meet.'

A few hours. Could this be because he hadn't even bought a ticket yet?

As I hung up the phone, I thought that time is not at all the big pink eraser people say it is.

Thirteen years was nothing.

For Brad. For me.

Thirteen years was a blink.

The voice was female, nasally and one hundred percent Brooklyn.

'I'm trying to reach Ms Emily Page.'

I gripped the receiver, head still planted on the pillow, clinging to fragments of an illusive dream starring Caroline Warwick in a Victoria's Secret underwear commercial.

'Yes. That's me.' My voice was froggy with sleep.

'I'm Latisha Johnson, representing the New York State Parole Board. You asked for phone notification of the Luke Cummings decision, correct?'

Oh my God, was that today? Was it already morning? What time was it? I glanced at the clock. Could it really be 10 a.m.?

That made it 11 a.m. New York time. I was going to be late to meet Brad if I didn't hurry. But I was frozen in place, immediately nauseous. Good news or bad news? In my experience, it always seemed like a 50-50 shot.

'Ma'am, are you still there?'

'Yes, I'm here. Yes, that's correct. I want to know.'

'The board has unanimously decided that Luke Cummings will be paroled one week from today. I'm sorry.'

'No, no, that's great news.' And it was. The relief surging through my veins was the kind I rarely experienced, a no-holds-barred euphoria that usually followed a five-mile run or a generous dose of Percocet or a baby born perfect.

'Good girl. I been at this job a long time and holding on to all that hate is a mistake. God bless and have a beautiful day.'

I'm sure Latisha wasn't supposed to drop the G word, but G bless her back.

A few seconds after we hung up, the phone rang again. Latisha must have forgotten something.

But no.

It was him.

Silent, as usual.

By now, his silence was as recognizable as Latisha's nasally voice.

I walked into Terminal B dripping wet, pissed off, and wanting to shoot dead the architects of the whirling dervish of roads that made up Dallas/Fort Worth International Airport.

Get over. Exit. Whoops, no, don't get over. What are you doing? Turn!

That's what the signs said. Well, that's what it *felt* like the signs said.

Add to that the aggressive redneck personalities of the Texas drivers scurrying around me for the last forty-five minutes. I learned fast that if you're in a black pickup truck, you get a free pass to signal *after* you slide into another lane. I vaguely remembered a Jerry Seinfeld riff on 'polite' Texas drivers. They weren't going to *stop* you from getting over, but they weren't going to help you, either. You were on your own, baby.

It's not that they were any worse than New York drivers. I just expected more.

Mike didn't know where I was, a good thing. He had been back on the job since 3 a.m., when a motorcycle wreck jerked him out of bed. The bike flipped on a highway exit ramp into Clairmont. It

290

was the first fatality for the young deputy who responded, and he was a mess, throwing up at the scene.

To add just a little more suck to Mike's life, the computer system continued to freeze, *Time* and *USA Today* were requesting interviews about Caroline's case, and Harry Dunn was bugging Mike to drop a DUI for a friend. There wasn't enough personnel for Mike to keep assigning a cop to the house, so, starting today, he'd parked an empty cruiser in the driveway. He wasn't happy with this as a permanent solution and mentioned that 'something else was in the works.'

My pocket vibrated, making me jump. Had Bradley already landed?

I tugged out my phone.

No.

Lucy.

'Hey, what's up?' I could hear in her tone that Lucy knew very well what was up.

'Why did you lie to me?' Hurt.

'I'm sorry, Luce. It's a . . . long story.'

'Brad called to confirm that I knew you. He said you wanted information on the murder of a guy you dated at Windsor. That you ended up getting screwed by a story he wrote. He wanted to know if you were the type to indulge in revenge fantasies.'

Inside, I was thinking: *He didn't tell Lucy about the rape or this would be a completely different conversation. Maybe he doesn't know.*

'I'm at the airport now,' I said. 'We're meeting in about ten minutes.'

'He told me. Emily, I really didn't call to ask you why you didn't tell me the truth. It just came out. I called to warn you that Bradley sounded a little too interested. And with a journalist like Bradley or me, that generally isn't a good thing.'

My iPhone recommended Tip o'the Hat as the best place for meeting a stranger on a plane in Terminal B. The 'Irish-Texas pub' was squeezed beside Bobo China's Express Waffle Buffet. I couldn't decide which was a weirder marriage, but the leprechaun doffing his cowboy hat on the neon bar sign might be tipping things in his favor.

No matter, both places were doing a rockin' business at high noon on an August day at DFW airport, while a long line for security snaked less than a hundred yards away. According to the TV screens, Bradley's flight from LaGuardia had landed six minutes ago.

My eyes roamed the dim bar, while Lucy's warning roamed my head. How crazy was I to meet a guy who had, in his own words, 'screwed' me? Maybe he wasn't the Bradley who accosted me on the steps all those years ago, but he could have sent the twerp who did. There was no reason to believe he wasn't involved.

Half of the men in this place could be Bradley, except not one of them was looking for me. Oddly,

I felt safer here than in my house. Safety in numbers, right? And in anonymity. I could hear twenty conversations going on around me and not make out a word anyone was saying.

Two stools along the bar opened up. I slid into one and sat my purse on the other, just in time to prevent a woman with pancake makeup and a gold and white Jessica Simpson carry-on from wiggling her bottom there.

'I'm holding it for my husband.' I smiled sweetly and placed a hand on my stomach. 'He's in the bathroom. Do you mind?'

'You can stop milking the baby crap. I've had five of them.' But she didn't put up a fight, and drifted off.

The bartender slapped down a shamrock-shaped coaster. 'I'm not sure I can serve a . . . pregnant lady. Texas law or something.' He barely looked legal himself.

'Tonic and lime. And see that woman over there glaring at me? Put whatever she's having on my tab.'

I fingered the curved edges of the coaster, which was printed with some kind of bar trivia game. You were supposed to read the quote on it aloud to your drinking buddies and ask them to identify whether it was Western or Irish.

I stopped spinning the coaster long enough to read it. THE PROBLEM WITH SOME PEOPLE IS THAT WHEN THEY AREN'T DRUNK THEY'RE SOBER. Hmm. Maybe John Wayne. I flipped it over.

William Butler Yeats. I thought he wrote strictly about dappled grass.

The bartender plunked down another coaster and set a plastic cup of half-fizzy water on it. A grayish lime wedge floated on top.

'Thirty-six fifty,' he said.

'That's one expensive glass of water.'

The voice was brusque, behind me. I willed myself not to flinch as a hand casually brushed my shoulder. I could smell him, of course. Exotic spices. Musk. A scent first extracted from the gland of a Himalayan deer.

When I turned, Brad was pretty much what I expected: tall, dark, handsome, with perfectly proportioned nostrils and a Louis Vuitton briefcase that he was probably vain enough to have picked out himself.

'That includes three martinis for the woman over there,' the bartender said, defensive. 'She ordered in advance when she found out you were paying, lady. Are you? Paying?'

I removed my purse from the stool, and the man immediately swapped himself in. He stuck out his hand. 'Emily, right? I'm Brad.' His grip was cool and firm. He held my hand a little too long.

Then he answered the question on my face.

'You're one of two women in here. You're pregnant in an airport bar and drinking overpriced water that you could find for half the cost in a less overpriced plastic bottle next door. Not that hard to deduce. Congratulations, by the way. I didn't know.'

He threw down two twenties.

'Did you bring your own car?'

I nodded.

'Then let's take a walk.'

Already, out of control.

CHAPTER 25

He didn't want to drive anywhere. He wanted to suck down a Coke from the vending machine and sit in my station wagon in a dark garage parking lot where no one could hear us. Hopefully, he would leave me alive.

'We've got about twenty minutes,' he said. 'It will take at least fifteen to get through that line at security. Should I start or you?'

My hand rested on the door handle while I reconsidered whether I should be in my car with a 200-pound, extremely fit man I didn't know who could reach across and strangle me before making his connection. Then I remembered Lucy. Yes, she warned me about him. But she said he was decent. I would cling to that, because I needed Bradley Hellenberger to be who she said he was. Who *he* said he was.

I felt like I no longer had time to waste, and plunged in. 'You know that Pierce Martin was a rapist.'

Silence. 'Yes, I had that general idea.'

'A few days ago, somebody left a present for me on my doorstep. A copy of a campus police report taken the night Pierce raped me.' Amazing how much easier it was getting to say. I should have tried this long ago. Maybe I wouldn't be such a wound-up, secretive, compulsive mess who never gave myself fully to anybody except when it came to sex. In bed, I had no trouble letting go entirely. I'd asked myself more than once why I was trying so hard to prove something to a dead man.

Brad's scent was getting to me, lighting my nerves. In the bad old days, before Mike, I would have leaned over and brushed his lips with mine. Brad's lips were currently curling into a frown. A tell. And it was telling me he didn't know anything about the present on my doorstep.

'I was wondering if his other . . . dates . . . got similar gifts or if this nut job is just interested in me. I've received hate mail about the murder for years. I always figured it was from Pierce's mother. More recently, there have been hang-ups.' Not to mention a congratulatory cigar, a message in a mirror, and a bloodred thumbprint obliterating my face, but we only had eighteen minutes and five seconds left.

'Do you have the letters with you?'

'No. I don't have anything with me. My husband's a cop. He's . . . keeping them.'

Brad reached inside his jacket pocket and pulled out a reporter's notebook.

'No writing,' I insisted. 'This isn't an on-the-record interview. This is me seeking information from *you*. Are you going to give me the full names of the other girls or not?'

Brad moved the passenger seat back to accommodate very long legs and supple Italian loafers splotched with a few dark spots. Too bad about that puddle.

He set the notebook on his lap. 'Tell me a little more.'

'All of this is off the record, agreed?'

'The reporter's notebook . . . it's just an old-fashioned habit. I practically have to special-order these now.' *Uh-huh.*

'The day the police interviewed Pierce's girlfriends about the murder, a guy posing as the renowned Bradley Hellenberger waited for me outside a history class.'

That got his attention.

'What? I've never met you until today.'

'He looked nothing like you. He threatened me.'

I fumbled with my wallet and handed him the dog-eared card. 'He gave me this.'

'OK, this is my card.' His voice was stony. 'Well, I guess that's a good reason why you wouldn't return my calls. What did he look like?'

'Skinny, splotchy face, glasses, weird nose.'

The lip curled up again. 'Nose like a Keebler Elf?'

'You know him? He's a friend?'

'No, not a friend. I can't remember his name, but I'm sure I could find it. I interviewed him after the murder. He was in the house of assholes. One of Pierce Martin's fraternity brothers. He stuck out. The rest of those preppy faces are a blur. But he was particularly helpful. And there was that puny nose. He gave me the names of several of the girls Pierce dated. Said he'd already given the names to the cops. What exactly did he say he wanted with you?'

'He demanded to know what I told the police. It was all in the guise of saving his – your – reputation as a journalist.'

Brad spoke thoughtfully. 'I'm sure I gave him my card in case he remembered anything else. I do that with every interview.'

'So?'

'I'm obviously curious about his motive for impersonating me. I don't mind giving you his name. I have to find it in my notes, though. In the meantime . . .' He pulled out his BlackBerry. 'Here it is. Renata Tadynski.' He picked up the reporter's notebook and scribbled in it, then ripped off the sheet.

Renata, I thought. *Renata. Rosary Girl.*

A crack of angry-God thunder resounded through the concrete ceiling and then hail, like a thousand tennis balls, pelted the roof. It was a little too much on cue.

'You're giving me one of the names,' I said.

'Yep. And a phone number. She said it was OK. That at least gives you a start.'

'You talked to her? When?'

Sweat was rolling from my armpits down my sides. I notched the air conditioner up all the way. Even rain in this state didn't bring relief from the heat. But, of course, that wasn't why I was sweating.

'We still talk from time to time. She was the only one of you girls to return my phone call back then. She dropped out of school shortly afterward. Like you.'

'Why?' I asked. 'I mean, why did she leave Windsor?'

'I presume for the same reason you did. She was . . . traumatized.'

'Still,' I said slowly, 'I don't understand why you'd keep in touch.'

'You don't believe me. Even though I'm sitting in your damn car about to miss my plane.' He glanced at his watch. 'You know, there's still no good reason I should believe *you*. Did you kill Pierce Martin thirteen years ago? Shoot twice in the chest, five times in the balls, and run like hell?'

My left hand squeezed into a tight fist.

'Yeah, you should probably punch me. And since you were going to do that with your left hand, you're officially eliminated.' Sarcastic. 'The killer was right-handed. Everything I just told you – these weren't details released to the press. I found out with an FOI request three years ago. It made the crime look very personal to the cops.'

'Why were you filing FOI requests three years ago? Why didn't you tell me that from the start? I don't understand why you're still close to this. You can find your old notes even though you probably live in a New York City apartment with storage the size of a cereal box. You have Rosary Gi – Renata's number in your BlackBerry.'

He turned purposefully toward me. My hand groped again for the door handle.

'Emily, relax. I'm just reaching for my briefcase in the backseat. See? As for your questions . . . what can I say? It's personal. I don't like to let a story go until I'm sure.'

'Sure about what?'

'That it's finished.'

The air-conditioning in my Volvo breathed such a deep sigh of relief when Brad took off through the parking lot to catch his plane that it stopped breathing entirely. I turned the keys in the ignition. Not a pretty sound.

I'd overheated the stupid car by sitting here with the air-conditioning on frigid for fifteen minutes. The garage was like a sauna set up inside a gas stove. I repeatedly punched the button to roll down the window. Nope.

I opened the door, got out, slammed it, and propped myself against the car. What was I going to do now? How would I explain this to Mike? My cell phone vibrated in my pocket. I looked at the screen.

Mike. Of course.

'Hey, babe, I hear Luke Cummings is a free man.' His voice sounded strained.

'Yes. In a week.'

'That's a huge relief, right? A door closed.' He didn't reprimand me for not calling and telling him right away, which was odd. I was busy manufacturing an excuse in my head about why not when he spoke again.

'We found Caroline.' It was like Mike to be abrupt, for so few words to say so much. 'I hate telling you on the phone. But I wanted to hear your voice, to know you're safe at home.'

Home. He thinks I'm home.

A car's brakes screeched on the ramp above me, and I jerked my neck around. I was grasping that the situation on the other end of the line wasn't good. I reminded myself that I had to work harder in this stifling garage to breathe.

'Emily, she's dead. It's ugly. I've got every cop on this. Otherwise, I'd send a car over to the house right now.'

My gut clenched. Caroline, dead. *Ugly.* I didn't want to know. Not now, not in this shadowy garage with hail pounding so violently on the roof that I could barely hear Mike, much less think.

'It's OK. I understand.' It was a ridiculous thing to say. I fought off terror and every question banging in my head. I needed to get the hell out of there, on my own. To make sure that my husband never knew I was dumb enough to meet a stranger, to risk my life and our baby's while a freak was roaming free. I yanked open the car door to grab my purse and was slapped in the face with the musky smell Brad left behind. It almost made me lose my breakfast. I stepped back out quickly, bending over to recover.

'You don't sound right,' Mike said. 'You've got

the security system turned on, right? All the doors locked?'

'Yes.' The truth.

'Em, I want you to understand that this is serious. Caroline's body was discovered buried at the far end of her property, around eleven this morning. The FBI is calling in a forensic specialist from Dallas. My guys had been back over that area yesterday and swear they saw nothing. A neighbor found her when her Doberman broke away on their morning walk and set off across Caroline's yard. She found the dog whining under a tree.' He hesitated. 'So the guy might still be nearby.'

The baby kicked, hard. 'Don't worry,' I forced out. 'I'll keep the doors locked.'

I imagined my Facebook profile picture flashed across a TV screen. The one in the borderline tank top. Stupid choice, but a happy day.

He was here, somewhere in the angled shadows of this garage. My stalker. Caroline's. It didn't matter. I'd be another cliché. A pretty girl gone missing in a dark airport garage. I only say pretty because all missing girls are pretty, right? I started walking shakily toward a group of travelers who appeared as if summoned by my prayers, dragging bags and a few errant children.

I can handle this.

Safety in numbers. Now, there was a cliché.

Mike wouldn't stop talking.

'Emily, whoever did this . . . Caroline was pretty

messed up. It was personal. The killer stuck a cross in the ground. Two sticks. The neighbor figured it was a bad job of burying a pet. She called animal control first. By the time they arrived, her dog had done a little digging.'

Elegant, bewitching Caroline, dug up by a dog.

'Let me check the security system again to be sure,' I said. 'I'll call you back.'

Such a good little liar.

I walked out into the hail. It felt like God was shooting bullets from the sky.

CHAPTER 26

Leticia Abigail Lee Dunn whipped her monster black Escalade into Terminal B's drop-off zone for the handicapped and slammed on the brakes.

It is a sign of how much God enjoys a good joke that Letty was the person I picked to come to the rescue. I had my reasons, of course, and number one was that I needed to get home before Mike found out I wasn't.

I tried other alternatives. Misty didn't pick up. Twelve out of twelve tow truck places said it would be ten to twenty-four hours before anyone could show up. The airport cabbies were reluctant to haul me all the way to Clairmont when they could make good dough with short hops in the rain. The rental car places in the terminal were booked solid unless I wanted to rent a red Ferrari for $900 a day.

Which reluctantly led me to Letty Dunn, now popping out of her vehicle in a lime velour tracksuit faster than the law of physics would say is possible. The rain pelted her frizzy head until she darted under the awning and wrapped me tight in pillowy arms like I was a child who had come back to Jesus. When she finally pulled away, her eyes were bloodshot. She held a wad of wet tissues in her hand.

'I totally, *totally* accept your apology for the other night. I always told the pageant girls that it's the crises that pull us together.' She honked into her Kleenex. 'It's terrible, about Caroline, isn't it? I can't believe she's gone. She was my *friend*.' Her shoulders heaved, while passengers rerouted themselves around her on the wet sidewalk like she was just another part of the airport obstacle course.

Surely this wasn't pretend. Letty appeared to be demonstrating genuine grief. 'Letty, it's OK.' I awkwardly rubbed her shoulder. 'You knew her for a long time. It has to be an enormous shock. We should go, though. I think you're about to get ticketed.' A security cop was determinedly wending his way toward the Escalade.

'I can't drive this thing of Harry's,' she wailed. 'It nearly killed me. My car's in the shop.'

'No problem.' I pried the keys out of her hand, which was slick with a substance that I hoped wasn't born in her nose, and pushed her toward the passenger door.

She sniffed loudly. 'It was a lot to ask me to come get you while I'm mourning the tragic murder of my best friend.'

'Yes, it certainly was. I owe you a big one.'

Letty seemed to be turning this idea over in her mind as I switched on the ignition. The car's friendly glowing readout confirmed that it was 3:33 p.m. and 97 degrees. Letty had agreed to come, but only if I'd wait three hours for her to get her hair highlighted. I pulled out, pretending not to see the security guard stepping off the curb and shouting at us to roll down our window. That was before Letty agreeably rolled down the window and shot him the finger. I stepped on the gas and took the first curve a little fast.

'Didn't you notice I've lost weight?'

I barely nodded. I was back in the airport circle of hell, while the windshield wipers slashed violently at the rain. North or south exit?

Letty grabbed the wheel and wrenched us into the right lane. 'North, honey, north.' I gasped, whipping the wheel back a little before we hopped a curb. Letty seemed not to notice.

'I'm trying this diet where you can eat all the bananas, hot dogs, and boiled eggs you want, but that's it. Nothing else but water. I've lost seven pounds in four days. I'm getting a little sick of it. I gag if I eat more than six eggs and three or four hot dogs at a time. But throwing up wouldn't be a bad deal, either. Maybe that's the secret part of the diet.'

'Great.' I tried not to imagine those items working either way through her intestinal system. 'Please don't touch the wheel, OK?'

'You haven't asked about Caroline,' she said accusatorily.

I sucked in a breath and pictured myself soaking

in a hot bath in exactly one hour, protected by a house full of laser beams.

'It's terrible,' I agreed. 'I can barely think about it, much less talk about it.'

'The club's gettin' itchy. Some people are saying it was the midget man at the front gate, but I bet it was that tramp of a maid. She left town. After all Caroline has done for her. She's right at the top of the suspect pool if you ask me. Or Jenny. Caroline's had the goods on her since sixth grade. Jenny is not a role model for the Republican Party. But Jenny'd have to rent some muscle to get Caroline out of that window. Maybe the five volunteer firemen in town she's screwed.'

'Maria's gone?' I was getting better at pinpointing which of Letty's rambling sentences to pay attention to.

'Yep, I heard from one of my friends who borrows her on Wednesdays that she and her family cleaned out their little Boon Hill shanty and took off. Suspicious, huh? Caroline's house is neat as a pin, but Lord only knows what Maria took with her. I tried to get in to do an inventory but a cop your husband has parked at the door wouldn't let me past the crime tape.' *So how does she know of its tidy condition?* I mentally high-fived Maria's escape. One less needy, angry person with hidden motives for me to deal with.

'Toll-tag lane!' Letty's voice sang out as her hand slung the wheel again, swerving us into the far right lane.

The driver behind us laid on his horn. My heart thumped, out of control. *Not good for Baby, not good for Baby.*

'See, Harry's got this electronic doo-dah on his visor. We don't have to pay. *Look.*'

I nodded without looking and breathed in deep from my toes. The air was suddenly infused with the smell of pineapple. Letty was digging a finger into a small pot designed in the shape of a coconut and animatedly smearing on lip gloss. This did not slow her down from talking in the slightest. 'They won't release her body until after the autopsy. She was *naked*. Did you know that? Somebody carved her up like a turkey. It makes me scared to go out and scared to stay in. Ever since she went missing, I've had my son Reggie's baseball bat at the door and this gun in my purse at all times.'

She smacked her lips together and pulled out a pearl-handled revolver that looked like a kid's toy gun just as we hit the highway. Suddenly the passenger-side window was wide open, bringing in a rush of traffic noise and damp, polluted wind. I hardly had time to wonder what the hell was happening when Letty took direct aim at a 70-mile-an-hour speed limit sign closing in on us. I heard a light pop.

'Right in the middle of the zero, going 65,' she said with satisfaction, drawing the gun back in. 'The sign says 70. You can speed up a little. I certainly haven't lost my touch since Daddy trained me on that little .22. If you don't believe me, turn

309

the car around and see the dent for yourself. Like a bullet through the heart.'

'No, that's OK. I believe you. Impressive. That's good, you're putting the gun away.'

It calmed my nerves to say that out loud, while inside I raged at myself for putting my unborn baby in the car with this lunatic. I'd consider myself safer with a killer who cut up people like they were Thanksgiving dinner than with this 250-pound, unpredictable housewife/former beauty queen on a boiled egg and nitrates diet. Unless they were one and the same person.

I trained my eyes on the taillights in front of me.

Only twenty more miles. Tub. Bubbles. Laser beams.

'Did I scare you, honey?' Letty asked. 'You look kind of green. Pull over up here at the Braum's. Now that the rain's stopped pissin', I can take the wheel. Maybe we could drive through for a scoop of peanut butter pretzel. It's amazing what can make you feel better. Four or five of those Little Debbie cakes always do the trick. I store up on the heart-shaped vanilla Valentine ones. I think they taste better than the Christmas trees or the Easter ones even though they are supposed to be exactly the same thing, just cut in different shapes. I don't think it would hurt too much if I ate a few of those tonight. I bet all this grief is burning extra calories.'

My hands clenched the wheel tighter. 'I'm fine, Letty. No problem driving.' *And no way in hell am I letting you take the wheel.*

Letty contemplated my rigid profile while I frantically punched radio buttons to break the tension or whatever it was now lodged between us. Maybe I shouldn't worry. Maybe this was a perfectly normal one-on-one atmosphere with Letty Dunn.

'How about a little music to relax us?' I asked. 'Or NPR?'

Letty slapped my hand away.

'Honey, let me do that. I only listen to country.' For the next fifteen minutes, Letty ignored me and sang along squeakily about how her give-a-damn was busted and how tequila makes her clothes fall off and how she'd happily pack a lunch and stuff Earl in the trunk 'cause Earl had to die. She nearly busted my eardrums with the chorus, 'I'd like to check you for ticks.'

My give-a-damn was temporarily busted, too. Country music was making sense. Just screw and drink and shoot if necessary. It was a life philosophy that the very poor and the very rich had in common.

'Sorry,' she said, during a commercial. 'I'm musical. Singing was my pageant talent. Now people can mostly hear me at First Baptist. You should come the next time I do "He Touched Me." I've saved a few souls for Jesus with that one. They stream down the aisles. The preacher likes to keep me in his pocket for revival time.'

'Uh-huh.' I turned onto the exit ramp for Clairmont.

Three more minutes and I'd be off this roller

coaster. I probably wasn't going to die today at the hands of Letty Dunn.

I braked the Escalade sharply at my front curb, and exhaled.

'Thank you.' Two soft words, intended for a higher power than Letty.

'You owe me one.' Letty unbuckled her seatbelt.

'Yes, I certainly do.' I cleared my throat. 'Letty, will you please do me a favor and not mention this to Mike? You know, about picking me up? The car stalling at the airport? I don't want him to worry about any of it. With the Caroline stuff going on.'

Letty narrowed her eyes at me. This Phi Beta Kappa pageant queen was nobody's fool.

'Honey, I won't tell Mike if you don't tell Harry. He thinks I'm at Pilates. Like I'm going to do that liberal shit.' She grinned. 'Now you owe me two.'

When she lurched over to embrace me, I had a fuzzy thought that she might be about to stick a knife in my ribs.

The next morning, wrapped in a robe, wet hair in a towel turban, my mind briefly, pleasantly repressing everything, I found the letter in the stack of yesterday's mail on the side table by the door. Mike must have dropped it there.

Stamped, no return address, careful print lettering in blue ink, every sentence on a single line, like a free-verse poem.

Dear Ms Emily:

I am taking your husband's advice.
We are leaving town to stay safe.
Those women are bitches.
The man you heard that day is helping me.
He turned out not so bad.
I read Ms Caroline's diaries from when she
was little.
I do not hate her anymore.
I understand.
My niece is writing this.
I did not find my file.
If you do, please burn it.
God forgive me for my sins.
Dios bendiga a su nino,

Maria

Dios bendiga a su nino.
I plugged the words into my iPhone app translator.
God bless your little boy.
Who was Maria's man? And what did she understand about Caroline after reading those diaries? Did they point to her killer? Was Maria hinting that I should tell Mike to forget the files and read the diaries?

Caroline's killer had cut her up, buried her in the backyard, and topped off her grave with a sarcastic makeshift cross like a decoration on a Halloween cupcake. For the last hour, I'd been trying to forget, to reacquaint myself with routine things: the cantankerous hot-cold shower, a cup of loose-leaf Fruta Bomba tea, the daisy wallpaper that now seemed comforting enough to leave stuck to the kitchen walls until the end of time.

But the carefully constructed dam I'd built in my head was bursting, flooding my head with horrible images. I considered Caroline's last unspeakable hours aboveground, *really* considered them, for the first time. Her lovely, fine-boned face twisted in pain. Her honeyed voice begging for mercy as the knife slid deeper into her like she was a stick of butter. I thought about how much I'd complicated things by digging into my past. If it was simple, like Mike said. If her killer was my stalker. If my past had nothing to do with all of this. The baby rolled over restlessly.

The other piece of paper I held in my hand was a note from Mike, left on his pillow, asking me to meet him for lunch. He signed it, *Love, Mike XXX.* Always three *X*'s for some reason, no more, no less, no *O*'s to water it down.

A versatile letter, the *X*.

Kisses.

Multiplication. The Roman numeral ten. The twenty-fourth letter in the modern Latin alphabet. The unknown African tribe Malcolm X descended from. The signature of an illiterate human being.

Christ.

At whatever ungodly hour Mike arrived home

last night, I was knocked out in a dark, dreamless sleep. I briefly remembered warm lips brushing my cheek, his hand tracing over my belly.

By some miracle of God, a Clairmont towing company named Hooker Services Inc. dropped the Volvo at a local service center long before Mike slipped into bed. Joe Ray Hooker was also a lay preacher at Sunset First Baptist. He asked for $219.23 and took my credit card over the phone. I told him to tip himself another $50 but to please not tell anyone where he picked up my car. He told me that was between 'you and the Lord.'

I pulled off the towel, shook loose my hair, and picked up my purse from the couch. The cell phone was in the front left pocket.

It was 10:30 a.m. here, and in Lawrence, Kansas. A perfectly respectable time to call. Cereal had been eaten, coffee had kicked in. If Brad wasn't lying, Renata Tadynski was expecting me. The first ring sent me to voicemail.

'Hi. It's Miss T. If you're a parent calling about a student, please remember that middle-schoolers are certifiably crazy, that grades don't really count until high school, and that Colin Powell was a C student in college. Then let me know when and where I can reach you and a brief message about why you're calling. Everyone else just leave a name and number.'

Breezy. Confident. Funny. She was a teacher. Not at all like the frightened girl rubbing the varnish off her rosary beads.

'Hello.' Then I babbled. 'This is an old

315

acquaintance of yours from Windsor. Emily Page. Well, I used to be Emily Waters – but then, I'm not sure you even knew my last name. Or remember my first. I think we both experienced something . . . terrible.'

Now, why, why did I say that? I readjusted, trying to sound more professional. 'Brad Hellenberger gave me your number. I need to speak with you. Please call me at this number as soon as possible.'

I clicked off without saying goodbye and sank into the couch. Belmont hopped onto what was left of my lap and stretched out comfortably, purring like an idling Harley, doing his part to hatch our egg. Love was a bit much to ask of him, but he was making more of an effort. Once a day, I'd smash his obnoxiously cute furry face up to mine, and say, 'Please love me, Belmont.' He would suffer through it. This morning, he lapped milk and I sipped coffee. We weighed together. I stood on the scale while he hung from my arms like a lazy dead thing, then stood on it without him. I subtracted from my large number to determine his large number. We needed to rethink the wet cat food and the red Doritos.

'Belmont, I think I'm going crazy.' I whispered it and scratched him behind one ear, wondering whether the cat could hear the baby's heartbeat and Baby could feel the vibration of Belmont's purring, if they enjoyed some private connection I couldn't share.

The phone rang, shrill and loud, shattering

the peace, and I banged my shins on the coffee table.

'Shit,' I said aloud, rubbing my legs. 'Get it together, Emily. Stop cussing.'

The phone rang again, and again, as grating to me as a crying baby who didn't share my DNA. Maybe like one who did.

I walked slowly toward the kitchen, praying that someone sane would be on the other end. That seemed a lot to ask.

Four rings. Five rings. Six rings. Seven rings.

I was in the kitchen now, staring at the machine.

PRIVATE CALLER.

My hand rested on the receiver.

Please let it be Aunt Tilda in Minnesota, complaining that her retirement center's cafeteria had switched from cream cheese to cream cheese *spread* and that she sure as heck wasn't paying $3,000 a month for cream cheese spread, now, was she?

Please, let it be her.

'Hello?'

'Hello,' he said.

Not a voice synthesized by a computer device, so easy to do in the comfort of your own home these days. Apparently, he wasn't worried about me recognizing it.

I didn't.

He cleared his throat.

It sounded like he had a cold. Or that he smoked a lot.

He clicked off.

He said hello.

My mind was light, like it was flying off into the field of daisies on the wall.

But it whispered one more thing.

X marks the spot.

I imagined brute hands holding a child's treasure map.

A red line that ran straight to the X that was me, and my baby.

CHAPTER 27

'That's it,' Mike said grimly. 'I'm putting a private tail on you when I'm not around. One of the guys is going to do it off the books. I'll pay for it myself.'

We sat across from each other in a booth at a small, family-owned barbecue joint on the outskirts of the town, waiting for a woman named Wanda to yell out our order. We met for a late lunch around two, plenty of time for me to buck up. Our only companions were a couple of farmers in dirty overalls sucking down freshly brewed Lipton tea chunked with ice. Unlimited refills for seventy-nine cents meant the tip would likely be more than the bill.

Charred air, French fry grease, and the sweet smell of sauce churned my stomach, but not enough to stop me from ordering up the Combo Chopped Beef Sandwich Plate with extra onions and dill pickles.

'You didn't recognize the voice.'

'Mike, we've been over this. I can't recognize a person based on the word *hello* and the sound of him clearing his throat.' I knew that he wanted me to mimic it. No chance in hell was that happening.

'I'm nowhere good on this. No discernible prints on anything we sent to the lab except for the thumbprint on your easel. Billie's running it in another database, but I don't have much hope on getting a hit.'

'What about the cigar?' I asked.

Mike hesitated.

'Tell me,' I demanded.

'Made in Kentucky. The brand's been around for at least a hundred and fifty years. Artesian springs. Dark, fertile soil. It all adds up to a damn fine cigar but not much else. You can buy them online.'

'So you *are* somewhere on this,' I said slowly. 'Caroline was from Kentucky.'

I was officially linked to Caroline's psycho. Mike had it right all along.

'Here's your lunch, honey.'

The *honey* was directed at Mike, although Wanda plopped a loaded plate in front of me, too. Crinkled French fries hung off three sides like suicide jumpers who'd changed their minds. The two onion rings perched on top were surprise bonus points. Eyeing the quarter-inch of breading, I was betting 600-calories-plus bonus points.

Wanda was pretty in a brittle kind of way, with a messy bleached-blond ponytail and a lot of Maybelline eyeliner. Tight Levi's, and an even tighter red T-shirt with BUBBA'S BARBE-Q stitched in white over her right breast. I estimated her age somewhere between thirty and fifty. A great body and a lot of years in the sun confused things. In the dark, two-stepping across some scarred honky-tonk floor, she could pass for twenty-five.

She nervously rearranged the ketchup bottle and salt and pepper shakers to the middle of the table.

'Y'all need anything else? Extra Bubba's sauce?'

'No, I think we're good,' I said. 'Thanks.'

But Wanda wasn't so easily dismissed.

'You're the new chief, right?' Before Mike could speak, she continued. 'I heard that rich lady was raped and cut real bad. There hasn't been something like this in Clairmont since that girl was found way back in pieces on the highway, her head stuffed into one of those jumbo Ziploc bags. My ten-year-old and her friends scare the bejesus out of each other telling that story in bed with the lights off. It's like legend. Do you think it's related? Do you think that a serial killer has been living in our mist all along, like the TV is saying? Should my boyfriend be spending the night?'

Wanda's drawl, low at first, now stretched and curled to every corner of the room. The two farmers a couple of booths away were sitting perfectly still, their heads turned slightly, eyes on the floor, tea glasses drained. Waiting for Mike's answer.

Mike pushed his plate forward a couple of inches. 'There is absolutely nothing at this point that makes me think there is a serial killer . . . in our

321

mist. The highway killer case you're talking about, that was eleven years ago. The girl disappeared in Boston and was dumped here randomly. The FBI unofficially tied her to another serial killer. That man died two years ago on death row.'

I was surprised at the detail he provided. I loved him for not making fun of the word *mist*, repeating it with a perfectly straight face.

'You think it was someone in that club? Those women are scary as hell. One of them goes out in the middle of the night every spring and butchers her ex-husband's Remember Me rosebushes. Like clockwork. It's kind of clever, but still. Of course, he's dumb enough to keep planting them.' Wanda bit her lip, revealing a row of braces on her bottom teeth. Purple rubber bands. 'Lots of us are glad there's finally a real professional in town running things. Someone who maybe can't be bought off and who isn't a cop just so's he can drive fast.'

Her face lit with a flirtatious grin. I callously reassessed her at a hard-lived thirty-two.

'You remind me of Bruce Willis before he started wearing glasses and doing those artsy-fartsy movies. Let me know if you need anything else, honey, and I'll bring it right over.'

Was I not sitting right here?

'I don't think you're in danger,' Mike told her. 'That doesn't mean you shouldn't lock your doors. You should be doing that anyway. No matter how it feels, it's not a small town anymore. And if your boyfriend doesn't piss you off too much, I'd say

322

it doesn't hurt to keep him warm until this is cleared up.'

Wanda, mollified, sashayed off, and even I was slightly mesmerized. I recovered.

'*Keep him warm?* You're even starting to talk like a Texan. And stop looking at her size four ass.' I shoved my plate over to the side. 'I don't think I can eat this. Visions of a head in a baggie.' I swigged some water. A slight bitter tang, like from a well. 'Was Caroline raped? You didn't answer that.'

'We don't know yet if it was sexual. No semen, but that doesn't always mean anything. The Ziploc on the other girl . . . not accurate. It was a cut-off dry-cleaning bag.'

'That makes me feel *much* better. I don't want to hear any more. But it was nice that you didn't correct her. A killer "in our mist."' I nipped off a tiny bite of the onion ring breading and decided it was going down OK. I pulled my plate back over. 'Actually, it's pretty apt when you think about it.'

Mike raised his eyebrows.

'Not Misty the person. I mean that we can't see our way through yet. The mist. Never mind. What else?'

'We're still wading into Caroline's files. There are only two people besides Billie that I completely trust at this point with sensitive information. So it's very slow going. And then there's the maid. She took off, but not before running Caroline's mansion like a crematorium. A pile of ashes in every one of the fireplaces. Ten in all. Three downstairs, and one in each of the seven bedrooms. She was burning books.'

'Not books,' I said softly. 'Caroline's old diaries. The ones I told you about. In that weird pink room.'

'It doesn't really matter because there's not a piece of useful evidence in the ashes. We did reach Caroline's ex. He lives alone on the estate up in Appalachia. Caroline deeded him the house. It's been in his name for years. He claims he got a phone call out of the blue from Caroline several months ago. He hadn't heard from her in years. She wanted to know the location of their son. He said she seemed a little . . . off.'

'By the way, *where the hell is the son?*' The farmers fell silent again, listening. Mike picked up on it and lowered his voice.

'Nobody knows, according to Richard Deacon. Their son never married. He calls up Dad when he needs some cash. Deacon says that in the last fifteen or so years, he's wired money to his son all over the country. New Mexico, California, and Nevada.'

OK, not hungry again. Done, kaput, no more grease going down this hatch. I covered my plate with a napkin for the official burial.

Mike traced a finger over my knuckle, an unusual public display of affection. 'I need to go up there. To Kentucky. I want to watch Deacon's face while we talk about the murder of his wife. He knows more than he's saying about his son. There's Caroline's sister, too. About sixty miles apart.'

I felt my skin go hot. 'You're going to leave me *here*?'

Wanda was venturing our way with the tea pitcher, and Mike waved her off.

'The opposite. I want you to come along. I think you're safer with me than without me in this circumstance. But I don't want you anywhere near Deacon. I'll figure something out.' He drained the last of his tea, and banged the cup on the table. 'So tell me about Bradley Hellenberger.'

A long, dangerous silence.

Mike held up a hand before I started in with the excuses. 'Save it. I'm not angry. Right now, a reporter is the least of my worries. My guy says he checks out. He's an asshole after a story. You're a victim after resolution. I get it.'

Mike had a guy. He didn't really trust me all that much, after all. Good for him.

He slid a ten under the corner of his plate. 'Did you ever hear of the Chessboard Killer?'

I shook my head, trying to figure out why Mike was giving me a free pass on Bradley Hellenberger.

'The Chessboard Killer was convicted in Russia of killing forty-eight people. Do you know why?'

I shook my head, still wondering where this was going.

'He wanted to mark off sixty-four squares on a chessboard. Each person he murdered was a square. He claimed he got to sixty. Only four more squares to go when he got caught. He was mad that the cops only gave him credit for forty-eight. When the judge asked him if he understood his life sentence, his response was: "I'm not deaf." '

'And you're bringing this up because . . .?'

'I use him as a barometer. That's the kind of evil that gets under my skin. When there's no logic. No remorse. No emotional connection to human life.'

He nodded his head toward Wanda, earning her tips, leaning her tight breasts a little closer than necessary to the head of Farmer One while she refilled his tea glass. Orthodontics was damned expensive.

'No matter what I told *her*,' Mike said, eyes on Wanda, 'my skin is crawling.'

I hesitated. 'How long did he keep Caroline alive?'

Mike pretended interest in a fly buzzing in the window.

'Mike?'

'At least four days.'

In my head, fragments. Caroline's bright red lipstick. A glistening knife. A chessboard and a row of pawns.

Mike's message, loud and clear.

Yes, the Queen is dead.

But the game is on.

I swung the Volvo into the driveway, apprehensive in a way I hadn't been before. The cigar connected me to Caroline. To a vicious murder. My stalker had spoken, a first. An escalation, I was sure. His malevolent spirit was now comfortably nesting in Mrs Drury's little frame house, and I was about to walk right in and say, *Hi, honey, I'm home.*

Across the street, a man in a camouflage hunting cap hunkered down in the front of a blue, beat-up Hyundai. A beautiful black German shepherd hung his head out of the backseat window, eyes alertly following me, and the squirrel on the sidewalk, with divided interest.

My new bodyguards. According to a text sent to Mike, they'd searched the house thoroughly ten minutes before I arrived.

Jesse Milligan was a Clairmont boy back from war, a twenty-one-year-old sniper who lost half his left leg in Iraq and wore a prosthetic from his knee down. He'd spent eight months recuperating in Brooke Army Medical Center before applying to the Clairmont police force. Mike said he picked Jesse to watch over me because he was, in random order of importance: a crack shot, the best at taking a direct order, and a trained soldier who would die to save me. Apparently, this Jesse plan was hatched well before our lunch today at Bubba's. The only thing Mike told me about the dog was that Jesse refused to go anywhere without him.

As I stepped out of the car, my body felt like I was carrying fifteen babies instead of one. All I wanted to do was sink into my bed and pull the lucky quilt up to my chin. I definitely wasn't ready for an official meet and greet with my new body-guards. I tossed Jesse an offhand wave and stepped quickly toward the back door, glancing around for anything out of the ordinary. The garden hose was still curled up like a snake. No new footprints in the mud. A hedge trimmer droned on the next street over.

The back door was locked, exactly as I had left it, the new alarm system blinking as cheerfully as Christmas. I punched in my mother's birthday, thinking it was really not a good idea that I now missed my mother every time I entered the house. I set my purse on the kitchen table, opened the cabinet under the sink, and reached behind a box of Cascade for the case that held my gun. The .22 was a present from Mike for my twenty-ninth birthday, along with ten lessons at a Westchester shooting range, the only place I'd ever fired it. As far as Mike knew, this gun was still packed in a moving box.

It felt cold, and smooth. I placed my finger on the trigger, and carried the gun to the front door. Locked. I inched down the hall to the bedroom, throwing open the closets, checking under the beds twice, wondering if obsessive compulsive disorder was taking root in the wild garden with all my other disorders.

'I have a gun!' I yelled stupidly into the air. I felt mad and not mad, like Hamlet. After all, my husband, a seasoned veteran of horror, had informed me over a barbecue sandwich that his skin was crawling. A soldier, trained in stealth, was sitting right outside.

I flipped on the light in the dark bathroom. My damp towel was still crumpled on the floor, my makeup scattered across the shelf over the sink. I ripped down the straggly piece of wallpaper that I'd picked at, leaving a jagged scar on the wall, revealing more sweet little girls in bonnets.

There wasn't a single part of me that wanted to venture farther down the hall to survey the sunroom. But I wanted complete assurance more. What if Jesse hadn't checked, just like the police the other day? I didn't have good feelings about that room. A few days ago, I had asked Mike to rig a chain lock on this side of the sunroom door, the side that faced into the hall. Mrs Drury had the right idea. We just feared different things from behind the door. She believed in ghosts. I believed in windows that gave up a perfect view of me, in evil flesh and blood fingers that could lift up those old, rusty latches.

It was a silly request with everything on Mike's mind and the thousands of dollars he'd just spent on home security. I turned the corner cautiously. Surprise. I was staring at a gleaming, industrial-looking brass door bolt that belonged on the back of a motel room door in case an angry pimp came to call. Latched tight. Not overkill as far as I was concerned. *When did Mike do this?*

My breathing eased. Red eyes blinked at me from the ceiling, from the doors, from the windowsills. I headed to my bed, carefully rested the .22 on the bedside table, pointed away, plopped down, kicked off my shoes. The baby rolled over inside his cocoon, which was sweet, sweet relief, because he hadn't budged for the last five hours. The books say these patches of stillness are nothing to worry about, but tell that to any warhorse of miscarriages.

I pulled the cell phone out of my pocket to silence it during my nap.

As if protesting, it buzzed, tickling my palm.

It buzzed again, setting off a chain reaction shiver.

RESTRICTED.

He'd never called on my cell phone.

My hands started to shake. It took three tries to slide the bar over to answer.

'Hello.' I kept my voice as even as possible, and my eyes on the gun. I imagined that dog outside digging his teeth into my stalker's face, disfiguring him, so everyone would always know on sight that *this* was a monster.

'Hi, Emily? You sound far away. It's Renata.'

CHAPTER 28

Twenty seconds into my conversation with Renata Tadynski I realized I liked her, a lot.

'Thank you so much for calling me back.' My voice was fused with relief.

'Why wouldn't I? I worked through that period of my life years ago. So what's up?'

'Do you remember me?'

'Yes. The pretty Catholic girl who sat beside me that day pretending to read *The Cider House Rules*. I was kind of mixed on the whole abortion thing at the time. You brought me some water when I felt a little dizzy. You told me everything was going to be OK.'

'How did you know I was Catholic?'

'You mouthed along with me to the Prayer of Saint Michael as I worked the hell out of those rosary beads. My grandmother gave them to me at my first holy communion. She loved that prayer.'

She began to recite in a melodic, practiced voice.

'*Saint Michael, the Archangel, defend us in battle; be our safeguard against the wickedness and snares of the Devil.*'

My eyes closed. My chin dropped. I fell into the river of her words.

'May God rebuke him, we humbly pray. And do thou, O prince of the heavenly host, by the power of God, thrust into hell Satan and all evil spirits who wander through this world seeking the ruin of souls.

'Amen,' she said.

'Amen,' I echoed. It was this kind of mystical moment that always overruled any of my doubts about believing in God. He showed up. He spoke through strangers. If only the holy rollers didn't give these experiences such a bad name.

I knew in a flash of certainty that Renata never exacted revenge on Pierce. She'd left that to a higher power.

'You're a nun.' I just knew.

'You can tell? Not sure if that's good or bad. Eleven years this January. Saved my sanity, literally. I help kids who have suffered more than I could ever imagine. And they help by letting me.'

She paused. 'You didn't call for my sappy life story.'

No, but it was somewhat comforting to hear. I broke out the little speech I'd rehearsed in my head.

'I've received some strange letters over the years. Hateful ones. I always thought they were from Pierce's mother. But recently I received a package in the mail. The campus police report from the night Pierce Martin . . . raped me. Nothing else. Just that report. I'd never seen it. I'd never told many people about Pierce. Even my husband. I just wondered if, well, if I was the only one.'

'That's weird. How scary for you, Emily. I've never received any letters. But I didn't report anything officially on . . . . my rape. My current address and phone number aren't listed. Someone has to go through the church to get to me unless they call my cell phone. And I only give that out to parents, a few students I worry about, and select friends and relatives.'

'I have to ask, why are you still talking to Brad? A reporter?' It came out a little accusing.

'Because he's much more than that. He saved my life. I was an hour away from killing myself after the episode with the police. I'd planned it. Bought the rope. Brad called for a quote while I sat on my dorm bed with a pair of scissors in my hand, figuring how many feet I needed. He could hear something in my voice, called my parents, biked over, and stayed with me until they got there nine hours later. He never got his quote.'

Brad saved lives. He biked. Over the phone line, he picked up that a good Catholic girl was calculating the number of inches of rope she needed to hang herself, while I sat inches from her the hour before and didn't have a clue.

'I was wondering if you knew the full names of any of the other girls,' I said weakly. 'I'd like to ask them the same thing. Maybe Brad told you . . . he thought it would be unethical for him to give me the names.'

'That doesn't surprise me. He's got the Jewish guilt thing going. Me, I'd like to help you, which is probably why he pointed you my way. I'll need to call my parents, though. I'm sure they saved the document with all the names in it. They save everything.'

'Document?'

'That lawsuit drawn up by one of the girls' fathers, some big-shot attorney. The sorority girl's dad. Brook . . . Everheart? I think that's it. Didn't you ever see it? I'm pretty sure your name was in it, along with the rest of the girls whose pictures ran in the paper. It was never filed. Just used as blackmail against Windsor officials to keep this whole thing quiet. Mr Everheart suggested to them that they were looking at a very large judgment. It was overkill – the university was bending over backward to make the situation right. They were horrified that our photos were printed in the school paper. Of course, I only knew all of this after the fact. I spent a couple of months at what my family likes to call a mental health spa. You didn't know about the document? Didn't Brook's father call your parents, too? He must have. I don't think they could have used your name in the suit otherwise.'

'I'm not sure,' I said slowly. 'I spent some time abroad after that.'

'Maybe your parents wanted to take care of it for you. Try to protect you from thinking about it. As if they could. Some nights when I'm staring at the ceiling, it *still* comes back. He put his pocketknife to my throat. There's a little scar there. I think if he'd moved the knife up a few inches and cut my face, I would have reported him to the police instead of trying to kill myself. It's weird. How guilt works.' Her voice quivered. 'I don't know about your parents, but mine were torn to pieces. That was the worst part. I honestly think my father would have killed Pierce if someone else hadn't beaten him to it.'

A high-pitched, drama-girl scream rang out in Renata Tadynski's world. She put a hand over the phone and her muffled voiced called out, 'Demitri Owens, knock it off!' Then, to me, 'My English lit class is filing in, so I've got to go. One of my best students just unhooked a girl's bra. Reached right under her shirt, two feet in front of a nun. It doesn't work to threaten them with burning in hell anymore. A little devil with horns doesn't seem that scary compared with some of their real-life daddies. I'll try to round up those names for you. In the meantime, I'll get some prayers going with Mary.'

I placed the phone gently on the nightstand, careful not to disturb the gun, and lay flat on the bed, staring up at the ceiling fan, hoping the spinning blades could lull me to sleep. The fan creaked and wobbled as the blades whipped around. I imagined it falling, crashing the plaster ceiling on top of me and the baby. That's how Mike would find his family, cut up by a killer fan.

Could I possibly have two stalkers? One who left the rape report and one who smoked cigars?

Maybe they could meet and duke it out. Take care of each other. In less than a minute, I sat at the kitchen table, powering up my laptop.

Brook Everheart.

I signed on to Facebook and searched for her name. Brook Everheart Marcum in Chicago, Illinois. A good guess. I thought for a second and typed a Facebook message to her:

Hi, Brook. We attended Windsor together thirteen years ago. I'm trying to find some of my fellow alums and sorority sisters.

Then I tacked an exclamation point to the end of every sentence because I figured that's what a sorority sister would do.

Vague enough. Only the sorority part wasn't true. I sent the message and made a friend request. Now I'd play the waiting game. I'm not sure what I expected to glean from viewing Brook's Facebook page if she confirmed our friendship. But something.

I punched in Black Patch Cigar Co., found the main website, and was rewarded with a picture of my pirate feminist. A link to a blog declared it one of the best cigars in North America. A twenty-count box cost upward of a $100, and a bizarre and confusing hexagonal chart said the cigar leaned more toward spice and nut than peat and cocoa. At least that's what I think it said. This was a whole new way to fall down the rabbit hole.

My cell phone sang and danced on the desk.

I breathed out slowly after reading the screen.

DUNN, LETICIA.

'Hi,' I said.

'This is Leticia Lee Dunn,' she said, as if we hadn't shared an awkward hug less than twenty-four hours ago. 'I am organizing a small memorial service for Caroline Warwick in my home, since that butcher from Dallas isn't going to give up her body anytime soon. Tonight at seven-thirty. I know it's late notice, but a lot of us are suffering. I expect you will be there?'

'Sure.' The word was out of my mouth before I could stop it.

'It's women only.'

When I didn't reply, she said, 'So don't bring Mike.'

'I got that.'

'Would you like to speak a few words?'

'No, no, I wouldn't.' I spoke firmly. 'I didn't know her that well. Actually, I'm not sure I can make it, after all.'

'If I can pick you up at the airport when I'm out-of-my-mind bereaved, you can show up and say a few words about Caroline. I'll put you down for five minutes. No, ten. Don't be late.'

At 7:29 p.m., I drew the station wagon to a stop at the end of a long line of vehicles parked in a string down the curb of a bland, upscale street called La Mirada. Both sides were crammed with million-dollar brick homes barely distinguishable from one another.

About twenty seconds later, Jesse pulled in behind me and switched off his motor and headlights. I flipped him a thumbs-up. I had briefly poked my head in his car window and met Parker the dog before heading off to Letty's express memorial.

Parker had licked my hand. Jesse had called me *ma'am*. Other than the *ma'am* and the 9 mm lying on the seat beside him, it sort of felt like a protective teenage brother had my back.

I walked quickly, scanning the numbers on the houses, pretty sure my destination was ten houses up with a large, glowing display of some kind in the front yard. The street was void of human life. My low heels clicked on the sidewalk. Not a tree big enough to hide anyone. The only other sound in the failing twilight was the hiss of a sprinkler system spitting on. I counted eight white Lexuses and five black BMWs before deciding it wasn't that interesting to count them.

Letty's cushy little neighborhood, made up of nondescript 5,000-square-foot houses and short lawns, wasn't in Caroline Warwick's astronomical league but it was more posh than any place I'd ever dreamed of living. The brick landscape grew up out of flat Texas farmland, one more layer of life on top of centuries-old Indian graves and thousand-year-old fossils and million-year-old dinosaur bones.

On time in Texas must mean *Get there early*. I picked up the pace, regretting my wardrobe choice

– a dark blue suit with the waist button undone, a gray blouse that gapped a little between the top buttons if I moved my arms too much, and my mother's pearls.

I used a Manolo Blahnik toe to scoot a Billabong skateboard left carelessly in the middle of the sidewalk onto a lawn. In Manhattan, it would have disappeared less than a minute after the kid abandoned it. Every kid on this block probably had at least one to spare.

I was right about one thing. The street address was unnecessary. Letty's house glowed with candles in every window, like a New England Christmas. She'd planted an enormous memorial wreath of red carnations in the middle of her lawn, lit in the dusk by the glare of a portable spotlight, its orange cord snaking across the grass. A white ribbon with CAROLINE splashed in glitter stretched across the front of the wreath. A plastic gold cross, about twice the size of a priest's, dangled from the top.

I twisted the doorknob, hoping to sneak in, and found myself in the entrance hall, struck dumb by a giant framed color photograph. Not of Letty's children. Not a family portrait. A blown-up, professional head shot of Letty in better days. Misty hadn't lied. The old Letty reminded me of a prettier, more feminine Cameron Diaz. Three candles flickered on the table underneath the portrait. The real memorial.

I followed the cacophony of voices to the back of the house, noting that Letty's interior design didn't match her flashy wardrobe. Tasteful but dull, and Letty was neither. She had handed someone a blank check and stayed out of the way. It felt light and airy, with creamy walls, flowered and paisley upholstery, and generic fine prints.

I stopped short at the entrance to the family room and kitchen. The atmosphere was electric, almost frenzied. The loud, dissonant sound of an orchestra warming up – only, the violins and bassoons and clarinets were forty women, shoulder to shoulder, chattering chaotically. A killer in *their* town.

Two sets of French doors led out to a brick patio and a pool filled with floating candles. White, rented folding chairs lined either side of the pool and the grassy area behind it. A small podium with a microphone was set up by the shallow end with a white baby grand piano beside it. The man in the tux on the piano bench appeared rented, too.

None of the guests turned her head to acknowledge me as I veered toward the kitchen. I slipped around to the mosaic-tiled kitchen island, big enough to lay a twin mattress on top and go to sleep, and grabbed a glass and one of the first bottles of wine out of a line of pewter ice buckets. I took a sip of decent pinot, stuffed a boiled shrimp in my mouth, and wondered about the inch-high plastic cups with lids lined up on the kitchen island like tiny party favors.

'Please feel free to take a sample. I've just started

selling. The company I work for is the Mary Kay of freeze-dried fruits and vegetables. It's the wave of the future, with terrorists and all.' The woman speaking at my elbow was slightly pudgy, about forty-five, in colorfully striped glasses and a black pantsuit.

She pried open one of the plastic containers to reveal a shriveled collection of dead things. A pea, a banana slice, a bit of carrot. I think I recognized a strawberry. And there was something brown and unrecognizable, like a tiny tick.

'They've got a shelf life of ten years. You soak them in water and they jump right back to life.' She picked up a nearby jar of water floating with small objects that looked like something drained out of the garbage disposal. 'Would you like a taste?'

'Tammy, I think Letty said she'd give you a few minutes to make your pitch at the *end* of the service, right? Do you even know this woman's name?' My rescuer, a schoolteacherish sort, placed her body between Tammy and me, like she was setting a basketball pick, and stuck out her hand. 'I'm Letty's cousin, Lee Ann Womack.'

'You always try to control everything, Lee Ann,' Tammy whined.

'I'm Emily Page, the new chief's wife.' I thought it might ease things to finally interject. 'Nice to meet you both.' This was a new thing for me, identifying myself by my husband's career, and I had no idea why in the hell I was doing it.

Tammy nodded, irritated, and stalked off. Lee Ann guided me to the center of the family room, where I was instantly mesmerized by the giant wedding portrait of Letty and Harry over the fireplace. Squint a little, and they morphed into Cameron Diaz and Hugh Jackman.

'It's a shock the first time you see it. You can't believe it's her, right? Well, it's her. Put the bitchy personality you know with that face and body up there, draw on a cheerleader uniform, and you'll pretty much have a picture of what I had to face every day in high school, not to mention all the torturous Easter dinners. But life's a wicked little bastard. I got my master's in library science from Harvard and she got Harry and an addiction to high fructose corn syrup.'

Before I could figure out my response to that, screeching feedback from the microphone outside sliced through the room like a dying cat. I plugged my right ear with a finger, because I held the wineglass in the other hand and there was no immediate place to put it down. Letty was visible through the open door to the patio, decked out in black evening pants and a black sequined top. She was teetering on seven-inch heels gallantly struggling to support her body mass. She grabbed the podium and thumped the microphone with her finger, making things worse, which seemed to be her self-assigned role in life.

'Ladies! Please be seated so we can begin.' The pianist hustled to work on the microphone, and in a few seconds worked it down to a soft, bee-like buzz.

The women streamed expectantly to the patio, a herd of clomping, designer heels. Caroline couldn't have planned the drama better herself. Two young Mexican women at each of the double French doors handed us programs with a fifteen-year-old glamour shot of Caroline on the front along with her date of birth and death. High-gloss paper. Raised, gold type. Caroline was only fifty-two. She seemed so much older. The matriarch. The Queen.

I sat in the first open chair I came to, on the aisle on the far side of the pool, and quickly glanced inside the program. Letty had listed me as the fourth and last speaker. Emily Page, Wife of the Police Chief. I tried to tamp down my irritation. This was printed way before she ever picked up the phone to invite me.

My only consolation: The program listed Gretchen Liesel as Primary Eulogist. Maybe she'd run over her time limit. Maybe she'd inspire something in me. I had no idea what I was going to say. I didn't recognize the names of the other two speakers. Letty planned to sing a solo to close things out. 'I'll Fly Away.' I had a feeling it would no longer be one of my favorite gospel hymns by the time the evening shut down.

'We are here to mourn our great friend Caroline Warwick.' Letty's voice boomed across the yard. 'Let us open with a moment of silence.' The crowd bowed their heads low.

'Hey, Letty,' someone called from the back. 'We hear that Caroline found out you aren't really descended from the General.'

'That is a lie,' Letty said calmly, head still bowed. 'This is not an appropriate place to talk about things like how you blew my husband at my daughter's middle-school prom.'

'Show some respect, y'all,' urged the tall woman sitting directly in front of me. 'Take your bitch fight to Twitter, where it belongs.' She turned around and whispered to me, 'This is why Yankees like you think Texans are lunatics.'

'I don't think that at all,' I murmured. *I just think Clairmont women are lunatics.*

The crowd was babbling, moving in their chairs like restless hyenas. All those secrets, ready to explode. Caroline's real legacy.

Gretchen hopped up out of her chair in the front row. She nudged Letty away from the microphone, quickly adjusting it, turning it down.

'Thank you, Letty.' She stared at her pointedly. Letty hesitated. Then she tottered away from the podium, back to her chair. 'Everybody *sit* down. *Shut up.*'

And they did. By the time Gretchen finished her tribute, tears and $35 mascara ran down the faces around me. Women shared tissues from their purses. Gretchen's story about a philanthropist and dear friend who never wanted credit were hard to square with the Caroline Warwick I knew. Not a peep about her being seriously psychotic. I

344

had to wonder whether half of these women were crying out of relief that their secrets might die with her.

Gretchen rolled on for about half an hour. After that, Letty announced that the next two speakers on the program hadn't shown. I wish I'd known that was an option.

'Next up is Emily Page, wife of our new police chief, who will share a few thoughts about Caroline and then she will update us on the tragic case.'

Shock, a little panic, followed by full-blown anger. No way could I offer up inside information on the murder. The murderer was possibly in the house.

I wanted to squeeze Letty's neck with my hands until her chubby head popped off. Instead, I stepped haltingly up to the podium as Letty brushed by me in a wave of thick, flowery perfume, sat down, and peered up at me expectantly, as did forty other faces.

I glanced down at my program, pretending that I was refreshing myself on notes that didn't exist. Then I gazed deliberately at each section of the crowd. Left, right, center, silently acknowledging them, a trick I learned in my high school speech class. Take a moment to possess yourself. Make them feel like you have a relationship with each one of them. I wondered whether my eyes had passed over Caroline's killer.

I didn't see Misty's face out there. Or Holly's or Tiffany's, for that matter. I easily spotted Lucinda in the far back corner, hiding under a black floppy hat, which only made her stand out more.

'First,' I said, 'I am unable to speak about the case. I think it would be . . . inappropriate on several levels.' Letty made a small, regurgitating sound. 'I would, however, like to share a prayer I've always found a comfort to me. I am Catholic, and I know many of you are Baptist, but I think it is universal. Please bow your heads.'

Everyone immediately bowed their heads. The power of the podium in the Bible Belt.

It wasn't hard to find this one lodged in my brain.

'Hail, Holy Queen, Mother of mercy, our life, our sweetness, and our hope. To thee we do cry, poor banished children of Eve, to thee do we send up our sighs, mourning and weeping in this valley of tears. Turn then, most gracious Advocate, thine eyes of mercy toward us, and after this our exile, show unto us the blessed fruit of thy womb, Jesus. Amen.'

'Amen,' the crowd repeated.

I sat down. Letty seemed stunned. This appeal to the Lord wasn't the big Hollywood finish she was expecting. But she was Letty, so she recovered quickly. She picked up a portable microphone resting at her feet on the ground, cued the pianist, and proceeded to blast out 'I'll Fly Away.'

Not as awful as I thought she'd be in a full-out performance. The pitch roamed a little beyond her reach, but she was at least on key and clearly had voice training.

She made the mistake in the first chorus of thinking the crowd was with her. She began to wander the aisles like a nightclub singer, sticking the microphone in people's confused faces for them to sing along before yanking it away a second later and yelling for everyone to clap along.

Letty's face glowed red-hot from her vocal effort and her anger at our lackluster participation as she bobbled around in her shiny sequins and skyscraper heels. She walked unsteadily back toward the podium, singing Tammy Wynette–style about God's celestial shore. She almost made it.

A few steps from the podium, her left heel caught on the leg of an empty chair. She flapped her arms desperately in that moment before disaster, when you can see it coming but can't stop it.

Gravity and about 250 pounds gave way, and Letty flopped backward into the pool like a human Shamu, taking four empty chairs with her. The splash soaked mourners sitting on the periphery of the water, who immediately let out shrieks, and at least one very loud 'Fuck!'

It might have been just a medium-sized disaster if, while Letty's head bobbed above the water, one of the passing votives hadn't caught her hair on fire.

I found myself at the side of the pool, leaping. For the half second I was suspended in mid-air, I wondered how my life had come to this. Then I hit the water – no small splash, either.

'Your hair is on fire!' I was yelling, reaching for Letty's head, dunking it under.

Her head popped up.

'Are you trying to drown me?' she screeched.

The fire was out. The left side of her hair was singed all the way to the scalp, with a splotch of skin turning newborn baby pink. She'd been lucky. The rest of her head had been too wet to light up. But Letty had at least six months of hair recovery in front of her.

I felt a diabolical urge to dunk her again, saying, *No, no, your hair is still on fire, Letty,* and then again and again, letting her bob up and down, until it stopped being funny.

It turned out that the two Mexican women who handed out the programs, Juanita and Lupe, had suffered in Letty's domestic service for the last ten years.

With Letty's grudging permission, Juanita dug into the back of her mistress's walk-in closet to find the smallest-sized clothing she owned, which turned out to be a lavender velour tracksuit in a size 16. It was wonderfully loose and cozy, and made me completely rethink my snotty attitude about velour.

Meanwhile, Lupe wrung out my clothes and hung them over several of the chairs outside. She then delivered a cup of hot cinnamon tea, which I sipped while Gretchen pumped up a blood pressure cuff on my arm, which she'd retrieved from her bag in the car.

After Gretchen briefly examined Letty's scalp and recommended a temporary fix of over-the-counter cortisone cream, Letty disappeared into the back wing of the house. The last of the guests were trickling out the front door.

'I'm glad you are delivering my baby,' I said to Gretchen, moving over on the couch to make more room for her. 'You seem calm in an emergency.'

'You're the one who jumped in to save the day.'

'Instincts. Wife of a cop. Former junior lifeguard.'

'Your blood pressure is good.' Gretchen stripped off the Velcro, sounding curt. 'Do you understand what the words *avoid stress* mean?'

It seemed rhetorical, so I didn't answer. And while I had Gretchen's attention, I meant to take full advantage. 'Did you know that the cops are going through files that Caroline kept on all of you?'

'I thought we were done with this conversation. But yes, rumors are all over town that cops are picking our lives apart. I never saw the file room, but I had a general idea. I thought of it as a fairly harmless hobby.'

'Did you know she snooped around your house and found the Nazi uniform?'

'You don't give up, do you? Yes, she eventually told me. That uniform left our house years ago. We donated it to the National World War II Museum in New Orleans. How did you find this out anyway? Is your husband letting you read the files?'

'No,' I said, sharply. 'Definitely not.'

'So?'

'So, I don't think Caroline's motives were all that pure. I told you in your office that someone left a package on my doorstep. It was the police report from the night I was raped in college.'

Gretchen's face remained impassive.

'Her husband and son are still alive.' Now I was just throwing darts at the wall.

No reaction.

'You knew,' I said.

'I know that Caroline didn't deserve to die the way she did.'

'Do you have any idea who hated her this much?'

'No.' She snapped her black medical bag shut and spoke gently. 'Caroline wouldn't taunt you about a rape. You're the victim. Whatever her methods, she was all about *helping* the victim.'

'Hi, y'all.' Letty's voice rang out cheerfully behind us, like this awful evening was just another day in the life.

She plopped beside me on the couch, the leather cushion offering up a helpless sigh. The yellow smiley faces on her flannel pajamas beamed at me. She wore a matching blue facial mask that cracked a little, like a series of mini-earthquakes, every time her mouth moved. She'd stuck a SpongeBob Band-Aid on the left side of her forehead and tucked her hair into a clear pink plastic shower cap.

'Did I hear y'all talking about that little package I left on Emily's doorstep a while back? By the way,

I'm going to want that outfit back tomorrow before noon. I think I'm close to fitting back into it.'

She patted the shower cap on her head distractedly.

'What are y'all staring at? I'm giving myself one of those Queen Helene Cholesterol Hot Oil Treatments from Walgreens. It's an old pageant-girl trick. My hair's under a lot of stress.'

CHAPTER 29

Letty had delivered the rape report to my doorstep. *Letty.* The revelation opened a yawning space in my brain. My ears hummed and the baby somersaulted while Letty's mouth moved and her blue face cracked in front of me like dry land in a drought. I wondered if it was going to explode and send bits of plaster into my eyes.

Letty delivered the package, just that one, at least that's what she said when I asked her, in a very faraway voice, about cigars and phone hang-ups. And what kind of person would voluntarily admit the one crazy thing and not the others?

She shrugged it off in the way only Letty could.

'I don't know what phone hang-ups you're talking about,' she said. 'It's rude to suggest it. And I don't smoke. Pageant girls don't. It makes your lips look like a horse's butt-hole. I was just doing my job for Harry as head of the background search committee for the new chief of police. It was a lot of work. Ten applicants. Harry asked me to check out wives, kids, relatives, friends. Turns out, I had a real knack for it.'

Gretchen and I watched, speechless, as Letty blathered on, oblivious to the effect on her audience. I wondered if she'd been born with a slice of her soul missing and if she stored bloody knives with her Little Debbie cakes.

'I checked out all your college records.' She studiously examined a chipped hot-pink nail. 'You went to a bunch. I figured you for some kind of a cheater who had to move around. But your transcripts didn't bear that out. Sweetie, you don't need to look so shocked about all this. A little money opens lots of doors, always has, always will, even at those Ivy League, stick-up-their-butt schools. I lucked into some student temp at Windsor University's police department, who was more than happy to help me. Called me back three days later. I guess it took some digging in the basement files to find your name. We agreed that I'd send her a hundred-dollar Urban Outfitters gift card and she'd mail me a copy.'

My secrets in exchange for a pair of skinny jeans.

Dry crumbs from Letty's face fell like blue dust onto the couch. 'Those scholarship kids are always quick to take a dime. Did you just make up the rape? That's sure what it sounded like.'

I couldn't breathe.

'Why would you do this, Letty?' Gretchen asked in a strained voice.

'Why the hell do you think? So Harry would have leverage with the new chief if he ever needed it. I was going to hold on to it in case it was ever useful. Small-town politics is a bitch. But then I got pissed when Emily arrived, all snotty and New Yorky, strutting around like a pregnant Demi, at least from the waist down. Not to be downright mean or anything, Emily, but your boobs wouldn't pass pageant muster. Anyway, it was like we weren't good enough for you. I thought it would be worth it to take you down a peg. She said I shouldn't do it, but Caroline wasn't always right about everything. Look what happened to her. Planted like a crocus bulb in her own backyard.'

'Caroline knew about the report?' I stammered.

'Yep. I showed her the day it arrived because she liked to keep track of things herself. She said it wasn't important. That we should feel sorry for you. I believe her exact words were, *Men are filthy pigs*.' Letty sat back on her own little haunches.

'I have to go,' I said.

Juanita appeared with a plastic garbage bag stuffed with my wet clothes. She held out my Manolo Blahniks, which didn't appear all that worse for taking a dip in Letty's saltwater pool.

'Keep them,' I said.

'Are you OK?' Gretchen walked beside me to the door, any tension between us erased by Letty's bizarre confession. She draped her arm around my shoulders, but I could barely feel it.

'I have to go,' I repeated.

Jesse's headlights chased me all the way home.

★   ★   ★

When I arrived at the house, Mike was preoccupied in a way I was all too familiar with when it came to his big, ugly cases. Distracted, when I told him that Letty admitted delivering the rape report to our door.

'That's good,' he said absently, as if it was something to be crossed off a list. He barely glanced up at my disheveled appearance.

A copy of Caroline's autopsy report was spread out to all four corners of the kitchen table. I had to turn away from the pictures. Gray, red, surreal. Mike made no effort to hide them. He pressed his palms on either side of his head like a vise. 'No forensic evidence. No hairs. No blood. No semen. She was drugged with Vicodin, half a bottle of Tylenol PM, and high-proof whiskey. Then he cut her. For four to five days, he toyed with her. There were plenty of wounds before he struck her heart. He stripped her naked and washed her in something that left traces of citric acid and non-fat dry milk. Then he stored her somewhere for a week.'

He was talking more to himself than to me, so I just walked away. He was still at it, making another batch of coffee, when my head hit the pillow. I wondered whether we were finally falling apart. Intellectually, I knew that solving this case was the best way he could love me. But right now, all I wanted were his arms around my baby.

I slept hard and woke up about seven the next morning to an unexpectedly cool, lazy breeze drifting through the screen. The wind rustled the leaves of the forty-year-old live oak outside the window, encouraging me to sink deeper under the birds. I knew that Jesse was on the job out front, so I let nature lull me in and out of a fitful consciousness until mid-morning.

I restlessly piddled around after that. People wonder why women stalked by boyfriends or husbands or strange creeps don't run. It's because there is nowhere to run. There's not enough money to run. Electronic trails everywhere. The only escape is death. His or yours.

Come and get us, jerk, said the little voice in my head, bravely. *We're ready.*

This time, I listened.

I slipped my gun out from under a pile of silk panties in my underwear drawer, where I had carelessly hidden it from Mike. I set it on the dresser while I unpacked a small box of jewelry and hooked earrings into place on a little plastic tree. I placed it on the kitchen counter while I washed Mike's cereal bowl and juice glass. I rested it on top of the dryer while I threw Letty's tracksuit into the washer. I eventually landed on the stool in front of the computer. I stuck the gun into one of the cubbyholes of Mrs Drury's desk and called up my email.

Brook Everheart Marcum added you as a friend on Facebook . . .

Did it matter anymore? Mike would say no, that I should just leave it alone.

I clicked the link. Brook had 796 friends. Brook

Everheart Marcum, bless her heart, was a friend to all.

Brook networked in Miami and Chicago. She was a stay-at-home mom, married, with two children. Her profile picture displayed her on a yacht with a broad grin and healthy cleavage. Arms outstretched, *Titanic*-style.

I scrolled down her wall.

Brook last recorded her status four hours and twenty minutes ago.

I just used a neti pot for the first time and it's totally gross but I HIGHLY recommend it.

Three hours later, one of her friends had replied with a link to a story about brain-killing amoebas lurking in neti pots – 53 likes.

Brook updated her status an average of three times a day. Yesterday, Brook made the best macaroni and cheese EVER. She provided a recipe link to Pinterest and a picture that looked like a plate of yellow crawling worms. In response, a friend posted a Pinterest link to a dog bed made out of her grandmother's old suitcase and a pillow. I moved on down.

In the space of twenty-four hours, Brook threw her iPhone out the car window, joined the group Chi-O-My alums, complained that half the PTA's Silent Auction committee made 'crap jam baskets' to sell, and was highly disturbed because she had finally gotten around to watching the DVD of *Slumdog Millionaire* and not one of her 796 friends had warned her that a kid got blinded by acid.

Ambient awareness. That's what social scientists say we create when we relate the most insignificant details of our lives to 796 people. I sat in a room for ten minutes with Brook Everheart thirteen years ago because we were raped by the same man and now I was suddenly aware of the current activity inside her mucus membranes.

Used to be, only mothers cared for this kind of detail, probably because they microscopically examined the texture and color of our baby poop for signs of crisis. But while one detail on its own is meaningless, all those details together builds an interesting picture. I knew this because of Mike, the master profiler. And, as a whole, six screens of Brook's wall, a mundane peek into the last ten days of her life, was revealing enough for my purposes.

If she was testing out neti pots and operating on her mucus only a few hours ago, then making it public, it was a pretty good guess she wasn't worried about a stalker.

I returned to my inbox.

An email from Brad.

Subject line: *Keebler Elf.*

One terse sentence: *Does the name Avery Crane mean anything to you?*

I typed a terse *No,* and sent it away just as the doorbell rang.

I glanced out the kitchen window. A FedEx van parked across the street. I wasn't expecting anything. Maybe a baby gift? How many more $60 infant pajamas could I fit in the drawers if I ever bothered to put anything in drawers?

When I cracked open the door, Jesse stood on the stoop with the delivery guy, flashing a badge, asking him to slowly lower a large envelope to the stoop.

'What do you think, that it's going to explode?' It was pretty heavy-duty sarcasm from a glorified mailman in Dockers shorts. 'That terrorists are striking Clairmont? You cops need to get your ass over to Iraq and see some real action.' He pronounced it *I-rack*.

Jesse didn't take the bait. He wore the same pleasant expression he always did. 'Don't drop it. Slow. That's it. Just set it right there. Ms Page, please step outside and walk to the cruiser. Parker is going to sniff this one out.'

He nodded toward the car. Parker's head was poking out the back window, black ears standing up like pert triangles.

'Whoa, I am frickin' outta here. I don't do cops. And I don't do dogs.' The FedEx man lit off across the lawn, his Dockers sliding down a few obscene inches.

'Come on out, ma'am.' Jesse reached out a hand. 'Please.'

I hesitated, thinking that my wardrobe wasn't really appropriate for a public walk across the lawn. Mike's old gray pajama pants and a too tight navy sports bra from the B cup era. Bare feet. Bare stomach area. A silver peace-sign toe ring, a going-away gift from Lucy, that I'd just found on the bedroom floor. 'I'm not really dressed . . .'

'It's all right, ma'am. I got sisters. Just head on down the walk with me and get in the passenger side of the car.'

'OK. Do you really think there's a bomb in there?' Pebbles bit into my heels on the stone walk as he urged me forward.

'Your husband's orders, ma'am. Examine all packages that arrive, human or otherwise. Parker here is a sniffer who worked in Iraq with a soldier friend of mine.'

'He seems like . . . a great dog.'

'They don't get better. Parker got a little screwed up after his master died in sniper fire. Survivor's guilt. He couldn't have prevented the shot that took Leonard. They say I couldn't have, either. But neither of us really believe that, so that's our bond. Parker was glued to Leonard's body until the medics dragged him off.'

'Mike told me about your leg. Is that when . . . it happened?'

'Yep, same damn sniper. They let me bring Parker home, and he's worth a lot more than my foot.' He grinned and lifted up the shoe that housed his prosthetic. 'Just can't run the mile in 6:52 anymore.'

I wasn't fooled. Keeping up the patter to distract me. Good guy. *Smart* guy.

'Parker's not official these days because of his breakdown, but I'd count on him more than a

360

posse of ten Clairmont cops.' His face reddened. 'No offense to your husband, ma'am. He wouldn't be one of the ten I'm referring to.'

'No offense taken.'

I moved around to the passenger side while Jesse opened Parker's door. The dog bounded out, straight for the porch. I slid onto the seat, immediately aware that the interior of Jesse's 1992 Hyundai was military pristine. Not a speck of dust on the dashboard. No fast-food wrappers or newspapers or books to entertain him. Jesse's focus was one hundred percent me.

At the door of the house, Parker was sniffing the package. As if it could protect me, I closed my eyes tight, and when I opened them, Parker had already run back to Jesse, who was feeding him a treat.

'Is that good or bad?' I yelled it out, leaning over to the driver's window.

'Good. You can get out. Parker won't move from the package if there's a problem. But if you don't mind, I'd like to open it.'

I had no problem with that. My knees wobbled. I ventured back up the walk, sitting awkwardly on the bottom porch step while Jesse stood about fifty feet away in the side yard turning over the package in his hands.

'It's got a little rattle,' he said. 'The return address is a church.' He slit open the envelope with a pocketknife and pulled out a wad of white tissue paper with the end of a chain dangling from it. I noticed that Jesse was wearing latex gloves.

'Sorry, ma'am, for the interference. This appears to be personal.' He walked closer, handed me the tissue and a small piece of white stationery, and whistled for Parker, who was now doing his business on my crepe myrtle. The two moved together in perfect rhythm toward the car, like the last scene of an old movie right before the credits roll.

I read the note first. Three scribbled names, because I already knew hers, and I knew mine.

Margaret Smith.

Brook Everheart.

Lisa Connors.

Add the two of us and you got Pierce's damaged little sorority of five.

At the bottom Renata had scribbled a short note.

I think you need this more than I do. God bless, R.

It fell into my palm like a trickle of cool water.

I knew without counting that there were exactly fifty-nine amethyst beads.

Renata had sent me her grandmother's rosary.

CHAPTER 30

For the next forty-eight hours, he didn't call. My stalker seemed to have forgotten me. The more he left me alone, the more I felt his presence.

The longer his silence, the louder my brain. I dwelled on ugly things. Misty's scars, the ones on her thighs, so parallel, so perfectly straight, so white, so unlike the random, disfiguring marks of a car accident. The six-inch line between her elbow and wrist. Neat. Precise. The opposite of the jagged fury that ripped Caroline's skin and nicked marks into the bone, like those left by a boy whittling at a stick. Mike told me that.

He postponed the trip to Kentucky. I was slowly suffocating to death in this tiny locked-up box of a house. When I opened the door, an oven of oppressive heat stole my breath. I felt like I was living on the last place on earth, trapped in an Edvard Munch painting with the cast of *Real Housewives*.

Mike was less and less communicative, obsessed, drawing deep inside himself to a place he always assured me I didn't want to go. I'd seen him this way on cases before. He made it home to shower and then passed a hand over my belly, poked his head in Jesse's window, and took off again. I guessed he was catching naps in his vanilla-colored office with the plain vanilla art. I wondered briefly whether he was sleeping with his vanilla-boobed secretary, and then I hated myself for wondering that.

Jesse seemed to need no sleep.

Sometimes for ten hours, my only human contact was with Jesse. We fell into a loose routine. I'd bring him an occasional soda or sandwich, even though he stored a fully loaded cooler in his trunk. Every now and then, he rapped on the door and sprung me from my prison, inviting me along on a walk around the neighborhood with Parker.

I liked Jesse. I liked the smooth youthfulness of his skin, his wide and genuine smile, the easiness of his drawl, the kind core of him. I tried to believe it all, even though his body told a different story. Not the limp. The limp I could barely notice. It was the taut awareness of every muscle. Poised. Ready for something bad. This was a man like my husband, who would never sleep deeply again.

By mid-afternoon on the third day, I worked up the nerve to drive to Misty's house, even though I knew it would infuriate Mike. Jesse nodded when I told him I was going to visit a friend, and turned the key in his ignition. No questions. He knew I was like a bird in a cage.

I justified this journey to myself. I thought my

head would explode if I didn't do something. Mike was getting nowhere he was willing to tell me about. Misty and Caroline were twisted up. The house was proof of that. All the other women I'd met or read about in those files hid secrets that fit into the machinery of a small town. But Misty and Caroline were aliens, like me, who ran from some-place else. It was curious that they were seen together fighting before one of them disappeared. Now one was dead, cut to pieces, while the other walked around with baffling wounds.

I pulled the station wagon up the winding driveway and parked in the mid-afternoon shade by the four-car garage. Jesse drew his car in behind me. The baby rolled around like a pinball against my vital organs.

I knocked, but no one answered. I twisted the knob. Open. I stepped inside. Apparently, I hadn't learned any lessons. I ventured a few feet. The great room furniture was still in place, but the gaping blank space over the fireplace grabbed my eye at once. *The Blue Rider*, missing. The horse had run off. I wondered, for the first time, whether it was one of Caroline's paintings. I involuntarily glanced to the table that held the picture of the little girl. Gone.

'Misty?' Tentative, then louder. 'Misty?'

The house felt the same, an empty movie set, waiting.

At the bottom of the swirling staircase, I hesi-tantly took a step. 'Misty!' My voice hung weighted in place, refusing to float up.

365

I kept climbing. At the top landing, a long, narrow hall led away. Rich, dark mahogany lined the floor. Dramatic black-and-white landscape photographs were carefully spaced on white walls. A couple were leaning against the wall, ready to be hung or packed up. I'd bet on the latter.

The sound of a shower fell like thick white noise somewhere deeper down the hall. A good one that ran hot and fast. I passed two square, empty bedrooms devoid of any furniture. They reminded me of small dance studios. Unmarred wood floors gleamed while dust danced in the patches of sunlight that fell through the casement windows. I walked on, beside rippled fields and surreal white clouds. These works were signed, unlike the photos downstairs. *M.R.*

Misty Rich? Before I had time to truly register this, the shower stopped abruptly, and so did I, two-thirds of the way to the end of the hall.

'Misty. It's Emily. Are you there? Is that you?'

My feet pressed forward until I reached a large room on the left, double the size of the others, clearly the master suite. A queen-sized mattress rested on the floor under giant double picture windows. No headboard, no box spring, and I remembered what Holly had said about mattresses on the floor. The bed was unmade, a soft cream-colored duvet tousled, with matching sheets. A feather pillow imprinted with the shape of a head. Everything was clean and colorless. Misty was the art, and she'd stepped off the canvas.

366

Three empty black suitcases lay open on the floor alongside neatly folded piles of clothes. At least ten pairs of shoes lined the wall opposite the bed. The little girl was here, sitting in her frame, on the floor next to the mattress. She kept company with a cheap travel alarm clock, a small halogen reading lamp, a *Vogue,* a magazine tabloid starring Katie Holmes, and a crossword puzzle book.

Nothing on the white walls in here. Not even nail holes. Just two large windows overlooking the pool, revealing the secret of the infinity edge: a stepped waterfall tirelessly doing its job, recirculating the water.

I had the feeling – no, I *knew* – that this room and the others upstairs hadn't changed much since she'd moved in. Misty never planned to stay. This was all for show.

The doorknob across the room turned, and my heart danced while my mind jabbed at me. My stalker had killed her. He had just washed himself clean of her blood in the hot, fast water. Now his hand was on the knob and that hand was going to kill me, too.

My feet stuck to the floor.

The door opened.

It was Misty, but my heart didn't stop its dance. She wore a short, white terry-cloth robe unbelted, allowing a two-inch, top to bottom view of white skin, bony cleavage, and a small dark patch of pubic hair.

Her body reacted like a startled animal, and she

fumbled for the belt of the robe, trying to gain her composure. She looked impossibly young and innocent, her face scrubbed of any disguise. The big, brown eyes were back. Her short dark hair was wet and wild, vigorously toweled off.

She didn't speak, so I did.

'I'm sorry. I'm so sorry. I didn't mean to . . . scare you. I've been worried. You didn't show at Letty's memorial. You didn't answer your phone. I called out for you on the stairs.' It sounded lame, even to me. I'd only tried to phone once. I'd only let it ring twice.

'Get out,' she said softly. 'I'm leaving. You should, too.'

'Misty, please.'

'You need to go,' she said. 'All of this was a mistake.'

Her eyes were red, glazed, not really focusing. The Misty who chewed her nails stood before me, not the one who twisted flowers in her hair, but, of course, one was just tangled up in the sheets with the other.

'Are you curious, Emily? Is that why you're here? Do you want to see?' I didn't like the way her voice sounded, and something inside me twittered a warning.

Too late.

Her hands tugged at the belt of her robe, opening it wide, and she stretched out her arms like white wings. The sun streamed cheerfully through the window, casting a gold glow on her skin and red tints into her dark hair.

A scarred angel.

I wanted to look away so badly, but I couldn't.

Whatever I'd imagined, it wasn't this.

Faded lines criss-crossed her flat torso, below her small breasts, above the dark patch of pubic hair.

Shallow cuts. Cruel cuts.

Chaotic and methodical at the same time, different shades of white, red, and pink. As if they were done one at a time, with plenty of time to think about them in between.

'Shall I turn around?' She asked it as if she were modeling a dress for the prom.

'No. No. Please.' I rushed over, closed her robe, tied the belt, and hugged her carefully, as if those scars still hurt. It wasn't welcome. She remained stiff, arms at her sides. I stood slightly back, but close enough that her warm breath blew on my cheek.

'If you're not careful, this could happen to you.' She whispered it, and I imagined a man, holding her down. Black bars on the windows. But that's not at all what she was saying.

'I did this.' Her finger almost prayerfully traced a half-moon scar high on her neck, under her ear, one I'd never noticed. 'And this.' She ran a finger-nail down the white line on her wrist. I felt a hot sensation on my arm, in the exact same place, as if she were touching me. 'I was supposed to be watching her that day. I was always supposed to be watching her.'

Mike had seen it. Misty was a cutter. Old scars. New ones. And Misty wasn't finished with herself.

'Who?' I asked wildly. 'Who were you supposed to be watching?'

'We're alike, you and me, Emily. We have different stories, but we're the same. Did you kill your rapist? I can understand if you did. I think about doing it all the time.'

I wasn't sure what she meant. Had she been raped, too? Or was she talking about killing herself? Inside my purse, my cell phone buzzed. Someone, reaching out a hand. My fingers scrambled around for it, never taking my eyes from Misty's, which were trained on me like a loaded weapon ready to go off.

'Hey, Emily.' Mike. Rushed. His at-work persona. 'Where are you?' he asked. 'Never mind. It doesn't matter, if Jesse's with you. Just wanted to let you know that we are flying to Kentucky Friday.' Misty dropped her robe and turned away. More pink and white lines in places I didn't know she could reach. Roads that went nowhere. She leaned over a suitcase and picked up a lacy purple bra. I averted my eyes, ashamed of myself for looking. 'Emily, are you there? Are you mad? Sorry I didn't make it home last night. Things are crazy. I'm here now picking up a few things.'

He was making an overture.

'That's OK.' I cleared my throat. 'Was Caroline's ex upset about her death?' I asked him on purpose, knowing full well that he was going to spring it on Richard Deacon in person.

Misty's head jerked at that like I expected. She angrily finished yanking on jeans and tugged a T-shirt over her head.

'Didn't I tell you?' Mike sounded confused. 'I want to confront him in person. Oh, and we did finally get to the right Todd Rich.'

'And?' I egged him on while Misty began to herd me out of the bedroom, her hand firm on my back.

'He's a man Misty met over a weekend in Vegas six months ago, a blackjack dealer going to law school. They were never married. He claims they slept together once after a night of tequila and slots. He said she insisted on taking a picture. He said he might not even have remembered her if they hadn't bonded over the same last name. She saw it on his name tag. Struck up a conversation. Frankly, he was a shit. Mostly bothered that she wouldn't take off her clothes during sex.' I thought of the framed snapshot of Misty and Todd, that vague feeling it had been taken in Europe. Fake Europe. Las Vegas. I thought that sleazy men like Todd Rich never kept the secrets of the women they slept with unless they forgot them. That they looked so normal until you were alone.

Misty ushered me down the stairs, her body inches from mine. She was leaning in, trying to make out what Mike was saying. I pressed the phone closer to my ear.

371

'We tried to question Misty last night. I asked her to drop by the station. She showed up, but that's about all I can say. She said she hadn't broken any laws and if we were arresting her, she wanted a lawyer. We let her go.'

'Mike, I'll call you later.'

I punched out without saying goodbye. By this time, Misty and I were halfway across the living room on a steady path to the front door.

'Thanks for stopping by,' Misty said with false brightness. One hand shoved me out, the other rested on the door handle. The door was already shutting in my face.

'Misty, I know about Todd.' I blurted it out. I stuck my hand purposefully on the frame so she'd have to make a choice about whether to break my fingers.

'You need to talk to me,' I pleaded. 'I can help. Mike can help. At least call me. Soon. Tomorrow. Before you leave.'

She moved her head slightly, an odd little smile, not a happy one, playing at her lips. *Yes or no?* I couldn't tell. Certainly not a promise.

'Caroline was my last hope.' I could barely hear her. 'I'm never going to know.'

Know what?

The massive door fell forward, like someone had shoved the lid of a coffin. My hand dropped away just in time. The door slammed hard, in my face. I stared at the wild, swirling oak grain, while the lock clicked.

I imagined Misty moving away, soft feet padding across the floor, back to the little girl waiting on the floor.

I wondered whether I would ever see her again.

CHAPTER 31

Three days later.

Nine hundred and fifty-three miles away.

I am staring at a roll of yellow crime tape. Blurry. I can only make out the C.

My body is shivering so violently I wonder whether the baby is going to drop right here onto the cold tile, even with my knees pulled up and shut together tight, my arms wrapped around my belly holding everything in.

Breathe. Don't look at him.

His name is Wayne. I know this, because somebody said, 'Hey, Wayne,' when he brushed by me coming in the door. I had immediately reached out for the wall and slid to the floor. The world had almost gone black, until I focused on the bright yellow circle under a desk.

'Emily, what's wrong?' Mike is kneeling, breathing in my ear. 'Is it the baby? Should we go to the emergency room?'

I shook my head. I'd been in this hell more than once. I needed him to be quiet, so I could time travel, imagine myself three minutes ahead of the moment, like a therapist once suggested. The same therapist who told me that almost every woman hid shame about a sexual encounter before age twenty-five. That they shoved it down, and never told.

Wayne leaned casually against a desk thirty feet from me, hat in hand. I am pretty sure that he knows exactly what is wrong. He isn't about to budge from this room because that's the kind of guy he is. He had touched me on purpose a few minutes ago, extending his arm ever so slightly as he passed so it grazed against my breast.

Most people would see a possible grandfather with slightly scratched wire-frame glasses and a belly that said he still liked to go out occasionally and drink on Friday nights. He might be that. But he is also something else.

I can smell a man who hates women. It is a very specific smell. It is sweet and sweaty and slightly acrid. That is how Wayne smells. Maybe Wayne has raped his wife. Maybe his high school girl-friend in the back of a pickup thirty years ago. He has stayed off the radar.

I can't tell Mike this. It is crazy. Wayne is fifty-five, minimum. He is wearing a Kentucky state trooper uniform. I've never seen him before in my life.

'I can't stay here.' My teeth chattered through the words. 'You have to take me with you.'

Five Kentucky troopers were grouped around us, gauging how this was going to go. Two of them were supposed to drive up the mountain with Mike and provide an introduction to Richard Deacon. Backup. I was supposed to stay here, in this Kentucky state police office hanging off a hill, with Bridget-who-filed-and-made-the-coffee.

Because it was safer.

Bridget brought me a Dixie cup of tepid water and an Oreo. By this time, I was sitting upright in a chair. My hand still wobbled enough that I gave up trying to bring the cup to my mouth. Bridget had draped a washcloth around my neck. It made my teeth click again, so it was hard to listen.

Mike stood within grabbing distance, grilling a trooper named Lloyd who was assigned to take him up to Richard Deacon's house. Waiting for me to recover. Wayne had parked himself at a desk across the room.

'Dickie's not real friendly, but he don't bother anyone,' Lloyd drawled. 'Keeps to hisself. Ain't seen his son for years.'

'His wife, Caroline. Has she been around recently?'

'Nah. Not since she dumped him years ago. Carrie was one of them debutantes in high school. You wouldn't know it to look at him now, but Dickie was a big state football star. Got her pregnant, and her parents set 'em up in that house on Butch Hill. Caroline came to town regular for her Valium. Always wore these real short skirts, like she wanted us to look. Their boy seemed OK, until that little girl went missing.'

Mike didn't react at all to this information, not even a slight twitch. The man could have been telling him where the bathroom was.

Lloyd directed his attention to Wayne, ostensibly concentrating on a computer screen.

'Wayne, weren't you on that case? How old was Dickie's boy back then? Fifteen?'

Wayne grunted affirmation. 'No real proof the boy took her, and he denied every minute of it. Things didn't set right, though. I found a box of knives in his closet. We'd had a rash of pets gone missin' that year, and people came forward to say they'd suspected Wyatt all along. You could tell his parents knew something. The prosecutor got him sent to juvie 'cause of the knives. Right before Carrie run out.'

Lloyd stuck his hat on his head. 'Ready to head up there?'

Mike didn't ask the next, most obvious question.

Instead, he cast his gaze to me, hopeful.

He didn't find what he was searching for in my eyes.

Our rental car climbed steadily at twenty miles an hour up an Appalachian mountain. We were spiraling toward the clouds to the house of the reclusive Richard Deacon, where Caroline had lived her other life.

I had refused to stay behind. I stared out the window now, silent, overwhelmed with guilt. I could feel Mike's anger and empathy punching it out inside him. I wasn't sure which one to root for this time. What could he do? It was all too much. *I* was too much.

An ancient forest hugged us on both sides. The paved road had long ago fallen into disrepair. Every pothole we hit made me think we were about to shimmy off the road and into the kudzu that draped and entwined the trees, determined to swallow the forest one leaf at a time. A blowout, and we'd careen in there, left for dead, strangled by the boa constrictor of green plants. Or, in a best case scenario, we'd have to change a tire on a slant. I pictured the car rolling back as Mike lay flat on the asphalt, struggling with the tools.

None of these awful things happened. The state police car with two troopers inside led the way, and we ascended gradually, rounding blind curves with mere inches between the car and a steep drop-off to a verdant valley of death.

Funny thing: Earlier, Mike had wanted me to stay back at the motel, a retro affair with every-thing original, including the semen stains on the mattress and the grandaddy of all roaches that I met on the end of my toothbrush this morning. I chose, insisted really, to be left at the state police office instead.

'How are you doing, Emily? You look much better.' He squeezed my knee. *Empathy*, I thought, *must have a killer left hook.* 'What are you thinking about?'

'Death,' I replied lightly. 'Semen. Roaches.' Anything but Wayne. 'How do you know Caroline's husband is up there right now?'

'The troopers placed a live-feed camera at the bottom of the hill the day after we found Caroline. Deacon drove in last night around ten in his pickup and hasn't come out. They don't see him in town for months, except when he needs supplies. He's a fan of blue Gatorade. Buys ten cases at a time.'

'What if it's a trap? What if his son, Wyatt, is up there, too?'

'It's a little ironic for you to be worrying about this now, don't you think?' I felt the edge of his anger. So it wasn't a complete knockout. 'No one else has come in or out. We know that Wyatt picked up a wire transfer of two thousand dollars from his dad in Denver six months ago. He maintains no permanent residence, apparently pays cash for everything, and switches cars frequently.'

Mike braked abruptly. The state troopers' car had slowed and was turning right at a dented mailbox almost hidden with fiery-red fall brush. The mailbox had met a drunken teenager wielding a baseball bat out of a car window, more than once.

The road sloped up to the top of a rise and the three-story brick and stone house nestled in the trees conjured up immediate déjà vu. Except for its age, the grime on the windows, and a general unkempt air, it reminded me of a mini-version of the house that Caroline eventually created – or re-created – for herself in Clairmont.

A tall, thin man appeared from behind a tree at the top of the drive, a shotgun gripped in both hands. It wasn't raised, but he was thinking about it. A bright orange cap, faded jeans, black work boots, a week's worth of stubble on his chin. Maybe he'd been hunting. Maybe not.

The trooper parked the car and powered down his window.

'Hey, there, Dickie,' he drawled. Friendly.

'Hi, Lloyd. What can I do for you?' Deacon didn't loosen his hold on the gun. A game of chicken, Kentucky-style.

Mike shoved my head down. Odd, how *this* situation didn't make me shake at all.

The trooper spoke in a lazy, casual tone, as if most of the citizens of Perry County greeted him with their finger on a trigger. 'This law officer behind me has come here all the way from Texas to bring you some news about your ex-wife. He'd like to get out and talk a bit. Probably in the house is best. That means you need to lay that shotgun on the ground.'

'I don't care about that bitch. I want all of you off my property. I got a God-given right to carry this gun.'

'You're sure right about that, Dickie. And it will be right where you left it after y'all talk. What is it? A Remington? Wasn't that your daddy's piece?'

Mike stepped out of the car without his gun drawn.

'Stay down until I get inside the house,' he told me tersely. '*Don't move* from this car.'

'But how will I know . . .' Mike had already shut the car door. I heard his feet crunch on gravel. Two other car doors opened and slammed.

My stomach was already cramping. Logically, I wouldn't be able to see when Mike went inside if my head was crammed at my knees. I rose up slightly and peered over the dashboard. The troopers leaned against the front of their car, arms folded, about ten feet from the old man. Master intimidators since grade school, I'd bet.

Mike was postured a foot away from Richard Deacon, with his hand out, waiting for a hand-shake. It wasn't reciprocated, and Mike lowered his arm, slowly.

'Do you know that your ex-wife, Caroline, was found murdered a week ago?' The first question, he'd told me, was sometimes the single best moment to assess the truth.

I couldn't see Richard Deacon's face, or see him crumple to his knees, but I heard the wail.

If he was faking, he was very good at it.

CHAPTER 32

I stood it as long as I could. My bladder was a
water balloon ready to burst.

Mike had pulled Dickie up, helped him to
the front door, and vanished behind it about
twenty minutes ago.

The troopers settled back in their shiny Dodge
Charger, pretty fancy for Appalachia. The officer
on the passenger side tapped cigarette ash out of
his window every ten seconds or so, while a Garth
Brooks song floated its way back to me.

Pretty nice stereo, too. There was no evidence
either officer figured me to be somebody to protect
or worry about.

I slid out of the car slowly, momentarily drunk
with the smell of fir trees and crisp oxygen. I briefly
considered finding a bush to squat behind. A
pregnant bladder knows no social boundaries. But
I really didn't want to provide a peep show for
Kentucky troopers. One foot had fallen asleep, so
I hopped a little on the way to their car. Lloyd,
the one in the driver's seat, readjusted the rearview
mirror to watch me approach. His deliberate cool-
ness struck me as bad cinematic drama.

His elbow jutted out of the open window.

'Sir,' I said. It was a word that rarely found itself in my mouth, but the South and his Dudley Doright hat inspired it. 'I'm going up there. I need to use the bathroom.' I pointed to my stomach and offered a smile. I felt ridiculous.

His expression said *too much information* and his lips said 'Go ahead,' almost taunting. I waited for him to offer to accompany me. He didn't.

In his low drawl, the *Go ahead* sounded like a dare. I banged three times on the arched oak door with my fist and waited a decent thirty seconds. No response. With a twist of the knob, the door swung open into a vestibule crowded with plastic lawn chairs and dried flower arrangements. A black lawn jockey with chipped paint and exaggerated African American features stood by the staircase, holding a lantern.

I wondered how two Southern-born men could send a pregnant woman in here alone. I was slammed with the powerful odor of mildew. A wide, sweeping staircase lined with the requisite family photos curled upward. I pinched my nose and breathed through my mouth.

To my left, a multithousand-dollar dust-and-cobweb-encrusted crystal chandelier dangled over a room that had abandoned the idea of hosting guests for dinner decades ago. Jumbles of clothes cloaked the floor, reminding me of the ball pit at Chuck E. Cheese, where kids jumped in and vanished. Hell, in this, I could disappear. I didn't

383

want to think about what was nesting underneath all of it.

To my right, it was a different story. The room was full of tidy trash. Recycling bins, with plastic cups and greasy take-out cartons tossed like a salad with empty cans, glass jars, and bottles. At least fifty rolls of unused toilet paper were stacked on the hearth. Yellowing old newspapers and stuffed black garbage bags with zip ties lined one wall. Neat. Compulsive.

The fear of throwing things away. *Disposophobia*, I remembered. A disease immortalized by the legendary Collyer brothers, who'd been found dead in their mess in a Harlem brownstone.

I remembered, too, that the Collyers used booby traps.

Mike's voice carried down the hall from the back of the house. Calm. Pleasant. A husky chuckle, and a snort back from Richard Deacon. My husband, working his magic.

My bladder hurt like hell. I needed to hurry this up and get back to the car before Mike knew I'd left it. I ventured down the hall, past stacks of encyclopedias, scrapbooks, papers, and enough old novels to start a used bookstore. So Richard Deacon was a reader. I glimpsed titles: *Robinson Crusoe, The Great Gatsby, Anna Karenina*. Dead authors. It made me think of Lucy, who read only novels by people who weren't alive.

I found a powder room to the right and flicked the switch. Nope. Bulb out. The hall light dimly spotlighted a blue pedestal sink nearly buried beneath an empty beer bottle, a can of Barbasol shaving cream, a flashlight, and a toothbrush with flattened bristles.

I pressed the button on the flashlight. Nothing. My eyes adjusted. At least it smelled better in here. No toilet paper, however, unless I wanted to make a trip back to the sitting room. On the tank of the toilet, Newt Gingrich's biography and *Miracles: A 52-Week Devotional.* I shut the door with my foot and squatted in absolute darkness, hopefully in the position I'd plotted out. Ironic that I'd just seen a sign in a truck stop bathroom this morning: LADIES, PLEASE REMAIN SEATED FOR THE ENTIRE PERFORMANCE.

Fat chance of that here or there. I wasn't touching a thing if I could help it. Something scuttled across the floor above my head, and I rapidly pulled up my maternity jeans. Thirty-three more pounds to go before they would burst apart.

My head spun a little in the dark. I realized I'd been holding my breath and released it in a ragged hiccup. I flushed and twisted the bathroom doorknob, using my sleeve. The door ran smack into Mike. Richard Deacon stood just a few steps behind him.

'What the hell are you doing?' Mike demanded.

'What does it look like I'm doing?'

'I asked you to wait in the car.'

'You didn't hear me knock?' Caroline's ex was much better up close. A decaying Daniel Craig in a fishing shirt from Goodwill. Once, a match for a debutante. 'I'm Mike's wife, Emily.' I slid into a deferential twang. 'Thank you so much for letting me use your powder room.'

'No problem at all, ma'am. I'm just embarrassed the place isn't a little better kept up for a lady. You might be noticin' my limp. No more climbin' poles for Kentucky Power. Live on disability. Would you like to come on back to the kitchen with us for a Tab?' Not so Daniel Craig-y. But polite.

Mike glared at me.

'Sure,' I said.

The spotless kitchen was completely unexpected. A gleaming avocado-green refrigerator and matching gas stove. Basic spices – garlic salt, minced onion, black pepper – lined up on the back ledge. An old, still-white Formica counter with a neat row of canned Del Monte green beans, shoepeg corn, and Le Sueur peas. A scrubbed yellow linoleum floor. A small kitchen table that reminded me of my grandmother's.

'This is where I live most the time. I sleep in the back bedroom. Hardly ever make it upstairs. Them roof rats are havin' a heyday up there.'

He set an ice-cold can of Tab in front of me before returning to the refrigerator. Instead of opening it, he reached up for a ceramic cookie jar shaped like a black cat, perched on top. He placed the jar gingerly in front of Mike.

'Mike and I were about to get to what's inside

here. I never wanted to turn on my son. He's my blood. But after gettin' to know Mike here a little, I feel that God led him up the mountain. Go on, open it.'

Mike carefully pulled off the head of the grinning cat. Inside, I could see what looked like a curled stash of papers.

'Go on, take 'em out. Ma'am, you might not want to look.' I watched Mike hesitate, no doubt wondering whether to touch them. Evidence. He slipped his forefinger and thumb inside and delicately pinched them out. I caught a glimpse of the one on top, right before the papers snapped back into a roll. The drawing of a prostrate body. Crude. Childish. Red. Red. Red.

'It makes me want to throw up, too,' Dickie apologized. 'This here's some of Wyatt's drawings after Caroline left us. I've been wanting to give these to the police ever since I was saved in the Motel 6 swimming pool a couple years ago.' Saved. *Baptized.* 'I'm going to wash my hands of Wyatt now and give him to the Lord.'

'Do you have a large Ziploc bag, Dickie?' Mike was frowning at the pages. 'I think it's better if I examine these drawings somewhere else. I appreciate your cooperation.'

'Sure, sure.' Dickie reached into a drawer. 'I feel bad. I thought I'd feel less guilty. I just feel more guilty.' Eyes shiny. Wet.

Dickie wasn't quite what I expected. More sympathetic. 'I was a . . . friend of Caroline's,' I said impulsively. 'I'd love to see those pictures on the staircase. We held a small memorial for her the other day and we had no mementoes of her past to display. Do you mind?'

'Sure, ma'am. Let's take a look. I never understood why Caroline didn't take those pictures with her. Guess she was in such a damn hurry. Haven't thought about them in years.'

Dickie led me to the staircase. Mike followed, holding his Ziploc bag of grisly drawings and staring a burning hole into my back. I began to climb the steps slowly, wondering why this had seemed like a good idea. It was impossible to see the details of the photos arrayed on the walls. The dust was so thick it appeared to be squares of brown woven cloth.

'Here.' Dickie tossed me a grimy T-shirt retrieved from the dining room floor. 'That should help clear things up.'

I caught it, deciding to be grateful that he threw me a shirt and not his underwear. I dusted off the first picture. A charcoal rendering of a young Caroline and a baby. She held the infant awkwardly, or else the artist was a novice, still inept at sketching human shapes. Arms are notoriously hard to draw.

I moved up a step, took another tentative swipe, sneezed, and uncovered the actual photograph used for the painting in Caroline's dining room, the one of her astride the horse. Every detail of the painting seemed identical. Had she been photographed at her parents' place? How far from here was that? I couldn't remember whether Mike said, just that it was essentially an estate.

Another step. The next three pictures recorded a boy growing up. Surely Wyatt, Caroline and Richard's son. A boy whose life would make perfect fodder for that dysfunctional modern fiction that Lucy so hated.

At two or three, Wyatt seemed impish, normal, unaware of anything worse than a transient wasp sting, posed in that silly way professionals insist on, leaning forward, two hands under his chin. A baby pinup.

At nine or ten, the blue eyes and blond hair were going dark, the nose sharpening, the smile not quite reaching his eyes. He gripped a wriggling dachshund puppy with about as much affection as his mother held him with, two pictures down. Maybe he'd wanted a less wimpy dog and more normal parents.

The next photo leapt several years ahead. I leaned in to see the writing etched in the corner with black pen. *Wyatt, 14.* Close to the time he'd been sent to the juvenile detention center. Tall for his age, a cut-off shirt baring lean muscles, jeans riding low, a hand-rolled cigarette dangling out of his mouth. Appalachian cool.

Wyatt was not classically good-looking, but cocky and magnetic and rife with hormones. The kind of guy who scared the shit out of me. He looked as if he knew I was on the other side of the glass and could yank me right into his world. His choice, always, not mine. I reminded myself he was alive somewhere on *this* side of the glass and approaching middle age, probably with a prescription for Crestor.

I fluffed the shirt at a few more pictures of dead ancestors before turning abruptly and bumping into Mike.

'Careful,' he warned, grasping my arm. In my ear, he whispered, 'We're leaving. *Now.*'

Richard Deacon was nowhere in sight.

'Where the hell did he go?' Mike muttered under his breath.

A wavery apparition appeared in a square patch of sunlight on the floor below. Mike instantly, firmly, placed one palm on the back of my neck, ever alert, ready to push me out of the way. His other hand, I knew, was on his holster.

Dickie emerged from the hallway.

'You can have this,' he told me, holding a fat photo album. 'To show her friends.'

I stepped onto the landing, and Dickie nervously thrust out the album, like maybe I wouldn't want it. I couldn't tell what color the album was, for all of the dust and age. Maybe green. Maybe not. My fingers grasped the edges, because it would have been rude not to.

A few gold letters broke through: *AM* and *BUM*. Perfect.

'Caroline kept up her picture albums and diaries pretty good. I used to say to her, "Nobody could have that much to say about hisself." She always told me I had ruint her dreams about being a writer or a movie star. Anyway, I don't want it back. I'm washin' myself of her, too.'

A pale brown spider was traveling up and over the corner of the album, on a speedy route to my hand. Mike caught the album in the air as I let it go, flicking the spider to the floor and crushing it with the heel of his boot.

Mike stuck out his hand to Dickie, and this time it was caught in a firm grip.

'When you find our son, you'll let me know?' Dickie asked, his eyes, the ones Caroline once stared into, still wet with tears.

'You'll be my first call.'

CHAPTER 33

I t was ninety minutes from Richard Deacon's place to the home of Caroline's sister. The tail end of the drive played out like a dreamy film reel of red and gold leaves, graceful horses, and white fences that stretched over rolling land into foggy infinity.

I knew it had been a stupid move to walk into Dickie's house on my own. I should have risked the chiggers and spiders and poison ivy and the possibility of mooning two strangers. Those troopers probably examined bare asses every night in the local strip joint and wouldn't think mine was anything special.

But Mike's mind was apparently not on me as we swept down the mountain curves. At the bottom, where the two-lane highway began, Mike pulled in at the Kitty Cat Quik Mart for gas. We had already checked out of The Mountain Motel, a place I never needed to see again.

The proprietor, a heavyset man who kept hiking up his pants, cheerfully pointed me to a bathroom that seemed like Shangri-La. There was plenty of light and soap. So what if the water was like ice and I had to shake my hands dry? At the counter, at my request, the owner obligingly gave me a few plastic bags and a large rubber band to package up the grimy photo album destined for the overhead compartment on the plane.

Mike had thoroughly brushed it off, and my fingers itched to explore the pages. Both of us had recognized the spider. A brown recluse, the kind that prefers to live in the dark, like vampires. His bite didn't hurt much at all. You died later, when the poison ate through your skin and ran around in your blood. Long after the eight-legged killer had retreated to dust and shadows.

The album, though, was stubbornly clinging to its mysteries. Prying open its pages was going to be a delicate, painstaking process. Definitely not a job for the car. The photographs were sandwiched between cheap, plastic sticky sheets popular before scrapbooking became a designer sport, the ones that yellowed and then melted the pictures to them. All the pages were stuck together. It was as if the book had been dunked in water, then broiled in the oven to a fine crisp.

Back on the road again, after prying off my shoes and tossing back my virgin swig of chocolate Yoo-hoo, I asked: 'Are you going to make me beg for details?' I tipped the drink again. Not bad. And fifteen percent calcium.

'No. You just seemed happy for a while there, so I didn't bug you. What do you want to know?' Mike's voice was easy.

'Your cop instinct about Dickie.'

'Depressed. Accommodating. Edgy.'

I wasn't in the mood to play. 'You didn't say *murderer.*'

'No, I didn't. As for the missing little girl, his story doesn't veer far from what Billie and the local cops told me. She disappeared from her poor mountain family. Not unusual in an area with so much poverty and desperation. But Wyatt was seen with her before she vanished.' So, Mike had known about the little girl before we got here. From Billie, the relentless digger.

The air was getting chillier, inside and out. I punched the heater button obsessively until the digital numbers read 80.

'Dickie said that Caroline paid off the family and local police to let it go. He assured me that whatever happened to the little girl was likely an accident. Claims the details are fuzzy because he was drunk all the time back then. That Caroline took off and didn't contact him – or Wyatt, as far as he knew – for almost twenty years. She did agree in the divorce decree to pay for their son's boarding school. After juvie.'

'All that would encourage a little resentment in a kid, even if he wasn't evil,' I pointed out. 'And especially if he was. I'd draw ugly pictures, too.'

'We'll see,' Mike said noncommittally. 'There are only two official incident reports on Wyatt before the little girl disappeared. Swiping some cigarettes from the Shell station. And an illegal road race ten miles out of town.'

'So you think Dickie is telling the truth?'

Mike shrugged. 'I don't know. He admits to drinking whiskey from his own still since puberty. That would fry a few brain cells. He credits his refrigerator full of Tab, grape Nehi, and blue Gatorade for his alcoholic recovery.'

I used a comb to slowly rip through my hair, tangled by the wind into stubborn knots on the ride down the mountain. 'They never found the little girl? The one who went missing?'

'No.' Mike eased on the brakes as a car whipped in front of us.

'I've been wondering whether Billie learned anything else about Misty.'

Just throwing it out there. We were both connecting a few crazy dots. Mike glanced over, unsure, like he didn't want to tell me something.

'I sent a couple of cops there for a drive-by yesterday. Misty's not answering her phone or door. A neighbor saw her dragging a few boxes to her car. We're working on getting a search warrant. One judge is on vacation, the other likes to see blood dripping out the windows before authorizing a search.' He tapped the heat back down to 73. 'I didn't tell you I was planning on a search because you seem attached to Misty. I didn't want you to warn her.' He glanced at me sharply. 'I still don't.'

He had every reason to worry about this.

He seemed relieved that I had nothing to say. I simply nodded.

I wanted him to search.

We learned within the first five minutes of meeting Caroline's sister why they looked absolutely nothing alike.

The woman who motioned us to sit down in her royally purple and blue brocaded living room was red-haired, bone thin, and bitterly confident that her rank in life was several notches above us.

'Caroline was adopted,' Sophia Browning told us. They were the first words out of her mouth after *Come on in*. She waved away a uniformed maid who set down a pitcher of raspberry iced tea that belonged on the cover of *Southern Living*. At least that part ran in the family.

'I'm not that surprised she ended up this way. Caroline had *psychological* problems.' She smiled at Mike, bringing to life ugly creases around her eyes and mouth. An enormous square-cut emerald hung loosely on a skeletal finger, poised to fall down a kitchen drain if Sophia Browning ever deigned to stand over one. Maroon fingernail polish startled translucent white skin, making me think of Dracula's bride.

'I heard from some woman in your town yesterday. Was it Libby? No, maybe she said she was Patty. Her last name escapes me. Anyway, she wants to handle the funeral arrangements. Claims to be a descendant of General Lee. She seemed to think that qualified her to be the one in charge of Caroline's burial. I told her to go right ahead. You know what, I think I'm going to need a real drink. Would you like one?'

Mike shook his head. Did Letty trace Caroline to Sophia on her own? Or had she known all along?

'The tea is delicious,' I ventured. Tarted up with lemon mint, sweet but not too sweet, three plump raspberries resting at the bottom of the glass.

'Taluhlah! Bring me my afternoon delight!' Sophia yelled it out, uncrossing toothpick legs, swallowed up in gray linen slacks. 'Gin and tonic,' she informed us. 'I thought I could wait, but I didn't realize this was going to be quite so hard on me.'

As far as I could tell, the conversation wasn't the slightest bit hard on her. Sophia seemed to be thoroughly enjoying herself. Her eyes wandered over Mike, predatory. 'I suppose you want to hear *all* about Caroline.'

'Anything you can tell me could be useful in finding her killer,' Mike said.

'I doubt that. I haven't seen her since the reading of Daddy's will. A fifty-fifty split.' Venom laced her voice. 'My parents died young. Daddy passed from a spell with cancer. Mama fell off a horse the year after and got pneumonia recuperating in bed.'

'I'm sorry,' Mike murmured. 'How old was Caroline when they adopted her?'

'Four, almost five. She was already set in concrete, everybody warned them. Daddy toured an orphanage in Lexington as part of a church elder event. He complained about going but when he spotted Caroline, he had to have her, just like one of his horses. Daddy was a compulsive collector. Caroline wasn't by any means a purebred, but she was a pretty little thing with a tragic story.'

The maid slipped back into the room with the 'afternoon delight,' and she offered me a half smile, which I returned.

'Thank you, Taluhlah.' Sophia removed a thick crystal tumbler off a tray weighed down by a decanter of gin, a half-empty bottle of tonic, a china plate of lime wedges, and a fresh pack of Marlboro Lights, the brand of choice for super-models and, apparently, rich Kentucky anorexics. 'Just leave the tray, Lula. I hope you've got the chicken on for supper. Mister wants to eat at five.'

'Yes, ma'am.'

I felt like I'd fallen back in time. Sophia eagerly resumed her story. 'Caroline came from the mountains. Her family's little lean-to burned up, killing her baby sister and her mother. Caroline's real daddy had fallen asleep with a Lucky Strike in his mouth – but, of course, he lived to tell, like all drunks do. He dumped Caroline in an orphanage with second-degree burns on her feet that hadn't been treated. My daddy spent a pretty penny on her plastic surgery at Duke.'

Sophia pulled the first cigarette out of the pack on the tray, removed an engraved silver lighter from her pocket, and lit up.

'Mama wasn't too happy about the idea of

adopting, but once she realized it wouldn't be any more work for her, that our maid Aida could just raise Caroline, too, she bought in. As long as she could go right back to her drinking and socializing, Mama was OK with it. My parents liked to show off what fine people they were, and Caroline was their long-shot Kentucky Derby horse. The little Appalachian girl they turned into a winner. They even set up a painting of her in the front hall and threw a cocktail party under it every year to raise money for orphans. Obscene really. Daddy told me while they hung it that she looked more blue-blood than I did.'

I used the armrest to push myself out of the deep-feather couch cushions and wandered over to the window. I was struggling to fit these pieces of Caroline with the others, while staring out at a back veranda supported by white colonial-style columns as big around as my current waistline, *Gone with the Wind*–style. The fields spread out before me, lush and green, perfectly groomed by cattle and horses better fed than most of the children in this county.

Mike glanced at his watch. Sophia jangled the ice in her empty glass, then poured herself another. Our plane left in three hours and an hour's drive stretched ahead of us. Mike had thought my feminine presence might loosen up Sophia, but he'd guessed wrong. She barely acknowledged I was in the room and seemed plenty loose already.

'Am I going too slow for you, Chief Page?' she

drawled. Her tongue might as well have been in his ear.

'Not at all,' he said. 'We have plenty of time. You were saying that Caroline had problems.'

'Yes. Caroline was a little off. At night in bed, she used to whisper to her dead sister, the one who burned up. And she always wrote like a fiend in those stupid diaries of hers. I stole one once and she near about went insane. My parents didn't pay attention, but Aida worried about her. Told her to stop living in her head or people would think she wasn't right and she'd get sent back.'

Sophia took a measured puff on the cigarette, exhaling coolly. I sat back down beside Mike, and she stared at my pregnant belly, annoyed, as if I might give birth all over her Persian rug.

'She straightened up a little.' Sophia blew another smoke stream at the ceiling. 'We had a good couple of years around fifteen, sixteen. We were only a year apart. Both of us made high school cheer-leader. Then she met Dickie, got pregnant, and her little life went up in flames again.'

'Why Dickie?' I couldn't hold back any longer. 'Wasn't it clear the kind of boy he was?'

'Oh, honey. It was *perfectly* clear.' She tossed her head back so the wrinkles melted into her skin. Sophia had never been beautiful, I was sure, but she had been coy, and that is enough for horny teenage males. 'Every girl in school wanted to taste that fire. Didn't you ever want a dangerous boy?'

She glanced slyly at Mike, then back at me. 'It

didn't hurt that Dickie knew how to catch a football and run all the way to Tennessee. He had a real shot at getting out. An Ohio State football scholarship. But he was set on getting into Caroline's pants. Told her they were alike deep down. Called her Sweet Caroline. Swore he was the only one who truly loved her. That might have been true, although, like I said, Aida had kind of a fondness for her. Caroline followed Dickie like a lost dog. And if you're wondering, I know most of this because I read it in her diaries.'

'So she married him and moved out at what . . . sixteen?'

I admired Mike's single-minded focus. I tried not to let my loathing for Sophia show.

'Yes, sixteen, almost seventeen. My parents built them that house near Hazard. They didn't disown Caroline, but they had an unspoken agreement she wasn't to come back. Reputation was everything to Mama. And, after all, Caroline wasn't blood. I think they saw the little bastard once, on his first birthday. Mama and Daddy mailed them a monthly check, and Christmas presents in a big box, all of 'em bought and wrapped by Aida.' Her eyes narrowed. 'I will say, the fifty-fifty split on the estate was a bit of a shock to me. Daddy's guilt money, I suppose. After the reading of the will, I didn't hear anything about Caroline for two years, until that little bastard of hers was connected to that missing girl. I've tried to stay as far away from that mess as possible. I heard she divorced

Dickie and moved to Texas. Now you guys show up after she's butchered to death. Not a fairy tale, is it?'

'I appreciate your time and straightforwardness.' Mike placed his hand on my knee, my clue that we were done here. Almost. 'Is there anything else you think I should know before taking off?'

Sophia leaned in closer. She'd been waiting for this. Her face was ugly with pleasure.

'I did see Daddy sneaking out of Caroline's bedroom late at night more than a few times.' She stubbed her cigarette in the flesh of a lime and, smirking, met Mike's eyes. 'I guess we'll never know, will we? I mean, whether her baby was Dickie's or Daddy's.'

It was the shocker she intended, even for Mike, whose shoulders tightened.

A trapped princess. A jealous sister. An ogre. No locks on the bedroom door. Who said this wasn't a fairy tale?

I tried not to picture Caroline as a child, with a sweet face and scarred feet, lying in bed every night, waiting to be raped.

One true thing rose up in my mind.

Caroline hadn't lied to me.

Her sister, her real sister, was dead. She died in a fire.

Mike snored and the baby tossed fitfully, leaving me to stare at the cracks in Mrs Drury's ceiling that reminded me of Sophia Browning's blueblood veins. I was home again, in the time it would take to watch a TV movie of the week.

I wondered how Mike could possibly sleep. In the morning, as soon as he left, I threw on some stretchy workout clothes, backed the station wagon out of the garage, waved to Jesse parked out front, and drove the ten minutes to Misty's house. As Jesse had pulled out behind me, I realized there was something unspoken between us, that he wasn't reporting my every movement.

I knew in my heart that she was gone, but I had to see for myself. I rolled to a stop at the curb. All the clues were there. Tall windows now black and shiny and uninviting. Three newspapers abandoned in the driveway. A yellow flyer already wedged in the door handle. The grass a hair too long.

Less than a week. How little time it took for a house to lose its spirit.

Where did you run, Misty? What is your story?

After several seconds, I shifted the car into gear. My mind was already jumping ahead to Caroline's photo album, still tightly wrapped up in white plastic bags and rubber bands. Lying on the kitchen table, waiting for me.

CHAPTER 34

My surgical instruments lay strewn across the table: an X-ACTO knife, an old butter knife, a sponge, and a small cereal bowl of warm, soapy water. I wiped the cover gently with a wrung-out sponge, revealing burgundy-colored plastic stamped with a fake leather grain. The words *FAMILY ALBUM* were almost worn off.

I ran the butter knife lightly under the three edges of the first page. So far, so good. In fact, that page opened fairly easily. My heart sank. Blank. I took a hit of mildew up my nose, then moved the knife to the second sheet.

This required a bit more negotiating, but I was rewarded with two black-and-white pictures of the same scene, different angles. An attractive couple and a girl in an old-fashioned frilly dress posed with a muscular Thoroughbred horse. The reins were held by a jockey about the same height as the girl. I recognized the girl as Caroline and her early, graceful handwriting underneath: *Kentucky Derby with Mama & Daddy.*

It was the first time I'd seen Caroline's father. I rubbed my thumb over his face, unsuccessfully trying to bring a picture blurry with age into better focus. He didn't strike me as a monster who would ask unspeakable things of a little girl; but then, isn't that exactly why most monsters succeed? This predator hid under handsome features, graying hair, and the hauteur that clings to the wealthy. Even if he didn't rape Caroline, he helped destroy her. His wife was a striking, fit woman who looked like she'd be comfortable riding either beast in the picture. The horse, or her husband.

The next seven or eight pages reflected a timeline of photographic technology and Caroline's privileged post-adoption childhood. Her parents owned a colonial-style mansion, eerily similar to Sophia's, plunked in the middle of a sprawling wonderland of grazing Thoroughbreds.

In one shot, their four barns were dressed with giant evergreen wreaths and twinkling white lights, every one of them nicer than almost every house I'd seen near Hazard.

Caroline had been launched from here onto another planet. Hazard was a depressing display of poverty and hopelessness, lawns littered like junkyards. It was hard to understand decent human beings banishing anyone to Hazard, especially a scared, pregnant sixteen-year-old.

But these were the early, quasi-happy times, and Caroline dashed off a few notes to record them.

The Christmas I got Izzie!!! under an image of Caroline and a gentle-looking horse with black socks.

My Best Friend, beneath a shot of a teenage Caroline and a grinning girl in a striped halter. They shared a hammock hung between giant oaks, their hair in French braids they'd probably fixed for each other.

I had almost reached the end of the album. Not a whisper that Sophia lived on the earth, much less in the same house.

The next page abruptly thrust me onto planet Hazard.

Baby pictures of Wyatt. Random, placed at careless angles, some merely thrown in, loose. No sentimental footnotes. A color Polaroid of a blasé Caroline and Dickie together on a plaid blanket by an open picnic basket, one of Dickie's hands a little too high on her thigh, a beer in the other. Caroline's eyes were dulled, too. Maybe she'd already made friends with Valium. A baby was crawling unattended off the corner of the blanket. I wondered who snapped the shot.

Sophia was right about one thing. The young Dickie oozed a lazy, James Dean sexuality. After flipping through more pages, I halted at the scene of a backyard birthday party. Someone had made a halfhearted effort with balloons and streamers. A grocery store birthday cake with thick, sugary icing sat on a picnic table, surrounded by a small tumble of presents. I counted thirteen candles.

Wyatt's face shone with genuine happiness, so much so that I felt an immediate, warm connection, which I pushed away. The boy stood in the center of a group of ten kids of varying heights and ages. Caroline posed reluctantly on the end, a few awkward feet from the children, wearing a flowered sundress with an apron. Her haggard face was blank, unsmiling.

I peered closer. I wiped the corner of the sponge over one of the tiny faces under the plastic sheet.

The smile, the curly blond hair, and the glow of her personality were unmistakable. The little girl under my finger was the same as the one in the framed picture in Misty's house.

It is the happiest day of my life, Misty had said about that picture in her great room, after snatching it out of my hands.

My eyes skipped quickly over the other faces. I stopped short at an older girl, about ten, her dark, stringy hair pulled in a ponytail. Petite. Harlequin face. In short shorts and a halter. Sunburned. Underfed. Mosquito bites ran up her bare legs and arms. No scars. Not yet.

The happiest day of my life. I'd misunderstood. But I knew for sure now. The little girl in that picture wasn't Misty.

I stared at the little blond girl. She was a little younger here. *Who are you? Are you the girl who disappeared?* She remained stubbornly silent, stuck in time, leaning into Wyatt Deacon, his arm draped over her shoulders, as if this were the most comfortable, safe place in the world. My eyes moved back over to Misty.

Misty, Caroline, Wyatt.

The little girl.
All linked from the very beginning.

Icy water dribbled in little rivers down my back, the old pipes cranky from a couple of days of disuse. They needed more time to heat up and get going than I had the patience for right now.

I had called Mike immediately. Things were happening.

As I soaped up with a bar of Ivory, my hand traveling over my newly protruding belly button bump, the old snapshot of Misty and the little girl was wending its way over the fax to the FBI in Louisville.

No messing with the local cops this time. Within three hours, the FBI would be knocking on doors and businesses to find out who they were. I sat down awkwardly in the cold tub, shivering, running the shower wand across my front and over my shoulders, a process that grew more difficult as I enlarged and battled an ever-changing center of gravity. My naked, swelling body was still a strange sight to me. I wondered without caring how much of this would be permanent: the widening hips and stomach, the flattening feet.

My eyes focused on the crosses formed by the lines of the tile grout. A grade-school nun had taught us to look for a cross at any moment of despair or worry. Windowpanes, electricity poles, fence posts. Once you began to look, crosses were everywhere. I sent up a prayer, for me, for Mike, for Misty, for Caroline, who didn't deserve to die that way, and for the smiling girl in the picture who probably never grew up.

No, I told Mike on the phone, there weren't any names written on the back of the photograph. Yes, I was sure it was the same girl. No, I hadn't heard from Misty. Yes, I was fine. Just fine. No need to worry about me.

I braced my hand on the edge of the tub as I stepped out, my feet slippery on the slick tile. I dried off with a faded blue-striped beach towel, the only one that now comfortably fit around me.

All at once, my brain felt drugged. A thin white cotton robe hung on the hook of the back door; it took all my effort to tie it around me and hang up the towel in its place.

I didn't feel like making dinner anymore, especially a solo one, but I wandered that direction, down the hall, to the kitchen, aimlessly opening and closing the refrigerator, the pantry, the freezer. The answering phone light blinked like a warning signal.

'*You have one unplayed message,*' a computer voice intoned before Jesse's voice rushed into the room.

'*Mrs Page, my niece had a seizure at a track meet in Nocona and my aunt can't get to the hospital as fast as I can. She's diabetic. My niece, I mean. She's already doing fine, but my aunt's on the edge of a stroke she's so worried no family is with her. I've got someone filling in for me here in about an hour, but don't leave the house without phoning the chief to make sure the new guy's in place, OK? The chief said you turn off your phone when you take a nap, that's why you aren't answering the cell.'*

I was instantly filled with concern for Jesse's niece. And then I started to giggle. This was just like the kind of movie I watched through my fingers. The lookout, misdirected. The girl in the underwear with the big breasts abandoned to her bloody fate. In my case, I wasn't wearing any underwear under the robe, and Letty said my breasts weren't that impressive. That made me laugh harder. I plopped down on a kitchen chair, gasping for air, tears running down my cheeks.

I stumbled out of the chair into the living room, and yanked up the window blind.

A cruiser sat comfortably at the curb, directly in the path of the front walk, its occupant reading a newspaper. Maybe not as vigilant as Jesse, but I wasn't alone.

Reinforcements already in place. Mike wouldn't leave me unprotected. My chest relaxed a little. My breathing slowed. Still raspy, but more normal.

I wish I could see what was gunning for me. The face. The weapon.

My rubbery legs made it to the kitchen sink. I promptly threw up. Bending my neck under the faucet, I let the cool water wash my face and run into my mouth. I sloshed it around and spit out the bitterness.

What to do now? I glanced at the clock on the microwave. A little past five. Mike wouldn't make it home before midnight, I bet.

I moved over to the desk and popped open my laptop, reassured to see the butt of my gun still peeking out of Mrs Drury's cubbyhole. I pulled the laptop out of its niche and powered it on. I deleted junk mail, read a nonsensical note from Lucy about a very bad date with a Saudi Arabian oil magnate, and a mass email from Letty inviting five hundred people to a memorial planned for Caroline next month. She requested we each bring a white balloon and recommended we buy them at the Albertsons on Highway 36, where she'd set up a group discount.

I was about to shut down the computer, when another email popped up.

Bhell@mojo.net.

Subject line: *Keebler Elf Unmasked.*

Something from my witty reporter friend Brad, with an attachment. He was thinking of me at this very moment. In a way, technology was so intimate.

Emily,

Left a message on your cell that I was sending this old picture of Avery Crane. Got it from a yearbook. Is he the man who impersonated me? He's the frat bro who was so forthcoming about Pierce's girlfriends. I've also included a current shot of him from his work profile. I've tried to get in touch with him, but he won't return my calls. I also wanted to let you know that Crane

*lives nearby, in Euless. He transferred there
several years ago. Life's a strange bitch, huh?*

*Hope all is well with you and the baby.
Brad*

My finger clicked on the attachment and, in
seconds, I stared numbly at the first picture of
Avery Crane. It was a posed fraternity-album
headshot of him in the requisite red tie and blue
jacket and plastered-on smile. I scrolled down
slowly and scrutinized the second image. Less hair,
the edge of a double chin, a smoother complexion.
A brief work biography offered up his job title, a
director of Global Services, followed by a list of
bullshit qualifications for 'team-building.'

His office: Mobile.

His location: Dallas/Fort Worth.

Forty-five miles away.

Life's a strange bitch.

*Fate is a compass inside us that takes our feet where
they need to go.*

Brad's words. My mother's words. Saying the
same, ominous thing.

I closed out of the attachment, hit 'reply,' typed
a single word answer, and punched 'send.'

Yes.

Yes, it was Avery Crane who accosted me that
day on campus, years ago. I shut the lid of the
laptop a little harder than necessary, not wanting
to chat further with Brad, a man whose agenda

was questionable. Not to think about the Keebler Elf, an hour's drive away. It must be a lie. I double-checked on the cruiser out front. Still there. Just as I started to twist the blinds shut, the cop turned his profile, and my stomach flipped. The new man on duty was none other than Cody Hill, the jerk who interviewed me after Caroline's disappearance. Maria's nemesis. *Rojo.*

The phone rang, jangly and intrusive. I don't remember crossing over to the receiver, but I found it in my hand.

'*What is it, you son of a bitch?*'

Silence.

'Emily, it's me.'

Mike.

'Are you OK?'

'Why did you pick *him* to watch over me?' I demanded, a little too shrilly.

'He's decent at what he does, Emily.'

Decent.

'Did you just call to check on me? I'm perfectly fine.'

'Uh-huh, you *sound* fine. Yes, I called to check on you. I also wanted to let you know the FBI hit the jackpot in Peggy's Salon in Hazard. The old girls napping under the hair dryers were only too happy to talk. Misty's sister is the blond child in the photo. The girl who went missing, the one connected to Wyatt Deacon. She was eight when she disappeared. Dirt poor. Misty got out of there as soon as she graduated high school. Was accepted at Berea, changed her last name, and never looked back.'

'Berea?'

'A college in Kentucky that takes in promising kids, mostly from Appalachia, no tuition required. Transforms their lives.' Where Misty was reborn, I realized, into someone who could fool me.

'We learned something else. Do you remember that Dickie wired money across the country to Wyatt?'

'Yes.'

'In every one of those towns on Dickie's list, two or three days after he wired the money, a little girl disappeared.'

I let this sink in, feeling sick.

I knew the answer, but I asked anyway.

'What did you say the girl's name was?'

'I don't think I did. It's Alice.'

Present tense. My decent, hopeful man.

Alice.

The name scribbled on the back of a fortune, the sweet face held hostage in a frame at Misty's. The girl at the birthday party with her killer's arm draped around her shoulders.

CHAPTER 35

I woke to darkness, reassured to see Mike's curled-up shape under the quilt next to me. The digital numbers on the clock reported that it was only 9:31.

I'd switched off the lamp at eight, as soon as my eyes blurred the words of last Sunday's *Times* book section. Reading on Mike's iPad always made me sleepy. It took about ten minutes before I shut it down, sunk into the pillow, and drifted off.

Mike must be as exhausted as I was to go to bed this early, probably more. And I had been so deeply asleep I hadn't even heard him come in.

Misty's face floated in my mind, a wisp of cotton candy. Her last name, Rich. Her childhood, poor beyond my imagining. I juggled myself over to face Mike, edging closer to spoon his back as closely as I could, the baby lodged between us. I didn't want to wake up either of them.

As soon as my hand fell across his waist, I knew.

Mike's body was built like a treacherous mountain, every muscle and crevice familiar to me.

This wasn't Mike.

This guy, this stranger in my bed, was like a taut rubber band.

I forced down the scream in my throat.

Was I dreaming? Finally, really losing it?

This had to be one of those wild nightmares that pregnant women everywhere were so familiar with. A dream within a dream.

I slowly rolled myself away, heart trip-hammering, desperate not to disturb the lump beside me just in case, desperate to pinch myself awake. I could feel my fingers squeezing my skin.

Too late.

In one swift movement, he grabbed my shoulders and shoved me down on my back. He slung himself on top of me. He bore his full weight painfully on my legs, assuring me that this was no dream.

For a second, I knew it was Pierce, who'd clawed his way out of hell. It was so strangely quiet as he hung over me. Just the squeak of the mattress as I flailed uselessly, a clumsy pregnant woman.

'Please. *Please.*' No response.

Then I screamed.

For Cody Hill, the obnoxious *rojo* who was supposed to be protecting me, for a neighbor, for anyone who could hear through the thick old walls of this house.

He was stuffing something thick and cottony in my mouth. A sock? I tried not to panic. To surrender, because breathing was important. I smelled lemons. Caroline was washed in something citrusy before she died. Or maybe after. Like it mattered at which point in the process she was washed. Or which particular killer was tying me up. My old stalker, or Caroline's.

So dark in here, like I was resting on the bottom of the ocean.

Swim toward the light.

Flick, flick, flick.

I knew that sound. Fingernail against plastic.

I had heard the same sound in Gretchen's office.

He leaned over, his chest tight against my belly. I slung myself up and grabbed for his eyes, snagging rough fabric.

A mask.

'Wyatt, why—?' My words were lost, suffocated.

He plunged the syringe into my arm.

CHAPTER 36

My little girl is running. Down the hill. As fast as she can. Calling for me.

I am reaching out my hand to touch her; instead, I touch the chill, gritty floor.

A hammer is pounding in my brain. Chemical fumes stinging my nose. My legs feel like they are not attached to me. I am aware of the world but can't see it. My consciousness is pushing slowly to the surface. I make out shapes.

Squares.

Boxes.

The man is busying himself in front of a vertical rectangle of gray light.

The sound of a sprinkler system spitting on and off.

Where am I? Not dead. Not raped.

I don't dare move, but I'm frantic to get a better view of my prison.

This couldn't be.

The sunroom.

My sunroom.

It wasn't a sprinkler system. The monster was

spray-painting the windows black, and he'd almost finished the job.

Before I could determine if my location was a good or bad omen for survival, something nudged my back.

The gag stifled my scream.

The monster worked at the window while the finger tickled my back, making circular motions.

Three of us.

Maybe this was his partner. Or vice versa – the man who plunged in the needle was behind me, and *his* partner was at the window. I steeled my body not to respond.

What if the thing behind me had a weapon? What if they were both just waiting for me to wake up to more fully enjoy themselves?

What if this rubbing thing on my back was a sexual prelude?

I fought down nausea, tried to calm my mind and remain perfectly still, watching the natural light and my hope disappear with each pass of the spray can. The finger continued to whirl away on my back.

Mike had been so careful for years, through every pregnancy, not to let me paint or change kitty litter, or touch any substance that could leach its way into my womb. And here I was, in an unventilated area with a sociopathic painter, and the fumes flooding my nose were the least of my worries.

Letters.

The finger was making letters.

Spelling something.

Rubbing it away with one pass of the hand, then starting over.

A game from elementary school days. I'd been good at this when I was little, when Robin, my Barbie friend, and I would lie on her bed and write silly messages on each other's backs. We graduated to the Helen Keller game, where we shut our eyes and signed into each other's hands.

The finger drew again, more insistently, a nail digging into my back.

The first letter was *N*.

No, *M*.

The second letter, *i*, the finger painfully punctuating the dot. The third letter was a snake. Easy. And then I knew. *Misty.* She kept going. Spelling her name. Rubbing it out. Spelling it again.

'Shit.' The man threw the can across the room, where it clattered against the wall. Instantly, the hand on my back stilled.

He'd run out of paint while working on the last window, black only half of the way down. He stalked purposefully toward us, and I squeezed my eyes shut, my heart twitching in my throat like a dying bird. He shined the blinding beam of a flashlight in my face and nudged my leg roughly with his foot. I kept my body limp, dead. He thrust a swift kick at something behind me. A groan. Misty. I felt a rush of guilt for thanking God that he kicked her instead of my baby.

'You girls have a nice time,' he said. 'I've got a few things to do.'

That voice. It was the same, but different.

The sunroom door slammed and the deadbolt shot into place, the extra-sturdy kind I'd wanted to make sure nothing could get out.

Misty, not moving.

My eyes, heavy, unable to stay open.

It didn't seem like this was the memory that should be bearing down on me. But there it was, running a loop in my brain. Four years after the rape, in a security line at the airport. Two men. Pierce's roommate, Haywood. And a thinner, older version. His father.

I stared. The older man nodded politely. His son stood two feet from me and pretended I did not exist, even though he'd heard me that night. He'd *heard* me.

I'd heard him, too. I'd heard his feet hit the floor when he slid off the top bunk. Saw the streak of light when he opened the door, and black when he quietly shut it. That was the moment I stopped fighting Pierce.

That was the moment I gave up.

Still curled on my side. A sharp pain shooting down my back. Eyes open, legs like lead. Unsure what was real. The man with the needle. The man at the window. If Misty was lying behind me. Any of it, none of it.

The room spun. I closed my eyes, the boxes and

blackened windows imprinted on my eyelids like a sick light show.

The sunroom door burst open, all those little panes of glass shaking and trembling. I opened my eyes.

He wore a black Nike T-shirt and black shorts. His legs were long, and lean. A runner's. I imagined them pumping up and down Appalachian hills. He was freakishly strong, wiry muscle formed by hard labor, not sculpted at a twenty-four-hour gym. Why hadn't I seen this before?

His mask was gone.

So were the scruff and the limp.

He didn't care anymore if I knew.

He wasn't the son.

He was the father.

CHAPTER 37

Richard Deacon stared at me clinically, like I was a butterfly he wasn't sure was pretty enough to put under glass. The small camping lantern he set on a box cast hideous shadows on the walls.

He knelt and rested his hand on my stomach, gently.

My breath snagged.

'Caroline got pregnant again.' His hand began to rub a circle. 'I bet she didn't tell you that. On the way out the door, she threw it in my face. That she'd killed my child. She aborted *my* child in *my* town.'

He bent over me, and whispered to Misty. I couldn't hear what he said, but her whimper sliced me like a knife. His arm was inches from my face, while his hand was busy with Misty behind me. I could smell the dank sweat of his armpit. See the black hair growing over a purple bruise near his wrist. Maybe Misty had fought back.

He was wearing a watch with a glowing digital readout. Not an ordinary watch. An expensive GPS runner's watch. It told me it was 12:43 a.m.

Another set of numbers was ticking down minutes and seconds. Mike carried a similar watch, in that black backpack.

'Misty and Caroline, Caroline and Misty. Deciding to give a damn after twenty years.' He straightened. 'I'm making a nice little surprise for your husband, Emily. Y'all are all going to heaven today.'

My mind was growing more alert; my body, still a beanbag.

'Don't make a sound.'

He shut the door, taking most of the light with him.

The moon straggled through the only patch of unpainted glass.

Lie still.

Don't make a sound.

Why was the house so silent? My body, so numb? What was he doing? How much time had passed?

Windows painted shut. Lock on the door.

Don't make a sound.

I floated like one of the clouds in Misty's glass house.

Over mountains. Trees.

Italy.

My parents' car accident.

The girl in that frat house bedroom.

Helpless. Pinned. Confused.

History, repeating.

★   ★   ★

I used my foot, the one tingling, to kick backward. To nudge her, wake her up. But she was already awake.

'I'm . . . sorry about your baby,' she said dully.

'What is he *doing*?' I spat out the words, angry. At her, for sounding helpless. At Dickie. At God.

'He has Alice.'

She's alive?

'I just wanted Caroline and Dickie to tell me *where*. Where their son took my sister. Where they have been hiding him. I love Alice so much.' She choked on a sob.

'Misty, we need to get out of here.' Trying not to scream it, urging my limp body to *move*.

'I didn't think Dickie would recognize me after twenty years.' Misty's voice trembled. 'I told him I was a photographer. That I wanted to take pictures on his land. Lies, so I could search that hill for her.'

'Can you move?' I asked. Impatient. Seconds escaping.

No response from Misty.

I pushed myself up a little. The moon had risen. Its yellow gleam shone near the windows, spotlighting a broken antique lamp of my mother's and an array of half-unpacked boxes. I could see the head of a blue stuffed dinosaur sticking out of one of them. Make out Mike's Sharpie scribble: *Baby's Room*.

My eyes traveled over the crib sheets, bottles, and Pampers stacked in a laundry basket in the corner.

A baby monitor, a shower gift, sat on the floor nearby. Brand-new, out of its packaging.

'Misty,' I said shakily, 'I think I'm going to pass out again.'

I watched the doorknob turn.

I scrambled back in slow, painful motion, against the wall, dragging Misty with me.

Dickie, with his lamp, bringing light. The receiver to the baby monitor in his other hand.

'I thought I told you *not to make a sound.*'

Listening to us. Getting off on our fear.

Dickie, at play.

Lying beside me in my bed. Cigars, and messages in the mirror.

I thought that Pierce was the worst that could happen to me. But this was worse. Because, this time, I should have *known.*

This man leering over me was not the hick with the shotgun that I met in that schizophrenic house, the guy with the loose Wrangler jeans, the old fishing shirt, the burned-out brain cells, and the limp that bought him disability. This man was the manipulative, smart athlete that Caroline fell in love with. He had played into every stereotype, and I'd bought every second of the performance.

'Please don't hurt my baby,' I begged, hating myself for it.

'Well, your husband should have thought of that. I lost mine.'

He stood over me, placing his black running shoe lightly on my belly. Pressing.

I kept my breath even.

'Not yet.' He removed his foot, glancing at his watch. 'Not yet.'

He moved to the other side of the room, kicking a box out of the way.

Now or never, I told myself.

Dickie stood near the windows, his back turned.

I pushed myself up, using the wall.

I was going to go out standing.

Make him feel something. Mike's voice in my head, urging me.

'But there were some . . . good times, right?' I stuttered. 'When you and Wyatt wore matching eye patches for Halloween? The trip you took to Dollywood? The picnics? The Christmas you gave Caroline the white dress?'

Dickie flipped around. Red-faced. Pissed.

'How do you know all that shit?' His mouth shifted into a knowing grin. 'Caroline told you. Did she also tell you I ripped that pretty white dress off her on Christmas night? She scrubbed and scrubbed, but couldn't get the blood out.'

I couldn't stop the hot, bitter hatred flooding into my face. 'Caroline didn't tell me, you asshole. You handed those pictures to me, pictures of your life you probably never bothered to look at once. *Pictures* that Caroline wished were *real.*'

I ventured a step, staggered. It took everything in me to remain upright.

427

'I don't know what you got in mind, Mrs Page, but come on over,' he jeered lazily. 'We can relive a few good times Caroline and I had in the bedroom.'

My fingers closed around the X-ACTO knife clutched at my side, the one I'd pulled out of my art supply box minutes before Dickie twisted the doorknob. Seconds after I saw the monitor sitting on the box I'd never unpacked.

The tiny green light glowing *on*.

Did he buy my lie over that monitor? That I was blacking out?

I would go for his throat. It wouldn't kill him, but I'd never let myself be a victim again.

'*No!*' Misty's shriek pierced the room. She threw herself forward. We were falling together, the knife clattering to the floor. '*He hasn't told me where Alice is.*'

Misty, sobbing. The skittering sound of the knife flying across the floor.

Dickie tugged a black remote from the pocket of his shorts. Placed his finger on the button.

I'm sorry, Mike. I love you so much. I tried.

I felt and heard the explosion simultaneously.

Icy fragments raining down on me like sleet, a torrent of hot air.

I tried.

Why don't I feel any pain?

'What the . . .' Dickie muttered.

The second shot drilled a small black hole in his left temple.

Dickie lurched sideways and fell, dead in a single, perfect second. I stared, disbelieving, at the window that he hadn't finished painting. It was shattered, wide open to the night and to a red bouffant wig with a mouth.

'I don't think I can fit through here, although I'm on the point system now.' Letty peered inside the room, lowering a rifle with a telescopic sight. 'I ate one of those Outback Bloomin' Onions today. Do you know there's fifty-six points in one of those? That's a lot of damn points.'

She wafted the rifle through the window in the general area of the dead Dickie. I prayed her finger wasn't on the trigger. 'He's an ugly-ass sum-bitch, as my grandaddy used to say. I would have got him with the first shot if I had my Recon 550. To be honest, I was aiming for his knee. I almost got a bead on him through the picture window a few minutes ago, but he lowered the blinds right as I got him in my crosshairs. I still kind of wondered at that point whether you were kidnapped or having an affair. But he looked sketchy. What's that blue shit on his tongue?'

Dickie's head rested in a glistening pool of blood, his tongue hanging like a lazy blue lizard. The ugly sum-bitch I'd thought looked a little like Daniel Craig.

'Gatorade.' My lips formed the word, but I'm not sure sound came out.

'What? Oh, never mind. You two are a damn mess.' Letty squinted at us critically from her perch. 'Y'all *really* owe me now. I'm kind of down in the dumps after filing the divorce papers. Do you know Harry's set up house in Phoenix with that Mexican maid? With my daddy's money? Says she's his *soul mate*. Bet it's blow jobs for breakfast, lunch, and dinner.'

The sound of sirens floated through the window, sweet music.

Letty tugged at her lopsided wig.

'Harry loses total brain function when there's a mouth on his penis. Not that I've ever provided that service for him. I told him right from the start, pageant girls don't do that.'

Letty is at the window.

Her red wig is bobbing in the moonlight. She is impossibly beautiful.

Misty is reciting something, but I cannot understand her.

My eyes land on the sunroom's French door, and the crosses formed by the molding. On the old, faded comic strips that Mrs Drury had pasted to each pane, the yellowed glue in the corners.

Dagwood and Blondie, Dennis the Menace, Calvin and Hobbes.

Misty and me, lying in a bed of shattered glass and a monster's blood.

Guernica in my own house.

'Emily, say something if you're awake,' Letty commanded. 'Misty, stop gibbering.'

'Something.' I croaked it out.

Letty had resumed her perch at the window after calling the Clairmont police to pass on the 'situation' and my warning that the house might be rigged to blow.

'Those sirens we heard were goin' the other way,' Letty informed us. 'I heard Cody was supposed to be watching your house, but I saw him in the Whataburger drive-through after my midnight workout at Cute Chubby Girls and he sure as hell wasn't here when I pulled up. By the way, the operator says your husband should be arriving any sec. She told me to hang out with you and keep you awake. Told me not to touch the house again. That's why I'm standing on this lawn chair a foot away, kind of shouting. It's going to take thirty minutes for the bomb squad copter to get here from Dallas. You need new lawn chairs. This one's crap. Don't forget the cops don't want you to move. You listening?'

'I need new lawn chairs.'

'Lucky I dropped by. I decided it was as good a time as any to stick a personal reminder invitation to Caroline's memorial service in your mailbox since you hadn't been polite enough to RSVP. I go up to the mailbox, put my ear to the door, and ask myself, *Why is Emily using power tools at midnight?* My spidey sense was tingling. I got my Ruger out of my trunk, and here we are.'

Letty's patter was constant, ludicrous, breathtakingly soothing.

I don't remember passing out, only coming to in Mike's arms.

Mike and Jesse unrigged an explosive on the back door and carried Misty and me to the waiting ambulance long before a bomb squad helicopter landed on our little suburban street. I'm pretty sure it scared off all of Mrs Drury's ghosts for good.

CHAPTER 38

Ten days later, the FBI exhumed the bodies of four girls from the wooded hill behind Dickie Deacon's place. One of the first bodies was almost certainly that of Alice, age eight, buried in a clearing near the top, four feet off a ragged path.

Misty identified the ring with an orange plastic gem that they dug out with the third set of bones. Her sister had won two rings in a gumball machine that final summer and never took them off. Alice had insisted they were lucky.

On the third story of Dickie's house, the FBI found these things: a nicely appointed bedroom with a satellite flat-screen TV, a master bathroom with twenty jars of lemon bath salts, an industrial washer and dryer, a closet of high-tech hunting gear and surveillance equipment, unopened Amazon boxes packed with stuffed animals, a portfolio of horrible, amateurish drawings of Caroline, and a museum-like room dedicated to Dickie's trophies and fading football jerseys. I know there was more in that house on the hill, but Mike refused to tell me about it. Search teams had settled in at the

Best Western, planning on wrestling the kudzu and mud on that hill for months.

The worst day for me was when they found Wyatt. Dug from a shallow grave in a horse stall in the crumbling barn behind Dickie's house. Forensic investigators estimated his age at death to be between eighteen and nineteen. His preliminary DNA test did not match Richard Deacon's. He'd been strangled to death, like all the little girls.

It left us to wonder: Did Dickie *know* that Wyatt wasn't his son? Sophia Browning has said through her fortress of lawyers that she won't in a million years offer her DNA for comparison. She's fighting an exhumation of her father.

Mike reminds me that in every terrible case, there would always be questions. The absolute truth dies with the victim. Mike says he just imagines the scenario that makes him happiest. I imagine that Wyatt found out about Alice and died trying to avenge her.

Dickie had told everyone that his no-good son had taken off, and everyone believed him. The official theory is that he wired money to himself around the country, picking it up in Wyatt's name, in case anyone ever got wise to his lifestyle or too curious about what happened to his missing son. A dead man on the run is easy to blame.

A few nights ago, Mike and I watched some old football film of Dickie in a state high school playoff game. The film canister arrived at the front door by UPS, in an anonymous brown cardboard box addressed to Mike, the number *88* drawn in Sharpie where the return address should have been.

No soundtrack. We watched every grainy moment.

In the final seconds of the game, the ball was soaring across the field, a Hail Mary pass. No. 88 leapt in the air, his hands reaching up for the impossible ball like a prayer to the gods.

It is hard to square that magnificent moment of grace with the man who, in some odd ritual that made sense only to him, washed his ex-wife in homemade bath salts before he murdered her. Liza Beth Tucker sold eight varieties of bath salts at her gas station in Hazard. She told police that Dickie bought a six-month supply of the lemon salts at a time. He told her his wife liked them, even though Liza Beth knew that his wife had left him years ago.

When serial killer fanatics found out about the bath salts – the kind of loonies who collect famous murderers' cards the way kids collect baseball cards – they ordered so much of the stuff by phone that Liza Beth set up an Internet site. The home page claims her products 'are original recipes loaded with healing properties from the salt dug out of a genuine Kentucky mine.'

If you order the lemon bath salts and pay an extra $5.95, she'll send you a small bag of dirt from Dickie's property and an overhead helicopter shot of his place, with hand-drawn X's where the bodies were discovered. I'd bet the salt is Morton's and the earth is from Liza Beth's own backyard.

What can I say? People are sick.

CHAPTER 39

I didn't think she'd show.

She held the strings of three dancing white balloons. Her filmy pale blue dress melted into a big sky of skittering clouds. She stood in a carpet of red leaves, about a hundred yards apart from the group of mourners. Her head was slightly turned, fighting the wind. Impressionistic. A Monet. A picture of Misty that almost wasn't painted.

Misty had tracked her way to Dickie's hill months ago, looking for her sister, twenty years after she disappeared. Dickie recognized her, and kicked her off. He didn't kill her then, but Misty had set her fate in motion. Her fate, Caroline's fate, *my* fate.

Those weren't roof rats over my head in Dickie's bathroom. It was Misty, hoping I'd hear, a fact I can't think about too much. After months of stalking, Dickie had grabbed Misty on the last night in the glass house. The day after she shut the door in my face. He trucked her back to the hill and planned to kill and bury her there, until Mike and I drove up. We apparently inspired him to a more apocalyptic fury.

Dickie spent a good deal of time on the road in the last month, tracking back and forth between his house in Kentucky and a motel in Fort Worth where he paid a monthly rate. A search of his room turned up prepaid cell phones and a scratch pad scribbled with the name and number of one of the security clones who worked on our house. It still isn't clear where Caroline died, or whether Dickie ever brought her back to the house where they began their story.

Misty had promised to come back and say goodbye, I just didn't expect her to do it today, at Caroline's second memorial. I stared past her, across the open ranchland, a beautiful piece of property owned by the Lee family trust. Letty had deemed it the appropriate place to scatter Caroline's ashes. It was turning out to be a simple, beautiful service, in part because Letty's Baptist reverend had gently encouraged her not to speak or sing. About two hundred people, a little prayer, a harp, a good strong wind that would carry the ashes, and not a word about how Caroline died.

I could see Lucinda's floppy black funeral hat in the back of the crowd. She'd lost the baby and left her bad-tempered husband three weeks ago. She stood near Holly and Tiffany, who had tied their balloons to their Gucci bags and linked their arms. I realized Caroline's club would go on without her, a crippled, handicapped centipede. My mother had liked centipedes. She said they were misunderstood.

When it was time, I let the string slip out of my fingers and turned to watch Misty. I didn't have to ask why there were three.

Alice. Wyatt. Caroline.

Rising together. Misty's head craned up until they mingled with the hundreds of other balloons sailing into the clouds. Then her eyes settled on me. Eight months pregnant, I was not too easy to miss.

'Give me a minute, OK?' I asked Mike.

He nodded, as people headed back to their cars, lined up on the dirt road behind us.

I hadn't seen Misty for six weeks. We'd exchanged a couple of brief emails and one stilted phone call about her sister Alice's burial. Misty had been recuperating in Kansas City, at a wonderful place that seeks to heal both the wounds of the body and the mind. When a serial killer's siege on my house exploded on the Internet, Renata was one of the first people to call my hospital room. She hooked Misty up with the clinic and the renowned psychiatrist who had treated her years ago after her rape and suicide attempt.

Misty and I met halfway across the grass. She held the picture of Alice in her hand, out of the prison of its frame. This time, I saw details: the plastic jewels on both fingers, the grape Kool-Aid around her lips, the crooked middle tooth.

Misty gave me a quick hug, a relief. I wasn't sure how she really felt about us. A friendship forged out of deception and guilt and redemption.

She was still bony, still recovering. A tiny silver cross hung where the encrusted dollar sign used to. No makeup. Her eyes, brown, like the first time.

'Everyone in my group therapy thinks I need to lock this picture away forever,' she told me. *For-evah.* I could hear the twang now, just the tiniest echo. 'They all agreed that it is holding me back. But I decided to give Alice one more outing. We buried her a week ago today. By my mother and father. I wish you could have been there.'

'Me, too.' Mike and Gretchen had laid down the law. No traveling.

She glanced at the photo. 'About a year ago, my aunt found this and mailed it to me. Out of the blue. I was sure it was Alice begging me to find her. A fever took over me, although truthfully, I can't remember ever *not* being angry. But what's the saying? "While seeking revenge, dig two graves, one for yourself."'

'Douglas Horton,' I replied. 'The guy who also famously taught thousands of teenage girls the fallacy that if you love something set it free.' Trying to sound light, not quite succeeding. 'I'm really surprised you're here, Misty. Mourning Caroline.'

'Not mourning exactly. Trying to forgive, maybe. After Dickie wouldn't help, I tried Caroline. It was almost like she'd been waiting for me. Like it was a *relief* to see me when I landed at her door. Begged me to stay so that we could work on finding Alice together. Put me up in that fortress of a house, paid for private investigators, said she'd make Dickie tell us where Wyatt was. Said not to say who I was or why I was there, of course, and told me to invent something about my past. Asked me to join her stupid club so people wouldn't ask questions if they saw us together. All of this, ostensibly to protect me from Wyatt. But Wyatt was nowhere. By the time I realized how off-balance Caroline was, it was too late to back out. Of course, I'm not one to talk about being off-balance.' She laughed softly. 'I hated lying to you, Emily.'

I nodded. 'Do you think she knew what happened to her son?'

'I like to think she didn't. That she was sincere about that, at least. I heard her make one of the calls to Dickie, telling him about the private investigator she hired. I do believe Caroline kept horrible secrets about him. Maybe she finally let Dickie know she couldn't keep them anymore. I try to look back and see all the things I must have missed when I was a kid. Wyatt's crappy life seemed so much better than my crappy life.' Her mouth twisted. 'This town. I stepped into it and went crazier than I already was. If it's any consolation, I'm on a new path. Renata's psychiatrist . . . *my* psychiatrist . . . says I have all the tools to become a highly functioning dysfunctional. And your gallery friend called. Wants to set up a show of my photographs. She says people will come because of my ugly past, but that I'll be successful because I'm good.'

'You *are* good,' I told her. 'And your photographs are stunning.'

'Not good like you. Not good like Wyatt. Emily, you *fought* that bastard. You came to my house that day, risked your life, to make sure I was OK. You're *still* helping me, after I went nuts and very nearly got your baby killed. Then there's Wyatt – he used his allowance to buy Alice and me food. Still, I didn't believe him when he told me he fixed Alice's bike tire, and she rode off. Wyatt looked guilty. Probably because he knew who was.'

I had to ask, even though I wasn't sure I wanted the answer. 'Why did Dickie obsess on me?'

'He saw you at the party, that first night. He was making plans to take Caroline.' Misty hesitated. 'He told me that you reminded him of her. When she was young. In the beginning.'

I was right. I didn't want to hear.

'You brought a friend.' I pointed to a tall, lanky figure in conversation with Mike by the car.

'Joe. He's a Kansas City cop. His wife died two years ago of cancer. We met on the plane on my way to the clinic. A lucky coincidence that they reassigned his seat.'

Fate is a compass.

Mike called him The Candy Man.

He was young and fresh-faced in blue scrubs, still cute and macho even with the medical shower cap, and when he slipped the epidural needle into my back after twelve hours of labor, I wanted to

442

give him everything I had except my newborn child.

Two weeks late, I was ready to pop, although our baby seemed perfectly happy to settle inside me for life. Reasonable really, considering what was out here. Every ultrasound, every test declared that he was still perfect.

My eyes roved over a six-foot-tall giraffe created, entirely by Letty's hand, out of diapers. Letty herself was camped in the waiting room, explaining some kind of vending-machine diet to a hostage crowd that included Holly and Lucinda. They had packed our refrigerator with food last night. Go figure.

Our baby had a name now. Adam. Middle name Lee, in Letty's honor. We made this decision with full knowledge that this fixed Letty to our lives forever, no matter how far we eventually traveled from Clairmont, Texas.

'I have something that might take your mind off the pain.' Mike held a plain brown manila envelope. I flinched. I knew the ugliness contained in innocent-looking envelopes.

'What is it?' My heart beeped faster, triggering an annoying sound effect from the heart monitor.

'I tracked down your little girl. I called in a favor from an FBI buddy. He faxed it today. I was going to give it to you tonight. I just didn't count on you going into labor. Honestly, I didn't think Adam was ever coming out.' He just said it, flat-out, like it was no big deal. I stared at him in disbelief, thinking he shouldn't have done it, shouldn't have involved the FBI. I fought this emotion with the one that wanted to tear the envelope out of his hand. I watched a contraction start its rise on the monitor, feeling nothing. The Candy Man had done his job.

'Just tell me.' I squeezed my eyes shut, then opened them. 'No, wait. Is this really the right time?'

'I've thought about that for the last twelve hours. I think it's the perfect time. Her name is Natalia.'

It was out. I couldn't make him put it back in. *Natalia.*

'Pretty.' My eyes blurred with tears. 'They picked a pretty name.'

'She was adopted at five weeks. Lives in Rome with her parents and two older brothers. Her father is a professor. Her mother, a journalist.'

Safe.

'She appears to have a very happy life,' he said. 'Her parents are well respected.'

'I don't want to mess that up.' I meant it. All these years, fearing she was dead or homeless, hungry or abused. Wanting to fling my arms around her and say *sorry, sorry, sorry.*

My eyes found the cross at the end of the bed, formed by the railing.

I watched my belly tighten under the soft blue gown, swelling again like a thing apart from me. Adam, working harder. I imagined him swimming, pushing his way through an underwater cave.

No other choice but to brave the surface.

CHAPTER 40

I hesitated at the door of a small 1970s ranch-style house.

It was planted in the middle of a nondescript middle-class neighborhood in the Fort Worth suburb of Euless – or 'Useless,' as the lady at the 7-Eleven joked when I stopped for a bottle of water.

A pot of pink geraniums on the stoop. Neatly trimmed bushes. A garden hose curled like a snake into a perfect circle.

Once again, walking up to the lair of a killer.

I considered turning on my heels and driving straight back to Adam. When I left him an hour ago, he was listening to Billie singing about the farmer in the dell.

But I knocked, and the door opened. Two men stood there, holding hands. One of them I recognized, even though he'd had work done on his nose.

Avery Crane stuck out his hand. I took it, thirteen years after he accosted me on the Windsor campus. He'd been redrawn since then. The tiny nose flared wider, the work of a competent plastic surgeon.

Still slim, but shoulders broader, like he'd met a weight set. Furtive eyes behind expensive, black rectangular frames.

'This is my partner, Dan. He's also my lawyer. Dan's going to sit with us while we talk.'

I pointed to the car at the curb. 'That's Jesse. My bodyguard. If I don't come out in twenty minutes, he comes in. You don't want him to come in.'

Avery nodded as if this were a perfectly acceptable arrangement.

The inside décor contrasted sharply with the outdoor shell. Track lighting, high-quality furniture on black hardwoods, edgy sculptures, and wall art from years of trolling gallery nights with a discerning eye.

We passed down a dark narrow hall to a small kitchen, which had been updated as much as possible without gutting the thing. Granite countertops, stainless appliances. Two huge, friendly black dogs pressed their noses against a sliding glass door that opened to a manicured lawn. Identical sets of keys with Mercedes remotes hung on two hooks by the back door. His and His.

Dan pulled out a chair at the table, one I'd seen in the latest IKEA catalog, and gently scooted me in. He oozed nice guy. Protector. I'm an expert in those.

'I did it.' Avery pushed his glasses up on his nose. His hands fluttered like nervous doves, trying to figure out where to settle. 'I killed Pierce. I'm sorry I tried to redirect the blame to you and the

446

other girls. I wasn't . . . well.' His face relaxed slightly. 'I've been waiting to say that for a long time. I think I'm a changed person now.'

'You are changed,' Dan said, like a faithful therapist.

Avery had given no hint of a confession in our short conversation on the phone, although he understood exactly why I was coming.

'That day . . . I accosted you . . . I was desperate to find out what the police knew. I made this big show with my fraternity brothers about all I was doing to find Pierce's killer so they wouldn't suspect me. It was stupid. They never thought for one moment that someone like me would have the guts.'

Dan placed his hand in the small of Avery's back. 'Tell her what happened.'

'I know.' I didn't want him to have to say it. 'Pierce raped you, too.'

A familiar expression crossed Avery's face, one I'd seen in my mirror.

'All the pledges got maps at midnight. The last three to arrive at the destination point had to clean the toilets in the house for the rest of the year, so nobody wanted to lose. Except everybody else's map ended up at IHOP. Mine led to a dark corner of the city park, where he was waiting.'

Dan gripped Avery's hand tighter. I noticed matching wedding bands with turquoise stones.

'I hadn't even acknowledged to myself that I was gay. But *he* knew.'

'You don't know what he knew,' Dan protested.

'It wasn't about sex. It was about power. How many times do I have to tell you that?'

'He made it clear that it would happen again, as many times as he wanted it. That otherwise he was going to tell everyone I was gay. My parents. I'd be blackballed. I let him rape me twice more after that.'

Avery's body was limp, resigned. 'I'm not making excuses. Just explaining.'

Dan's eyes pleaded with me. 'He thinks he has to turn himself in. Ever since that reporter from New York showed up.'

'Brad?' I asked.

'Yes, he interviewed Avery. He called back to say he wasn't going to write a story, but Avery thinks it's inevitable. He's a damn reporter. I say wait and see. It doesn't do anybody any good at this point. Pierce's parents weren't exactly looking for the truth. Besides, Pierce's mother died a month ago of a stroke.'

'She did? Elizabeth Martin? Are you sure?'

'I don't remember her name,' he said. 'The reporter told us. He'd been running searches on everyone related to the case.'

Elizabeth Martin, dead.

My first stalker, I was sure.

Three weeks ago, I had pulled out Renata's scribbled list of names and dialed up the other women raped by Pierce Martin at Windsor University. At least the ones I knew about. Lisa Connors Johnston, the pre-med student, was now a stem cell researcher at the University of Michigan. Margaret Smith Yodel, the yogi, ran a night shelter in downtown Cincinnati.

Both of them willing, even eager, to talk when I called. Brook Everheart had messaged me her number through Facebook, cheerfully declaring herself 'just a mom.' Not one of them had received a single threatening letter over the years. I was more certain than ever that Pierce's mother had channeled all her rage at me, the girl she'd encountered at the casket. She'd probably gone into the ground denying the truth about her son.

'You're looking to me for redemption?' I asked Avery, disbelieving.

He was such a sad little man, and I don't think anything – not a loving partner, not a hundred years of therapy, not paying for his sins in prison, and certainly not my forgiveness – would ever change that.

But I could give him something.

'Don't you dare turn yourself in.' I stood up to go, suddenly overcome with an intense longing to hold Adam. 'He never would have stopped.'

'See,' Dan told Avery. 'That's exactly what that reporter said.'

EPILOGUE

Not very often, I have a bad day.

I hear something on the news that reminds me. Of little girls lying in the dark, and running down hills as fast as their legs can, riding off on shiny, new bikes and standing at birthday parties with the arm of their killer's son draped around their shoulders. Little girls who do not know what terrible things await them.

Of women lying on concrete floors and in the biting gravel of alleys, in soft beds and in fragrant, grassy parks, wondering how this could ever happen to them. How they could be careless enough to let that much hate and loathing and evil find its way into such an ordinary, safe life.

Of men with black hearts, making their plans for tonight or tomorrow or the next day. College boys who will spot a shy, pretty girl in the library and sit down beside her. Casual dates who will push that extra martini or glass of wine. Husbands who will slip into fresh sheets beside a terrorized wife pretending to be asleep.

I'm at the park under an ancient, leafy tree. Adam is in the stroller, wrapped in a pale yellow blanket, waving a fist at the sun spying at him through the leaves, catching the first breaths of spring, his mouth a perfect little O.

Today is a good day.

Still, I want to shout at the woman running by in pink jogging shorts, and the one tying her little boy's shoe.

Tell your girls. Tell them, tell them, tell them.

Tell them to fight and scratch and yell his name. Tell them not to be ashamed. To break the necklace of women who've kept their rapist's secret *because they know him.* Grandmothers and mothers, daughters and sisters, aunts and best friends. Century after century, decade after decade, year after year. Heartbeat after heartbeat.

In my hand, I hold a brush. I think of my own little girl, a rose that grew in a violent storm. Marked, some would say, from the moment of conception. On my good days and my bad ones, I choose to believe something different.

An easel is propped in front of me. My brush lingers over the canvas, stroking her hair, brown like mine. I curve her lips into a smile, sharpen the point of the steeple that rises behind her. I throw gold into the sky, green onto the earth under her feet.

I know I will never convince myself she is safe, until she tells me so.

My little girl is not running. She stands on the hill, waiting.

★   ★   ★

Hundreds of miles away, at the edge of a Kentucky forest, he's watching.

She's barely visible, playing an elaborate game of pretend under the sheets blowing on her mother's clothesline. She'll turn five tomorrow.

He sweeps low, dropping a gift at her feet.

A plastic ring.

It is old and dirty, but she can see the promise of a little sparkle underneath. She slips it on her finger and scrambles up, waving, as the crow soars higher and higher into the clouds, an inky smudge, until he disappears.

AUTHOR'S NOTE

When I sat down to write *Lie Still*, I had no idea that the first sentence Emily spoke would be about a rape in college that haunts her. I didn't know that this book would take me to uncomfortable places inside myself. That I would learn how much 'date rape' or 'acquaintance rape' is misunderstood, and how lasting are its effects. As I was putting the finishing touches on this book, two Congressional candidates confirmed that wild misperceptions about this crime are still alive, one by suggesting that a woman's body is able to reject a 'legitimate rape' pregnancy. I'd like to thank those men for bringing such ignorance about rape to the forefront (and the voters who kept them out of Washington).

Along those lines, my own knowledge was boosted by journalist Tim Madigan, who wrote a three-part series in the *Fort Worth Star-Telegram* last year debunking the myths of acquaintance rape. I'm also grateful to his sources, who are doing such excellent work in this area: sex crimes expert Russell Strand; University of Massachusetts psychologist and researcher David Lisak; Fort

453

Worth police Sgt. Cheryl Johnson; and Roger Canaff, a former special victims prosecutor in New York and an anti-violence advocate.

A postscript: Clairmont, Texas, does not exist. None of the crazy, diabolical Southern women in this book are based on a real person. Most of the Texas women I know are quite nice, thank you, and don't go around eating Little Debbie cakes with a rifle riding in the trunk of their cars.